DIANA PALMER

BOUND *by* HONOR

HQN™

ISBN 0-373-77182-7

BOUND BY HONOR

Copyright © 2006 by Harlequin Books S.A.

The publisher acknowledges the copyright holder of the
individual works as follows:

MERCENARY'S WOMAN
Copyright © 2000 by Diana Palmer

THE WINTER SOLDIER
Copyright © 2001 by Diana Palmer

This edition published by arrangement with Harlequin Books S.A.

® and TM are trademarks of the publisher. Trademarks indicated with
® are registered in the United States Patent and Trademark Office, the
Canadian Trade Marks Office and in other countries.

www.HQNBooks.com

Printed in U.S.A.

CONTENTS

MERCENARY'S WOMAN

CHAPTER ONE

EBENEZER SCOTT STOOD beside his double-wheeled black pickup truck and stared openly at the young woman across the street while she fiddled under the hood of a dented, rusted hulk of a vehicle. Sally Johnson's long blond hair was in a ponytail. She was wearing jeans and boots and no hat. He smiled to himself, remembering how many times in the old days he'd chided her about sunstroke. It had been six years since they'd even spoken. She'd been living in Houston until July, when she and her blind aunt and small cousin had moved back, into the decaying old Johnson homestead. He'd seen her several times since her return, but she'd made a point of not speaking to him. He couldn't really blame her. He'd left her with some painful emotional scars.

She was slender, but her trim figure still made his heartbeat jump. He knew how she looked under that loose blouse. His eyes narrowed with heat as he recalled the shocked pleasure in her pale gray eyes when he'd touched her, kissed her, in those forbidden places. He'd meant to frighten her so that she'd stop teasing him, but his impulsive attempt to discourage her had succeeded all too well. She'd run from him then, and she'd kept running. She was twenty-three now, a woman; probably an experienced woman. He mourned for what might have been if she'd been older and he hadn't just come back from leading a company of men into the worst bloodbath of his career. A professional soldier of fortune was no match for a young and very innocent girl. But, then, she hadn't known about his real life—the one behind the facade of cattle ranching. Not many people in this small town did.

It was six years later. She was all grown-up, a school-teacher here in Jacobsville, Texas. He was…retired, they called it. Actually he was still on the firing line from time to time, but mostly he taught other men in the specialized tactics of covert operations on his ranch. Not that he shared that information. He still had enemies from the old days, and one of them had just been sprung from prison on a technicality—a man out for revenge and with more than enough money to obtain it.

Sally had been almost eighteen the spring day he'd sent her running from him. In a life liberally strewn with regrets, she was his biggest one. The whole situation had been impossible, of course. But he'd never meant to hurt her, and the thought of her sat heavily on his conscience.

He wondered if she knew why he kept to himself and never got involved with the locals. His ranch was a model of sophistication, from its state-of-the-art gym to the small herd of purebred Santa Gertrudis breeding cattle he raised. His men were not only loyal, but tight-lipped. Like another Jacobsville, Texas, resident—Cy

Parks—Ebenezer was a recluse. The two men shared more than a taste for privacy. But that was something they kept to themselves.

Meanwhile, Sally Johnson was rapidly losing patience with her vehicle. He watched her push at a strand of hair that had escaped from the long ponytail. She kept a beef steer or two herself. It must be a frugal existence for her, supporting not only herself, but her recently blinded aunt, and her six-year-old cousin as well.

He admired her sense of responsibility, even as he felt concern for her situation. She had no idea why her aunt had been blinded in the first place, or that the whole family was in a great deal of danger. It was why Jessica had persuaded Sally to give up her first teaching job in Houston in June and come home with her and Stevie to Jacobsville. It was because they'd be near Ebenezer, and Jessica knew he'd protect them. Sally had never been told what Jessica's profession actually was, any more than she knew what Jessica's late husband, Hank Myers, had once done for a living. But even if she had known, wild horses wouldn't have dragged Sally back here if Jessica hadn't pleaded with her, he mused bitterly. Sally had every reason in the world to hate him. But he was her best hope of survival. And she didn't even know it.

In the five months she'd been back in Jacobsville, Sally had managed to avoid Ebenezer. In a town this size, that had been an accomplishment. Inevitably they met from time to time. But Sally avoided eye contact with him. It was the only indication of the painful memory they both shared.

He watched her lean helplessly over the dented fender of the old truck and decided that now was as good a time as any to approach her.

Sally lifted her head just in time to see the tall, lean man in the shepherd's coat and tan Stetson make his way across the street to her. He hadn't changed, she thought bitterly. He still walked with elegance and a slow, arrogance of carriage that seemed somehow foreign. Jeans didn't disguise the muscles in those long, powerful legs as he moved. She hated the ripple of sensation that lifted her heart at his approach. Surely she was over hero worship and infatuation, at her age, especially after what he'd done to her that long-ago spring day. She blushed just remembering it!

He paused at the truck, about an arm's length away from her, pushed his Stetson back over his thick blond-streaked brown hair and impaled her with green eyes.

She was immediately hostile and it showed in the tautening of her features as she looked up, way up, at him.

He raised an eyebrow and studied her flushed face. "Don't give me the evil eye," he said. "I'd have thought you had sense enough not to buy a truck from Turkey Sanders."

"He's my cousin," she reminded him.

"He's the Black Plague with car keys," he countered. "The Hart boys wiped the floor with him not too many years back. He sold Corrigan Hart's future wife a car that fell apart when she drove it off the lot. She was lucky at that," he added with a wicked grin. "He sold old lady Bates a car and told her the engine was optional equipment."

She laughed in spite of herself. "It's not a bad old truck," she countered. "It just needs a few things…"

He glanced at the rear tire and nodded. "Yes. An overhauled engine, a paint job, reupholstered seats, a tailgate that works. And a rear tire that isn't bald." He pointed toward it. "Get that replaced," he said shortly. "You can afford a tire even on what you make teaching."

She gaped at him. "Listen here, Mr. Scott…" she began haughtily.

"You know my name, Sally," he said bluntly, and his eyes were steady, intimidating. "As for the tire, it isn't a request," he replied flatly, staring her down. "You've got some new neighbors out your way that I don't like the look of. You can't afford a breakdown in the middle of the night on that lonely stretch of road."

She drew herself up to her full height, so that the top of her head came to his chin. He really was ridiculously tall…

"This is the twenty-first century, and women are capable of looking after themselves…." she said heatedly.

"I can do without a current events lecture," he cut her off again, moving to peer under the hood. He propped one enormous booted foot on the fender and studied the engine, frowned, pulled out a pocketknife and went to work.

"It's *my* truck!" she fumed, throwing up her hands in exasperation.

"It's half a ton of metal without an engine that works."

She grimaced. She hated not being able to fix it herself, to have to depend on this man, of all people, for help. She wouldn't let herself think about the cost of having a mechanic make a road service call to get the stupid thing started. Looking at his lean, capable hands brought back painful memories as well. She knew the tenderness of them on concealed skin, and her whole body erupted with sensation.

Less than two minutes later, he repocketed his knife. "Try it now," he said.

She got in behind the wheel. The engine turned noisily, pouring black smoke out of the tailpipe.

He paused beside the open window of the truck, his pale green eyes piercing her face. "Bad rings and valves," he pointed out. "Maybe an oil leak. Either way, you're in for some major repairs. Next time, don't buy from Turkey Sanders, and I don't give a damn if he is a relative."

"Don't you give me orders," she said haughtily.

That eyebrow lifted again. "Habit. How's Jess?"

She frowned. "Do you know my aunt Jessie?"

"Quite well," he said. "I knew your uncle Hank. He and I served together."

"In the military?"

He didn't answer her. "Do you have a gun?"

She was so confused that she stammered. "Wh…what?"

"A gun," he repeated. "Do you have any sort of weapon and can you use it?"

"I don't like guns," she said flatly. "Anyway, I won't have one in the house with a six-year-old child, so it's no use telling me to buy one."

He was thinking. His face tautened. "How about self-defense?"

"I teach second grade," she pointed out. "Most of my students don't attack me."

"I'm not worried about you at school. I told you, I don't like the look of your neighbors." He wasn't adding that he knew who they were and why they were in town.

"Neither do I," she admitted. "But it's none of your business…"

"It is," he returned. "I promised Hank that I'd take care of Jess if he ever bought it overseas. I keep my promises."

"I can take care of my aunt."

"Not anymore you can't," he returned, unabashed. "I'm coming over tomorrow."

"I may not be home…"

"Jess will be. Besides, tomorrow is Saturday," he said. "You came in for supplies this afternoon and you don't teach on the weekend. You'll be home." His tone said she'd better be.

She gave an exasperated sound. "Mr. Scott…"

"I'm only Mr. Scott to my enemies," he pointed out.

"Yes, well, Mr. Scott…"

He let out an angry sigh and stared her down. "You were so young," he bit off. "What did you expect me to do, seduce you in the cab of a pickup truck in broad daylight?"

She flushed red as a rose petal. "I wasn't talking about that!"

"It's still in your eyes," he told her quietly. "I'd rather have done it in a way that hadn't left so many scars, but

I had to discourage you. The whole damned thing was impossible, you must have realized that by now!"

She hated the embarrassment she felt. "I don't have scars!"

"You do." He studied her oval face, her softly rounded chin, her perfect mouth. "I'll be over tomorrow. I need to talk to you and Jess. There have been some developments that she doesn't know about."

"What sort of developments?"

He closed the hood of the truck and paused by her window. "Drive carefully," he said, ignoring the question. "And get that tire changed."

"I am not a charity case," she said curtly. "I don't take orders. And I definitely do not need some big, strong man to take care of me!"

He smiled, but it wasn't a pleasant smile. He turned on his heel and walked back to his own truck with a stride that was peculiarly his own.

Sally was so shaken that she barely managed to get the truck out of town without stripping the gears out of it.

JESSICA MYERS WAS IN HER BEDROOM listening to the radio and her son, Stevie, was watching a children's after-school television program when Sally came in. She unloaded the supplies first with the help of her six-year-old cousin.

"You got me that cereal from the TV commercial!" he exclaimed, diving into bags as she put the perishable items into the refrigerator. "Thanks, Aunt Sally!" Although they were cousins, he referred to her as his aunt out of affection and respect.

"You're very welcome. I got some ice cream, too."

"Wow! Can I have some now?"

Sally laughed. "Not until after supper, and you have to eat some of everything I fix. Okay?"

"Aw. Okay, I guess," he muttered, clearly disappointed.

She bent and kissed him between his dark eyes. "That's my good boy. Here, I brought some nice apples and pears. Wash one off and eat it. Fruit is good for you."

"Okay. But it's not as nice as ice cream."

He washed off a pear and carried it into the living room on a paper towel to watch television.

Sally went into Jessica's bedroom, hesitating at the foot of the big four-poster bed. Jessica was slight, blond and hazel-eyed. Her eyes stared at nothing, but she smiled as she recognized Sally's step.

"I heard the truck," she said. "I'm sorry you had to go to town for supplies after working all day and bringing Stevie home first."

"I never mind shopping," Sally said with genuine affection. "You doing all right?"

Jessica shifted on the pillows. She was dressed in sweats, but she looked bad. "I still have some pain from the wreck. I've taken a couple of aspirins for my hip. I thought I'd lie down and give them a chance to work."

Sally came in and sat down in the wing chair beside the bed. "Jess, Ebenezer Scott asked about you and said he was coming over tomorrow to see you."

Jessica didn't seem at all surprised. She only nodded. "I thought he might," Jessica said quietly. "I had a call from a former colleague about what's going on. I'm afraid I may have landed you in some major trouble, Sally."

"I don't understand."

"Didn't you wonder why I insisted on moving down here so suddenly?"

"Now that you mention it—"

"It was because Ebenezer is here, and we're safer than we would be in Houston."

"Now you're scaring me."

Jessica smiled sadly. "I wouldn't have had this happen for the world. It isn't something that comes up, usually. But these are odd circumstances. A man I helped put in prison is out pending retrial, and he's coming after me."

"You...helped put a man in prison? How?" Sally asked, perplexed.

"You knew that I worked for a government agency?"

"Well, of course. As a clerk."

Jessica took a deep breath. "No, dear. Not as a clerk." She took a deep breath. "I was a special agent for an agency we don't mention publicly. Through Eb and his contacts, I managed to find one of the confidants of drug lord Manuel Lopez, who was head of an international drug cartel. I was given enough hard evidence to send Lopez to prison for drug dealing. I even had copies of his ledgers. But there was one small loophole in the chain of evidence, and the drug lord's attorneys jumped on it. Lopez is now out of prison and he wants the person responsible for helping me put him away. Since I'm the only one who knows the person's identity, I'm the one he'll be coming after."

Sally just sat there, dumbfounded. Things like this only happened in movies. They certainly didn't happen in real life. Her beloved aunt surely wasn't involved in espionage!

"You're kidding, right?" Sally asked hopefully.

Jessica shook her head slowly. She was still an attractive woman, in her middle thirties. She was slender and she had a sweet face. Stevie, blond and dark-eyed, didn't favor her. Of course, he didn't favor his father, either. Hank had had black hair and light blue eyes.

"I'm sorry, dear," Jessica said heavily. "I'm not kidding. I'm not able to protect myself or you and Stevie anymore, so I had to come home for help. Ebenezer will keep us safe until we can get the drug lord back on ice."

"Is Ebenezer a government agent?" Sally asked, astounded.

"No." Jessica took a deep breath. "I don't like telling you this, and he won't like it, either. It's deeply private. You must swear not to tell another soul."

"I swear." She sat patiently, almost vibrating with curiosity.

"Eb was a professional mercenary," she said. "What they used to call a soldier of fortune. He's led groups of highly trained men in covert operations all over the world. He's retired from that now, but he's still much in demand with our government and foreign governments as a training instructor. His ranch is well-known in covert circles as an academy of tactics and intelligence-gathering."

Sally didn't say a word. She was absolutely speechless. No wonder Ebenezer had been so secretive, so reluctant to let her get close to him. She remembered the tiny white scars on his lean, tanned face, and knew instinctively that there would be more of them under his clothing. No wonder he kept to himself!

"I hope I haven't shattered any illusions, Sally," her aunt said worriedly. "I know how you felt about him."

Sally gaped at her. "You...know?"

Jessica nodded. "Eb told me about that, and about what happened just before you came to live with Hank and me in Houston."

Her face flamed. The shame! She felt sick with humiliation that Ebenezer had known how she felt all the time, and she thought she was doing such a good job of hiding it! She should have realized that it was obvious, when she found excuse after excuse to waylay him in town, when she brazenly climbed into his pickup truck one lovely spring afternoon and pleaded to be taken for a ride. He'd given in to that request, to her surprise. But barely half an hour later, she'd erupted from the passenger seat and run almost all the half-mile down the road to her home. Too ashamed to let anyone see the state she was in, she'd sneaked in the back door and gone straight to her room. She'd never told her parents or anyone else what had happened. Now she wondered if Jessica knew that, too.

"He didn't divulge any secrets, if that's why you're so quiet, Sally," the older woman said gently. "He only said that you had a king-size crush on him and he'd shot you down. He was pretty upset."

That was news. "I wouldn't ever have guessed that he could be upset."

"Neither would I," Jessica said with a smile. "It came as something of a surprise. He told me to keep an eye on you, and check out who you went out with. He could have saved himself the trouble, of course, since you never went out with anyone. He was bitter about that."

Sally averted her face to the window. "He frightened me."

"He knew that. It's why he was bitter."

Sally drew in a steadying breath. "I was very young," she said finally, "and I suppose he did the only thing he could. But I was leaving Jacobsville anyway, when my parents divorced. I only had a week of school before graduation before I went to live with you. He didn't have to go to such lengths."

"My brother still feels like an idiot for the way he behaved with that college girl he left your mother for," Jessica said curtly, meaning Sally's father, who was Jessica's only living relative besides Sally. "It didn't help that your mother remarried barely six months later. He was stuck with Beverly the Beauty."

"How are my parents?" Sally asked. It was the first time she'd mentioned either of her parents in a long while, She'd lost touch with them since the divorce that had shattered her life.

"Your father spends most of his time at work while Beverly goes the party route every night and spends every penny he makes. Your mother is separated from her second husband and living in Nassau." Jessica shifted on the bed. "You don't ever hear from your parents, do you?"

"I don't resent them as much as I did. But I never felt that they loved me," she said abruptly. "That's why I felt it was better we went our separate ways."

"They were children when they married and had you," the other woman said. "Not really mature enough for the responsibility. They resented it, too. That's why you spent so much time with me during the first five years you were alive." Jessica smiled. "I hated it when you went back home."

"Why did you and Hank wait so long to have a child of your own?" Sally asked.

Jessica flushed. "It wasn't…convenient, with Hank overseas so much. Did you get that tire replaced?" she added, almost as if she were desperate to change the subject.

"You and Mr. Scott!" Sally exploded, diverted. "How did you know it was bald?"

"Because Eb phoned me before you got home and told me to remind you to get it replaced," Jessica chuckled.

"I suppose he has a cell phone in his truck."

"Among other things," Jessica replied with a smile. "He isn't like the men you knew in college or even when you started teaching. Eb is an alpha male," she said quietly. "He isn't politically correct, and he doesn't even pretend to conform. In some ways, he's very old-fashioned."

"I don't feel that way about him anymore," Sally said firmly.

"I'm sorry," Jessica replied gently. "He's been alone most of his life. He needs to be loved."

Sally picked at a cuticle, chipping the clear varnish on her short, neat fingernails. "Does he have family?"

"Not anymore. His mother died when he was very young, and his father was career military. He grew up in the army, you might say. His father was not a gentle sort of man. He died in combat when Eb was in his twenties. There wasn't any other family."

"You said once that you always saw Ebenezer with beautiful women at social events," Sally recalled with a touch of envy.

"He pays for dressing, and he attracts women. But he's careful about his infrequent liaisons. He told me once that he guessed he'd never find a woman who could share the life he leads. He still has enemies who'd like to see him dead," she added.

"Like this drug lord?"

"Yes. Manuel Lopez is a law unto himself. He has millions, and he owns politicians, law enforcement people, even judges," Jessica said irritably. "That's why we were never able to shut him down. Then I was told that a confidant of his wanted to give me information, names and documents that would warrant arresting Lopez on charges of drug trafficking. But I wasn't careful enough. I overlooked one little thing, and Lopez's attorneys used it in a petition for a retrial. They got him out. He's on the loose pending retrial and out for vengeance against his comrade. He'll do anything to get the name of the person who sold him out. Anything at all."

Sally let her breath out through pursed lips. "So we're all under the gun."

"Exactly. I used to be a crack shot, but without my vision, I'm useless. Eb will have a plan by tomorrow." Her face was solemn as she stared in the general direction of her niece's voice. "Listen to him, Sally. Do exactly what he says. He's our only hope of protecting Stevie."

"I'll do anything I have to, to protect you and Stevie," Sally agreed at once.

"I knew you would."

She toyed with her nails again. "Jess, has Ebenezer ever been serious about anyone?"

"Yes. There was a woman in Houston, in fact, several years ago. He cared for her very much, but she dropped him flat when she found out what he did for a living. She married a much-older bank executive." She shifted on the bed. "I hear that she's widowed now. But I don't imagine he still has any feelings for her. After all, she dropped him, not the reverse."

Sally, who knew something about helpless unrequited love, wasn't so quick to agree. After all, she still had secret feelings for Ebenezer...

"Deep thoughts, dear?" Jessica asked softly.

"I was remembering the reruns we used to see of that old TV series, *The A-Team,*" she recalled with an audible laugh. "I loved it when they had to knock out that character Mr. T played to get him on an airplane."

"It was a good show. Not lifelike, of course," Jessica added.

"What part?"

"All of it."

Jessica would probably know, Sally figured. "Why didn't you ever tell me what you did for a living?"

"Need to know," came the dry reply. "You didn't, until now."

"If you knew Ebenezer when he was still working as a mercenary, I guess you learned a lot about the business," she ventured.

Jessica's face closed up. "I learned too much," she said coldly. "Far too much. Men like that are incapable of lasting relationships. They don't know the meaning of love or fidelity."

She seemed to know that, and Sally wondered how. "Was Uncle Hank a mercenary, too?"

"Yes, just briefly," she said. "Hank was never one to rush in and risk killing himself. It was so ironic that he died overseas in his sleep, of a heart condition nobody even knew he had."

That was a surprise, along with all the others that Jessica was getting. Uncle Hank had been very handsome, but not assertive or particularly tough.

"But Ebenezer said he served with Uncle Hank."

"Yes. In basic training, before they joined the Green Berets," Jessica said. "Hank didn't pass the training course. Ebenezer did. In fact," she added amusedly, "he was able to do the Fan Dance."

"Fan Dance?"

"It's a specialized course they put the British commandos, the Special Air Service, guys through. Not many soldiers, even career soldiers, are able to finish it, much less able to pass it on the first try. Eb did. He was briefly 'loaned' to them while he was in army intelligence, for some top secret assignment."

Sally had never thought very much about Ebenezer's profession, except that she'd guessed he was once in the military. She wasn't sure how she felt about it. A man who'd been in the military might still have a soft spot or two inside. She was almost certain that a commando, a soldier for hire, wouldn't have any.

"You're very quiet," Jessica said.

"I never thought of Ebenezer in such a profession," she replied, moving to look out the window at the November landscape. "I guess it was right there in front of me, and I didn't see it. No wonder he kept to himself."

"He still does," she replied. "And only a few people know about his past. His men do, of course," she added, and there was an inflection in her tone that was suddenly different.

"Do you know any of his men?"

Jessica's face tautened. "One or two. I believe Dallas Kirk still works for him. And Micah Steele does consulting work when Eb asks him to," she added and smiled. "Micah's a good guy. He's the only one of Eb's old colleagues who still works in the trade. He lives in Nassau, but he spends an occasional week helping Ebenezer train men when he's needed."

"And Dallas Kirk?"

Jessica's soft face went very hard. At her side, one of her small hands clenched. "Dallas was badly wounded in a firefight a year ago. He came home shot to pieces and Eb found something for him to teach in the tactics courses. He doesn't speak to me, of course. We had a difficult parting some years ago."

That was intriguing, and Sally was going to find out about it one day. But she didn't press her luck. "How about fajitas for supper?" she asked.

Jessica's glower dissolved into a smile. "Sounds lovely!"

"I'll get right on them." Sally went back into the kitchen, her head spinning with the things she'd learned about people she thought she knew. Life, she considered, was always full of surprises.

CHAPTER TWO

EBENEZER WAS A MAN of his word. He showed up early the next morning as Sally was out by the corral fence watching her two beef cattle graze. She'd bought them to raise with the idea of stocking her freezer. Now they had names. The white-faced Black Angus mixed steer was called Bob, the white-faced red-coated Hereford she called Andy. They were pets. She couldn't face the thought of sitting down to a plate of either one of them.

The familiar black pickup stopped at the fence and Ebenezer got out. He was wearing jeans and a blue checked shirt with boots and a light-colored straw Stetson. No chaps, so he wasn't working cattle today.

He joined Sally at the fence. "Don't tell me. They're table beef."

She spared him a resentful glance. "Right."

"And you're going to put them in the freezer."

She swallowed. "Sure."

He only chuckled. He paused to light a cigar, with one big booted foot propped on the lower rung of the fence. "What are their names?"

"That's Andy and that's…Bob." She flushed.

He didn't say a word, but his raised eyebrow was eloquent through the haze of expelled smoke.

"They're watch-cattle," she improvised.

His eyes twinkled. "I beg your pardon?"

"They're attack steers," she said with a reluctant grin. "At the first sign of trouble, they'll come right through the fence to protect me. Of course, if they get shot in the line of duty," she added, "I'll eat them!"

He pushed his Stetson back over clean blond-streaked brown hair and looked down at her with lingering amusement. "You haven't changed much in six years."

"Neither have you," she retorted shyly. "You're still smoking those awful things."

He glanced at the big cigar and shrugged. "A man has to have a vice or two to round him out," he pointed out. "Besides, I only have the occasional one, and never inside. I have read the studies on smoking," he added dryly.

"Lots of people who smoke read those studies," she agreed. "And then they quit!"

He smiled. "You can't reform me," he told her. "It's a waste of time to try. I'm thirty-six and very set in my ways."

"I noticed."

He took a puff from the cigar and studied her steers. "I suppose they follow you around like dogs."

"When I go inside the fence with them," she agreed. She felt odd with him; safe and nervous and excited, all at once. She could smell the fresh scent of the soap he used, and over it a whiff of expensive cologne. He was close at her side, muscular and vibrating with sensuality. She wanted to move closer, to feel that strength all around her. It made her self-conscious. After six years, surely the attraction should have lessened a little.

He glanced down at her, noticing how she picked at her cuticles and nibbled on her lower lip. His green eyes narrowed and there was a faint glitter in them.

She felt the heat of his gaze and refused to lift her face. She wondered if it looked as hot as it felt.

"You haven't forgotten a thing," he said suddenly, the cigar in his hand absently falling to his side, whirls of smoke climbing into the air beside him.

"About what?" she choked.

He caught her long, blond ponytail and tugged her closer, so that she was standing right up against him. The scent of him, the heat of him, the muscular ripple of his body combined to make her shiver with repressed feelings.

He shifted, coaxing her into the curve of his body, his eyes catching hers and holding them relentlessly. He could feel her faint trembling, hear the excited whip of her breath as she tried valiantly to hide it from him. But he could see her heartbeat jerking the fabric over her small breasts.

It was a relief to find her as helplessly attracted to him as she once had been. It made him arrogant with pride. He let go of the ponytail and drew his hand against her cheek, letting his thumb slide down to her mouth and over her chin to lift her eyes to his.

"To everything, there is a season," he said quietly.

She felt the impact of his steady, unblinking gaze in the most secret places of her body. She didn't have the experience to hide it, to protect herself. She only stood staring up at him, with all her insecurities and fears lying naked in her soft gray eyes.

His head bent and he drew his nose against hers in the sudden silence of the yard. His smoky breath whispered over her lips as he murmured, "Six years is a long time to go hungry."

She didn't understand what he was saying. Her eyes were on his hard, long, thin mouth. Her hands had flattened against his broad chest. Under it she could feel thick, soft hair and the beat of his heart. His breath smelled of cigar smoke and when his mouth gently covered hers, she wondered if she was going to faint with the unexpected delight of it. It had been so long!

He felt her immediate, helpless submission. His free arm went around her shoulders and drew her lazily against his muscular body while his hard mouth moved lightly over her lips, tasting her, assessing her experience. His mouth became insistent and she stiffened a little, unused to the tender probing of his tongue against her teeth.

She felt his smile before he lifted his head.

"You still taste of lemonade and cotton candy," he murmured with unconcealed pleasure.

"What do you mean?" she murmured, mesmerized by the hovering threat of his mouth.

"I mean, you still don't know how to do this." He searched her eyes quietly and then the smile left his face.

"I did more damage than I ever meant to. You were seventeen. I had to hurt you to save you." He traced her mouth with his thumb and scowled down at her. "You don't know what my life was like in those days," he said solemnly, and for once his eyes were unguarded. The pain in them was visible for the first time Sally could remember.

"Aunt Jessica told me," she said slowly.

His eyes darkened. His face hardened. "All of it?"

She nodded.

He was still scowling. He released her to gaze off into the distance, absently lifting the cigar to his mouth. He blew out a cloud of smoke. "I'm not sure that I wanted you to know."

"Secrets are dangerous."

He glanced down at her, brooding. "More dangerous than you realize. I've kept mine for a long time, like your aunt."

"I had no idea what she did for a living, either." She glared up at him. "Thanks to the two of you, now I know how a mushroom feels, sitting in the dark."

He chuckled. "She wanted it that way. She felt you'd be safer if she kept you uninvolved."

She wanted to ask him about what Jessica had told her, that he'd phoned her about Sally before the painful move to Houston. But she didn't quite know how. She was shy with him.

He looked down at her again, his eyes intent on her softly flushed cheeks, her swollen mouth, her bright eyes. She lifted his heart. Just the sight of her made him feel welcome, comforted, cared for. He'd missed that. In all his life, Sally had been the first and only person who could thwart his black moods. She made him feel as if he belonged somewhere after a life of wandering. Even during the time she was in Houston, he kept in touch with Jessica, to get news of Sally, of where she was, what she was doing, of her plans. He'd always expected that she'd come back to him one day, or that he'd go to her, despite the way they'd parted. Love, if it existed, was surely a powerful force, immune to harsh words and distance. And time.

Sally's face was watchful, her eyes brimming over with excitement. She couldn't hide what she was feeling, and he loved being able to see it. Her hero worship had first irritated and then elated him. Women had wanted him since his teens, although some loved him for the danger that clung to him. One had rejected him because of it and savaged his pride. But, even so, it was Sally who made him ache inside.

He touched her soft mouth with his fingers, liking the faint swell where he'd kissed it so thoroughly. "We'll have to practice more," he murmured wickedly.

She opened her mouth to protest that assumption when a laughing Stevie came running out the door like a little blond whirlwind, only to be caught up abruptly in Ebenezer's hard arms and lifted.

"Uncle Eb!" he cried, laughing delightedly, making Sally realize that if she hadn't been around Ebenezer since their move from Houston, Jessica and Stevie certainly had.

"Hello, tiger," came the deep, pleasant reply. He put the boy back down on his feet. "Want to go to my place with Sally and learn karate?"

"Like the 'Teenage Mutant Ninja Turtles' in the movies? Radical!" he exclaimed.

"Karate?" Sally asked, hesitating.

"Just a few moves, and only for self-defense," he assured her. "You'll enjoy it. It's necessary," he added when she seemed to hesitate.

"Okay," she capitulated.

He led the way back into the house to where Jessica was sitting in the living room, listening to the news on the television.

"All this mess in the Balkans," she said sadly. "Just when we think we've got peace, everything erupts all over again. Those poor people!"

"Fortunes of war," Eb said with a smile. "How's it going, Jess?"

"I can't complain, I guess, except that they won't let me drive anymore," she said, tongue-in-cheek.

"Wait until they get that virtual reality vision perfected," he said easily. "You'll be able to do anything."

"Optimist," she said, grinning.

"Always. I'm taking these two over to the ranch for a little course in elementary self-defense," he added quietly.

"Good idea," Jessica said at once.

"I don't like leaving you here alone," Sally ventured, remembering what she'd been told about the danger.

"She won't be," Eb replied. He looked at Jessica and

one eye narrowed before he added, "I'm sending Dallas Kirk over to keep her company"

"*No!*" Jessica said furiously. She actually stood up, vibrating. "No, Eb! I don't want him within a mile of me! I'd rather be shot to pieces!"

"This isn't multiple choice," came a deep, drawling voice from the general direction of the hall.

As Sally turned from Jessica's white face, a slender blond man with dark eyes came into the room. He walked with the help of a fancy-looking cane. He was dressed like Eb, in casual clothes, khaki slacks and a bush jacket. He looked like something right out of Africa.

"This is Dallas Kirk," Eb introduced him to Sally. "He was born in Texas. His real name is Jon, but we've always called him Dallas. This is Sally Johnson," he told the blond man.

Dallas nodded. "Nice to meet you," he said formally.

"You know Jess," Eb added.

"Yes. I...know her," he said with the faintest emphasis in that lazy Western drawl, during which Jess's face went from white to scarlet and she averted her eyes.

"Surely you can get along for an hour," Eb said impatiently. "I really can't leave you here by yourself, Jess."

Dallas glared at her. "Mind telling me why?" he asked Eb. "She's a better shot than I am."

Jessica stood rigidly by her chair. "He doesn't know?" she asked Eb.

Eb's face was rigid. "He wouldn't talk about you, and the subject didn't come up until he was away on assignment. No. He doesn't know."

"Know what?" Dallas demanded.

Jessica's chin lifted. "I'm blind," she said matter-of-factly, almost with satisfaction, as if she knew it would hurt him.

The look on the newcomer's face was a revelation. Sally only wished she knew of what. He shifted as if he'd sustained a physical blow. He walked slowly up to her and waved a hand in front of her face.

"Blind!" he said huskily. "For how long?"

"Six months," she said, feeling for the arms of the chair. She sat back down a little clumsily. "I was in a wreck. An accident," she added abruptly.

"It was no accident," Eb countered coldly. "She was run off the road by two of Lopez's men. They got away before the police came."

Sally gasped. This was a new explanation. She'd just heard about the wreck—not about the cause of it. Dallas's hand on the cane went white from the pressure he was exerting on it. "What about Stevie?" he asked coldly. "Is he all right? Was he injured?"

"He wasn't with me at the time. And he's fine. Sally lives with us and helps take care of him," Jess replied, her voice unusually tense. "We share the chores. She's my niece," she added abruptly, almost as if to warn him of something.

Dallas looked preoccupied. But when Stevie came running back into the room, he turned abruptly and his eyes widened as he stared at the little boy.

"I'm ready!" Stevie announced, holding out his arms to show the gray sweats he was wearing. His dark eyes were shimmering with joy. "This is how they look on television when they practice. Is it okay?"

"It's fine," Eb replied with a smile.

"Who's he?" Stevie asked, big-eyed, as he looked at the blond man with the cane who was staring at him, as if mesmerized.

"That's Dallas," Eb said easily. "He works for me."

"Hi," Stevie said, naturally outgoing. He stared at the cane. "I guess you're from Texas with a name like that, huh? I'm sorry about your leg, Mr. Dallas. Does it hurt much?"

Dallas took a slow breath before he answered. "When it rains."

"My mama's hip hurts when it rains, too," he said. "Are you coming with us to learn karate?"

"He's already forgotten more than I know," Eb said in a dry tone. "No, he's going to take care of your mother while we're gone."

"Why?" Stevie asked, frowning.

"Because her hip hurts," Sally lied through her teeth. "Ready to go?"

"Sure! Bye, Mom." He ran to kiss her cheek and be hugged warmly. He moved back, smiling up at the blond man who hadn't cracked a smile yet. "See you."

Dallas nodded.

Sally was staggered by the resemblance of the boy to the man, and almost remarked on it. But before she could, Eb caught her eyes. There was a look in them that she couldn't decipher, but it stopped her at once.

"We'd better go," he said. He took Sally by the

arm. "Come on, Stevie. We won't be long, Jess," he called back.

"I'll count the seconds," she said under her breath as they left the room.

Dallas didn't say anything, and it was just as well that she couldn't see the look in his eyes.

IT WAS IMPOSSIBLE TO TALK in front of Stevie as they drove through the massive electronic gates at the Scott ranch. He, like Sally, was fascinated by the layout, which included a helipad, a landing strip with a hangar, a swimming pool and a ranch house that looked capable of sleeping thirty people. There were also target ranges and guest cabins and a formidable state-of-the-art gym housed in what looked like a gigantic Quonset hut like those used during the Second World War in the Pacific theater. There were several satellite dishes as well, and security cameras seemingly on every available edifice.

"This is incredible," Sally said as they got out of the truck and went with him toward the gym.

"Maintaining it is incredible," Eb said with a chuckle. "You wouldn't believe the level of technology required to keep it all functioning."

Stevie had found the thick blue plastic-covered mat on the wood floor and was already rolling around on it and trying the punching bag suspended from one of the steel beams that supported other training equipment.

"Stevie looks like that man, Dallas," she said abruptly.

He grimaced. "Haven't you and Jess ever talked?"

"I didn't know anything about Dallas and my aunt until you told me," she said simply.

"This is something she needs to tell you, in her own good time."

She studied the youngster having fun on the mat. "He isn't my uncle's child, is he?"

There was a rough sound from the man beside her. "What makes you think so?"

"For one thing, because he's the image of Dallas. But also because Uncle Hank and Aunt Jessie were married for years with no kids, and suddenly she got pregnant just before he died overseas," she replied. "Stevie was like a miracle."

"In some ways, I suppose he was. But it led to Hank asking for a combat assignment, and even though he died of a heart condition, Jess has had nightmares ever since out of guilt." He looked down at her. "You can't tell her that you know."

"Fair enough. Tell me the rest."

"She and Dallas were working together on an assignment. It was one of those lightning attractions that overcome the best moral obstacles. They were alone too much and finally the inevitable happened. Jess turned up pregnant. When Dallas found out, he went crazy. He demanded that Jess divorce Hank and marry him, but she wouldn't. She swore that Dallas wasn't the father of her child, Hank was, and she had no intention of divorcing her husband."

"Oh, dear."

"Hank knew that she'd been with another man, of

course, because he'd always been sterile. Dallas didn't know that. And Hank hadn't told Jessica until she announced that she was expecting a child." He shrugged. "He wouldn't forgive her. Neither would Dallas. When Hank died, Dallas didn't even try to get in touch with Jess. He really believed that Stevie was Hank's child. Until about ten minutes ago, that is," he added with a wry smile. "It didn't take much guesswork for him to see the resemblance. I think we won't go back for a couple of hours. I don't want to walk into the firefight he's probably having with Jess even as we speak."

She bit her lower lip. "Poor Jess."

"Poor Dallas," he countered. "After the fight with Jessie, he took every damned dangerous assignment he could find, the more dangerous the better. Last year in Africa, Dallas was shot to pieces. They sent him home with wounds that would have killed a lesser man."

"No wonder he looks so bitter."

"He's bitter because he loved Jess and though she felt the same, she wasn't willing to hurt Hank by leaving him. But in the end, she still hurt him. He couldn't live with the idea that she was having some other man's child. It destroyed their marriage."

She grimaced. "What a tragedy, for all of them."

"Yes."

She looked toward Stevie, smiling. "He's a great kid," she said. "I'd love him even if he wasn't my first cousin."

"He's got grit and personality to boot."

"You wouldn't think so at midnight when you're still trying to get him to sleep."

He smiled as he studied her. "You love kids, don't you?"

"Oh, yes," she said fervently. "I love teaching."

"Don't you want some of your own?" he asked with a quizzical smile.

She flushed and wouldn't look at him. "Sure. One day."

"Why not now?"

"Because I've already got more responsibilities than I can manage. Pregnancy would be a complication I couldn't handle, especially now."

"You sound as if you're planning to do it all alone."

She shrugged. "There is such a thing as artificial insemination."

He turned her toward him, looking very solemn and adult. "How would it feel, carrying the child of a man you didn't even know, having it grow inside your body?"

She bit her lower lip. She hadn't considered the intimacy of what he was suggesting. She felt, and looked, confused.

"A baby should be made out of love, the natural way, not in a test tube," he said very softly, searching her shocked eyes. "Well, not unless it's the only way two people can have a child," he added. "But that's an entirely different circumstance."

Her lips parted on the surge of emotion that made her heart race. "I don't know...that I want to get that close to anyone, ever."

He seemed even more remote. "Sally, you can't let the past lock you into solitude forever. I frightened you because I wanted to keep you at bay. If I didn't discourage you somehow I was afraid that the temptation might prove too much for me. You were such a baby." He scowled bitterly. "What happened wouldn't have been so devastating if you'd had even a little experience with men. For God's sake, didn't they ever let you date anyone?"

She shook her head, her teeth clenched tightly together. "My mother was certain that I'd get pregnant or catch some horrible disease. She talked about it all the time. She made boys who came to the house so uncomfortable that they never came back."

"I didn't know that," he said tautly.

"Would it have made any difference?" she asked miserably.

He touched her face with cool, firm fingers. "Yes. I wouldn't have gone nearly as far as I did, if I'd known."

"You wanted to get rid of me…"

He put his thumb over her soft mouth. "I wanted you," he whispered huskily. "But a seventeen-year-old isn't mature enough for a love affair. And that would have been impossible in Jacobsville, even if I'd been crazy enough to go all the way with you that day. You were almost thirteen years my junior."

She was beginning to see things from his point of view. She hadn't tried before. There had been so much resentment, so much bitterness, so much hurt. She looked at him and saw, for the first time, the pain of the memory in his face.

"I was desperate," she said, speaking softly. "They told me out of the blue that they were divorcing each other. They were selling the house and moving out of town. Dad was going to marry Beverly, this girl he'd met at the college where he taught. Mom couldn't live in the same town with everybody knowing that Dad had thrown her over for someone younger. She married a man she hardly knew shortly afterward, just to save her pride." She stared at his mouth with more hunger than she realized. "I knew that I'd never see you again. I only wanted you to kiss me." She swallowed, averting her eyes. "I must have been crazy."

"We both were." He cupped her face in his hands and lifted it to his quiet eyes. "For what it's worth, I never meant it to go further than a kiss. A very chaste kiss, at that." His eyes drifted down involuntarily to the soft thrust of her breasts almost touching his shirt. He raised an eyebrow at the obvious points. "That's why it wasn't chaste."

She didn't understand. "What is?"

He looked absolutely exasperated. "How can you be that old and know nothing?" he asked. He glanced over her shoulder at Stevie, who was facing the other way and giving the punching bag hell. He took Sally's own finger and drew it across her taut breast. He looked straight into her eyes as he said softly, "That's why."

She realized that it must have something to do with being aroused, but no one had ever told her blatantly that it was a visible sign of desire. She went scarlet.

"You greenhorn," he murmured indulgently. "What a babe in arms."

"I don't read those sort of books," she said haughtily.

"You should. In fact, I'll buy you a set of them.

Maybe a few videos, too," he murmured absently, watching the expressions come and go on her face.

"You varmint…!"

He caught her top lip in both of his and ran his tongue lazily under it. She stiffened, but her hands were clinging to him, not pushing.

"You remember that, don't you, Sally?" he murmured with a smile. "Do you remember what comes next?"

She jerked back from him, staggering. Her eyes found Stevie, still oblivious to the adults.

Eb's eyes were blatant on the thrust of her breasts and he was smiling.

She crossed her arms over her chest and glared up at him. "You just stop that," she gritted. "I'll bet you weren't born knowing everything!"

He chuckled. "No, I wasn't. But I didn't have a mother to keep my nose clean, either," he said. "My old man was military down to his toenails, and he didn't believe in gentle handling or delicacy. He used women until the day he died." He laughed coldly. "He told me that there was no such thing as a good woman, that they were to be enjoyed and put aside."

She was appalled. "Didn't he love your mother?"

"He wanted her, and she wouldn't be with him until they got married," he said simply. "So they got married. She died having me. They were living in a small town outside the military base where he was stationed. He was overseas on assignment and she lived alone, isolated. She went into labor and there were complications. There was nothing that could have been done for her by the time she was found. If a neighbor hadn't come to look in on us, I'd have died with her."

"It must have been a shock for your father," she said.

"If it was, it never showed. He left me with a cousin until I was old enough to obey orders, then I went to live with him. I learned a lot from him, but he wasn't a loving man." His eyes narrowed on her soft face. "I followed his example and joined the army. I was lucky enough to get into the Green Berets. Then when I was due for discharge, a man approached me about a top secret assignment and told me what it would pay." He shrugged. "Money is a great temptation for a young man with a domineering father. I said yes and he never spoke to me again. He said that what I was doing was a perversion of the military, and that I wasn't fit to be any officer's son. He disowned me on the spot. I didn't hear from him again. A few years later, I got a letter from his post commander, stating that he'd died in combat. He had a military funeral with full honors."

The pain of those years was in his lean, hard face. Impulsively she put a hand on his arm. "I'm sorry," she told him quietly. "He must have been the sort of man who only sees one side of any argument."

He was surprised by her compassion. "Don't you think mercenaries are evil, Miss Purity?" he asked sarcastically.

CHAPTER THREE

SALLY LOOKED UP INTO PAIN-LACED green eyes and without thinking, she lifted her hand from his arm and raised it toward his hard cheek. But when she realized what she was doing, she drew it back at once.

"No, I don't think mercenaries are evil," she said quickly, embarrassed by the impulsive gesture that, thankfully, he didn't seem to notice. "There are a lot of countries where atrocities are committed, whose governments don't have the manpower or resources to protect their people. So, someone else gets hired to do it. I don't think it's a bad thing, when there's a legitimate cause."

He was surprised by her matter-of-fact manner. He'd wondered for years how she might react when she learned about what he did for a living. He'd expected everything from revulsion to shock, especially when he remembered how his former fiancée had reacted to the news. But Sally wasn't squeamish or judgmental.

He'd seen her hand jerk back and it had wounded him. But now, on hearing her opinion of his work, his heart lifted. "I didn't expect you to credit me with noble motives."

"They are, though, aren't they?" she asked confidently.

"As a matter of fact, in my case, they are," he replied. "Even in my green days, I never did it just for the money. I had to believe in what I was risking my life for."

She grinned. "I thought maybe it was like on television," she confessed. "But Jess said it was nothing like fiction."

He cocked an eyebrow. "Oh, I wouldn't say that," he mused. "Parts of it are."

"Such as?"

"We had a guy like 'B.A. Barrabas' in one unit I led," he said. "We really did have to knock him out to get him on a plane. But he quit the group before we got inventive."

She laughed. "Too bad. You'd have had plenty of stories to tell about him."

He was quiet for a moment, studying her.

"Do I have a zit on my nose?" she asked pleasantly.

He reached out and caught the hand she'd started to lift toward him earlier and kissed its soft palm. "Let's get to work," he said, pulling her along to the mat. "I'll change into my sweats and we'll cover the basics. We won't have a lot of time," he added dryly. "I expect Jess to call very soon with an ultimatum about Dallas."

JESS AND DALLAS HAD SQUARED OFF, in fact, the minute they heard the truck crank and pull out of the yard.

Dallas glared at her from his superior height, leaning heavily on his cane. He wished she could see him, because his eyes were full of anger and bitterness.

"Did you think I wouldn't see that Stevie is the living image of me? My son," he growled at her. "You had my son! And you lied to me about it and wouldn't ask Hank for a divorce!"

"I couldn't!" she exclaimed. "For heaven's sake, he adored me. He'd never have cheated on me. I couldn't bring myself to tell him that I'd had an affair with his best friend!"

"I could have told him," he returned furiously. "He was no angel, Jess, despite the wings you're trying to paint on him. Or do you think he never strayed on those overseas jaunts?" he chided.

She stiffened. "That's not true!"

"It is true!" he replied angrily. "He knew he couldn't get anybody pregnant, and he was sure you'd never find out."

She put a hand to her head. She'd never dreamed that Hank had cheated on her. She'd felt so guilty, when all the time, he was doing the same thing—and then judging her brutally for what she'd done. "I didn't know," she said miserably.

"Would it have made a difference?"

"I don't know. Maybe it would have." She smoothed the dress over her legs. "You thought Stevie was yours from the beginning, didn't you?"

"No. I didn't know Hank was sterile until later on. You told me the child was Hank's and I believed you. Hell, by then, I couldn't even be sure that it was his."

"You didn't think—" She stopped abruptly. "Oh, dear God, you thought you were one in a line?" she exploded, horrified. "You thought I ran around on Hank with any man who asked me?"

"I knew very little about you except that you knocked me sideways," he said flatly. "I knew Hank ran around on you. I assumed you were allowed the same freedom." He turned away and walked to the window, staring out at the flat horizon. "I asked you to divorce Hank just to see what you'd say. It was exactly what I expected. You had it made—a husband who tolerated your unfaithfulness, and no danger of falling in love."

"I thought I had a good marriage until you came along," she said bitterly.

He turned, his eyes blazing. "Don't make it sound cheap, Jess," he said harshly. "Neither of us could stop that night. Neither of us tried."

She put her face in her hands and shivered. The memory of how it had been could still reduce her to tears. She'd been in love for the first time in her life, but not with her husband. This man had haunted her ever since. Stevie was the mirror image of him.

"I was so ashamed," she choked. "I betrayed Hank. I betrayed everything I believed in about loyalty and duty and honor. I felt like a Saturday night special at the bordello afterward."

He scowled. "I never treated you that way," he said harshly.

"Of course you didn't!" she said miserably, wiping at tears. "But I was raised to believe that people got married and never cheated on each other. I was a virgin when I married Hank, and nobody in my whole family was ever divorced until Sally's father, my brother, was." She shook her head, oblivious to the expression that washed over Dallas's hard, lean face. "My parents were happily married for fifty years before they died."

"Sometimes it doesn't work," he said flatly, but in a less hostile tone. "That's nobody's fault."

She smoothed back her short hair and quickly wiped away the tears. "Maybe not."

He moved back toward her and sat down in a chair across from hers, putting the cane down on the floor. He leaned forward with a hard sigh and looked at Jessica's pale, wan face with bitterness while he tried to find the words.

She heard the cane as he placed it on the floor. "Eb said you were badly hurt overseas," she said softly, wishing with all her heart that she could see him. "Are you all right?"

That husky softness in her tone, that exquisite concern, was almost too much for him. He grasped her slender hands in his and held them tightly. "I'm better off than you seem to be," he said heavily. "What a hell of a price we paid for that night, Jess."

She felt the hot sting of tears. "It was very high," she had to admit. She reached out hesitantly to find his face. Her fingers traced it gently, finding the new scars, the new hardness of its elegant lines. "Stevie looks like you," she said softly, her unseeing eyes so full of emotion that he couldn't bear to look into them.

"Yes."

She searched her darkness with anguish for a face she

would never see again. "Don't be bitter," she pleaded. "Please don't hate me."

He pulled her hand away as if it scalded him. "I've done little else for the past five years," he said flatly. "But maybe you're right. All the rage in the world won't change the past." He let go of her hand. "We have to pick up the pieces and go on."

She hesitated. "Can we at least be friends?"

He laughed coldly. "Is that what you want?"

She nodded. "Eb says you've given up overseas assignments and that you're working for him. I want you to get to know Stevie," she added quietly. "Just in case…"

"Oh, for God's sake, stop it!" he exploded, rising awkwardly from the chair with the help of the cane. "Lopez won't get you. We aren't going to let anything happen to you."

She leaned back in her chair without replying. They both knew that Lopez had contacts everywhere and that he never gave up. If he wanted her dead, he could get her. She didn't want her child left alone in the world.

"I'm going to make some coffee," Dallas said tautly, refusing to think about the possibility of a world without her in it. "What do you take in yours?"

"I don't care," she said indifferently.

He didn't say another word. He went into the kitchen and made a pot of coffee while Jessica sat stiffly in her own living room and contemplated the direction her life had taken.

"YOU HAVE GOT…TO BE KIDDING!" Sally choked as she dragged herself up from the mat for the twentieth time. "You mean I'm going to spend two hours falling down? I thought you were going to teach me self-defense!"

"I am," Eb replied easily. He, too, was wearing sweats now, and he'd been teaching her side breakfalls, first left and then right. "First you learn how to fall properly, so you don't hurt yourself landing. Then we move on to stances, hand positions and kicks. One step at a time."

She swept her arm past her hip and threw herself down on her side, falling with a loud thud but landing neatly. Beside her, Stevie was going at it with a vengeance and laughing gleefully.

"Am I doing it right?" she puffed, already perspiring. She was very much out of condition, despite the work she did around the house.

He nodded. "Very nice. Be careful about falling too close to the edge of the mat, though. The floor's hard."

She moved further onto the mat and did it again.

"If you think these are fun," he mused, "wait until we do forward breakfalls."

She gaped at him. "You mean I'm going to have to fall deliberately on my face? I'll break my nose!"

"No, you won't," he said, moving her aside. "Watch."

He executed the movement to perfection, catching his weight neatly on his hands and forearms. He jumped up again. "See? Simple."

"For you," she agreed, her eyes on the muscular body

that was as fit as that of a man half his age. "Do you train all the time?"

"I have to," he said. "If I let myself get out of shape, I won't be of any use to my students. Great job, Stevie," he called to the boy, who beamed at him.

"Of course he's doing a great job," she muttered. "He's so close to the ground already that he doesn't have far to fall!"

"Poor old lady," he chided gently.

She glared in his direction as she swept her arm forward and threw herself down again. "I'm not old. I'm just out of condition."

He looked at her, sprawled there on the mat, and his lips pursed as he sketched every inch of her. "Funny, I'd have said you were in prime condition. And not just for karate."

She cleared her throat and got to her feet again. "When did you start learning this stuff?"

"When I was in grammar school," he said. "My father taught me."

"No wonder it looks so easy when you do it."

"I train hard. It's saved my life a few times."

She studied his scarred face with curiosity. She could see the years in it, and the hardships. She knew very little about military operations, except for what she'd seen in movies and on television. And as Jess had told her, it wasn't like that in real life. She tried to imagine an armed adversary coming at her and she stiffened.

"Something wrong?" he asked gently.

"I was trying to imagine being attacked," she said. "It makes me nervous."

"It won't, when you gain a little confidence. Stand up straight," he said. "Never walk with your head down in a slumped posture. Always look as if you know where you're going, even if you don't. And always, always, run if you can. Never stand and fight unless you're trapped and your life is in danger."

"Run? You're kidding, of course?"

"No," he said. "I'll give you an example. A man of any size and weight on drugs is more than a match for any three other men. What I'm going to teach you might work on an untrained adversary who's sober. But a man who's been drinking, or especially a man who's using drugs can kill you outright, regardless of what I can teach you. Don't you ever forget that. Overconfidence kills."

"I'll bet you don't teach your men to run," she said accusingly.

His eyes were quiet and full of bad memories. "Sally, a recruit in one of my groups emptied the magazine of his rifle into an enemy soldier on drugs at point-blank range. The enemy kept right on coming. He killed the recruit before he finally fell dead himself."

Her lower jaw fell.

"That was my reaction, too," he informed her. "Absolute disbelief. But it's true. If anyone high on drugs comes at you, don't try to reason with him…you can't. And don't try to fight him. Run like hell. If a full automatic clip won't bring a man down, you certainly can't. Neither can even a combat-hardened man, alone. In that sort of situation, it's just basic common sense to get out of the way as quickly as possible if there's any chance of escape, and pride be damned."

"I'll remember," she said, all her confidence vanishing. She could see in Eb's eyes that he'd watched that recruit die, and had to live with the memory forever in his mind. Probably it was one of many nightmarish episodes he'd like to forget.

"Sometimes retreat really is the better part of valor," he said, smiling.

"You're educational."

He smiled slowly. "Am I, now?" he asked, and the way he looked at her didn't have much to do with teaching her self-defense. "I can think of a few areas where you need...improvement."

She glanced at Stevie, who was still falling on the mat. "You shouldn't try to shoot ducks in a barrel," she told him. "It's unsporting."

"Shooting is not what I have in mind."

She cleared her throat. "I suppose I should try falling some more." She brightened. "Say, if I learn to do this well, I could try falling on an adversary!"

"Ineffective unless you want to gain three hundred pounds," he returned. He grinned. "Although, you could certainly experiment on me, if you want to. It might immobilize me. We won't know until we try it. Want me to lie down and let you practice?" he added with twinkling eyes.

She laughed, but nervously. "I don't think I'm ready to try that right away."

"Suit yourself. No hurry. We've got plenty of time."

She remembered Jess and the drug lord and her eyes grew worried. "Is it really dangerous for us at home...?"

He held up a cautioning hand. "Stevie, how about a soft drink?"

"That would be great!"

"There are some cans of soda in the fridge in the kitchen. How about bringing one for me and your aunt as well?"

"Sure thing!"

Stevie took off like a bullet.

"Yes, it's dangerous," Eb said quietly. "You aren't to go alone, anywhere, at night. I'll always have a man watching the house, but if you have to go to a meeting or some such thing, let me know and I'll go with you."

"Won't that cramp your social life?" she asked without quite meeting his eyes.

"I don't have a social life," he said with a faint smile. "Not of the sort you're talking about."

"Oh."

His face tautened. "Neither do you, if I can believe Jess."

She shifted on the mat. "I haven't really had much time for men."

"You don't have to spare my feelings," he told her quietly. "I know I've caused you some sleepless nights. But you've waited too long to deal with it. The longer you wait, the harder it's going to be to form a relationship with a man."

"I have Jess and Stevie to think about."

"That's an excuse. And not a very good one."

She felt uncomfortable with her memories. She wrapped her arms around her chest and looked at him with shattered dreams in her eyes.

He took a sharp breath. "It will never be like that again," he said curtly. "I promise you it won't."

She averted her eyes to the mat. "Do you think Jess and Dallas have done each other in by now?" she asked, trying to change the subject.

He moved closer, watching her stiffen, watching her draw away from him mentally. His big, lean hands caught her shoulders and he made her look at him.

"You're older now," he said, his voice steady and low. "You should know more about men than you did, even if you've had to learn it through books and television. I was fiercely aroused that day, it had been a long, dry spell, and you were seventeen years old. Get the picture?"

For the first time, she did. Her eyes searched his, warily, and nodded.

His hands contracted on her soft arms. "You might try it again," he said softly.

"Try what?"

"What you did that afternoon," he murmured, smiling tenderly. "Wearing sexy clothes and perfume and making a beeline for me. Anything could happen."

Her eyes were sadder than she realized as she met his even gaze. "I'm not the same person I was then," she told him. "But you still are."

The light seemed to go out of him. His pale eyes narrowed, fastened to hers. "No," he said after a minute.

"I've changed, too. I lost my taste for commando work a long time ago. I teach tactics now. That's all I do."

"You're not a family man," she replied bravely.

Something changed in his face, in his eyes, as he studied her. "I've thought about that a lot recently," he contradicted. "About a home and children. I might have to give up some of the contract work I do, once the kids came along. I won't allow my children anywhere near weapons. But I can always write field manuals and train teachers in tactics and strategy and intelligence-gathering," he added.

"You don't know that you could settle for that," she pointed out.

"Not until I try," he agreed. His gaze fell to her soft mouth and lingered there. "But then, no man really wants to tie himself down. It takes a determined woman to make him want it."

She felt as if he were trying to tell her something, but before she could ask him to clarify what he'd said, Stevie was back with an armful of soft drinks and the moment was lost.

JESS AND DALLAS WEREN'T SPEAKING at all when the others arrived. Dallas was toying with a cup of cold coffee, looking unapproachable. When Eb came in the door, Dallas went out it, without a word or a backward glance.

"I don't need to ask how it went," Eb murmured.

"It would be pretty pointless," Jessica said dully.

"Mama, I learned to do breakfalls! I wish I could

show you," Stevie said, climbing into his mother's lap and hugging her.

She fought tears as she cuddled him close and kissed his sweaty forehead. "Good for you! You listen when Eb tells you something. He's very good."

"Stevie's a natural," Eb chuckled. "In fact, so is your niece." He gave Sally a slow going-over with his eyes.

"She's a quick learner," Jessica said. "Like I was, once."

"I have to get back," Eb said. "There's nothing to worry about right now," he added, careful not to speak too bluntly in front of the child. "I have everything in hand. But I have told Sally to let me know if she plans to go out alone at night, for any reason."

"I will," Sally promised. She didn't want to risk her aunt's life, or Stevie's, by being too independent.

Eb nodded. "We'll keep the lessons up at least three times a week," he told Sally. "I want to move you into self-defense pretty quickly."

She understood why and felt uneasy. "Okay."

"Don't worry," he said gently. "Everything's going to be fine. I know exactly what I'm doing."

She managed a smile for him. "I know that."

"Walk me to the door," he coaxed. "See you, Jess."

"Take care, Eb," Jessie replied, her goodbye echoed by her son's.

On the front porch, Eb closed the door and looked down into Sally's wide gray eyes with concern and something more elusive.

"I'll have the house watched," he promised. "But you have to be careful about even normal things like opening the door when someone comes. Always keep the chain lock on until you know who's out there. Another thing, you have to keep your doors and windows locked, curtains drawn and an escape route always in mind."

She bit her lip worriedly. "I've never had to deal with anything like this."

His big, warm hands closed over her shoulders. "I know. I'm sorry that you and Stevie have been put in the line of fire along with Jess. But you can handle this," he said confidently. "You're strong. You can do whatever you have to do."

She searched his hard, lean face, saw the deep lines and scars that the violence of his life had carved into it, and knew that he would never lie to her. Her frown dissolved. His confidence in her made her feel capable of anything. She smiled.

He smiled back and traced a lazy line from her cheek down to her soft mouth. "If Stevie wasn't so unpredictable, I'd kiss you," he said quietly. "I like your mouth under mine."

Her caught breath was audible. There had never been anyone who could do to her with words what he could.

He traced her lips, entranced. "I used to dream about that afternoon with you," he said in a sensuous tone. "I woke up sweating, swearing, hating myself for what I'd done." He laughed hollowly. "Hating you for what I'd done, too," he added. "I blamed us both. But I couldn't forget how it was."

She colored delicately and lowered her eyes to his broad chest under the shirt he wore. The memories were so close to the surface of her mind that it was impossible not to glimpse them from time to time. Now, they were blatant and embarrassing.

His lean hands moved up to frame her face and force her eyes to meet his. He wasn't smiling.

"No other man will ever have the taste of you that I did, that day," he said roughly. "You were so deliciously innocent."

Her lips parted at the intensity of his tone, at the faint glitter of his green eyes. "That isn't what you said at the time!" she accused.

"At the time," he murmured huskily, watching her mouth, "I was hurting so much that I didn't take time to choose my words. I just wanted you out of the damned truck before I started stripping you out of those tight little shorts you were wearing."

The flush in her cheeks got worse. The image of it was unbelievably shocking. Somehow, it had never occurred to her that at some point he might undress her, to gain access...

"What an expression," he said, chuckling in spite of himself. "Hadn't you considered what might happen when you came on to me that hard?"

She shook her head.

His fingers slid into the blond hair at her temples where the long braid pulled it away from her face. "Someone should have had a long talk with you."

"You did," she recalled nervously.

"Long and explicit, the day afterward," he said, nodding. "You didn't want to hear it, but I made you. I liked to think that it might have saved you from an even worse experience."

"It wasn't exactly a bad experience," she said, staring at his shirt button. "That was part of the problem."

There was a long, static silence. "Sally," he breathed, and his mouth moved down slowly to cover hers in the silence of the porch.

She stood on tiptoe to coax him closer, lost in the memory of that long-ago afternoon. She felt his hands on her arms, guiding them up around his neck before they fell back to her hips and lifted her into the suddenly swollen contours of his muscular body.

She gasped, giving him the opening he wanted, so that he could deepen the kiss. She felt the warm hardness of his mouth against hers, the soft nip of his teeth, the deep exploration of his tongue. A warm flood of sensation rushed into her lower abdomen and she felt her whole body go tense with it. It was as if her body had become perfectly attuned to this man's years ago, and could never belong to anyone else.

He felt her headlong response and slowly let her back down, lifting his mouth away from hers. He studied her face, her swollen, soft mouth, her wide eyes, her dazed expression.

"Yes," he said huskily.

"Yes?"

He bent and nipped her lower lip sensuously before he pushed her away.

She stared up at him helplessly, feeling as if she'd just been dropped from a great height.

His eyes went to her breasts and lingered on the sharp little points so noticeable at the front of her blouse, the fabric jumping with every hard, quick beat of her heart.

She met that searching gaze and felt the power of it all the way to her toes.

"You know as well as I do that it's only a matter of time," he said softly. "It always has been."

She frowned. Her mind seemed to have shut down. She couldn't quite focus, and her legs felt decidedly weak.

His eyes were back on her breasts, swerving to the closed door, and to both curtained windows before he stepped in close and cupped her blatantly in his warm, sensuous hands.

Sally's mouth opened on a shocked gasp that became suddenly a moan of pleasure.

"I won't hurt you," he whispered, and his mouth covered hers hungrily.

It was the most passionate, adult kiss of her life, even eclipsing what had come before. His hands found their way under her sweatshirt and against lace-covered soft flesh. Her body responded instantly to the slow caresses. She curled into his body, eagerly submissive.

"Lord, what I wouldn't give to unfasten this," he groaned at her mouth as his fingers toyed with the closure at her back. "And sure as hell, Stevie would come outside the minute I did, and show and tell would take on a whole new meaning."

The idea of it amused him and he lifted his head, smiling down into Sally's equally laughing eyes.

"Ah, well," he said, removing his hands with evident reluctance. "All things come to those who wait," he added.

Sally blushed and moved a little away from him.

"Don't be embarrassed," he chided gently, his green eyes sparkling, full of mischief and pleasure. "All of us have a weak spot."

"Not you, man of steel," she teased.

"We'll talk about that next time," he said. "Meanwhile, remember what I said. Especially about night trips."

"Now where would I go alone at night in Jacobsville?" she asked patiently.

He only laughed. But even as she watched him drive away she remembered an upcoming parents and teachers meeting. There would be plenty of time to tell him about that, she reminded herself. She turned back into the house, her mouth and body still tingling pleasantly.

CHAPTER FOUR

JESSICA WAS SUBDUED AFTER the time she'd spent with Dallas. Even Stevie noticed, and became more attentive. Sally cooked her aunt's favorite dishes and did her best to coax Jess into a better frame of mind. But the other woman's sadness was blatant.

With her mind on Jessica and not on time passing, she forgot that she had a parents and teachers meeting the next Tuesday night. She phoned Eb's ranch, as she'd been told to, but all she got was the answering machine and a message that only asked the caller to leave a name and number. She left a message, doubting that he'd hear it before she was safely home. She hadn't really believed him when he'd said the whole family was in danger, especially since nothing out of the ordinary had happened. But even so, surely nothing was going to happen to her on a two-mile drive home!

She sent Stevie home with a fellow teacher. The business meeting was long and explosive, and it was much later than usual when it was finally over. Sally spoke to the parents she knew and left early. She wasn't thinking about anything except her bed as she drove down the long, lonely road toward home. As she passed the large house and accompanying acreage where her three neighbors lived, she felt a chill. Three of them were out on their front porch. The light was on, and it looked as if they were arguing about something. They caught sight of her truck and there was an ominous stillness about them.

Sally drove faster, aware that she drew their attention as she went past them. Only a few more minutes, she thought, and she'd be home...

The steering wheel suddenly became difficult to turn and with horror she heard the sound of a tire going flatter and flatter. Her heart flipped over. She didn't have a spare. She'd rolled it out of the bed to make room for the cattle feed she'd taken home last week, having meant to ask Eb to help her put it back in again. But she'd have to walk the rest of the way, now. Worse, it was dark and those creepy men were still watching the truck.

Well, she told herself as she climbed out of the cab with her purse over her shoulder, they weren't going to give her any trouble. She had a loud whistling device, and she now knew at least enough self-defense to protect herself. Confident, despite Eb's earlier warnings, she locked the truck and started walking.

The sound of running feet came toward her. She looked over her shoulder and stopped, turning, her mouth set in a grim line. Two of the three men were coming down the road toward her in a straight line. Just be calm, she told herself. She was wearing a neat gray pantsuit with a white blouse, her hair was up in a French twist, and she lifted her chin to show that she wasn't afraid of them. Feeling her chances of a physical defense waning rapidly as she saw the size and strength of the two men, her hand went nervously to the whistle in her pocketbook and brought it by her side.

"Hey, there, sweet thing," one of the men called. "Got a flat? We'll help you change it."

The other man, a little taller, untidy, unshaved and frankly unpleasant-looking, grinned at her. "You bet we will!"

"I don't have a spare, thank you all the same."

"We'll drive you home," the tall one said.

She forced a smile. "No, thanks. I'll enjoy the walk. Good night!"

She started to turn when they pounced. One knocked the whistle out of her hand and caught her arm behind her back, while the other one took her purse off her shoulder and went through it quickly. He pulled out her wallet, looked at everything in it, and finally took out a bill, dropping her self-defense spray with the purse.

"Ten lousy bucks," he muttered, dropping the bag as he stuffed the bill into his pocket. "Pity Lopez don't pay us better. This'll buy us a couple of six-packs, though."

"Let me go," Sally said, incensed. She tried to bring her elbow back into the man's stomach, as she'd seen an instructor on television do, but the man twisted her other arm so harshly that the pain stopped her dead.

The other man came right up to her and looked her up and down. "Not bad," he rasped. "Quick, bring her over here, off the road," he told the other man.

"Lopez won't like this!" The man on the porch came

toward them, yelling across the road. "You'll draw attention to us!"

One of them made a rude remark. The third man went back up on the porch, his footsteps sounding unnaturally loud on the wood.

Sally was almost sick with fear, but she fought like a tigress. Her efforts to break free did no good. These men were bigger and stronger than she was, and they had her helpless. She couldn't get to her whistle or spray and every kick, punch she tried was effectively blocked. It occurred to her that these men knew self-defense moves, too, and how to avoid them. Too late, she remembered what Eb had said to her about overconfidence. These men weren't even drunk and they were too much for her.

Her heart beat wildly as she was dragged off the road to the thick grass at the roadside. She would struggle, she would fight, but she was no match for them. She knew she was in a lot of danger and it looked like there was no escape. Tears of impotent fury dripped from her eyes. Helpless while one of the men kept her immobilized, she remembered the sound of her own voice telling her aunt just a few weeks ago that she could handle anything. She'd been overconfident.

A sound buzzed in her head and at first she thought it was the prelude to a dead faint. It wasn't. The sound was growing closer. It was a pickup truck. The headlights illuminated her truck on the roadside, but not the struggle that was going on near it.

It was as if the driver knew what was happening

without seeing it. The truck whipped onto the shoulder and was cut off. A man got out, a tall man in a shepherd's coat with a Stetson drawn over his brow. He walked straight toward the two men, who released Sally and turned to face the new threat. Eb!

"Car trouble?" a deep, gravelly voice asked sarcastically.

One of the men pulled a knife, and the other one approached the newcomer. "This ain't none of your business," the taller man said. "Get going."

The newcomer put his hands on his lean hips and stood his ground. "In your dreams."

"You'll wish you had," the taller of them replied harshly. He moved in with the knife close in at his side.

Sally stared in horror at Eb, who was inviting this lunatic to kill him! She knew from television how deadly a knife wound in the stomach could be. Hadn't Eb told her that the best way to survive a knife fight was to never get in one in the first place, to run like hell? And now Eb was going to be killed and it was going to be all her fault for not taking his advice and getting that tire fixed…!

Eb moved unexpectedly, with the speed of a striking cobra. The man with the knife was suddenly writhing on the ground, holding his forearm and sobbing. The other man rushed forward, to be flipped right out into the highway. He got up and rushed again. This time he was met with a violent, sharp movement that sent him to the ground, and he didn't get up.

Eb walked right over the unconscious man, ignoring

the groaning man, and picked Sally up right off the ground in his arms. He carried her to his truck, balancing her on one powerful denim-covered thigh while he opened the passenger door and put her inside.

"My…purse," she whispered, giving in to the shock and fear that she'd tried so hard to hide. She was shaking so hard her speech was slurred.

He closed the door, retrieved her purse and wallet from the ground, and handed it in through his open door. "What did they take, baby?" he asked in a soft, comforting tone.

"The tall one…took a ten-dollar bill," she faltered, hating her own cowardice as she sobbed helplessly. "In his pocket…"

Eb retrieved it, tossed it to her and got in beside her.

"But those men," she protested.

"Be still for a minute. It's all right. They look worse than they are." He took a cell phone from his pocket, opened it, and dialed. "Bill? Eb Scott. I left you a couple of assailants on the Simmons Mill Road just past Bell's rental house. That's right, the very one." He glanced at Sally. "Not tonight. I'll tell her to come see you in the morning." There was a pause. "Nothing too bad; a couple of broken bones, that's all, but you might send the ambulance anyway. Sure. Thanks, Bill."

He powered down the phone and stuck it back into his jacket. "Fasten your seat belt. I'll take you home and send one of my men out to fix the truck and drive it back for you."

Her hands were shaking so badly that he had to do it

for her. He turned on the light in the cab and looked at her intently. He saw the shock, the fear, the humiliation, the anger, all lying naked in her wide, shimmering gray eyes. Last, his eyes fell to her blouse, where the fabric was torn, and her simple cotton brassiere was showing. She was so upset that she didn't even realize how much bare skin was on display.

He took off the long-sleeved chambray shirt he was wearing over his black T-shirt and put her into it, fastening the buttons with deft, quick hands over the ripped blouse. His face grew hard as he saw the evidence of her ordeal.

"I had a…a…whistle." she choked. "I even remembered what you taught me about how to fight back…!"

He studied her solemnly. "I trained a company of recruits a few years ago," he said evenly. "They'd had hand-to-hand combat training and they knew all the right moves to counter any sort of physical attack. There wasn't one of them that I couldn't drop in less than ten seconds." His pale green eyes searched hers. "Even a martial artist can lose a match. It depends on the skill of his opponent and his ability to keep his head when the attack comes. I've seen karate instructors send advanced students running with nothing more dangerous than the yell, a sudden quick sound that paralyzes."

"Those two men…they couldn't…touch you," she pointed out, amazed.

His pale eyes had an alien coldness that made her shiver. "I told you to get that damned tire fixed, Sally."

She swallowed. Her pride was bruised almost beyond

bearing. "I don't take orders," she said, trying to salvage a little self-respect.

"I don't give them anymore," he returned. "But I do give advice, and you've just seen the results of not listening. At least you had the sense to leave a message on my answering machine. But what if I hadn't checked my messages, Sally? Would you like to think where you'd be now? Want me to paint you a picture?"

"Stop!" She put her face in her hands and shivered.

"I won't apologize," he told her abruptly. "You did a damned stupid thing and you got off lucky. Another time, I might not be quick enough."

She swallowed and swallowed again. "The...conquering male," she choked, but she wasn't teasing now, as she had been that afternoon when he'd told her to get the tire fixed.

He drew her hands away from her face and looked into her eyes steadily. "That's right," he said curtly, and he wasn't kidding. "I've been dealing with vermin like that for almost half my life. I told you there was danger in going out alone. Now you understand what I meant. Get that damned tire fixed, and buy a cell phone."

Her head was spinning. "I can't afford one," she said unsteadily.

"You can't afford not to. If you'd had one tonight, this might never have happened," he said forcefully. The heat in his eyes made her shiver. "A man is physically stronger than a woman. There are some exceptions, but for the most part, that's the honest truth. Unless you've trained for years, like a policewoman or a federal agent, you're not going to be the equal of a man who's drunk or on drugs or just bent on assault. Law enforcement people know how to fight. You don't."

She shivered again. Her hair was disheveled. She felt bruises on her arms where she'd been restrained by those men. She was still stunned by the experience, but already a little of the horror of what might have happened was getting to her.

He let her wrists go abruptly. His lean face softened as he studied her. "But I'll say one thing for you. You've got grit."

"Sure. I'm tough," she laughed hollowly, brushing a strand of loose hair out of her eyes. "What a pitiful waste of self-confidence!"

"Who the hell taught you about canned self-defense?" he asked curiously, referring to the can of spray on the ground.

"There was this television self-defense training course for women," she said defensively.

"Anything you spray, pepper or chemical, can rebound on you," he said quietly. "If the wind's blowing the wrong way, you can blind yourself. If you don't hit the attacker squarely in the eyes, you're no better off, either. As for the whistle, tonight there would have been no one close enough to hear it." He sighed at her miserable expression and shook his head. "Didn't I tell you to run?"

She lifted a high-heeled foot eloquently.

He leaned closer. "If you're ever in a similar situation again, kick them off and try for the two-minute mile!"

She managed a smile for him. "Okay."

He touched her wan, drawn face gently. "I wouldn't have had that happen to you for the world," he said bitterly.

"You were right, I brought it on myself. I won't make that mistake again, and at least I got away with everything except my pride intact," she said gamely.

He unfastened her seat belt, aware of a curtain being lifted and then released in the living room. "I sent Dallas straight here as soon as I got the message," he explained, "to watch out for Jess and Stevie. You should have let me know about this night meeting much sooner."

"I know." She was fighting tears. The whole experience had been a shock that she knew she'd never get over. "There was a third man, on the porch. He said that Lopez wouldn't like what they were doing, calling attention to themselves."

He stared at her for a long moment, seeing the fear and terror and revulsion that lingered in her oval face, watching the way her hands clenched at the shirt he'd fastened over her torn bodice. He glanced at the window, where the curtain was in place again, and back to Sally's face.

"Come here, sweetheart," he said tenderly, pulling her into his arms. He cuddled her close, nuzzling his face into her throat, letting her cry.

Her clenched fist rested against his black undershirt and she sobbed with impotent fury. "Oh, I'm so…mad!" she choked. "So mad! I felt like a rag doll."

"You do your best and take what comes," he said at her ear. "Anybody can lose a fight."

"I'll bet you never lost one," she muttered tearfully.

"I got the hell beaten out of me in boot camp by a little guy half my size, who was a hapkido master. Taught me a valuable lesson about overconfidence," he said deliberately.

She took the handkerchief he placed in her hands and wiped her nose and eyes and mouth. "Okay, I get the message," she said on a broken sigh. "There's always somebody bigger and you can't win every time."

"Nice attitude," he said, approving.

She wiped away the last trace of tears and looked up at him from her comfortable position across his lap. "Thanks for the hero stuff."

He shrugged. "Shucks, ma'am, t'weren't nothin'."

She laughed, as she was meant to. Her eyes adored him. "They say that if you save a life, it becomes yours."

His lips pursed and he looked down at where the jacket barely covered her torn blouse. "Do I get that, too?"

"Too?"

He opened the shirt very slowly and looked at the pale flesh under the torn blouse. There was a lot of it on view. Sally didn't protest, didn't grab at cover. She lay very still in his arms and let him look at her.

His pale eyes met hers in the faint light coming from the house. "No protest?"

"You saved me," she said simply. She sighed and smiled with resignation. "I belonged to you, anyway. There's never been anyone else."

His long, lean fingers touched her collarbone, his eyes narrow and solemn, his expression serious, intent. "That could have changed, tonight," he reminded her quietly. "You have to trust me enough to do what I tell you. I don't want you hurt in this. I'll do anything I have to, to protect you. That includes having a man follow you around like a visible appendage if you push me to it. Think what your principal would make of *that!*"

"I won't make any more stupid mistakes," she promised.

"What would you call this?" he mused, nodding toward the ripped fabric that left one pretty, taut breast completely bare.

"Cover me up if you don't like what you see," she challenged.

He actually laughed. She was constantly surprising him. "I think I'd better," he murmured dryly, and pulled the shirt back over her, leaving her to button it again. "Dallas is at the window getting an education."

"And I can tell how much he needs it," she said with dry humor as Eb helped her back into her own seat.

"That makes two of you," Eb told her. His eyes were kind, and now full of concern. "Will you be all right?"

"Yes." She hesitated with her hand on the doorknob. "Eb, is it always like that?"

He frowned. "What?"

She looked up into his eyes. "Physical violence. Do you ever get to the point that it doesn't make you sick inside?"

"I never have," he said flatly. "I remember every face, every sound, every sick minute of what I've done in my life." He looked at her, but he seemed to go far away. "You'd better go inside. I'll take you and Stevie out to the ranch Thursday and Saturday and we'll put in some more time."

"For all the good it will do me," she managed to say nervously.

"Don't be like that," he chided. "You got overpowered. People do, even 'big, strong' men. There's no shame in losing a fight when you've given it all you've got."

She smiled. "Think so?"

"I know so." He touched her disheveled French knot. "You wore your hair down that spring afternoon," he murmured softly. "I remember how it felt on my bare chest, loose and smelling of flowers."

Her breath seemed to stick in her throat as she recalled the same memory. They had both been bare to the waist. She could close her eyes and feel the hair-roughened muscles of his chest against her own softness as he kissed her and kissed her...

"Sometimes," he continued, "we get second chances."

"Do we?" she whispered.

He touched her mouth gently. "Try not to dwell on what happened tonight," he said. "I won't let anyone hurt you, Sally."

That felt nice. She wished she could give him the same guarantee, but it seemed pretty ridiculous after her poor performance.

He seemed to read the thought right in her mind, and he burst out laughing. "Listen, lady, when I get through with you, you'll be eating bad men raw," he promised. "You're just a beginner."

"You aren't."

"That's true. And not only in self-defense," he added dryly. "You'd better go in."

"I suppose so." She picked at the buttons of the shirt he'd loaned her. "I'll give it back. Eventually."

"You look nice in it," he had to admit. "You can keep it. We'll try some more of my clothes on you and see how they look."

She made a face at him as she opened the door. "Eb, do I have to go and see the sheriff?"

"You do. I'll pick you up after school. Don't worry," he said quietly. "He won't eat you. He's a nice man. But you must see that we can't let Lopez's people get away with this."

She felt a chill go down her arms as she remembered who Lopez was. "What will he do if I testify against his men?"

"You let me worry about that," Eb told her, and his eyes were like green steel. "Nobody touches you without going through me."

Her heart jumped right up into her throat as she stared at him. She was a modern woman, and she probably shouldn't have enjoyed that passionate remark. But she did. Eb was a strong, assertive man who would want a woman to match him. Sally hadn't been that woman at seventeen. But she was now. She could stand up to him and meet him on his own ground. It gave her a sense of pride.

"Debating if it's proper for a modern woman to like being protected?" he chided with a wicked grin.

"You said yourself that none of us are invincible," she

pointed out. "I don't think it's a bad thing to admire a man's strength, especially when it's just saved my neck."

He made her feel confident, he gave her joy. It had been years since she'd laughed so much, enjoyed life so much. Odd that a man whose adult years had been imbued with such violence could be so tender.

"Okay now?" he asked.

She nodded. "I'm okay." She glanced toward the road and shivered a little. "They won't come looking for me?"

"Not in that condition they won't," he said matter-of-factly. "And they're very lucky," he added, his whole face like drawn cord. "Ten years ago, I wouldn't have been so gentle."

Both eyebrows went up at the imagery.

"You know what I was," he said quietly. "Until comparatively recent years, I lived a violent, uncertain life. Part of the man I was is still in me. I won't ever hurt you," he added. "But I have to come to grips with the old life before I can begin a new one. That's going to take time."

"I think you're saying something."

"Why, yes, I am," he mused, watching her. "I'm giving notice of my intentions."

"Intentions?"

"Last time I stopped. Next time I won't."

Her mind wasn't quite grasping what he was telling her. "You mean, with those men...?"

"I mean with you," he said gently. "I want you very badly, and I'm not walking away this time."

"You and what army?" she asked, aghast.

"I won't need an army. But you might." He smiled. "Go on in. I'm having the house watched. You'll be safe, I promise."

She pulled his shirt closer. "Thanks, Eb," she said.

He shrugged. "I have to take care of my own. Try to sleep."

She smiled at him. "Okay. You, too."

He watched her go up onto the porch and into the house, waiting for Dallas, who came out tight-lipped with barely a word to Sally as he passed her.

He got into the truck with Eb and slammed the door.

"What happened to Sally?" he asked, putting his cane aside.

"Lopez's men rushed the truck when she had a flat. I don't know if it was premeditated," he added coldly. "They could have lain in wait for her and caused the flat. The tire was almost bald, but it could have gone another few hundred miles."

"She looked uneasy."

"They assaulted her and may have raped her if I hadn't shown up," Eb said bluntly as he backed the truck and pulled out into the road. "I want to have another look, if the ambulance hasn't picked them up yet."

"You sent for an ambulance?" Dallas asked with mock surprise. "That's new."

"Well, we're trying to blend in, aren't we?" came the terse reply. He glared at the tall blond man. "Difficult to blend in if we let people die on the side of the road."

"If you say so."

They drove to where Sally's pickup truck was still sitting, but there was no sign of the two men. The house nearby was dark. There wasn't a soul in sight.

As Eb digested that, red lights flashed and a big boxy ambulance pulled up behind the pickup truck, followed closely by a deputy sheriff in a patrol car.

Eb pulled off the road and got out. He knew the deputy, Rich Burton, who was one of the department's ablest members. They shook hands.

"Where are the victims?" Rich asked.

Eb grimaced. "Well, they were both lying right there when I took Sally home."

The deputy and the ambulance guys looked toward the flattened grass, but there weren't any men lying there.

"Unless one of you needs medical attention, we'll be on our way," one of the EMTs said with a wry glance.

"Both of the perps did," Eb said quietly. "At least one of them has broken bones."

The EMT gave him a wary look. "Not their legs, by the look of things."

"No. Not their legs."

The EMTs left and Rich joined Eb and Dallas beside the truck.

"Something's going on at that house," Rich said quietly. "I've had total strangers stop me and tell me they've seen suspicious activity, men carrying boxes in and out. That's not all. Some holding company bought a huge tract of land adjoining Cy Parks's place, and it's filling up with building supplies. There's a contractor been hired and a plan has gone to the county commission's planning committee about a business starting up there."

"How much do you know about the men who live here?" Eb asked coolly.

Rich shrugged. "Not as much as I'd like to. But my contacts tell me that there's a drug lord named Manuel Lopez, and the talk is that these guys belong to him. They're mules. They run his narcotics for him."

Eb and Dallas exchanged quiet glances.

"What sort of business are we talking about?" Eb queried.

"Don't know. There's a huge steel warehouse going up behind Parks's place," Rich replied, and he looked worried. "If I were making a guess, and it is just a guess, I'd say somebody had distribution in mind."

CHAPTER FIVE

"A DISTRIBUTION CENTER," Eb said curtly. "With Manuel Lopez, the head of the most violent of the international drug cartels, behind it! That's just what we need in Jacobsville."

"That's right," the younger man replied. He scowled. "How do you know about Lopez?"

Eb didn't answer. "Thanks, Rich," he said. "If I hear anything about the men who attacked Miss Johnson, I'll give you a call."

"Thanks. But I'd bet that they're long gone," he said carelessly. "They'd be crazy to stick around and face charges like attempted rape in a town this size. Lopez wouldn't like the notoriety."

"My guess exactly. So long," Eb said, motioning to Dallas. Rich drove off with a wave of his hand. Eb hesitated, and once Rich was out of sight, he looked for and found a board with new nails sticking through it. It was lying point-side down, now, but the wood was new and there was a long cord attached to it. Evidently it had been placed in the road just as Sally approached, and then jerked away once Sally had run over it. That meant that there had to be a fourth man involved, besides the man on the porch and the two men who'd assaulted Sally. That disturbed Eb.

"They set a trap," Dallas guessed. "She ran over this. That's how she got the flat."

"Exactly." Eb threw the board in the bed of the truck before he climbed in under the wheel. "There were at least four men in on it, and I don't think assault was the sole object of the exercise. I think I'll go over and have a talk with Cy Parks first thing in the morning. He may know something about that new construction behind his place."

CY PARKS WAS GRUMPY. He hadn't been able to sleep the night before, and he was groggy. Even after four years, he still had nightmares about the loss of his wife and five-year-old son in a fire back home in Wyoming. He'd moved here to Jacobsville, where Ebenezer Scott lived, more for someone to talk to than any other reason. Eb was not only a former comrade at arms, but he was also the only man he knew who could listen to the un-abridged horror of the fire without losing his supper. It kept him sane, just having someone to talk to. And not only could he talk about the death of his family at Lopez's henchmen's hands but also he had someone to help him exorcise the nightmares of the past that he and Ebenezer shared.

The knock on the door came just as he was pouring his second cup of coffee. It was probably his foreman. Harley Fowler was an adventurer wannabe who fancied himself a mercenary. He was forever reading a magazine for armchair adventurers and once he'd actually answered one of the ads for volunteers and, supposedly, had taken a job during his summer vacation. He'd come back from his vacation two weeks later grinning and bragging about his exploits overseas with a group of world-beaters and lording it over the other ranch hands who worked for Cy. Harley had become the overnight hero of the men. Cy watched him with amused cynicism. None of the men he'd served with had ever returned home strutting and bragging about their exploits. Nor had any of them come home smiling. There was a look about a man who'd seen combat. It was unmistakable to anyone who'd been through it. Harley didn't have the look.

None of the ranch hands knew that Cy Parks hadn't always been a rancher. They knew about the fire that had cost him his family—most people locally did. But they didn't know that he was a former professional mercenary and that Lopez was responsible for the fire. Cy wanted to keep it that way. He was through with the old life.

He opened the front door with a scowl on his lean, tanned face, but it wasn't Harley who was standing on his porch. It was Ebenezer Scott.

Cy's eyes, two shades darker green than Eb's, narrowed. "Lost your way?" he taunted, running a hand through his thick unruly black hair.

Eb chuckled. "Years ago. Got another cup?"

"Sure." He opened the door and let Eb in. The living room, old-fashioned and sparsely furnished, was neat as a pin. So were the formal dining room—never used—

and the big, airy kitchen with not a spot of dirt or grime anywhere.

"Tell me you hired a housekeeper," Eb murmured.

Cy got down an extra cup and poured black coffee into it, handing it across the table before he sat down. "I don't need a housekeeper," he replied. "Why are you here?" he added with characteristic bluntness.

"Did you keep in touch with any of your old contacts when you got out of the business?" Eb asked at once.

Cy shook his head. "No need. I gave it up, remember?" He lifted the cup to his wide, chiseled mouth.

Eb sipped coffee, nodded at the strength of it, and put the mug down on the Formica tabletop with a soft thud. "Manuel Lopez is loose," he said without preamble. "We think he's in the vicinity. Certainly some of his henchmen are."

Cy's face hardened. "Are you certain?"

"Yes."

"Why is he here?"

"Because Jessica Myers is here," Eb replied. "She's living with her young son and her niece, Sally Johnson, out at the old Johnson place. She got one of Lopez's accomplices to rat on Lopez without giving himself away. She had access to documents and bank accounts and witnesses willing to testify. Now Lopez is out and he's after Jess. He wants the name of the henchman who sold him out."

Cy made an impatient gesture. "Fighting out in the open isn't Lopez's style. He's the original knife-in-the-back boy."

"I know. It worries me." He sipped more coffee. "He had three, maybe four, of his thugs living in a rental place near Sally's house. Two of them attacked her last night when her truck had a flat tire just down the road from them. It was no accident, either. They've obviously been gathering intelligence, watching her. They knew exactly where she was and exactly when she'd get as far as their place." His face was grim. "I think there are more than four of them. I also think they may have the same sort of surveillance equipment I maintain at the ranch. What I don't know is why. I don't know if it's solely because Lopez wants to get to Jessica."

"Is Sally all right?"

Eb nodded. "I got to her in time, luckily. I broke a couple of bones for her assailants, but they got away and now the house seems to be without tenants—temporarily, of course. Have you noticed any activity on your northern boundary?"

"As a matter of fact, I have," Cy replied, frowning. "All sorts of vehicles are coming and going. They've graded about an acre, and a steel warehouse is going up. The city planning commission chairman says it's going to be some sort of production and distribution center for a honey concern. They even have a building permit." He sighed angrily. "Matt Caldwell has been having hell with the planning commission about a project of his own, yet this gang got what they wanted immediately."

"Honey," Eb mused.

"That isn't all of it," Cy continued. "I investigated the holding company that bought the land behind me. It doesn't belong to anybody local, but I can't find out who's behind it. It belongs to a corporation based in Cancún, Mexico."

Eb's eyes narrowed. "Cancún? Now, that's interesting. The last report I had about Lopez before he was arrested was that he bought property there and was living like a king in a palatial estate just outside Cancún." He stopped dead at the expression on his friend's face. Cy and Eb had once helped put some of Lopez's men away.

Cy's breathing became rough, his green eyes began to glitter like heated emeralds. "Lopez! Now what the hell would he want with a honey business?"

"It's evidently going to be a front for something illegal," Eb assured him. "He may have picked Jacobsville for a distribution center for his 'product' because it's small, isolated, and there are no federal agencies represented near here."

Cy stood up, his whole body rigid with hatred and anger. "He killed my wife and son...!"

"He had Jessica run off the road and almost killed," Eb added coldly. "She lived, but she was blinded. She came back here from Houston, hoping that I could protect her. But it's going to take more than me. I need help. I want to set up a listening post on your back forty and put a man there."

"Done," Cy said at once. "But first I'm going to buy a few claymores..."

It took a minute for the expression on Cy's face, in his eyes, in the set of his lean body to register. Eb had only seen him like that once before, in combat, many years before. Probably that was the way he'd looked when his wife and son died and he was hospitalized with severe burns on one arm, incurred when he'd tried to save them from the raging fire. He hadn't known at the time that Lopez had sent men to kill him. Even in prison, Lopez could put out contracts.

"You can't start setting off land mines. You have to think with your brain, not your guts," Eb said curtly. "If we're going to get Lopez, we have to do it legally."

"Oh, that's new, coming from you," Cy said with biting sarcasm.

Eb's broad shoulders lifted and fell as he sat down again, straddling the chair this time. "I'm reformed," he said. "I want to settle down, but first I have to put Lopez away. I need you."

Cy extended the hand that had been so badly burned.

"I know about the burns," Eb said. "If you recall, most of us went to see you in the hospital afterward."

Cy averted his eyes and pulled the sleeve down over his wrist, holding it there protectively. "I don't remember much of it," he confessed. "They sent me to a burn unit and did what they could. At least I was able to keep the arm, but I'll never be much good in a tight corner again."

"You mean you were before?" Eb asked with howling mockery.

Cy's eyes widened, narrowed and suddenly he burst out laughing. "I'd forgotten what a bunch of sadists you and your men were," he accused. "Before every search and destroy mission, somebody was claiming my gear and asking about my beneficiary." Cy drew in a long breath. "I've been keeping to myself for a long time."

"So we noticed," came the dry reply. "I hear it took a bunch of troubled adolescents to drag you out of your cave."

Cy knew what he meant. Belinda Jessup, a public defender, had bought some of the property on his boundary for a summer camp for youthful offenders on probation. One of the boys, an African-American youth who'd fallen absolutely in love with the cattle business, had gotten through his shell. He'd worked with Luke Craig, another neighbor, to give the boy a head start in cowboying. He was now working for Luke Craig on his ranch and had made a top hand. No more legal troubles for him. He was on his way to being foreman of the whole outfit, and Cy couldn't repress a tingle of pride that he'd had a hand in that.

"Even assuming that we can send Lopez back to prison, that won't stop him from appointing somebody to run his empire. You know how these groups are organized," Cy added, "into cells of ten or more men with their chiefs reporting to a regional manager and those managers reporting to a high-level management designee. The damned cartels operate on a corporate structure these days."

"Yes, I know, and they work complete with pagers, cell phones and faxes, using them just long enough to avoid detection," Eb agreed. "They're efficient and they're merciless. God only knows how many undercover agents the drug enforcement people have lost, not to mention those from other law enforcement agencies. The drug lords make a religion of intimidation, and they have no scruples about killing a man and his entire family. No wonder few of their henchmen ever cross them. But one did, and Jessica knows his name. I don't expect Lopez to give up. Ever."

"Neither do I. But what are we going to do about Lopez's planned operation?" Cy wanted to know.

Eb sobered. "I don't have a plan yet. Legally, we can't do anything without hard evidence. Lopez will be extra careful about covering his tracks this time. He won't want anything that will connect him on paper to the drug operation. From what I've been able to learn, Lopez has already skipped town, forfeiting the bond. Believe me, there's no way in hell he'll ever get extradited from Mexico. The only way we'll ever get him back behind bars again is to lure him back here and have him nabbed by the U.S. Marshals Service. He's at the top of the DEA's Most Wanted list right now." He finished his second cup of coffee. "If we can get a legal wiretap on the phones in that warehouse once it's operating, we might have something to take to the authorities. I know a DEA agent," Eb said thoughtfully. "In fact, he and his wife are neighbors of yours. He's gung-ho at his job, and he's done some undercover work before."

"Most of Lopez's people are Hispanic," Cy pointed out.

"This guy could pass for Hispanic. Good-looking devil, too. His wife's father left her that small ranch…"

"Lisa Monroe," Cy said, and averted his eyes. "Yes, I've seen her around. Yesterday she was heaving bales of hay over the fence to her horse," he added in the coldest tones Eb had ever heard him use. "She's thinner than she should be, and she has no business trying to heft bales of hay!"

"When her husband's not home to do it for her…"

"Not home?" Cy's eyes widened. "Good God, man, he was standing ten feet away talking to a leggy blond girl in an express delivery uniform! He didn't even seem to notice Lisa!"

"It's not our business."

Cy moved abruptly, standing up. "Okay. Point taken. Suppose we ride up to the boundary and take a look at the progress on that warehouse," he said. "We can take horses and pretend we're riding the fence line."

Eb retrieved high-powered binoculars from the truck and by the time he got to the stable, Cy's young foreman had two horses saddled and waiting.

"Mr. Scott!" Harley said with a starstruck grin, running a hand absently through his crew-cut light brown hair. "Nice to see you, sir!" He almost saluted. He knew about Mr. Scott's operation; he'd read all about it in his armchair covert operations magazine, to say nothing of the top secret newsletter to which he subscribed.

Eb gave him a measuring glance and he didn't smile. "Do I know you, son?"

"Oh, no, sir," Harley said quickly. "But I've read about your operation!"

"I can imagine what," Eb chuckled. He stuck a cigar into his mouth and lit it.

Cy mounted offside, from the right, because there

wasn't enough strength in his left arm to permit him to grip the saddle horn and help pull himself up. He hated the show of weakness, which was all too visible. Up until the fire, he'd been in superb physical condition.

"We're going to ride up to the northern boundary and check the fence line for breaks," Cy said imperturbably. "Get Jenkins started on the new gate as soon as he's through with breakfast."

"He'll have to go pick it up at the hardware store first," Harley reminded him. "Just came in late yesterday."

Cy gave him a look that would have frozen running water. He didn't say anything. But, then, he didn't have to.

"I'll just go remind him," Harley said at once, and took off toward the bunkhouse.

"Who is he?" Eb asked as they rode out of the yard.

"My new foreman." Cy leaned toward him with mock awe. "He's a real *mercenary*, you know! Actually went on a mission early this summer!"

"My God," Eb drawled. "Fancy that. A real live hero right here in the boonies."

"Some hero," Cy muttered. "Chances are what he really did was to camp out in the woods for two weeks and help protect city campers from bears."

Eb chuckled. "Remember how we were at his age?" he asked reminiscently. "We couldn't wait for people to see us in our gear. And then we found out that the real mercs don't advertise."

"We were like Harley," Cy mused. "All talk and hot air."

"And all smiles." Eb's eyes narrowed with memory. "I hadn't smiled for years by the time I got out. It isn't romantic and no matter how good the pay is, it's never enough for what you have to do for it."

"We did do a little good in the world," came the re-joinder.

"Yes, I guess we did," Eb had to admit. "But our best job was breaking up one of Lopez's cocaine processing plants in Central America and helping put Lopez away. And here he is back, like a bad bouncing ball."

"I knew his father," Cy said unexpectedly. "A good, honest, bighearted man who worked as a janitor just up the road in Victoria and studied English at home every night trying to better himself. He died just after he found out what his only child was doing for a living."

Eb stared off into space. "You never know how kids will turn out."

"I know how mine would have turned out," Cy said heavily. "One of his teachers was in an accident. Not a well-liked teacher, but Alex started a fund for him and gave up a whole month's allowance to start it with." His face corded like wire. He had to swallow, hard, to keep his voice from breaking. The years hadn't made his memories any easier. Perhaps if he could help get Lopez back in prison, it might help.

"We'll get Lopez," the other man said abruptly. "Whatever it takes, if I have to call in markers from all over the world. We'll get him."

Cy came out of his brief torment and glanced at his comrade. "If we do, I get five minutes alone with him."

"Not a chance," Eb said with a grin. "I remember

what you can do in five minutes, and I want him tried properly."

"He already was."

"Yes, but he was caught and tried back east. This time we'll manage to apprehend him right here in Texas and we'll stack the legal deck by having the best prosecuting attorney in the state brought in to do the job. The Hart boys are related to the state attorney general—he's their big brother."

"I'd forgotten." He glanced at Eb. His eyes were briefly less tormented. "Okay. I guess I can give the court a second chance. Not their fault that Lopez can afford defense attorneys in Armani suits, I guess."

"Absolutely. And if we can catch him with enough laundered money in his pockets and invoke the RICO statutes, we can fund some nice improvements for our drug enforcement people."

They'd arrived at the northernmost boundary of Cy's property, and barely in sight across the high-wire fence was a huge construction site. From their concealed position in a small stand of trees near a stream, Eb took his binoculars and gave the area a thorough scrutiny. He handed them to Cy, who looked as well and then handed them back.

"Recognize anybody?" Cy asked.

Eb shook his head. "None of them are familiar. But I'll bet if you looked in the right places, you could find a rap sheet or two. Lopez isn't too picky about pedigrees. He just likes men who don't mind doing whatever the job takes. Last I heard, he had several foreign nationals in his employ." He sighed. "I sure as hell don't want a drug distribution network out here."

"Neither do I. We'd better go have a word with Bill Elliott at the sheriff's office."

Cy shrugged. "You'd better have a word with him by yourself, if you want to get anywhere. I'd jinx you."

"I remember now. You had words with him over Belinda Jessup's summer camp."

"Hard words," Cy agreed uncomfortably. "I've mellowed since, though."

"You and the KGB." He pulled his hat further over his eyes. "We'd better get out of here before they spot us."

"I can see people coming."

"They can see you coming, too."

"That should worry them," Cy agreed, grinning.

Eb chuckled. It was rare these days to see a smile on that hard face. He wheeled his horse, leaving Cy to follow.

THAT AFTERNOON, EB DROVE over to the Johnson place to pick up Sally and Stevie for their self-defense practice.

Sally's eyes lit up when she saw him and he felt his heart jump. She made him feel warm inside, as if he finally belonged somewhere. Stevie ran past his aunt to be caught up and swung around in Eb's muscular arms.

"How's Jess?" Eb asked.

Sally made a face and glanced back toward the house. "Dallas got here just before you did. It's sort of unarmed combat in there. They aren't even speaking to each other."

"Ah, well," he mused. "Things will improve eventually."

"Do you gamble?" she teased. "I feel a lucky streak coming on."

He chuckled as he loaded them into the pickup. No, he wasn't willing to bet on friendlier relations on that front. Not yet, anyway.

"How much do you know about surveillance equipment?" Sally asked unexpectedly.

He gave her a look of exaggerated patience. "With my background, how much do you think I know?"

She laughed. "Sorry. I wasn't thinking. Can a microphone really pick up voices inside the house? Jess tried to convince me that they could hear us through the walls and we had to be very careful what we discussed. I mentioned that Lopez man and she shushed me immediately."

He glanced at her as he drove. "You've got a lot to learn. I suppose now is as good a time as any to teach you."

When he parked the truck at the front door, he led her inside, parking Stevie at the kitchen table with Carl, his cook, who dished up some ice cream for the child while Eb led Sally down the long hall and into a huge room literally crammed with electronic equipment.

He motioned her into a chair and keyed his security camera to a distant view of two cowboys working on a piece of machinery halfway down a rutted path in the meadow.

He flipped a switch and she heard one cowboy muttering to the other about the sorry state of modern tools and how even rusted files were better than what passed for a file today.

They weren't even talking loud, and if there was a microphone, it must be mounted on the barn wall outside. She looked at Eb with wide, frankly disbelieving eyes.

He flipped the switch and the screen was silent again. "Most modern sound equipment can pick up a whisper several hundred yards away." He indicated a shelf upon which sat several pairs of odd-looking binoculars. "Night vision. I can see anything on a moonless night with those, and I've got others that detect heat patterns in the dark."

"You have got to be kidding!"

"We have cameras hidden in books and cigarette packs, we have weapons that can be broken down and hidden in boots," he continued. "Not to mention this."

He indicated his watch, a quite normal looking one with all sorts of dials. Normal until he adjusted it and a nasty-looking little blade popped out. Her gasp was audible.

He could see the realization in her eyes as the purpose of the blade registered there. She looked up at him and saw the past. His past.

His green eyes narrowed as they searched hers. "You hadn't really thought about exactly what sort of work I did, had you?"

She shook her head. She was a little paler now.

"I lived in dangerous places, in dangerous times. It's only in recent years that I've stopped looking over my shoulder and sitting with my back against a wall." He touched her face. "Lopez's men can hear you through a wall, with the television on. Don't ever forget. Say nothing that you don't want recorded for posterity."

"This Lopez man is very dangerous, isn't he?" she asked.

"He's the most dangerous man I know. He hires killers. He has no compassion, no mercy, and he'll do absolutely anything for profit. If his henchman hadn't sold him out, he'd never have been taken into custody in this country. It was a fluke."

She looked around her curiously. "Could he overhear you in here?"

He smiled gently. "Not a chance in hell."

"It looks like something out of *Star Wars,*" she mused.

He grinned. "Speaking of movies, how would you and Stevie like to go see a new science fiction flick with me Saturday?"

"Could we?" she asked.

"Sure." His eyes danced wickedly at the idea of sitting in a darkened theater with her....

CHAPTER SIX

SALLY FOUND THE WORKOUTS easier to do as they progressed from falls to defensive moves. Not only was it exciting to learn such skills, but the constant physical contact with Eb was delightful. She couldn't really hide that from him. He saw right through her diversionary tactics, grinning when she asked for short breaks.

Stevie was also taking to the exercise with enthusiasm. It wasn't hard to teach him that such things had no place at school, either. Even at his young age, he seemed to understand that martial arts were for recreation after school and never for the playground.

"It goes with the discipline," Eb informed her when she told him about it. "Most people who watch martial arts films automatically assume that we teach children to hurt each other. It's not like that. What we teach is a way to raise self-esteem and self-confidence. If you know you can handle yourself in a bad situation, you're less likely to go out and try to beat somebody up to prove it. It's lack of self-confidence, lack of self-esteem, that drives a lot of kids to violence."

"That, and a very sad lack of attention by the adults around them," Sally said quietly. "It takes two incomes to run a household these days, but it's the kids who are suffering for it. Any gang member will tell you the reason he joined a gang was because he wanted to be part of a family. But how do we change things so that parents can earn a living and still have enough free time to raise their children?"

He put both hands on his narrow hips and studied her closely. "If I could answer that question, I'd run for public office."

She grinned at him. "I can see you now, mopping the floor with the criminal element on the streets."

He shrugged. "Piece of cake compared to what I used to do for a living."

Her pale eyes searched his lean, scarred face while Stevie fell from one side of the mat to another practicing his technique. "I rented one of those old mercenary films and watched it. Do you guys really throw grenades and use rocket launchers?"

A dark, odd look came into his pale eyes. "Among other things," he said.

"Such as?" she prompted.

"High-tech equipment like the stuff you saw in my office. Plastic explosive charges, small arms, whatever we had. But most of what we do now is intelligence-gathering and tactics. And intelligence-gathering," he told her dryly, "is about as exciting as two-hour-old cereal in milk."

She was surprised. "I thought it was like war."

He shrugged. "Only if you get caught gathering intelligence," he replied on a laugh. "We were good at what we did."

"Dallas was one of your guys, wasn't he?"

He nodded. "Dallas, Cy Parks and Callie Kirby's stepbrother Micah Steele, among others."

Her mouth fell open. "Cy Parks was a mercenary?!"

His eyebrows levered up. "You didn't notice that he has a hard time interacting with other people?"

"It's hard to miss. But in the condition he's in…"

"I know. That's one reason that he isn't in our line of work anymore. He was one of the group that helped put Lopez's organization away a little over two years ago—so was I. It was Jess who got to the man himself. But Lopez appealed the verdict and only went to prison six months ago. As you can see, he's out now,' he added dryly.

"Two years ago—that was about the time Cy came to Jacobsville," she recalled.

"Yes. After one of Lopez's goons torched his house in Wyoming. The idea was to kill all three of them, not just Cy's wife and child," he added, seeing the horror in her eyes. "But Cy wasn't asleep, as they'd assumed. He got out."

She grimaced. "But why would Lopez burn his house down?"

"That's how he gets even with people who cross him," he said simply. "He doesn't take out just the person responsible, but the whole family, if he can get to it. There have been slaughters like you wouldn't believe down in Mexico when anyone tried to stand against him. He does usually stop short of children, however; his one virtue."

"I never knew people like him existed," she said sorrowfully.

"I wish I could say the same," he told her. "We don't live in a perfect world. That's why I want you to learn how to defend yourself."

"Fat lot of good it would have done me the night I had the flat tire," she pointed out. "If you hadn't come along when you did..." She shuddered.

"But I did. Don't look back. It's unproductive."

Her soft, worried eyes searched his scarred face quietly.

"What are you thinking?" he asked with a faint smile.

She shrugged. "I was thinking what a false picture I had of you all those years ago," she admitted. "I suppose I was living in a dream world."

"And I was living in a nightmare," he replied. "That unforgettable spring day six years ago, I'd just come home from a bloodbath in Africa, trying to help an incumbent government fight off a military coup by a very nasty native communist general. I lost most of my unit, including several friends, and the incumbent president's office was blown up, with him in it. It wasn't a good time."

She named the country, to his surprise. "We were studying that in a political science class at the time," she said. "I had no idea what you did for a living, or that you were involved. But we all thought it was an idealistic resistance," she added with a smile.

"Idealistic," he agreed. "And very costly, as most ideas are when you try to put them into practice." His eyes were very old as they met hers. "After that, I began to concentrate on intelligence and tactics. War isn't noble. Only the resolution of it is that."

She recalled the fresh scars on his face that day, scars

that she'd attributed to ranch work. She studied him with obvious interest, smiling sheepishly when one of his eyebrows levered up.

"Sorry," she murmured.

He moved a step closer to her, forcing her to raise her chin so that she could see his face. The contact, barely perceptible, made her heart race. It wasn't so much the proximity as the way he was looking at her, as if he'd like to press her against him and kiss her until she couldn't stand up.

She moved a step back, her gaze going involuntarily to her cousin, who was giving the punching bag a hard time.

"I hadn't forgotten he was there," Eb said in a velvety tone. His pale eyes fell to her mouth and lingered. Even without makeup and with her long hair disheveled, she was pretty. "One night soon I'm going to take you out to dinner. Dallas can keep an eye on Jess and Stevie while you're away."

Until he said that, she'd actually forgotten the danger for a few delightful minutes. It all came rushing back.

He smoothed out the frown between her thin eyebrows. "Don't brood. I've got everything under control."

"I hope so," she said uneasily. "Does Mr. Parks know that Lopez is out of prison?"

"He knows," Eb replied. He ran a hand through his thick hair. "He's the one loose cannon I'm going to have to watch. Even in the old days, Cy never had much patience. He and his wife weren't much of a pair, but he loved that boy to death. He won't rest until Lopez is caught, and if he gets to him first, we can forget about a trial. You can't ever afford to act in anger," he added quietly. "Anger clouds reason. It can get you killed."

"You can't really blame him for the way he feels. Poor man," she sympathized.

"Pity would be wasted on him," he murmured with a smile. "Even crippled, he's more man than most."

"I don't think of him as crippled," she said genuinely. "He's very attractive."

He glared down at her. "You're off-limits."

Her eyes widened. "What?"

"You heard me."

"I'm not property," she began.

"Neither am I, but don't start thinking about Cy, nevertheless. You can concentrate on me." He took one of her hands in his and looked at it, turning it over gently to study it. "Nice hands," he said. "Short nails, well-kept. No rings."

"I have several of them, mostly silver and turquoise, but I don't wear them very much."

His lean fingers rubbed gently over her ring finger and he looked thoughtful, absorbed.

Her own fingers went to the onyx-and-gold signet ring on the little finger of his left hand with the letter *S* in gold script embossed in the onyx.

"It was my father's," Eb told her solemnly. "He was a hell of a soldier, even if he wasn't the best father in the world."

"Do you miss him?" she asked gently.

He nodded. "I suppose I do, from time to time." He

touched the ring. "This will go to my son, if I ever have one."

The thought of having children with Eb made Sally's knees weak, but she didn't speak. Eb seemed about to, when they were interrupted.

"Hey, Sally, look what I can do!" Stevie called, and executed a kick that sent the bag reeling.

"Very nice!" Eb said, grinning. "You're a quick study, young man."

"I got to learn to do it real fast," he murmured, sending another kick at the bag.

"Why?" Eb asked curiously.

"So I can hit that big blond man who makes my mama cry," he said, oblivious to the shocked and then amused looks on the faces of the adults near him.

"Dallas?" Sally asked.

"That's him," Stevie agreed, and his dark eyes glimmered. "Mama was crying last night and I asked her why, and she said that man hates her."

Eb joined the young boy at the bag and went on one knee beside him, his eyes very solemn. "Your mother and Dallas knew each other a long time ago," he told him in an adult way. "They had a fight, and they never made up. That's why she cried. They're both good people, Stevie, but sometimes even good people have arguments."

"Why are they mad at each other?"

"I don't know," Eb replied not quite factually. "That's for them to say, if they want you to know. Dallas isn't a bad man, though."

"He's all banged up," Stevie replied solemnly.

"Yes, he is. He was shot."

"Shot? Really?" Stevie moved closer to Eb and put a small hand on his shoulder. "Who shot him?"

"Some very bad men," Eb told him. "He almost died. That's why he has to use a walking stick now. It's why he has all those scars."

Stevie touched Eb's face. "You got scars, too."

"Yes, I have."

"You ever been shot?" he wanted to know.

"Several times," Eb replied honestly. "Guns can be very dangerous. I suppose you know that."

"I know it," Stevie said. "One of my friends shot himself with his dad's pistol playing war out in the yard. He was hurt pretty bad, but he's okay now. Mama told me that children should *never* touch a gun, even if they think it's not loaded."

"Good for your mom!"

"That man doesn't like my mama," he continued worriedly. "He frowns and frowns at her. She can't see it, but I see it."

"He wouldn't ever hurt her," Eb said firmly. "He's there to protect her when you're away from home," he added wryly.

"That's right, I protect her at home. I'm very strong. See what I did to the bag?"

"I sure did!" Eb grinned at him. "Those were nice kicks, but you need to snap them out from the knee. Here—" he got to his feet "—let me show you."

Sally watched them with lazy pleasure, smiling at the born rapport between them. It was a pity that Stevie didn't like Dallas. That would matter one day. But she had enough problems of her own to worry about.

EB STOPPED BY THE LOCAL sandwich shop and bought frozen yogurt cones for all three of them, a reward for the physical punishment, he told them dryly.

While the two adults sat at a table and ate their yogurt cones, Stevie became engrossed in some knick-knacks on sale in the same store.

"He's a natural at this," Eb remarked.

"I'll bet I'm not," she mused, having had to repeat several of the moves quite a number of times before she did them well enough to suit her companion.

"You're not his age, either," he pointed out. "Most children learn things faster than adults. That's why they teach foreign languages so early these days."

"Do you speak any other languages?" she asked suddenly.

"Only a handful," he replied. "The romance languages, several dialects of African languages, and Russian."

"My goodness."

"Languages will get you far in intelligence work these days," he told her. "If you're going to work in foreign countries, it's stupid not to speak the language. It can get you killed."

"I had to have a foreign language series as part of my degree," she said. "I chose Spanish, because that's pretty necessary around here, with such a large Hispanic population. I hated it at first, and then I learned how to read in it." Her eyes brightened. "It's the most exciting thing in the world to read something in the language the author created it in. I never dreamed how delightful it would be to read *Don Quixote* as Cervantes actually wrote it!"

"I know what you mean. But the older the novel, the more difficult the translation. Words change meaning. And a good number of the more modern novels are written in the various dialects of Spanish provinces."

She grinned. "Like Blasco-Ibañez, who used a regional dialect for his matador hero, Juan Gallardo, in dialogue."

"Yes."

She finished her cone and wiped her hands. "I became really fascinated with bullfighting after I read the book, so I found a Web site that had biographies of all the matadors. I found the ones mentioned in the book, who fought in the corridas of Spain around the turn of the century."

"Until you read Blasco-Ibañez, you have no idea how dangerous bullfighting really is," Eb agreed. "He must have seen some of the corridas."

"A number of Spanish authors did. Lorca, for example, wrote a famous poem about the death of his friend Sanchez Mejias in the bullring."

He brushed back a strand of gold-streaked brown hair and smiled. "I've missed conversations like this, although a good many of the men I train are well-educated. In fact, Micah Steele, who does consulting work for me, was a resident doctor at one of the bigger Eastern hospitals when he joined my unit."

"Why did he give up a profession that he must have studied very hard for?"

"Nobody knows, and he won't talk. Mostly what we know about him we found out from his father, who used to be a bank president until his heart attack. Micah's stepsister, Callie, looks after old man Steele these days. He and Micah haven't spoken for years, not since he and Callie's mother divorced."

"Do you know why they did?"

He shrugged. "Local gossip had it that Micah's father caught Micah and his stepmother in a compromising position and threw them both out of the house."

"Poor man."

"Poor Callie. She worshiped the ground Micah walked on, but he won't even speak to her these days."

"That name sounds familiar," she commented.

"It should. Callie's a paralegal. She works for Barnes and Kemp, the trial lawyers here in town."

"It's so nice to have a lazy day like this," she murmured, watching Stevie browse among the party decorations on a shelf. "It makes me forget the danger."

"I'm surprised that Lopez hasn't made any more moves lately," he said. "And a little disturbed. It isn't like him to back off."

"Maybe he was afraid those two men who attacked me would be arrested and they'd tell on him," she said.

He laughed mirthlessly. "Dream on. Lopez would have them disposed of before they had time to rat on him." He pursed his lips. "That could be what happened to them. You don't make a mistake when you belong to that particular cartel. No second chances. Ever."

She shivered. "We do keep all the doors locked," she

said. "And we're very careful about what we say. Well, Jessica is," she amended sheepishly. "Until you taught me about surveillance equipment, I didn't know that a whisper could be heard half a mile away."

"Never forget it," he told her. "Never drop your guard, either. I'll always have someone close enough to run interference if you get into trouble, but you have to do your part to keep the house secure."

"And let you know when and where I'm going," she agreed. "I won't forget again."

He reached across the table and folded his fingers into hers, liking the way they clung. His thumb smoothed over the soft, moist palm while he searched her eyes.

"You haven't had an easy time of it, have you?" he asked conversationally. "In some ways, your whole life has been in turmoil since you were seventeen."

"In transition, at least," she corrected, smiling gently. "If there's one thing I've learned, it's that everything changes."

"I suppose so." His fingers tightened on hers and the look in his eyes was suddenly dark and mysterious and a little threatening. "I've learned a few things myself," he said quietly.

"Such as?" she whispered daringly.

He glanced down at their entwined fingers. "Such as never taking things for granted."

She frowned, puzzled.

He laughed and let go of her fingers. "I told you that I was engaged once, didn't I?" he asked.

She nodded.

"I never told her what I did for a living. She never questioned where my money came from. In fact, when I tried to tell her, she stopped me, saying it wouldn't matter, that she loved me and she'd go wherever my job took me." He leaned back in his chair, his expression reflective and solemn. "Her parents were dead. She and an older boy were fostered at the same time to a wealthy woman. They spent years together, but he and Maggie weren't close, so I made all the wedding arrangements and paid for her gown and the rings, everything." His eyes darkened with remembered pain. "I still felt uncomfortable about having secrets between us, though, so the night before the wedding, I told her what I did for a living. She put the rings on the coffee table, got her stuff, and left town that same night. She married two months later…a man twice her age."

She knew about his ex-fiancée, but not how much he'd cared about the woman. The expression in his eyes told her that the pain hadn't gone away. "Didn't she send you a letter, or phone you after she'd had time to think it over?" she asked.

He shook his head. "Until I ran into her in Houston a week ago, I had no idea where she was. Her adoptive mother died just after we broke up. Tough break."

Her heart stopped in her chest. "You…saw her…in Houston?"

He nodded, oblivious to the shock in her eyes. "As luck would have it, she's a new junior partner in an investment firm I use, and widowed."

He stared at her until she looked up, and he wasn't smiling. "You're in a precarious situation, and we've been thrown together in a rather unconventional way. We're friends, but you don't have to live with what I do."

All her hopes and dreams and wild expectations crumbled to dust in her mind. Friends. Good friends. Of course they were! He was teaching her martial arts, he was helping her to survive a potential attack by a ruthless drug lord. That didn't mean he wanted her to share his life. Quite the opposite, it seemed now.

"If a woman cared enough, surely she could give it a chance?" she asked, terrified that her anguish might show.

Apparently it didn't. He leaned back in his chair with a long sigh, reflective and moody. "No. She said she wanted a career, anyway," he replied. "It suited her to have her own money and be independent."

"My parents never shared their paychecks, or anything else," she said carelessly. She glanced at Stevie. "Stevie, we'd better go, sweetheart."

He came running, smiling as he leaned against her and looked across at Eb, who was still brooding. "Can we take Mama a cone?"

"Of course we can," Sally said gently. She dug out two dollars. "Here. Get her a cup of that fat-free Dutch chocolate, okay? And make sure it has a lid."

"Okay!"

He ran off with his grubstake, feeling very adult. Sally watched him, smiling.

"I could have done that," Eb commented.

"Yes, you could, but it wouldn't help teach him responsibility. Six isn't too young to start learning independence. He's going to be a fine man," she added, her voice softer as she watched him.

He didn't comment. He was feeling claustrophobic and he didn't know why. He got up and dealt with the used napkins. By the time he was finished, Stevie came back carrying a small white sack with Jessica's treat inside.

There wasn't much conversation on the way back to the Johnson house, and even then it was completely impersonal. Sally realized that it must have hurt Eb to recall how abruptly his fiancée had rejected him. She might have loved him, but the constant danger of his profession must have been more than she could handle. Now that he was retired from the danger, it might not be such an obstacle.

That was a depressing thought. His ex-fiancée was a widow and he was in a secure profession, and they'd recently seen each other. It was enough to get Sally out of the truck with Stevie and off into the house with only a quick thank-you and a forced smile.

Eb, driving away down the road, felt a vague regret for the loss of the rapport he and Sally had seemed to share. He couldn't understand what had made her so distant this afternoon.

Eb had already contacted a man he knew in the Drug Enforcement Administration on a secure channel and told him what he knew about Lopez and his plans for Jacobsville. He'd also asked about the possibility of having a man go undercover to infiltrate the operation and was told only that the DEA was aware of Lopez's construction project. He wouldn't tell Eb anything more than that.

Understanding government work very well, Eb had assumed that the undercover operation was already underway. He wasn't about to mention that to anyone he knew. Not even Cy.

He had Dallas monitoring some sensitive equipment that gave them direct audio and visual information from Sally's house. Nobody would sneak up on it without being noticed. He'd also had Dallas bug the telephone. That night, he was glad he had.

In the early hours of the morning, Sally was brought wide-awake by the insistent ringing of the telephone. The number was unlisted, but that didn't stop telemarketers. Ordinarily, though, they didn't call at this hour. It wasn't a good marketing strategy, especially in Sally's case. She'd hardly slept after the discussion with Eb in the yogurt shop. She wasn't in the mood to talk to strangers.

"Hello?" she asked belligerently.

"You'll never see us coming," a slow, ice-cold voice said in her ear. "But unless Jessica gives up the name by midnight Saturday, there will be serious repercussions."

Sally was so shocked that she fumbled with the phone and cut off the caller. She stood holding the receiver, blinking in astonishment. That softly accented tone had chilled her to the bone, despite the flannel gown she was wearing.

No sooner had she righted the telephone than it rang again. This time, she hesitated. Her heart was pounding like mad. She was almost shaking with the force of it.

Her mouth was dry. Her palms began to sweat. There was an uncomfortable knot in the pit of her stomach.

She wanted to ignore it. She didn't dare. Quickly, before she lost her nerve, she lifted it.

"She has one last chance," the voice continued, as if the connection hadn't been cut. "She must phone this number Saturday night at midnight exactly and give a name. One minute after midnight, you will all suffer the consequences." He gave the number and hung up. This time the connection was cut even more rapidly. Sally dropped the receiver back into the cradle with icy fingers. She stared down at it with growing horror. Surely Eb and Dallas and the others would be watching. But were they listening as well?

The phone rang a third time, but now she was angry and she didn't hesitate. She jerked it up. "Hello…?"

"We couldn't get a trace," Eb said angrily. "Are you all right?"

She swallowed, closed her eyes, took a deep breath, and swallowed again. "Yes," she said calmly. "I'm all right. You heard what he said?"

"I heard. Don't worry."

"Don't worry?" she parroted. "When a man's just threatened to kill everyone in my house?"

"He won't kill anybody," he assured her. "And he's through making threats for tonight. I'm going to find out where that phone is. Go to sleep. It's all right."

The receiver went dead. "I am sick and tired of men throwing out orders and hanging up on me!" she told the telephone earpiece.

It did no good, of course, except that voicing her irritation made her feel a little better. She climbed back into bed and lay awake, wide-eyed and nervous, until dawn. Just before she and Stevie left for school, out of the child's hearing range, she told Jessica what had happened.

"Eb and the others are watching us," Sally assured her quickly. "But be careful about answering the door."

"No need," Jessica said. "Lopez may be certifiable, but he's predictable. He never takes action until his demands haven't been met. We have until midnight Saturday to think of something."

"Wonderful," Sally said on a sigh. "We have today and tomorrow. I'm sure we'll have Lopez and all his cohorts in jail by then."

"Sarcasm doesn't suit you, dear," Jessica said with a smile. "Go to work. I'll be fine."

"I wish I could guarantee that all of us would be fine," Sally murmured to herself as she went out the door behind Stevie.

Somehow she knew that life would never be the same again. It had been bad enough hearing Eb talk about the woman he'd loved who had rejected him at the altar, and knowing from the way he spoke of it that he hadn't gotten over her. But now, she had drug dealers threatening to kill Jessica and Stevie as well as herself. She wondered how in the world she'd ended up in such a nightmare.

It didn't help when Eb phoned again and told her that the phone number she'd been given was that of a stolen cell phone, untraceable until it was answered, and it rang and rang unnoticed now. There would be no time to run a trace precisely at midnight. It was the most disheartening news Sally had received in a long time.

CHAPTER SEVEN

EB WAS DISTURBED BY THE MESSAGE he'd intercepted from Lopez. He knew, even better than Sally did, that it wasn't an idle threat. The drug lord, like his minions, was merciless. He'd had countless enemies neutralized, and he wouldn't hesitate because Jessica was a woman. Just the month before his arrest, he'd had the leader of a drug-dealing gang disposed of for cheating him. It was chilling even for a professional soldier to know what depths a human being could sink to in the name of greed.

He and Dallas started planning for the certainty of an attack. The Johnson homeplace was isolated, but it had plenty of cover where men could hide. Eb intended having people in place long before Lopez's hired goons could find a safe passage to the house to carry out the madman's orders. Anything else would be impossible, since he knew Jessica would never sacrifice her informant's life, even to save herself and her family.

"I think we can safely assume that these men aren't professionals," Dallas said quietly. "Their way will be to wade in shooting."

Eb's pale eyes narrowed. "I wouldn't bet the lives of two women and a child on that," he replied. "Lopez knows I'm here, and that I have trained professionals working for me. He also knows that I'm why Jessica talked Sally into moving back here in the first place. He's ruthless, but he isn't stupid. When he comes after Jessica, he'll send the best people he's got."

"Point taken," Dallas said heavily. "I suppose it was wishful thinking." He glanced worriedly at Eb. "We could bring all three of them over here."

"Sure we could. But it would only postpone the inevitable. Lopez doesn't quit. He'll look on it as a setback and find another way to get to them. Besides, they can't stay here indefinitely. Sally has a job and Stevie has to go to school."

Dallas stared into the distance, quiet and thoughtful. "Stevie doesn't like me," he murmured. "He told his mother he was learning karate so that he could work me over." He shot a half-amused glance in Eb's direction. "Spunky kid."

"Yes, he is," Eb agreed. "Pity he has to grow up without a father. And before you fly at me," he interrupted Dallas's exclamation, "I know Jessica didn't tell you whose child he was. But you know now."

"I know," Dallas muttered irritably, "for all the good it does me. She won't even discuss it. The minute I walk in the door, she clams up and stays that way until I leave. I can barely get her to say hello and goodbye!"

"Then she cries herself to sleep at night because you hate her."

The blond man's dark eyes widened. *"What?"*

"That's why Stevie wants to deck you," Eb said simply. "He's very protective of his mother."

Dallas seemed to calm down a little. "Imagine that," he mused. "Well, well. So she isn't quite as disinterested as she pretends." He stuck his hands into his pockets and leaned back against the wall. "No chance she'll turn in the guy who ratted on Lopez, I gather?"

"Not one in a million." He studied the other man for a moment. "You're really worried."

"Of course I am. I've seen the aftermath of Lopez's vendettas," Dallas said curtly. "What worries me most is that if someone's willing to trade his life or his freedom to get you, he can. No protection is adequate against a determined killer."

"Then ours will make history," Eb promised him. "Let's go over to Cy Parks's place. I want to see if he's got a way to contact that guy in Mexico who used to work as a mercenary with Dutch Van Meer and Diego Laremos back in the eighties. He went on to do work infiltrating drug cartels."

"J.D. Brettman led that mercenary group," Dallas recalled, grinning. "He's a superior court judge in Chicago these days. Imagine that!"

"I heard that Van Meer lives with his wife and kids in the northwestern Rocky Mountains on a ranch. What about Laremos?" Eb asked.

"He and his family live in the Yucatán. He's given up soldiering, too." He shook his head. "Those guys were younger than us when they started and they made fortunes."

"It was a different game back then. Times have changed. So have the rules. We'd never get away with some of the stunts those guys pulled." Eb felt in his pocket for his truck keys. "All of us met them, but Cy and Diego Laremos got to know each other well several years back when Cy was doing a little job down around Cancún for a wealthy yachtsman. He may know the professional soldier who helped a friend of Laremos's escape some nasty pothunters and a kidnapper."

"Do I know this friend?" Dallas wanted to know as they headed out the door.

"You probably know *of* him—Canton Rourke."

"Good Lord, Mr. Software?" Dallas exclaimed. "The guy who lost everything and then regrouped and now has a corporation in the Fortune 500?"

"That's him." Eb nodded. "Turns out the new Mrs. Rourke's parents are university professors who devote summers to Mayan digs in the Yucatán. It's a long story, but this Mexican agent does a little freelance work. He'd be an asset in this sort of operation."

"He might even have some contacts we could use?"

"That's so." Eb got in and started the truck. He glanced at Dallas. "Besides that, he's done undercover work on narcotics smuggling for the Mexican government and lived to tell about it. That proves how good he is. A lot of undercover people get killed."

"He'd be just what we need, if we can get him. I don't imagine the DEA is going to tell us who their undercover guy is, or what he finds out."

"Exactly. That's where I hope Cy's going to come in. He doesn't like any of the old associations very much anymore, but considering the danger Lopez poses, he might be willing to help us."

"Pity about his arm."

Eb shot him a wry glance. "Yes, but it's a lucky break it wasn't the arm he uses."

They drove over to Cy Parks's ranch, and found him watching his young foreman, Harley, doctoring a sick bull yearling in the barn. He was lounging against one of the posts that supported the imposing structure, his hat low over his eyes, his arms folded over a broad chest, one booted foot resting on a rail of the gate that enclosed the stall where his man was busy.

He turned as Cy and Dallas strode down the neat chipped bark covered floor to join him.

"You two out sightseeing?" Cy drawled without smiling, his green eyes narrowed and curious.

"Not today. We need a name."

"Whose?"

"The guy who worked with your friend Diego Laremos out near Chichén Itzá. I think he might be just what we need to infiltrate Lopez's cartel."

Cy's eyebrows lifted. "Rodrigo? You must be out of your mind!" he said at once.

"Why?"

"Good God," Cy burst out, "Diego says that he's such a renegade, nobody will hire him anymore, not even for black ops!"

"What did he do?" Dallas asked, aware that the

young man in the stall had perked up and was suddenly listening unashamedly.

"For a start, he crashed a Huey out in the Yucatán last year," Cy said. "That didn't endear him to a certain government agency which was running him. Then he blew up an entire boatload of powder cocaine off Cozumel that the authorities were trying to confiscate—millions' worth. In between he wrecked a few hired cars in various chases, hijacked a plane, and broke into a government field office. He walked off with a couple of classified files and several thousand dollars' worth of high-tech listening devices that you can't even buy unless you're in law enforcement. After that, he went berserk in a bar down in Panama and put two men in the hospital, just before he absconded with a suitcase full of unlaundered drug money that belonged to Manuel Lopez…"

"Are we talking about the same Rodrigo that the feds used to call 'Mr. Cool'?" Eb asked with evident surprise.

"That isn't what they call him these days," Cy said flatly. "Mr. Liability would be more like it."

"He was with Laremos and Van Meer in Africa back in the early eighties," Eb recalled. "They left, but he signed on with another outfit and kept going."

"That's when he started working freelance for the feds," Cy continued. "At least, that's what Diego said," he added for Harley's benefit. He didn't want his young employee to know about his past.

"Anybody know why Rodrigo went bananas in Panama?" Dallas asked.

Cy shrugged. "There are a lot of rumors—but nothing concrete." He studied the other two with pursed lips. "If you want him for undercover work to indict Lopez, he'd probably pay you to hire him on. He hates Lopez."

Eb glanced past Cy at Harley, whose mouth was hanging open.

"Don't mind him," Cy told his companions with a mocking smile. "He's a mercenary, too," he added dryly.

Harley scrambled to his feet. "Can't I hire on?" he burst out. "Listen, I know those names—Van Meer and Brettman and Laremos. They were legends!"

"Put the top back on the medicine before you spill it," Cy told the young man calmly. "As for the other, that's up to Eb. It's his party."

Harley fumbled the lid back on the bottle. "Mr. Scott?" he asked, pleading.

"I guess we could find you something to do," Eb said, amused. Then the smile faded, and his whole look was threatening. "But this is strictly on the QT. You breathe one word of it locally and you're out on your ear. Got that?"

Harley nodded eagerly. "Sure!"

"And you'll work for him only after you do your chores here," Cy said firmly. "I run cattle, not commandos."

"Yes, sir!"

Cy exchanged a complicated glance with Eb. "I've got the last number I had for Rodrigo in my office. I'll go get it."

He left the other three men in the barn. Harley was almost dancing with excitement.

"I'll be an asset, sir, honestly," he told Eb. "I can shoot anything that has bullets, and use a knife, and I know a little martial arts…!"

Eb chuckled. "Son, we don't need an assassin. We're collecting intelligence."

The boy's face fell. "Oh."

"Running gun battles aren't a big part of the business," Dallas said without cracking a smile. "You shoot anybody these days, even a criminal, and you could find yourself behind bars."

Harley looked shocked. "But…but I read about it all the time; those exciting battles in Africa…"

"Exciting?" Eb's eyes were steady and quiet.

"Why, sure!" Harley's eyes lit up. "You know, testing your courage under fire."

The boy's eyes were gleaming with excitement, and Eb knew then for certain that he'd never seen anyone shot. Probably the closest he'd come to it was listening to an instructor—probably a retired mercenary—talking about combat.

Harley noticed his employer coming out of the house and he grimaced. "I hope Mr. Parks meant what he said. He's not much on adventure, you see. He's sort of sarcastic when I mention where I went on my vacation, out in the field in Central America with a group of mercenaries. It was great!"

"Cy wasn't enthusiastic, I gather?" Eb probed.

"Naw," Harley said heavily. "He's just a rancher. Even if he knows Mr. Laremos, he sure doesn't know what it's like to really be a soldier of fortune. But we do, don't we?" he asked the other two with a grin.

Eb and Dallas glanced at each other and managed not to laugh. Quite obviously, Harley believed that Cy's information about Rodrigo was secondhand and had no idea what Cy did before he became a rancher.

Cy joined them, presenting a slip of paper with a number on it to Eb. "That's the last number I have, but they'll relay it, I'm sure."

"You still hear from Laremos?" Eb asked his friend.

"Every year, at Christmas," Cy told him. "They've got three kids now and the eldest is in high school." He shook his head. "I'm getting old."

"Not you," Eb chuckled.

"We'd better go," Dallas said, checking his watch.

"So we had."

"What about me?" Harley asked excitedly.

"We'll be in touch, when the time comes," Eb promised him, and, oddly, it sounded more like a threat.

Cy saw them off and came back to take one last look at the bull. "Good job, Harley," he said, approving the treatment. "You'll make a rancher yet."

Harley closed the bull in his stall and latched the gate. "How do you know Mr. Laremos, sir?" he asked curiously.

"Oh, we had a mutual acquaintance," he said without meeting the other man's eyes. "Diego still keeps in touch with the old group, so he knows what's going on in the intelligence field," he added deliberately.

"I see. I thought it was probably something like that,"

Harley said absently and went to work on the calf with scours in the next stall, reaching for the pills that were commonly called "eggs" to dose it with.

Cy looked after the smug younger man with amusement. Harley had his boss pegged as a retiring, staid rancher with no backbone and only an outsider's familiarity with the world of covert operations. He'd think that Cy had gotten all that information from Laremos, and, for the present, it suited Cy very well to let him think so. But if Harley had in mind an adventure with Eb and the others, he was in for a real shock. In the company of those men, he was going to be more uncomfortable than he dreamed right now. Some lessons, he told himself, were better learned through experience.

WHEN THEY GOT BACK TO THE ranch, Eb phoned the number Cy had given him. There was a long pause and then a quick, deep voice giving instructions. Eb was to leave his name and number and hang up immediately. He did. Seconds later, his phone rang.

"You run that strategy and tactics school in Texas," the deep voice said evenly.

"Yes."

"I read about it in one of the intelligence sitreps," he returned, shortening the name for situation reports. "I thought you were one of those vacation mercs who sat at a desk all week and liked to play at war a couple of weeks a year, until I spoke to Laremos. He remembers you, along with another Jacobsville resident named Parks."

"Cy and I used to work together, with Dallas Kirk and Micah Steele," Eb replied quietly.

"I don't know them, but I know Parks. If you're looking for someone to do black ops, I'm not available," he said curtly, with only a trace of an accent. "I don't do overseas work anymore, either. There's a fairly large price on my head in certain Latin American circles."

"It isn't a foreign job. I want someone to go undercover here in Texas and relay intelligence from a drug cartel," Eb said flatly.

There was a long pause. "I'd find someone with a terminal illness for that sort of work," Rodrigo replied. "It's usually fatal."

"Cy Parks told me you'd probably jump at the chance to do this job."

"Oh, that's rich. And what job would that be?"

"The drug lord I want intelligence on is Manuel Lopez. I'm trying to put him back in prison permanently."

The intake of breath on the other end was audible, followed by a description of Lopez that questioned his ancestry, his paternity, his morals, and various other facets of his life in both Spanish and English.

"That's the very Lopez I'm talking about," Eb replied dryly. "Interested?"

"In killing him, yes. Putting him back in prison… well, he can still run the cartel from there."

"While he's in there, his organization could be successfully infiltrated and destroyed from within," Eb suggested, dangling the idea like a carrot on a string. "In fact, the reason we're under the gun in Jacobsville right now is because a friend of our group is protecting the identity of an intimate of Lopez who sold him out to the DEA."

"Keep talking," Rodrigo said at once.

"Lopez is trying to kill a former government agent who coaxed one of his intimate friends to help her get the hard evidence to put him in prison. He's only out on a legal technicality and he's apparently using his temporary freedom to dispose of her and her informant."

"What about the so-called hard evidence?" Rodrigo asked.

"My guess is that it'll disappear before the retrial. If he manages to get rid of the witnesses and destroy the evidence, he'll never go back to prison. In fact, he's already skipped bond."

"Don't tell me. They set bail at a million dollars and he paid it out of petty cash," came the sarcastic reply.

"Exactly."

There was a brief hesitation and a sigh. "Well, in that case, I suppose I'm working for you."

Eb smiled. "I'll put you on the payroll."

"Fine, but you can forget about retirement benefits if I go undercover."

Eb chuckled softly. "There's just one thing. We've heard that you and Lopez had a common interest at one time," he said, putting it as delicately as he could. "Does he know what you look like?"

There was another pause and when the voice came back, it was strained. "No, you can be sure of that."

"This won't be easy," Eb told him. "Be sure you're willing to take the risk before you agree."

"I'm quite sure. I'll see you tomorrow." The line went dead.

Eb took Sally out to dinner that night, driving the sleek new black Jaguar S that he liked to use when he went to town.

"We'll go to Houston, if that suits you?"

She agreed. He looked devastating in a dinner jacket, and she was shy and uneasy with him, after what she'd learned about his fiancée. In fact, she'd told herself she wasn't going to be alone with him ever again. Yet here she sat. Resolve was hard when emotions were involved. His feelings for the woman he'd planned to marry were unmistakable in his voice when he talked about her, and now that she was free, he might have a second chance. Knowing that part of him had never gotten over his fiancée's defection, Sally was reluctant to risk her heart on him again. She kept a smiling, pleasant, but determined distance between them.

Eb noticed the reticence, but didn't understand its purpose. He could hardly take his eyes off her tonight. His green eyes kept returning to linger on her pretty black cocktail dress under the long red-lined black velvet coat she wore with it. Her hair was in a neat chignon at her nape, and she looked lovely.

"Are you sure this is a good idea?" Sally asked him. "I know Dallas will take care of Jess and Stevie, but it seems risky to go out at night with Lopez and his men around."

"He's a vicious devil," he replied, "but he is absolutely predictable. He'll give Jessica until exactly midnight Saturday. He won't do one thing until the deadline.

At one minute past midnight," he added curtly, "there will be an assault."

Sally wrapped her arms closer around her body. "How do we end up with people like that in the world?"

"We forget that all lives are interconnected in some way, and that selfishness and greed are not desirable traits."

"What good will it do Lopez to kill Jessica and us?" she asked curiously. "I know he's angry at her, but if she's dead, she can't tell him anything!"

"He's going to be setting an example," he said. "Of course, he probably thinks she'll give up the name to save her child." He glanced at Sally. "Would you?"

"I wouldn't have a hard time choosing between my child and someone who's already turned against his own people," she admitted.

"Jessica says there are extenuating circumstances," he told her.

She stared at her fingers. "I know. She won't even tell me who the person was." She glanced at him. "She's probably covering all her bases. If I knew who it was…"

He made a sound deep in his throat. "You'd turn the person over to Lopez?"

She shifted restlessly. "I might."

"Cows might fly."

He knew her too well. She laughed softly. "I wish there was another way out of this, that's all. I don't want Stevie hurt."

"He won't be." He reached across to clasp her cool hand gently in hers and press it. "I'm putting together a network. Lopez isn't going to be able to move without being in someone's line of sight from now on."

"I wish…" she began.

"Don't wish your life away. You have to take the bad with the good—that's what life is. Good times don't make us strong."

She grimaced. "No. I guess they don't." She leaned her head back against the headrest and drank in the smell of the leather. "I love the way new cars smell," she said conversationally. "And this one is just super."

"It has a few minor modifications," he said absently.

She turned her head toward him with a wicked grin. "Don't tell me—the headlights retract and become machine gun ports, the tailpipe leaves oil slicks, and the passenger seat is really an ejectable projectile!"

He laughed. "Not quite."

"Spoilsport."

"You need to stop watching old James Bond movies," he pointed out. "The world has changed since the sixties."

Her eyes studied his profile quietly. He was still handsome well into his thirties, and he glorified evening clothes. She knew that she couldn't look forward to anything permanent with him, but sometimes just looking at him was almost enough. He was devastating.

He caught that scrutiny and glanced at her, enjoying the shy admiration in her gray eyes. "Can you dance?" he asked.

"I'm not in the class with Matt Caldwell on a dance floor," she teased, "but I can hold my own, I suppose. Are we going dancing?"

"We're going to a supper club where they have an orchestra and a dance floor," he said. "A sophisticated place with a few carefully placed friends of mine."

"I should have known."

"You'll like it," he promised. "You'll never spot them. They blend in."

"You don't blend," she murmured dryly.

He chuckled. "If that's a compliment, thank you," he said.

"It was."

"You won't blend, either," he said in a low, soft tone.

She clutched her small bag tightly in her lap, feeling the softness right through her body. It made her giddy to think of being held in his arms on a dance floor. It was something she'd dreamed about in her senior year of high school, but it had never happened. As if it would have. She couldn't really picture Eb at a high school prom.

"You're sure Jess and Stevie will be okay?" she asked as he pulled off the main highway and onto a Houston city street.

"I'm sure. Dallas is inside and I have a few people outside. But I meant what I said," he added solemnly. "Lopez won't do a thing until midnight tomorrow."

She supposed that was a sort of knowledge of the enemy that came from long experience in a dangerous profession. But she couldn't help worrying about her family. If anything happened while she was away, she'd never forgive herself.

THE CLUB WAS JUST OFF A MAIN thoroughfare, and so discreet that it wouldn't have drawn attention to itself. The luxury cars in the parking lot were an intimation of what was inside.

Inside, the sounds of music came from a room off the main hallway. There was a bar and a small coffee shop, apart from the restaurant. Inside, an employee in a dinner jacket led them into the restaurant, which ringed a central dance floor, where a small jazz ensemble played lazy blues tunes for several couples who were dancing.

"This is really spectacular," she told Eb when they were seated near a small indoor waterfall with tropical plants blooming around it.

"It is, isn't it?" he asked, leaning back to study her with a warm smile. "I have to admit, it's one of my favorite haunts when I'm in Houston."

"I can see why." She searched his eyes in a long, tense silence.

He didn't smile. His eyes narrowed as they locked into hers. She could almost hear her own heart beating, beating, beating...!

"Why, Eb!" came a soft voice from behind Sally. "What a coincidence to find you here, at one of our favorite night spots."

Without another word being spoken, Sally knew the identity of the newcomer. It couldn't be anyone except Eb's ex-fiancée.

CHAPTER EIGHT

"HELLO, MAGGIE," EB SAID, standing up to greet the pretty green-eyed brunette who took possession of his arm and smiled up at him.

"It's good to see you again so soon!" she said with obvious pleasure. "You remember Cord Romero, don't you?" She indicated a tall, dark-haired, dark-eyed man beside her without meeting his eyes. "He and I were fostered together by Mrs. Amy Barton, the Houston socialite."

"Sure. How are you, Cord?" Eb asked.

The other man, his equal in height and build, nodded. Sally was curious about Maggie's obvious uneasiness around the other man.

"Sally, this is Maggie Barton and Cord Romero. Sally Johnson." They all acknowledged the introductions, and Eb added, "Won't you join us?"

Sally's heart plummeted as she saw Maggie's eyes light up at the invitation and knew she wouldn't refuse.

"We may be intruding," Cord said with a pointed look at Sally.

"Oh, not at all," Sally said at once.

"I thought Sally needed a night out," Eb said easily

and with a warm smile in Sally's direction. "She's an elementary schoolteacher."

The man, Cord, studied her with open curiosity while Eb seated Maggie.

"Allow me," Cord said smoothly, standing behind Sally's chair.

Sally smiled at the old-world courtesy. "Thank you."

Eb glanced at them with unreadable eyes before he turned back to Maggie, who was flushed and avoided looking at the other couple. "Quite a coincidence, running into you here," he said in a neutral tone.

"It was Cord's idea," Maggie said. "He felt like a night on the town and he doesn't date these days. Better your foster sister than nobody, right, Cord?" she added with a nervous laugh and a smile that didn't touch her eyes.

Cord shrugged broad shoulders indolently and didn't say a word, but his distaste for her reference was there, in those unblinking dark eyes.

Sally was curious about him. She wondered what he did for a living. He was very fit for a man his age, which she judged to be about the same as Eb's. His hands were rough and callused, as if he worked physically rather than sat behind a desk. He had the same odd stare that she'd noticed in Eb and Dallas and even Cy Parks, a probing but unfocused distant stare that held a strange hollowness.

"How are things going at the ranch?" Maggie asked gently. "I heard that you had Dallas out there with you."

"Yes," he replied. "He's doing some consulting work for me."

"Shot to pieces, wasn't he?" Cord asked abruptly, his eyes on Sally's face.

"That happens when a man doesn't keep his mind on his work," Eb said with a pointed glance at Cord, who averted his eyes.

"One of my friends is hosting a huge party down in Cancún for Christmas," Maggie murmured, drawing a lazy polished nail across the back of Eb's hand. "Why don't you take some time off and go with me?"

"No time," Eb said with a smile to soften the words. "I'm not a man of leisure."

"Baloney," she replied. "You could retire on what you've got squirreled away."

"And do what?" came the dry response. "Do I look like a lounge lizard to you?"

"I didn't mean that," she said, and her eyes searched his face for a long moment. "I meant that you could give up walking into danger if you wanted to."

"That's an old argument and you know what the answer is," Eb told her bluntly.

She withdrew her hand from his with a sad little sigh. "Yes, I know," she said wearily. "It's in your blood and you can't stop." Involuntarily she glanced at Cord.

Eb frowned a little as he watched her wilt. Sally saw it and knew at once that he and Maggie had gone through that very argument years ago when she'd broken their engagement. It wasn't their emotions that had split them up. It was his job that he wouldn't quit, not even for a woman he'd loved enough to marry.

She felt helpless. She'd known at some level that he

was carrying a torch for Maggie. She stared at her own short, unpolished nails and compared them with Maggie's long, red-stained, beautiful ones. The difference was like the women themselves—one colorful and flamboyant and drawing attention, the other reclusive and practical and...dull. No wonder Eb hadn't wanted her all those years ago. Beside the exotic Maggie, she was insignificant.

"What subject is your specialty, Miss Johnson?" Cord asked curiously.

"History, actually," she said. "But I teach second grade, so I'm not really using it."

"No ambition to teach higher grades?" he persisted.

She shook her head and smiled wryly. "I tried it when I did my practice-teaching," she confessed. "And by the end of the day, my classroom was more like a zoo than a regimented place of learning. I'm afraid I don't have the facility to handle discipline at a higher level."

Cord's lean face lightened just a little as he studied her. "I had the facility, but the principal and the school board didn't like my methods," he replied.

"You teach?" she asked, enthused to find a colleague in such an unlikely place.

"I taught high school science for a year after I got out of college," he said. "But it wasn't a profession I could love enough to continue." He shrugged. "I found I had an aptitude in a totally unrelated area."

Maggie's hand clenched on her water glass and she took a quick sip.

"What do you do?" she asked, fascinated.

He glanced at Eb, who was openly glaring at him. "Ask Eb," he said on a brief, deep laugh, with a cold glance in Maggie's direction. "Can we order now?" he asked, lifting the menu. "I haven't even had lunch today."

Eb signaled a waiter and brought Sally's conversation with Cord to an end.

It was the longest and most tense meal Sally could remember having sat through. Maggie and Eb talked about places and people that they shared in memory while Sally concentrated on her food.

Cord was polite, but he made no further attempt at conversation. At the end of the evening, as the two couples parted outside the restaurant, Maggie held on to Eb's hand until he had to forcibly draw it away from her.

"Can't you come up and have dinner with us again one evening?" Maggie asked plaintively.

"Perhaps," Eb said with a careless smile. He glanced at Cord. "Good to see you."

Cord nodded. He glanced down at Sally. "Nice to have met you, Miss Johnson."

"Same here," she said with a smile.

Maggie hesitated and looked uneasy as Cord deliberately took her arm and propelled her away. She went with him, but her back was arrow-straight and she looked as if she was walking on hot coals and on the way to her own execution.

Eb stared after them for a long moment before he put Sally into the sleek Jaguar and climbed in under the wheel. He gave her a look that could have curdled milk.

"Don't encourage him," he said at once.

Her mouth fell open. "Wh...what?"

"You heard me." He started the car, and turned toward Sally. His eyes went over her like sensual fingers, brushing her throat, her bare shoulders under the coat, the shadowy hollow in her breasts revealed by the low-cut dress. "He has a weakness for blondes. He was ravishing you with his eyes."

She didn't know how to respond. While Sally was trying to come up with a response, he moved closer and slid a hand under her nape, under the heavy coil of hair, and pulled her face up toward his.

"So was I," he whispered roughly, and his mouth went down on her lips, burrowing beneath them, pressing them apart, devouring them. At the same time, his free hand slid right down into the low bodice of her dress and curved around her warm, bare breast.

"Eb!" she choked, stiffening.

He was undeterred. He groaned, overcome with desire, and his fingers contracted in a slow, heated, sensual rhythm that brought Sally's mouth open in a tiny gasp. His tongue found the unprotected heat of it and moved inside, in lazy, teasing motions that made her whole body clench.

He felt her nervous fingers fumble against the front of his dress shirt. Impatiently, he unfastened three buttons and dragged her hand inside the shirt, over hair-roughened muscles down to a nipple as hard as the one pressing feverishly into the palm of his hand.

She was devastated by the passion that had kindled so unexpectedly. She couldn't find the strength or the voice to protest the liberties he was taking, or to care that they were in a public parking lot. She didn't care about anything except making sure that he didn't stop. He couldn't stop. He mustn't stop, he mustn't…!

But he did, suddenly. He held her hands together tightly as he moved a little away from her, painfully aware that she was trying to get back into his arms.

"No," he said curtly, and shook her clenched hands.

She stared into his blazing eyes, her breath rustling in her throat, her heartbeat visible at the twin points so blatantly obvious against the bodice of her dress.

He glanced down at her and his jaw clenched. His own body was in agony, and this would only get worse if he didn't stop them now. She was too responsive, too tempting. He was going to have to make sure that he didn't touch her that way when they were completely alone. The consequences could be devastating. It was the wrong time for a torrid relationship. If he let himself lose his head over Sally right now, it could cost all of them their lives.

Forcefully, he put her back into her own seat and fastened the seat belt around her.

She just stared at him with those huge, soulful gray eyes that made him feel hungry and guilt-ridden all at the same time.

"I have to get you home," he said tersely.

She nodded. Her throat was too tight for words to get out. She clutched her small purse in her hands and stared out the window as he put the car into gear and pulled out into traffic.

It was a long, and very silent, drive back to her house.

He was preoccupied, as distant as she remembered him from her teens. She wondered if he was thinking about Maggie and regretting the decision he'd made that put her out of his life. She was mature now, but beautiful as well, and it didn't take a mind reader to know that she was still attracted to Eb. How he felt was less obvious. He was a man who knew how to hide what he felt, and that skill was working overtime tonight.

"Why did Maggie introduce Cord as a foster child at first and then refer to him as her brother? Are they related?" she asked.

"They are not," he returned flatly. "His parents died in a fire, and she came from a severely dysfunctional family. Mrs. Barton adopted both of them. Maggie took her name, but Cord kept his own. His father was a rather famous matador in Spain until his death. Maggie does usually try to present Cord as her brother. She's scared to death of him, despite the fact that they've kept in close touch all these years."

That was a surprise. "But why is she scared of him?"

He chuckled. "Because she wants him, although she's apparently never realized it," he returned with a quick glance. "He's been a colleague of mine for a long time, and I always thought that Maggie got engaged to me to put Cord out of the reach of temptation."

She pondered that. "A colleague?"

"That's right. He still works with Micah Steele," he said. "He's a demolitions expert."

"Isn't that dangerous?"

"Very," he replied. "His wife died four years ago.

Committed suicide," he added shockingly. "He never got over it."

"Why did she do something so drastic?" she asked.

"Because he was working for the FBI when they married and he got shot a few months after the wedding. She hadn't realized his work would be so dangerous. He was in the hospital for weeks and she went haywire. He wouldn't give up a job he loved, and she found that she couldn't live with the knowledge that he might end up dead. She couldn't give him up, either, so she took what she considered the easy way out." His face set grimly. "Easy for her. Hell on him."

She drew in a sharp breath. "I suppose he felt guilty."

"Yes. That was about the time Maggie broke up with me," he added. "She said she didn't want to end up like Patricia."

"She knew Cord's wife?"

"They were best friends," he said shortly. "And something happened between Cord and Maggie just after Mrs. Barton's funeral. I never knew what, but it ended in Maggie's sudden marriage to a man old enough to be her father. I don't know why, but I think it had something to do with Cord."

"He's unique."

He glared at her. "Yes. He's a hardened mercenary now. He gave up law enforcement when Patricia died and took a job with an ex-special forces unit that went into freelance work. He started doing demolition work and now it's all he does."

Her eyes softened. "He wants to die."

"You're perceptive," he mused. "That's what I think, too. Hell of a pity that he and Maggie don't see each other. They're a lot alike."

She looked at her purse. "You aren't still carrying a torch for her?"

He chuckled. "No. She's a kind, sweet woman and I probably would have married her if things had been different. But I don't think she could have lived with me. She takes things too much to heart."

"Don't I?" she fished.

He smiled. "At times. But you're spunky, Miss Johnson, and despite the scare you had with your two neighbors, you don't balk at fighting back. I like your spirit. When I lose my temper, and I do occasionally, you won't be looking for a closet to hide in."

"That might be true," she confessed. "But if you were into demolition work, I think I'd run in the opposite direction when I saw you coming."

He nodded. "Which is exactly what Maggie did," he replied. "She ran from Cord and got engaged to me."

That was heartening. If the woman was carrying a torch for another man, it might stop Eb from falling back into his old relationship with her.

"Jealous?" he murmured with a sensuous glance.

Her heart raced. She moved one shoulder a little and avoided his eyes. Then she sighed and said, "Yes."

He chuckled. "Now that really is flattering," he said. "Maggie is part of the past. I have no hidden desire to rekindle old flames. Except the one you and I shared," he qualified.

Sally turned her head and met his searching gaze. Her breath caught in her throat as she stared back at him hungrily.

"Watch it," he said, not quite jokingly. "When we drive up in your yard, we'll be under surveillance. I don't want an audience for what we were doing in the parking lot at that restaurant."

She laughed delightedly. "Okay."

"On the other hand," he added, "we could find a deserted road."

She hesitated. It was one thing for it to happen spontaneously, but quite another to plan such a sensual interlude. And she wasn't sure of her own protective instincts. Around Eb, she didn't seem to have any.

"Don't make such heavy weather of it," he said after a minute. "There's no hurry. We've got all the time in the world."

"Have we?" she wondered, remembering Lopez and his threats.

"Don't gulp down your life, Sally," he said. "Take it one minute at a time. I'm not going to let anything happen to you or Jessica or Stevie. Okay?"

She swallowed. "Sorry. I panic when I think about how dangerous it is."

"I've been handling danger for a long time," he reminded her. "I have a state-of-the-art surveillance system. Nothing is going to get past it."

She managed a weak smile. "He's very ruthless."

"He's been getting away with murder," he said simply. "He doesn't think the justice system can touch him. We're going to prove to him that it can."

"How do you bring a man to justice when he's rich enough to buy a country?"

"You cut off the source of his wealth," he said simply. "Without its head, the snake can't go far."

"Good point."

"Now stop worrying."

"I'll try."

He reached across the seat for her hand and locked it into his big, warm one. "I enjoyed tonight."

"So did I," she said gently.

"Maggie isn't my future, in case you were wondering," he added in a soft tone.

Sally hoped fervently that it was true. She wanted Eb with all her heart.

His fingers tightened on hers. "I think it might be a good idea if I start driving you and Stevie to school and picking you up in the afternoons."

Her heart leaped. "Why?"

He glanced at her. "Because Lopez wouldn't hesitate to kidnap either or both of you to further his own ends. Even two miles is a long distance when you don't have any sort of protection."

She stared at him worriedly. "Why didn't Jess leave well enough alone?" she asked miserably. "If she hadn't gotten that person to talk…"

"Hindsight is wonderful," he told her. "But try to remember that Lopez's operation supplies about a quar-

ter of all narcotics sold in the States. That's a lot of ad-
dicted kids and a fair number of dead ones."

She grimaced. "Sorry. I was being selfish."

"It isn't selfish to be concerned for the welfare of
people you love," he told her. "But getting Lopez behind
bars, and cutting his connections, will help make the
world a better place. A little worry isn't such a bad
trade-off, considering."

"I guess not."

He brought the back of her hand to his mouth and
kissed it warmly. "You looked lovely tonight," he said.
"I was proud of you."

Her face flushed at the rare compliment. "I'm always proud of you," she replied softly.

He chuckled. "You're good for my ego."

"You're good for mine."

He kept his eyes on the road with an effort. He
wanted to pull the car onto a side road and make passionate love to her, but that was impractical, given the
circumstances. All Lopez's men needed was an opportunity. He wasn't going to give them one, despite his
teasing comment to Sally about it.

When they pulled up in her driveway, the lights were
all on in the house and Dallas was sitting in the front
porch swing, smoking like a furnace.

"Have a nice time?" he asked as Eb and Sally came
up the steps.

"Very nice," Eb replied. "I ran into Cord Romero."

"I thought he was overseas, helping detonate unex-
ploded land mines?"

"Not now," Eb told him. "He's in Houston. Between jobs, maybe. Why are you sitting out here?"

Dallas stared at the red tip of his cigarette. "Jessica has a cough," he replied. "I didn't want to aggravate it."

"Are the two of you speaking?" Eb drawled.

Dallas laughed softly. "Well, she's stopped trying to throw things at me, at least."

Sally's eyes went enormous. That didn't sound like her staid aunt.

"What was she throwing?" Eb asked.

"Anything within reach that felt expendable," came the dry reply. "Stevie thought it was great fun, but she wouldn't let him play. He's gone to bed. She's pretending to watch television."

"You might talk to her," Eb suggested.

"Chance," Dallas replied, "would be a fine thing. She doesn't want to talk, thank you." He finished the cigarette. "I'll be out in the woods with Smith."

"Watch where you walk," Eb cautioned.

"Mined the forest, did we?" Dallas murmured wickedly.

Eb grinned. "Not with explosives, at least."

Dallas shook his head and went down the steps, to vanish in the direction of the woods at the edge of the yard.

Sally rubbed her arms through the coat, shivering, and it wasn't even that cold. She felt the danger of her predicament keenly and wished that she could have done something to prevent the desperate situation.

"You're doing it again," Eb murmured, drawing her

against him. "You have to trust me. I won't let anything happen to any of you."

She looked up at him with wide, soft eyes. "I'll try not to worry. I've never been in such a mess before."

"Hopefully you never will again," he said. He bent and kissed her very gently, nipping her lower lip before he lifted his head. "I'll be somewhere nearby, or my men will be. Try to get some sleep."

"Okay." She touched her fingers to his mouth and smiled wanly before she turned and walked to the door. "Thanks for supper," she added. "It was delicious."

"It would have been better without the company," he said, "but that was unavoidable. Next time I'll plan better."

She smiled at him. "That's a deal."

He watched her walk inside the house and lock the door behind her before he turned and got back into his truck. Less than twenty-four hours remained before Lopez would make good his threat. He had to make sure that everyone was prepared for a siege.

SALLY PAUSED IN THE DOORWAY of the living room with her eyes wide as she saw the damage Jessica had inflicted with her missiles.

"Good Lord!" she exclaimed.

Jess grimaced. "Well, he provoked me," she muttered. "He said that I'd gotten lazy in my old age, just lying around the house like a garden slug. I do not lie around like a garden slug!"

"No, of course you don't," Sally said, placating her

while she bent to pick up pieces of broken pottery and various other objects from the floor.

"Besides, what does he expect me to do without my eyesight, drive the car?"

Sally was trying not to smile. She'd never seen her aunt in such a tizzy before.

"He actually accused me of insanity because I won't give up the name to Lopez," she added harshly. "He said that a good mother wouldn't have withheld a name and put her child in danger. That's when I threw the flowerpot, dear. I'm sorry. I do hope it hit him."

Sally made a clucking sound. "You're not yourself, Jess."

"Yes, I am! I'm the result of all his sarcasm! He can't find one thing about me that he likes anymore. Everything I do and say is wrong!"

"He doesn't seem like a bad man," Sally ventured.

"I didn't say he was bad, I said he was obnoxious and condescending and conceited." She pushed back a strand of hair. "He was laughing the whole time."

Which surely made things worse, Sally mused silently. "I expect it was wails of pain, Jess."

"You couldn't hurt him," she scoffed. "You'd have to stick a bomb up his shirt."

"Drastic surely?"

Jess sighed and leaned back in the chair, looking drained. "I hate arguments. He seems to thrive on them." She hesitated. "He taught Stevie how to braid a rope," she added unexpectedly.

"That's odd. I thought Stevie wanted to beat him up."

"They had a talk outside the room. I don't know what was said," Jess confessed. "But when they came back in here, Dallas had several lengths of rawhide and he taught Stevie how to braid them. He was having the time of his life."

"Then what?"

"Then," she said, her lips compressing briefly, "he just happened to mention that I could have taught him how to braid rope and a lot of other things if I'd exert myself occasionally instead of vegetating in front of a television that I can't see anyway."

"I see."

"Pity I ran out of things to throw," she muttered. "I was reaching for the lamp when he called a draw and said he was going to sit on the front porch. Then Stevie decided to go to bed." She gripped the arms of her chair hard. "Everybody ran for cover. You'd think I was a Chinese rocket or something."

"In a temper, there is something of a comparison," Sally chuckled.

The older woman drew in a long breath. "Anyway, how was your date?"

"Not bad. We ran into his ex-fiancée at the restaurant."

"Maggie?" Jess asked, wide-eyed. "How is she?"

"She's very pretty and still crazy about Eb, from all indications. I think she'd have followed us home if her dark and handsome escort hadn't half dragged her away."

"Cord was there?"

"You know him?" Sally asked curiously.

Jess nodded. "He was a handsome devil. I had a yen

for him once myself, but he married Patricia instead. She was a little Dresden china doll, blonde and absolutely gorgeous. She worshipped Cord. They'd only been married a few months when he was involved in a shoot-out with a narcotics dealer. She couldn't take it. When Cord came home from the hospital, she was several days dead, with a suicide note clutched in her fingers. He found her. He was like a madman after that, looking for every dangerous job he could find. I don't suppose he's over her yet. He loved her desperately."

"Eb says he works with Micah Steele."

"He does, and there's a real coincidence. Micah also has a stepsister, Callie. You know her, she works in Mr. Kemp's law office."

"Yes. We went to school together. But Micah doesn't have anything to do with her or his father since his father divorced Callie's mother. They say," she murmured, "that old Mr. Steele caught Micah with his new wife in a very compromising position and tossed them both out on their ears."

"That's the obvious story," Jessie said dryly. "But there's more to it than that."

"How does Callie feel about Micah's work, do you think?"

"The way any woman would feel," Jessie replied gently. "Afraid."

Sally knew that Jess was talking about Dallas, and how she'd regarded his work as a soldier of fortune. She stared at the darkened window, wondering how she'd feel under the same circumstances. At least Eb wasn't involved in demolition work or actively working as a mercenary. She knew that she could adjust to Eb's lifestyle. But the trick was going to be convincing Eb that she could—and that he needed her, as much as she needed him.

CHAPTER NINE

SALLY FOUND HERSELF JUMPING at every odd noise all day Saturday. Jessica could feel the tension that she couldn't see.

"You have to trust Eb," she told her niece while Stevie was watching cartoons in the living room. "He knows what he's doing. Lopez won't succeed."

Sally grimaced over her second cup of coffee. Across the kitchen table from her, Jess looked serene. She wished she could feel the same way.

"I'm not worried about us," she pointed out. "It's Stevie…"

"Dallas won't let anything happen to Stevie," came the quiet reply.

Sally smiled, remembering the broken objects in the living room the night before. She drew a lazy circle around the lip of her coffee cup while she searched for the right words. "At least, the two of you are speaking."

"Yes. Barely," her aunt acknowledged wryly. "But Stevie likes him now. They started comparing statistics on wrestlers. They both like wrestling, you see. Dallas knows all sorts of holds. He wrestled on his college team."

"Wrestling!" Sally chuckled.

"Apparently there's a lot more to the professional matches than just acting ability," Jessica said dryly. "I'm finding it rather interesting, even if I can't see what they're doing. They explained the holds to me."

"Common threads," Sally murmured.

"And one stitch at a time. What did you think of Cord Romero?"

"He's the strangest ex-schoolteacher I've ever met," Sally said flatly.

"He was never cut out for that line of work," Jessica said, sipping black coffee. "But demolition work isn't much of a profession, either. Pity. He'll be two lines of type on the obituary page one day, and it's such a waste."

"Eb says Maggie's running from him."

"Relentlessly," Jess said dryly. "I always thought she got engaged to Eb just to shake Cord up, but it didn't work. He doesn't see her."

"He's in the same line of work Eb was," Sally pointed out, "and Eb said that his job was why she called off the wedding."

"I think she just came to her senses. If you love a man, you don't have a lot to say about his profession if it's a long-standing one. Cord's wife was never cut out for life on the edge. Maggie, now, once had a serious run-in with a couple of would-be muggers. She had a big flashlight in her purse and she used it like a mace." She laughed softly. "They both had to have stitches before they went off to jail. Cord laughed about it for weeks afterward. No, she had the strength to marry Eb—she simply didn't love him."

Sally traced the handle of her cup. "Eb says he isn't carrying a torch for her."

"Why should he be?" she asked. "She's a nice woman, but he never really loved her. He wanted stability and he thought marriage would give it to him. As it turned out, he found his stability after a bloody firefight in Africa, and it was right here in Jacobsville."

"Do you think he'll ever marry?" she fished.

"When he's ready," Jess replied. "But I don't think it will be Maggie. Just in case you wondered," she teased.

Sally pushed back a wisp of hair from her eyes. "Jess, do you know where your informant is now, the one that Lopez wants you to name?"

She shook her head. "We lost touch just after Lopez was arrested. I understand that my informant went back to Mexico. I haven't tried to contact…the person."

"What if the informant betrays himself?"

"You're clutching at straws, dear," Jessica said gently. "That isn't going to happen. And I'm not giving a witness up to the executioner in cold blood even to save myself and my family."

Sally smiled. "No. I know you wouldn't. I wouldn't, either. But it's scary to be in this situation."

"It is. But it will be over one day, and we'll get back to normal. Whatever happens, happens." Jess reminded her niece, "It's like that old saying, when your time's up, it's up. We may not know what we're doing, but God always does. And He doesn't have tunnel vision."

"Point taken. I'll try to stop worrying."

"You should. Eb is one of the best in the world at what he does. Lopez knows it, too. He won't rush in headfirst, despite his threat."

"What if he has a missile launcher?" Sally asked with sudden fear.

Miles away in a communications hot room, a man with green eyes nodded his head and shot an order to a subordinate. It wouldn't hurt one bit to check out the intelligence for that possibility. Sally might be nervous, but she had good instincts. And a guardian angel in cowboy boots.

MANUEL LOPEZ WAS A SMALL man with big ambition. He was nearing forty, balding, cynical and mercenary to the soles of his feet. He stared out the top floor picture window of his four-story mansion at the Gulf of Mexico and cursed. One of his subordinates, shifting nervously from one foot to the other, had just brought him some unwelcome news and he was livid.

"There are only a handful of men," the subordinate said in quiet Spanish. "Not a problem if we send a large force against them."

Lopez turned and glared at the man from yellow-brown eyes. "Yes, and if we send a large force, the FBI and the DEA will also send a large force!"

"It would be too late by then," the man replied with a shrug.

"I have enough federal problems in the United States as it is," Lopez growled. "I do not anticipate giving them an even better reason to send an undercover unit after me here! Scott has influence with his government. I want the name of the informant, not to wade in and kill the woman and her protectors."

The other man stared at the spotless white carpet. "She will never give up the name of her informant," he said simply. "Not even for the sake of her child."

Lopez turned fully to look at the man. "Because now it is only words, the threat. We must make it very real, you understand? At midnight tonight in Jacobsville, precisely at midnight, you will have a helicopter fly over the house and drop a smoke bomb. A big one." His eyes narrowed and he smiled. "This will be the attack they anticipate. But not the real one, you understand?"

"They will probably have missiles," the man said quietly.

"And they are far too soft to use them," came the sneering reply. "This is why we will ultimately win. I have no scruples. Now, listen. I will want a man to remove one of the elementary school janitors. He can be drugged or threatened, I have no interest in the method, just get him out of the way for one day. Then you will have one of our men take his place. The substitute must know what the child looks like and which class he is in. He is to be taken very covertly, so that nothing out of the way is projected until it is too late and we have him. You understand?"

"Yes," the man replied respectfully. "Where is he to be held?"

Lopez smiled coldly. "At the rental house near the Johnson home," he said. "Will that not be an irony to end all ironies?" His eyes darkened. "But he is not to be harmed. That must be made very clear," he added in tones that chilled. "You remember what happened to the man who went against my orders and set fire to my enemy's house in Wyoming without waiting for the man to be alone, and a five-year-old boy was killed?"

The other man swallowed and nodded quickly.

"If one hair on this boy's head is harmed," he added, "I will see to it that the man responsible fares even worse than his predecessor. I am a violent man, but I do not kill children. It is, perhaps, my only virtue." He waved his hand. "Let me know when my orders have been carried out."

"Yes. At once."

He watched the man go and his odd yellow-brown eyes narrowed. He had watched his mother and siblings die at the hands of a guerrilla leader at the age of four. His father had been a poor laborer who could barely earn enough to provide one meal a day for the two of them, so his childhood had been spent scavenging for food like an animal, hiding in the shadows to avoid being tortured by the invaders. His father had not been as fortunate, but the two of them had managed to work their way to the States, to Victoria, Texas, when he was ten. He watched his father scrape and bow as a janitor and hated the sight. He had vowed that when he was a man, he would never know poverty again, regardless of what it cost him. And despite his father's anguish, he had embarked very quickly on a path to easy money.

He looked down at the white carpet, a dream of his from youth, and at the wealth with which he surrounded himself. He dealt in drugs and death. He was wealthy and immensely powerful. A word from him could topple heads of state. But it was an empty, cold, bitter existence. He had lived at first only for vengeance, for the ability and the means to avenge his mother and his baby brother and sister. That accomplished, he wanted wealth and power. One step led to another, until he was in over his head, first as a murderer, then as a thief, and finally, as a drug lord. He was ruthless and he knew that one day his sins would catch up with him, but first he was going to know who had sold him out to the authorities two years before. What irony that vengeance had led him to power, and now it was vengeance that had almost brought him down. He cursed the woman Jessica for refusing to give him the name. He had only discovered her part in his arrest six months before. She would pay now. He would have the name of his betrayer, whatever the cost!

He stared down at the rocks and winced as he saw once again, in his memory, the floating white dress and the equally white face and open, dead eyes of the woman he'd wanted even more than the name of the person who had betrayed him. Isabella, he thought with anguish. He had never loved, not until Isabella came into his home as a housekeeper, the sister of one of his lieutenants' friends. She had talked to him, admired him, teased him as if he were a boy. She had made herself so necessary to him that he told her things that he told no one else. She had made him want to be clean, to give up his decadent life, to have a family, a home. But when he had approached her ardently, she had suddenly wanted no part of him. In a fit of rage when she pushed him away at a party on his yacht, he hit her. She went over the rails and into the ocean, vanishing abruptly under the keel of the boat.

He had immediately regretted the act, but it was too late. His men had searched for her in the water until daybreak before he let them give up the search, only to find her washed up on the beach, dead, when he arrived back at his mansion. Her death had cheapened him, cheapened his life. He was deeply sorry that his temper had pushed him to such an act, that he cost himself the most precious thing in his life. He had killed her. He was damned, he thought. Damned eternally. And probably he deserved to be.

Since that night, two years ago, just before his arrest in the United States for narcotic trafficking, he had no other thought than to find the man who had betrayed him. Nothing made him happy since her loss, not even the pretty young woman who sang at a club in Cancún just recently. He had taken a fancy to her because she reminded him of Isabella. He had ordered his henchmen to bring her to him one night after her performance. He had enjoyed her, but her violent revulsion had angered him and she, too, had felt his wrath. She had taken her own life, jumped from a high balcony rather than submit to him a second time. Her death had wounded him, but not as deeply as the loss of Isabella. Nothing, he was certain, would ever give him such anguish and remorse again. He thought of the woman Jessica and her son, of the fear she would experience when he had her child. Then, he thought angrily, she would give him the name of her informant. She would have to. And, at last, he would have his vengeance for the betrayal that had sent him to an American prison.

EB HADN'T COME NEAR the house all day. After Stevie was tucked up in bed, Jessica and Sally sat together in the dimly lit living room and watched the clock strike midnight.

"It's time," Sally said huskily, stiff with nerves.

Jessica only nodded. Like Sally, her frame was rigid. She had made her decision, the only decision possible. Now they were all going to pay the consequences for it.

Even as the thought crawled through her mind, she heard the sudden whir of a helicopter closing in.

"Get down!" Jessica called to Sally, sliding onto the big throw rug full-length. She felt Sally beside her as the helicopter came even closer and a flash, followed by an explosion, shook the roof.

Smoke came down the chimney, filling the room. Outside, the whir of the helicopter was accompanied by small arms fire and the sounds of bullets hitting something hard. Then that sound was abruptly interrupted by a sudden whooshing sound. Right on the heels of that came a violent explosion that lit up the whole sky and then the unmistakable sound of falling debris.

"There went the chopper," Jessica said huskily. "Sally, are you all right?"

"Yes. We have to get out," she said, coughing. "The smoke is going to choke us!"

She helped Jessica to her feet and started her down

the hall to the front door while she went to grab Stevie up out of his bed and rush down the same hall with him in her arms. It was like a nightmare, but she didn't have time to count the cost or worry about the outcome. She was doing what was necessary to save them, in the quickest possible time. She could only pray that they wouldn't run out right into the arms of Lopez's men.

She caught up with Jess, who was feeling her way along the wall. Taking her by the arm, with Stevie close, she propelled them to the front door, unlocked it, and rushed out onto the porch.

Eb was running toward them, but an Eb that Sally didn't recognize at first. He was dressed completely in black with a face mask on, carrying a small automatic weapon. Other men, similarly dressed, were already going around the back of the house.

"Come with me," Eb called, herding them into the forest and into a four-wheel-drive vehicle. "Lock the doors and stay put until we check out the house," he said.

He was gone even as the words died on the air. Stevie huddled close to his mother while Sally watched Eb's stealthy but rapid approach toward the house, her heart racing madly. Even though the attack had been expected, it was frightening.

A tap on the window next to Jessica on the passenger side made them all jump. Dallas pulled off his face mask, smiling as he replaced a walkie-talkie in his belt. "Open the window," he said.

Sally fumbled with the key in the ignition and powered the passenger side window down.

"We got the chopper," he said. "But it's only a smoke bomb in the house, irritating but not deadly. Lopez is a man of his word. He did attack at midnight. Pity about the chopper," he added with glittery eyes. "That will set him back a little small change."

Sally didn't ask the obvious question, but she knew that somebody had to be piloting that helicopter. She felt sick inside, now that the danger was past.

"Is everyone all right?" Jessica asked. "We heard shots."

"The chopper was well-equipped with weapons," Dallas said. "But he wasn't a very good shot."

"Thank God," Jessica said heavily.

Dallas reached in and touched her face gently, pausing to run a rough hand over Stevie's tousled hair. "Don't be afraid," he said softly. "I won't let anything happen to you."

Jessica held his hand to her cheek and choked back a sob. Dallas bent to touch his mouth to her wet eyes.

Impulsively Stevie leaned across his mother to hug the big blond man, too. Watching them, Sally felt empty and alone. They were already a family, even if they hadn't realized it.

Dallas's walkie-talkie erupted in a burst of static. "All clear," Eb's voice came back to them. "I'm phoning the sheriff while the others open the windows and turn on the attic fan to get this smoke out of here. Then I'll lock up."

"What about…" Dallas began.

"We'll take the women and Stevie home with us," he

said. "No sense in leaving them here for the rest of the night. Sally?"

Dallas moved the walkie-talkie to her mouth. "Yes?" she said, shaken.

"Come in and help me find what you need in the way of clothes for all three of you. Dallas, take Jess and Stevie back to the house. We'll catch up."

"Sure thing."

Sally got out of the vehicle, still in her jeans and sneakers and sweatshirt, her long hair falling out of its braid. Dallas got in under the wheel as she walked back to the house. She heard the engine roar and glanced back to see the utility vehicle pull out of the yard. At least Jess and Stevie were safe. But she felt shaken to the soles of her sneakers.

Eb was in the smoky living room, having just hung up the phone. His mask was in one hand, dangling along with the small machine gun. He looked tough and angry as he glanced at Sally's white face. He didn't say a word. He just held out his arm.

Sally ran to him, and he gathered her up in his arms and held her tight while she shivered from the shock of it all.

"I'm no wimp, honest," she whispered in a choked attempt at humor. "But I'm not used to people bombing my house."

He chuckled deeply and hugged her close. "Only a smoke bomb, baby," he said gently. "Noisy and frightening, but not dangerous unless it set fire to something. He had to make a statement, you see. Lopez is a man of his word."

"Damn Lopez," she muttered.

"Amen."

Around them, men were pouring over the house. Eb escorted Sally down the hall to her bedroom.

"Get what you need together," he said, "but only essentials. I'd like to get you out of here very soon after the sheriff arrives."

"The sheriff…?"

"It's his jurisdiction," he told her. "I'm sanctioned, if that's what the worried look is about," he added when he saw her face. He smiled. "I wouldn't take the law into my own hands. Not in this country, anyway," he added with a grin.

"Thank goodness," she said heavily. "I had visions of trying to bail you out of jail."

"Would you?" he teased.

"Of course."

She looked so solemn that the smile faded from his lips. He gathered a handful of her thick blond hair and pulled her wan face under his. His grip was a little tight, and the look in his green eyes was glittery. "Danger is an aphrodisiac, did you know?" he whispered roughly, and bent to her mouth.

He hadn't kissed her that way before. His mouth was hard and demanding on her lips, parting them ruthlessly as his body shifted and one arm pushed her hips deliberately into the changing contours of his own.

She felt helpless. Her mouth opened for him. Her body arched up, taut and hot, in the grip of madness. She returned his kiss ardently, moaning when his legs parted so that he could maneuver her hips between them, letting her feel the power of his arousal.

His tall, fit body shuddered and she could feel the sharp indrawn breath he took.

After a few wild seconds, he dragged his mouth away from hers without letting her move away even a fraction of an inch. He looked down at her with intent, searching her wide, soft gray eyes hungrily. The arm that was holding her was like a steel rod at her back, but against her legs, she felt the faintest tremor in his.

"I've gone hungry for a long time," he whispered gruffly.

She didn't know how to reply to such a blatant statement. Her eyes searched his in an odd silence, broken only by the whir of the attic fan in the hall and the muffled sound of voices as Eb's men searched the house. She reached up and touched his hard mouth tenderly, loving the immediate response of his lips to the caress.

He bent, nuzzling his face against hers to find her mouth. He kissed her urgently, but with restraint, nibbling her lower lip sensuously. Both arms went around her, riveting her to him. Her own slid under his arms and around his hard waist, holding him close. She closed her eyes, savoring the wondrous contact. The fierce hunger he felt was quite obvious in the embrace, but it didn't frighten her. She wanted him, too.

"When I heard the explosion," he said at her ear, his voice tight with tension, "I didn't know what we were going to find when I ran toward the house. We'd planned for any eventuality, but the chopper came in under radar.

We didn't even hear the damned thing until we could see it, and then the launcher jammed…!"

She hadn't imagined that Eb would be afraid for her. It was wonderful. She hugged him closer and felt him shiver.

"We were a little shaken," Sally whispered. "But we're all okay."

"I didn't expect to feel like this," he said through his teeth.

She lifted her head and looked up at his strained face. "Like…this?"

His green gaze met her soft gray one and then fell to her mouth, to her soft breasts flattened against him. "Like this," he whispered and moved deliberately against her while he held her eyes.

She blushed, because it was blatant.

But he didn't smile. "I knew you were going to be trouble six years ago," he said through his teeth. He bent and kissed her again, fiercely, before he put her away from him and stood trying to get his breath.

She was shivering a little in the aftermath of the most explosive sensuality she'd ever felt. She searched his face quietly, despite the turmoil inside her awakened body.

"You've never felt like that before, have you?" he asked in a hushed tone.

She shook her head, still too shaken for words.

"If it's any consolation, it gets steadily worse," he continued. "Think about that."

He turned and went out into the hall with her puzzled eyes following him. She touched her swollen lips gingerly and wondered what he meant.

THE SHERIFF, BILL ELLIOTT, and two deputies pulled up in the yard, took statements and looked around with Eb and the other men. Sally was questioned briefly, and when the house was secure, Eb drove her back to his house with the rest of his men remaining in the woods.

"I don't think Lopez has any idea of trying again tonight," he said, "but I'm not taking any chances. I've already underestimated him once."

"He does keep his word," she said huskily.

"Yes."

"What do we do now?"

"I take you and Stevie to school and Jess stays at my house. In fact, you all stay at my house," he said curtly. "I'm not putting you at risk a second time."

She was stunned at the emotion in his voice. He was really concerned about her. She felt a warm glow all the way to her toes.

He glanced at her with slow, sensuous eyes. "At least at my own house, I can find one room with no bugs." His eyes went to her breasts and back to her face. "I'm starving."

She knew he wasn't talking about food, and her heart began racing madly.

He caught her hand in his free one and worked his fingers slowly between hers, pressing her palm to his. "Don't worry. I won't let things go too far, Sally."

She wasn't worried about that. She was wondering how she was going to go on living if he made love to her and then walked away.

WHEN THEY GOT TO THE HOUSE, Jessica and Dallas were in the small bedroom Eb's male housekeeper had given Stevie, tucking him in.

Eb had his housekeeper show the others to their rooms and he excused himself, tugging Sally along with him, to Dallas's obvious amusement.

"Where are we going?" Sally asked.

"To bed. I'm tired. Aren't you?"

"Yes."

She supposed he was giving her a room further down the hall, but he didn't stop at any of the closed doors. He led her around a corner and through two double doors into a huge room with Mediterranean furnishings and green and gold and brown accessories. He closed the double doors, locking them, before he turned to the dresser and pulled out a pair of blue silk pajamas.

"You can wear the pajama top and I'll wear the bottoms," he said matter-of-factly.

Her breath escaped in a rush. "Eb…"

He drew her into his arms and kissed her slowly, with deliberate sensuality, making nonsense of her protests with his hands as they skimmed under the sweatshirt and up to find her taut breasts.

She moaned, feeling the fever rise in her as he unfastened the bra and touched her hungrily. Her body arched, helping him, inviting him. Her hands gripped hard against the powerful muscles of his upper arms, drowning in waves of pleasure.

His mouth lifted fractionally. "I won't hurt you," he breathed. "Not in any way. But you're sleeping in my arms tonight."

She started to protest, but his mouth was already covering hers, muffling the words, muffling her brain.

His hands removed the sweatshirt and the bra and he looked at her with quiet, possessive eyes, drinking in the soft textures, the smooth skin, the beauty of her. He touched her gently, smiling as her body reacted to his skilled hands.

His mouth slid down to her breasts and kissed them slowly, each caress more ardent than the one before. He had her out of her jeans and sneakers and down to her briefs before she realized what was happening.

He moved away just long enough to pick up the pajama top and slip it over her head, still buttoned. He lifted her, dazed, in his arms and paused, balancing her on one knee, to pull the covers back so that he could tuck her into bed. He leaned over her, balancing on his hands, and searched her flushed, fascinated face.

"I'll be in after I've talked to Dallas and reset the monitors."

She didn't bother to protest. Her gray eyes searched his and she sighed a little unsteadily. "All right."

His eyes kindled with pleasure. He smiled, because he knew she was accepting anything he proposed. It was humbling. He kissed her eyelids closed. "Sleep well."

She watched him go, uncertain if that meant he was sleeping elsewhere. She was so tired that she fell asleep almost as soon as the doors closed behind him, wrapped in sensuous dreams.

CHAPTER TEN

SALLY HAD VIOLENT, PASSIONATE DREAMS that night. She moved helplessly under invisible caressing hands, moaning, arching up to prolong their warm, sweet contact. Her body burned, swelled, ached. She whispered to some faceless phantom, pleading with it not to stop.

There was soft, deep laughter at her ear and the rough warmth of an unshaven face moving against her skin, where her heart beat frantically. Slowly it occurred to her that it felt just a little too vivid to be a dream…

Her eyes flew open and blond-streaked brown hair came into focus under them in the pale dawn light filtering in through the window curtains. Her hands were enmeshed in its thick, cool strands and when she looked down, she realized that her pajama top was open, baring her to a marauding mouth.

"Eb!" she exclaimed huskily.

"It's all right. You're only dreaming," he whispered, and his mouth slid up to cover her lips as the hair-roughened skin of his muscular chest slid over her bare breasts. She felt his legs entwining with her own, felt the throb of his body, the tenderness of his hands, his mouth, as he learned her by touch and taste.

"Dreaming?"

"That's right." He lifted his lips from hers and looked down into misty gray eyes. He smiled. "And a lovely dream it is," he added in a whisper as he lifted away enough to give his eyes a stark view of everything the pajama top no longer covered. "Lovelier than I ever imagined."

"What time is it?" she asked, dazed.

"Dawn," he told her, smoothing her long hair back away from her flushed face. "Everyone else is still asleep. And there are no bugs, of any sort, in here with us," he added meaningfully.

She touched his rough cheek gently, studying him as he'd studied her. He was still wearing the pajama trousers, but his broad chest was bare. Like her own.

He rolled over onto his back, taking her with him. He guided her hands to his chest with a quiet smile. "I was going to let you wake up alone," he murmured. "But I didn't have enough willpower. There you lay, blond hair scattered over my pillows, the pajama top half off." He shook his head. "You can't imagine how lovely you look in the dawn light. Like a fairy, all creamy and gold. Irresistible," he added, "to a man who's abstained as long as I have."

She traced the pattern of hair over his breastbone. "How long have you abstained?"

"Years too long," he whispered, searching her eyes. "And that's why I set the alarm in Dallas's room to go off five minutes from now. It will wake him and he'll wake Jess and Stevie. Stevie will come looking for you."

He grinned. "See how carefully I look after your virtue, Miss Johnson?"

She gave her own bare torso a poignant glance and met his eyes again.

He lifted an eyebrow. "Virtue," he emphasized, "not modesty. I don't seduce virgins, in case you forgot."

She couldn't quite decide whether he was playing or serious.

He saw that in her face and smiled gently. "Sally, the hardest thing I ever did in my life was to push you away one spring afternoon six years ago," he said softly. "I had passionate, vivid dreams about you in some of the wildest places on earth. I'm still having them." His hand swept slowly down her body, watching it lift helplessly to his touch. "So are you, judging by the sounds you were making in your sleep when I came to bed about ten minutes ago. I crawled in beside you and you came right up against me and touched me in a way I won't tell you about."

She searched his eyes blankly. "I did what?"

"Want to know?" he asked with an outrageous grin. "Okay." He leaned close and whispered it in her ear and she cried out, horrified.

"No need to feel embarrassed," he chided. "I loved it."

She knew her face was scarlet, but he looked far more pleased than teasing.

He traced her lower lip lazily. "For a few tempestuous seconds I forgot Lopez and last night, and just about everything else of any immediate importance." His eyes darkened as he held her poised above him. "I've lived on dreams for a long time. The reality is pretty shattering."

"Dreams?"

He nodded. He wasn't smiling. "I wanted you six years ago. I still do, more than ever." He brushed back her disheveled hair and looked at her with eyes that were tender and possessive. "I'm your home. Wherever I go, you go."

She didn't understand what he meant. Her face was troubled.

He rolled her over onto her back and propped himself above her. "From what I know of you, my lifestyle isn't going to break you. You've got spirit and courage, and you're not afraid to speak your mind. I think you'll adjust very well, especially if I give up any work that takes me out of the country. I can still teach tactics, although I'll cut down my contract jobs when the babies start coming along."

"Babies?" She looked completely blank.

"Listen, kid," he murmured dryly, "what we're doing causes them." He frowned. "Well, not exactly what we're doing. But if we were wearing less, and doing a little more than we're doing, we'd be causing them."

Her whole body tingled. She searched his eyes with a feeling of unreality. "You want to have a child with me?" she asked, awed.

"Oh, yes. I want to have a lot of children with you," he whispered solemnly.

She laid her hands flat on his broad chest, savoring its muscular warmth as she considered what he was saying. She frowned, because he hadn't mentioned love or marriage.

"What's missing?" he asked.

"I teach school," she said worriedly. "My reputation..."

Now he was frowning. "God Almighty, do you think I'm asking you to live in sin with me, in Jacobsville, Texas?" he asked, with exaggerated horror.

"You didn't say anything about marriage," she began defensively.

He grinned wickedly. "Do you really think I spent so much time on you just to give you karate lessons?" he drawled. "Darlin', it would take years of them to make you proficient enough to protect yourself from even a weak adversary. I brought you over here for practice so that I could get my arms around you."

Her eyes brightened. "Did you, really?"

He chuckled. "See what depths I've sunk to?" he murmured. He shook his head. "I had to give you enough time to grow up. I didn't want a teenager who was hero worshiping me. I wanted a woman, a strong woman, who could stand up to me."

She smoothed her hands up to his broad shoulders. "I think I can do that," she mused.

He nodded. "I think you can, too. Can you live with what I do?"

She smiled. "Of course."

He drew in a slow breath and his eyes were more possessive than ever. "Then we'll get Jess out of harm's way and then we'll get married."

She pulled him down to her. "Yes," she whispered against his hard mouth.

Seconds later, they were so close that she wasn't certain he'd be able to draw back at all, when there was a loud knock at the door and the knob rattled.

"Aunt Sally!" came a plaintive little voice. "I want some cereal and they haven't got any that's in shapes and colors. It's such boring cereal!"

Sally laughed even as Eb managed to drag himself away from the tangle of their legs with a groan that was half amusement and half agony.

"I'll be right there, Stevie!"

"Why's the door locked?" he called loudly.

"Come on here, youngster, and let's see if we can find something you'd like to eat," came a deep, amused adult voice.

"Okay, Dallas!"

The voices retreated. Eb lay shivering a little with reaction, but he grinned when Sally sat up and looked down at him with love glowing in her eyes.

"Close call," he whispered.

"Very," she agreed.

He took a long, hungry last look at her breasts and resolutely sat up and fastened her buttons again with a rueful smile. "Maybe food is a bearable substitute for what I really want," he mused.

She leaned forward and kissed him gently. "I'll make you glad we waited," she whispered against his mouth.

Several heated minutes later, they joined the others at the breakfast table, but Eb didn't mention future plans. He was laying down ground rules for the following week, starting with the very necessary trip Sally and Stevie must take to school the next day.

"We could keep him out of school until this is over," Dallas said tersely, glancing at the child who was sitting between himself and Jessica. "I don't like having him at risk."

"Neither do I," Jessica said heavily. "But it's possible that he won't be. Lopez has a weakness for children," she said. "It's the only virtue he possesses, but he's a maniac about abusive adults. He'd never hurt Stevie, no matter what."

"I'd have to agree with that," Eb said surprisingly.

"Then life goes on as usual," Jessica said. "And maybe Lopez will make a mistake and we'll have him. Or at least," she added, "a way of getting at him."

"What about Rodrigo?" Dallas asked abruptly.

"He phoned me late last night," Eb told him. "He's already in town, in place. Fast worker. It seems he has a relative, a 'mule' who works for Lopez in Houston, a distant relative who doesn't know what Rodrigo really does for a living. He got Rodrigo a job driving a truck for the new operation here." He let out a breath through his teeth. "Once we get Lopez's attention away from Jess," he added, "that operation is going to be our next priority."

"Can't you just send the sheriff over there to arrest them?" Sally asked.

"It's inside the city limits. Chief Chet Blake has jurisdiction there, and, of course, he'd help if he could," Eb told her. "But so far, all we have on Lopez's employees is a distant connection to a drug lord. Unless we can catch them in the act of receiving or shipping cocaine, what would we charge them with? Building a warehouse is legal, especially when you have all the easements and permission from the planning commission."

"That's why we're going to stake out the place, once this is over," Dallas added. He glanced from Jessica to Stevie with worried eyes. "But first we have to solve the more immediate problem."

Jess felt for his hand on the table beside her and tangled her fingers into it. "We'll get through this," she said in a soft tone. "I can't cold-bloodedly give a human being's life up to Lopez, no matter what the cost. The person involved risked everything to put him away. And even then, his attorneys found a loophole."

"Don't forget that it took them a couple of years to do that," Eb reminded her. "He won't be easy to catch a second time. He has enough pull with the Mexican government to keep them from extraditing him back here for trial."

"I hear DEA's going to put him on their top ten Most Wanted list," Dallas said. "That will turn up the heat a little, especially with a fifty-thousand dollar reward to sweeten the deal."

"Lopez would double their bounty out of his pocket change to get them off his tail, even if we could find someone crazy enough to go down to Cancún after him," Eb said.

"Micah Steele would, in a second," Dallas replied.

Eb chuckled. "I imagine he would. But he's been working on a case overseas with Cord Romero and Bojo Luciene."

"Bojo, the Moroccan," Dallas recalled. "Now there's a character."

Eb was immediately somber. "Okay, tomorrow morning I'll follow Sally and Stevie in to school. Dallas can tail them on the way home. We'll stay in constant contact and hope for the best."

"The best," Dallas replied, "would be that Lopez would give up."

"It won't happen," Eb assured him.

"Have you considered contacting your informant?" Dallas asked Jessica. "If we could get him back to the States, we could arrange around-the-clock protection and get him into the witness protection program, where even Lopez couldn't find him."

She grimaced. "I thought of that, but I honestly don't know how to locate my informant," she said sadly. "The people who could have helped me do it are dead."

Eb scowled. "All of them?"

Jessica nodded with a sigh. "All of them. About six months ago. Just before my accident."

"Rodrigo might be able to dig something up," Dallas said.

"That's very possible," Eb agreed. "Jessica, you could trust him with the name. I know, you don't want to put your informant in danger. But if we can't find him, how can we protect him?"

She hesitated. Then she shifted in her chair, clinging even more tightly to Dallas's big hand. "Okay," she said finally. "But he has to promise to keep the information to himself. Can I trust him to do that?"

"Yes," Eb said with certainty.

"All right, then. When can we do it?"

"Tomorrow after school," Eb said. "I'll get Cy Parks to run into him 'accidentally' and slip him a note, so that Lopez won't get suspicious."

Jessica's head moved to rest on Dallas's shoulder. "I wish I'd done things differently. So many people at risk, all because I didn't do my job properly."

"But you did," Dallas said at once, sliding a protective arm around her. "You did what any one of us would do. And you did put Lopez away. It's not your fault that he slipped out of the country."

Jessica smiled. "Thanks."

"You going to marry my mama, Dallas?" Stevie piped up.

"Stevie!" Jessica exclaimed.

"Yes, I am," Dallas said, chuckling at Jessica's red face. "She just doesn't know it yet. How do you feel about that, Stevie?"

"That would be great!" he said enthusiastically. "You and me can watch wrestling together!"

"Yes, we can." Dallas kissed Jess's hair gently and looked at his son with proud, possessive eyes.

Sally, watching them, knew that everything was going to be all right for Jessica, once they were out of this mess. She'd be free to marry Eb and she'd never have to worry about her aunt or her cousin again. Even more important, Jessica would be loved. That meant everything to Sally.

EB FOLLOWED THEM TO school the next morning, keeping a safe distance. But there were no attempts on them along the way, and once they were inside the building, Sally felt safe. She and Stevie went right along to her class, smiling and greeting teachers and other children they knew.

"It's gonna be all right, isn't it, Aunt Sally?" Stevie asked at the door to her classroom.

"Yes, I think it is," she said with a warm smile.

She checked her lesson plan while the students filed into the classroom. A boy at the back of the room made a face and caught Sally's attention.

"Miss Johnson, there's a puddle of something that smells horrible back here!"

She got up from her desk and went to see. There was, indeed, a puddle. "I'll just go and get one of the janitors," she said with a smile.

But as she started out the door, a tall, quiet man appeared with a mop and pail.

"Hi, Harry," she said to him.

"Hard to be inside today when it's so nice outside," he said with a rueful smile. "I should be sitting on the river in my boat right now."

She smiled. "I'm sorry. But it's a good thing for us that you're here."

He started to wheel the bucket and mop away when one of the wheels came off the bucket. He muttered something and bent to look.

"I'll have to carry it. Can I get one of these youngsters to help me carry the mop?" he asked.

"I'll go!" Stevie volunteered at once.

"Yes, of course," Sally said. "Would you rather I went with you?"

He shook his head. "No need. This strong young man can manage a mop, can't you, son?" he asked with a big grin.

"Sure can!" Stevie said, hefting the mop over one shoulder.

"Let's away then, my lad," the man joked. "I'll send him right back, so he won't miss any class," he promised.

"Okay."

She watched Stevie go down the crowded hall behind Harry. It wasn't quite time for class to start, and she didn't think anything of the incident. Until five minutes later, when Stevie hadn't reappeared.

She left a monitor in charge of her class and went down the hall to the janitor's closet. There was the broken bucket, and the mop, but Stevie was nowhere in sight. But the janitor was. He'd been knocked out. She went straight to the office to phone Eb and call the paramedics. Fortunately Harry only had a slight concussion. To be safe, he was taken to the hospital for observation. Sally felt sick. She should have realized that Lopez might send someone to the school. Why had she been so gullible?

Eb arrived at the front office with the police chief, Chet Blake, and two of his officers. They went from door to door, combing the school. But Stevie was no longer there. One of the other janitors remembered seeing a stranger leave the building with the little boy and get into a brown pickup truck in the parking lot.

With that information, the police put out a bulletin. But it was too late. They found the pickup truck minutes later, abandoned in another parking lot, at a grocery store. Stevie was nowhere to be seen.

THEY WAITED BY THE telephone that afternoon for the call that was sure to come. When it did, Eb had to bite down hard on what he wanted to say. Jessica and Sally had been in tears ever since he brought Sally home to the ranch.

"Now," the voice came in a slow, accented drawl, "Stevie's mother will give me the name I want. Or her son will never come home."

"She had to be sedated," Eb said, thinking fast. "She's out cold."

"You have one hour. Not a second longer." The line went dead.

Eb cursed roundly.

"Now what do we do?" Sally asked.

He phoned Cy Parks. "Did you get that message sent for me?" he asked.

"Yes. Scramble the signal."

Eb touched a button on the phone. "Shoot."

Cy gave him a telephone number. "He should be there by now. What can I do to help?"

Eb didn't have to be told that the news about Stevie's abduction was all over town. "Nothing. Wish me luck."

"You know it."

He hung up. Eb dialed the other number and waited. It rang once. Twice. Three times. Four times.

"Come on!" Eb growled impatiently.

On the fifth ring, the receiver was lifted.

"Rodrigo?" Eb asked at once.

"Yes."

"I'm going to put Jessica on the line, and leave the room. She'll give you a name. You know what to do with it."

"Okay."

Eb gave the receiver to Jessica and motioned everybody out of the communications room. He closed the door.

Jessica felt the receiver in her hands and took a deep breath. "The name of my informant was Isabella Medina," she said quietly. "She worked as a housekeeper for…"

There was an intake of breath on the other end of the line. "But surely you knew?" he asked at once.

"Knew what?" Jessica stammered.

"Isabella was found washed up on the rocks in Cancún, just before Lopez's capture," Rodrigo said abruptly. "She is long dead."

"Oh, good Lord," Jessica gasped.

"How could you not know?" he demanded.

Jessica wiped her forehead with a shaking hand. "I lost touch with her just before the trial. I assumed that she'd gone undercover to escape vengeance from Lopez. She wasn't going to testify, after all. She only gave me sources of hard information that I could use to prosecute him. Afterward, there were only three people who knew about her involvement, and they died under rather…mysterious circumstances."

"This is the name Lopez wants?" he asked.

"Yes," she said miserably. "He's got my son!"

"Then you lose nothing by giving him the name," he said quietly. "Do you?"

"No. But he may not even remember her…"

"He was in love with her," Rodrigo said coldly. "His women have a habit of washing up on beaches. The last, a young singer in a Cancún nightclub, died only weeks ago at his hands. There is no proof, of course," he added coldly. "The official cause of death was suicide."

He sounded as though the matter was personal. She hesitated to ask. "You knew the singer?" she ventured.

There was a pause. "Yes. She was…my sister."

"I'm very sorry."

"So am I. Give Lopez the name. It will pacify him and spare your son any more adventures. He will not harm the boy," he added at once. "I think you must know this already."

"I do. At least he has one virtue among so many vices. But it doesn't ease the fear."

"Of course not. Tell Scott I'll be in touch, and not to contact me again. When I have something concrete, I'll call him."

"I'll tell him. Thank you."

"*De nada.*" He hung up.

She went into the other room, feeling her way along the wall.

"Well?" Sally asked.

"My informant is dead," Jessica said sadly. "Lopez killed her, and I never knew. I thought she'd escaped and maybe changed her name."

"What now?" Sally asked miserably.

"I give Lopez the name," Jessica replied. "It will harm no one now. She was so brave. She actually worked in his house and pretended to care about him, just so that she could find enough evidence to convict him. Her father and mother, and her sister, had been gunned down in their village by his men, because they spoke to a government unit about the drug smuggling. She was sick with fear and grief, but she was willing to do anything to stop him." She shook her head. "Poor woman."

"A brave soul," Eb said quietly. "I'm sorry."

"Me, too," Jessica said. She wrapped her arms around herself, feeling chilled. "What if Lopez won't believe me?"

"You know," Eb said quietly, "I think he will."

"Let's hope so," Dallas agreed, his eyes narrow and dark with worry.

Sally put a loving arm around her aunt. "We'll get Stevie back," she said gently. "Everything's going to be okay."

Jessica hugged her back tearfully. "What would I do without you?" she whispered huskily.

Sally exchanged a long look with Dallas. She smiled. "I think you're going to find out very soon," she teased. "And I'll be your bridesmaid."

"Matron of honor," Eb corrected with soft, tender eyes.

"What?" Jessica exclaimed.

"I'm going to marry your niece, Jess," Eb said gently. "I always meant to, you know. And," he added with mock solemnity, "it does seem the least I can do, considering that she's saved herself for me all these years, despite the blatant temptations of college life…"

"Temptations," Sally chuckled. "If you only knew!"

"Explain that," Eb challenged.

She let go of Jessica and went close to him, sliding her arms naturally around his hard waist. "As if there's a man on the planet who could compare with you," she murmured, and reached up to kiss his chin. Her eyes literally glowed with love. "There never was any competition. There never could be."

Eb lifted an eyebrow. "I could return the compliment," he said in a deep, quiet tone. "You're in a class all your own, Sally mine."

She laid her cheek against his hard chest. "They'll give Stevie back, won't they?" she asked after a minute.

"Yes," he said, utterly certain.

Sally glanced at Jessica, who was close beside Dallas now, leaning against him. They looked as if they'd always belonged together. Things had to turn out all right for them. They just had to. Lopez might have one virtue, but Sally wasn't at all sure that Eb was right. She only prayed that Stevie would be returned when Jess gave up the informant's name. If Lopez did keep his word, and that seemed certain, there was a chance. She had to hope it was a good one.

CHAPTER ELEVEN

IN EXACTLY AN HOUR FROM THE time Lopez hung up, the phone rang again. Eb let Jessica answer it.

"Hello," she said quietly.

"The name," Lopez replied tersely.

She took a slow breath. "I want you to understand that I would never have given up my informant under ordinary circumstances. But nothing I say can harm her now. I only found out today that she's beyond your vengeance. So it doesn't matter anymore if you know who she was."

"Who...she was?" Lopez asked, his voice hesitant.

"Yes. Was. Her name was Isabella..."

His indrawn breath was so harsh that Jessica almost felt it. "Isabella," he bit off. There was a tense pause. "Isabella."

"I lost touch with her before your trial," Jessica said curtly. "I assumed that she'd gone away and taken on another identity to escape being found out. I didn't know that she was dead already."

Still, Lopez said nothing. The silence went on for so long that Jessica thought the connection was cut.

"Hello?" she asked.

There was another intake of breath. "I loved her," he spat. "In my life, there was no other woman I trusted so much. But she wanted nothing to do with me. I should have known. I should have realized!"

"You killed her, didn't you?" Jessica said coldly.

"Yes," he said, and he didn't sound violent. He sounded oddly subdued. "I never meant to. But I lashed out in a moment's rage, and then it was too late, and all my regrets would not bring her back to life." He drew another breath. "She was close enough to me that she knew things no one else was permitted to know. It occurred to me that she was asking far too many questions, but I was conceited enough to believe she cared for me." There was another brief pause. "The boy will be returned at once. You will find him at the strip mall in the toy store in five minutes. He will not be harmed. You have my word. Nor will you ever be threatened by me again. I…regret…many things," he added in an odd tone, and the line went dead abruptly.

Jessica caught her breath, still holding the receiver in her hand, as if it had life.

"Well?" Dallas asked impatiently.

She felt for the instrument and replaced the receiver with slow deliberation. "He said that Stevie would be in the toy store in the strip mall, in five minutes, unharmed." Her eyes closed. "Unharmed."

Eb motioned Dallas toward Jessica.

"Let's go," he said tersely.

"What if he lied?" Jessica asked as Dallas escorted her out to the big sports utility vehicle Eb drove.

"We both know that Lopez is a man of his word, regardless of his bloody reputation," Dallas said tersely. "We have to hope that he told the truth."

Jessica nibbled on her fingernails all the way to the mall, which was only about six minutes away from Eb's ranch. She sat close beside Dallas in the back seat, holding his hand tightly. Sally glanced back at them, silently praying all the way, worried for all of them, but especially for little Stevie. Her hand felt for Eb's and he grasped it tightly, sparing her a reassuring smile.

The minutes seemed like hours as they sped into town. Eb had no sooner parked the vehicle in the parking lot than Jessica was out the door, hurrying with Dallas right beside her to guide her steps.

Eb and Sally followed the couple into the small toy store, and there was Stevie, sitting on the floor, playing with a mechanical elephant that walked and lifted its trunk and trumpeted.

"It's Stevie," Dallas said huskily. "He's...fine!"

"Where? Stevie!" Jessica called brokenly, holding out her arms.

"Hi, Mom!" Stevie exclaimed, leaving the toy to run into her arms. "Gosh, I was scared, but the man taught me how to play poker and gave me a soda! He said I was brave and he admired my courage! Were you scared, Mom?"

Jessica was crying so hard that she could barely speak at all. She hugged her child close and couldn't seem to let him go, even when he wiggled.

"Let his dad have a little of this joyful reunion," Dallas murmured dryly, holding out his arms.

Stevie went right into them and hugged him hard. "I don't have a real dad now," he said, "but you're going to be a great dad, Dallas! You and me will go to all the wrestling matches and take Mom and describe everything to her, won't we?"

"Yes," Dallas said, his voice husky, his eyes bright as he rocked his child in his arms with mingled relief and affection. "We'll do that."

Jessica felt her way into Dallas's arms with Stevie and pressed there for a long moment. Beside them, Sally held tight to Eb's hand and smiled with pure relief.

"I had an adventure," Stevie said when his parents let go of him. "But it's nice to be home again. Can I have that elephant? He sure is neat!"

"You can have a whole circus if I can find one for sale," Dallas laughed huskily. "But for now, I think we'll go back to the ranch."

They paid for the elephant and got into the truck with Eb and Sally.

"Can you drop us off at our house?" Jessica asked Eb.

There was a hesitation. She heard it and smiled.

"Lopez said that he had no more business with me," Jessica told him. "He didn't even question what I told him," she added. "He said that Isabella was always asking him questions and pretending to care about him. He knew she didn't. He did sound very sorry that he killed her. Perhaps the small part of him that's still human can feel remorse. Who knows?"

"One day," Dallas said curtly, "we'll catch up with him. This isn't over, you know, even if he is through making threats toward you and Stevie. He's going to pay for this. And, somehow, we're going to stop him from setting up business in Jacobsville."

"We have Rodrigo in place," Eb agreed, "and Cy watching the progress of the warehouse. It won't be easy, but if we're careful, we may cut his source of supply and his distribution network right in half. Cut off the head and the snake dies."

"Amen," Dallas replied.

DALLAS GOT OUT OF THE sports utility vehicle with Jessica and Stevie, waving the other couple off with a big smile.

"You really believe Lopez meant it when he said he was quits with Jessica?" Sally asked, still not quite convinced of the outlaw's sincerity.

"Yes, I do," Eb replied, glancing at her with a smile. "He's a snake, but his word is worth something."

Sally turned her head toward Eb and studied his profile warmly, with soft, covetous eyes.

He glanced over and met that look. His own eyes narrowed. "A lot has happened since last night," he said quietly. "Do you still mean what you told me at dawn?"

"That I'd marry you?" she asked.

He nodded.

"Oh, yes," she said, "I meant every word. I want to live with you all my life."

"It won't bother you to have professional mercenaries running around the place at all hours for a while?" he teased.

She grinned. "Why should it? I am, after all, a mercenary's woman."

"Not quite yet," he murmured with a wry glance. "And very soon, a mercenary's wife."

"That sounds very respectable," she commented.

"I'm glad you waited for me, Sally," he said seriously.

"So am I." She slid her hand into his big one and held on tight. It tingled all the way up her arm.

"We've had enough excitement for today," he said. "But tomorrow we'll see about getting the license. Do you want a justice of the peace or a minister to marry us?"

"A minister," she said at once. "I want a permanent marriage."

He nodded. "So do I. And you have to have a white gown with a veil."

Her eyebrows arched.

"You're not just a mercenary's woman, you're a virtuous mercenary's woman. I want to watch you float down the aisle to me covered in silk and satin and lace, and with a veil for me to lift after we've said our vows."

She smiled with her whole heart. "That would be nice. There's a little boutique…"

"We'll fly up to Dallas and get one at Neiman-Marcus."

She gasped.

"You're marrying a rich man," he pointed out. "Humor me. It's going to be a social event. Let me deck you out like a comet."

She laughed. "All right. I'd really love a white wedding, if you don't mind."

"And we'll both wear rings," he added. "We'll get those in Dallas, too."

Her eyes were full of dreams as she looked at her future husband hungrily. There was only one small worry. "Eb, about Maggie…"

"Maggie is a closed chapter," he told her. "I adored her, in my way, but she was never in love with me. I stood in Cord's shadow even then, and she never realized it. She still hasn't." He glanced at her and smiled. "I love you, you know," he murmured, watching her eyes light up. "I'd never have proposed if I hadn't."

"I love you, too, Eb," she said solemnly. "I always will."

His fingers curled tighter into hers. "Dreams really do come true."

She wouldn't have argued with that statement to save her life, and she said so.

IT WAS THE SOCIETY EVENT of the year in Jacobsville, eclipsed only by Simon Hart's wedding with the governor giving Tira away. There were no major celebrities at Eb and Sally's wedding, but Eb did have a conglomeration of mercenaries and government agents the like of which Jacobsville had never seen. Cord Romero was sitting with Maggie on the groom's side of the church, along with a tall, striking dark-haired man with a small mustache and neat brief beard. Beside him was a big blond man who made even Dallas look shorter. On the pew across from him, on Sally's side of the church, was a blue-eyed brunette who avoided looking at the big blond man. Sally recognized her as Callie, the stepsister of the big blond man, who was Eb's friend Micah Steele.

A number of men in suits filled the rest of the groom's pews. Some were wearing sunglasses inside. Others were watching the people on the bride's side of the church, which wasn't packed, since Sally hadn't been back in Jacobsville long enough to make close friends in the community. Jessica was there with Stevie and Dallas, of course.

Sally walked down the aisle all by herself, since she hadn't contacted either of her parents about her wedding. They had their own lives now, and neither of them had written to Sally since the breakup of their family when she moved in with Jessica. She didn't really mind going it alone. Somehow, under the circumstances, it even seemed appropriate. She wore a dream of a wedding gown, with yards and yards of delicate lace and a train, and a veil that accentuated her blond beauty.

Eb stood at the altar waiting for her, in a gray vested suit with a white rose in his lapel. He turned as she joined him, and looked down at her with eyes that made her knees weak.

The ceremony was brief, but poignant, and when Eb lifted the veil to kiss her for the first time as her husband, tears welled up in her eyes as his mouth tenderly claimed hers. They held hands going back down the aisle, wearing matching simple gold bands. Outside the church, they were pelted with rice and good wishes. Laughing, Sally tossed her bouquet and Dallas intercepted it to make sure it landed in Jessica's hands.

They climbed into the rented limousine and minutes later, they were at Eb's ranch, pausing just long enough to change into traveling clothes and rush to the private airstrip to board a loaned Learjet for the trip to Puerto Vallarta, Mexico, for their brief honeymoon.

The trip was tiring, and so was the aftermath of the day's excitement. Sally climbed into the huge whirlpool bath while Eb made dinner reservations for that evening.

She didn't realize that she wasn't alone until Eb climbed down into the water with her. He chuckled at her expression and then he kissed her. Very soon, she forgot all about her shock at the first sight of her un-clothed bridegroom in the joy of an embrace that knew no obstacles.

He kissed her until she was clinging, gasping for breath and shivering with pleasure.

"Where?" he whispered, stroking her tenderly, enjoy-ing her reactions to her first real intimacy. "Here, or in the bed?"

She could barely speak. "In bed," she said huskily.

"That suits me."

He got out and turned off the jets, lifting her clear of the water to towel them both dry. He picked her up and carried her quickly into the bedroom, barely taking time to strip down the covers before he fell with her onto crisp, clean sheets.

She knew that first times were notoriously painful, embarrassing, and uncomfortable, but hers was a nota-ble exception. Eb was skillful and slow, arousing her to a hot frenzy of response before he even began to touch her intimately. By the time his body slid down against hers in stark possession, she was lifting toward him and pleading for an end to the violent tension of pleasure he'd aroused in her.

Her breath jerked out at his ear at the slow, steady invasion of her most private place in a silence that magnified the least little sound. She heard his heartbeat, and her own, increase with every careful thrust of his hips. She heard his breathing, erratic, rough, mingling with her own excited little moans.

She felt one lean hand sliding up her bare leg as he turned and shifted his weight against her, and when he touched her high on her inner thigh in a rhythm like the descent of his body, she arched up toward him and groaned in anguish.

He laughed softly at her temple while he increased the rhythm and caressed her in the most outrageous ways, all the while whispering things so shocking that she gasped. Tossed between waves of pleasure that grew with each passing second, she found herself suddenly suspended somewhere high above reality as she went over some intangible cliff and fell shuddering with ecstasy into a white-hot oblivion.

She felt him there with her, felt his pleasure in her body, felt his own release even as hers threatened to last forever. She wondered dimly if she was going to survive the incredible delight of it. She shivered helplessly as pleasure washed over her and she clung harder to the source of it, pleading for him not to stop.

When she was finally exhausted and barely able to

catch her breath, he tucked her close in his arms and pulled the sheet over them.

"Sleep now," he whispered, kissing her forehead.

"Like this?" she asked unsteadily.

"Just like this." He wrapped her closer. "We'll sleep a little. And then…"

"And then."

The dinner reservations went unclaimed. Through the long night, she learned more than she'd ever dreamed about men and bodies and lovemaking. For a first time, she told her delighted husband, it was quite extraordinary.

They had breakfast in bed and then set out to explore the old city. But by evening, they were exploring each other again.

A WEEK LATER, THEY ARRIVED back home at Eb's ranch, to find a flurry of new activity. A local undercover DEA agent, whose wife Lisa Monroe lived on a ranch next door to Cy Parks, had been found murdered. Apparently he'd infiltrated Lopez's organization and been discovered. Rodrigo was still undercover, and Eb was concerned for him. The warehouse next door to Cy was in the final stages of construction. Things were heating up in Jacobsville.

"At least we had a honeymoon," Eb murmured dryly, hugging his new wife close.

"So we did," she agreed. She looked up at him lovingly. "And now you're back off adventuring."

"Well, so are you," he pointed out. "After all, isn't teaching second-graders a daily adventure as well?"

She hugged him close. "Being married to you is the biggest adventure, but you have to promise not to ever get shot at again."

"I give you my word as a Girl Scout," he murmured dryly.

She punched him in the stomach. "And if you wade into battle, I'll be right there beside you holding spare cartridges."

He searched her eyes. "You really are a hell of a woman," he murmured.

She grinned. "I'm glad you noticed."

"Lucky me," he said only half facetiously, and bent to kiss her with unbridled passion. "Lucky, lucky me!" he added while he could manage speech.

Sally wrapped her arms around him and held on tight, as intoxicated with pleasure as he was. There would always be the threat of danger, but nothing that the mercenary and his woman couldn't handle. But for the moment, she had her soldier of fortune right where she wanted him—in her gentle, loving arms.

THE WINTER SOLDIER

CHAPTER ONE

IT WAS MONDAY, the worst day in the world to try to get a prescription filled. Behind the counter, the poor harassed male druggist was trying to field the telephone calls, fill prescriptions, answer questions from patrons and delegate duties to two assistants. It was always like this after the weekend, Cy Parks thought with resignation. Nobody wanted to bother the doctor on his days off, so they all waited until Monday to present their various complaints. Hence the rush on the Jacobsville Pharmacy. Michael, the pharmacist on duty, was smiling pleasantly despite the crush of customers, accustomed to the Monday madness.

That group putting off a visit to the doctor until Monday included himself, Cy mused. His arm was throbbing from an encounter with one of his angry Santa Gertrudis bulls late on Friday afternoon. It was his left arm, too, the one that had been burned in the house fire back in Wyoming. The angry rip needed ten stitches, and Dr. "Copper" Coltrain had been irritated that Cy hadn't gone to the emergency room instead of letting it wait two days and risking gangrene. The sarcasm just washed right off; Coltrain could have saved his breath. Over the years, there had been so many wounds that Cy hardly felt pain anymore. With his shirt off, those wounds had been apparent to Coltrain, who wondered aloud where so many bullet wounds came from. Cy had simply looked at him, with those deep green eyes that could be as cold as Arctic air. Coltrain had given up.

Stitches in place, Coltrain had scribbled a prescription for a strong antibiotic and a painkiller and sent him on his way. Cy had given the prescription to the clerk ten minutes ago. He glanced around him at the prescription counter and thought he probably should have packed lunch and brought it with him.

He shifted from one booted foot to the other with noticeable impatience, his glittery green eyes sweeping the customers nearest the counter. They settled on a serene blond-haired woman studying him with evident amusement. He knew her. Most people in Jacobsville, Texas, did. She was Lisa Taylor Monroe. Her husband, Walt Monroe, an undercover narcotics officer with a federal agency, had recently been killed. He'd borrowed on his insurance policy, so there had been just enough money to bury him. At least Lisa had her small ranch, a legacy from her late father.

Cy's keen eyes studied her openly. She was sweet, but she'd never win any beauty contests. Her dark blond hair was always in a bun and she never put on makeup. She wore glasses over her brown eyes, plastic-framed ones, and her usual garb was jeans and a T-shirt when she was working around the ranch. Walt Monroe had loved the ranch, and during his infrequent visits home, he'd set out improving it. His ambitions had all but bankrupted it, so that Lisa was left after his death with a small savings account that probably wouldn't even pay the interest on the loans Walt had obtained.

Cy knew something about Lisa Monroe because she was his closest neighbor, along with Luke Craig, a rancher who was recently married to a public defender named Belinda Jessup. Mrs. Monroe there liked Charolais, he recalled. He wasn't any too fond of foreign cattle, having a purebred herd of Santa Gertrudis cattle, breeding bulls, which made him a profitable living. Almost as prosperous as his former sideline, he mused. A good champion bull could pull upward of a million dollars on the market.

Lisa had no such livestock. Her Charolais cattle were steers, beef stock. She sold off her steer crop every fall, but it wouldn't do her much good now. She was too deeply in debt. Like most other people, he felt sorry for her. It was common gossip that she was pregnant, because in a small town like Jacobsville, everybody knew everything. She didn't look pregnant, but he'd overheard someone say that they could tell in days now, rather than the weeks such tests had once required. She must be just barely pregnant, he mused, because those tight jeans outlined a flat stomach and a figure that most women would covet.

But her situation was precarious. Pregnant, widowed and deeply in debt, she was likely to find herself homeless before much longer, when the bank was forced to foreclose on the property. Damned shame, he thought, when it had such potential for development.

She was clutching a boxed heating pad to her chest, waiting her turn in line at the second cash register at the pharmacy counter.

When Lisa was finally at the head of the line, she put down her heating pad on the counter and opened her purse.

"Another one, Lisa?" the young female clerk asked her with an odd smile.

She gave the other woman an irritated glance as she dug in her purse for her checkbook. "Don't you start, Bonnie," she muttered.

"How can I help it?" the clerk chuckled. "That's the third one this month. In fact, that's the last one we have in stock."

"I know that. You'd better order some more."

"You really need to do something about that dog," Bonnie suggested firmly.

"Hear, hear!" the other clerk, Joanne, seconded, peering at Lisa over her glasses.

"The puppy takes after his father," Lisa said defensively. He did, she mused. His father belonged to Tom Walker, and the mostly German shepherd dog, Moose, was a local legend. This pup was from the first litter he'd sired—without Tom's knowledge or permission. "But he's going to be a lot of protection, so I guess it's a trade-off. How much is this?"

Bonnie told her, waited while she wrote the check, accepted it and processed it. "Here you go," she told the customer. She glanced down at the other woman's flat stomach. "When are you due?"

"Eight months and two weeks," Lisa said quietly, wincing as she recalled that her husband, away from home and working undercover, had been killed the very night after she'd conceived, if Dr. Lou Coltrain had his numbers right. And when had Lou ever missed a due date? He was uncanny at predicting births.

"You've got that Mason man helping you with the ranch." Bonnie interrupted her thoughts. "You shouldn't need a dog with him there. Can't he protect you?"

"He only comes on the weekends," Lisa replied.

Bonnie frowned. "Luke Craig sent him out there, didn't he? But he said the man was supposed to spend every night in the bunkhouse!"

"He visits his girlfriend most nights," Lisa said irritably. "And better her than me! He doesn't bathe!"

Bonnie burst out laughing. "Well, there's one bright side to it. If he isn't staying nights, you only have to pay him for the weekends...Lisa," she added when she saw the guilty expression on the other woman's face, "you aren't still paying him for the whole week?"

Lisa flushed. "Don't," she said huskily.

"Sorry." Bonnie handed her a receipt. "It's just I hate the way you let people take advantage of you, that's all. There are so many rotten people in the world, and you're a walking, talking benevolence society."

"Rotten people aren't born, they're made," Lisa told her. "He isn't a bad man, he just didn't have a proper upbringing."

"Oh, good God!" Cy said harshly, glaring at her, having kept his mouth shut as long as possible without imploding. The woman's compassion hit him on a raw spot and made him furious.

Lisa's eyes were brown, big and wide and soft through the plastic frames of her glasses. "Excuse me?"

"Are you for real?" he asked curtly. "Listen, people dig their own graves and they climb into them. Nothing excuses cruelty."

"You tell her!" Bonnie said, agreeing.

Lisa recognized her taciturn neighbor from a previous encounter, long ago. He'd come right up to her when she'd been pitching hay over the fence to her cattle one day and told her outright that she should leave heavy work to her husband. Walt hadn't liked that comment, not at all. It had only been a few days after he'd let her do the same thing while he flirted with a pretty blond parcel delivery employee. Worse, Walt thought that Lisa had encouraged Cy's interference somehow and they'd had a fight—not the first in their very brief marriage. She didn't like the tall man and her expression told him so. "I wasn't talking to you," she pointed out. "You don't know anything about my business."

His eyebrows rose half an inch. "I know that you overpay the hired help." He looked pointedly at her flat belly. "And that you're the last person who should be looked upon as a walking benevolence society."

"Hear, hear!" Joanne said again from behind Bonnie.

Lisa glared at her. "You can be quiet," she said.

"Let your erstwhile employee go," he told her. "I'll send one of my men over to spend nights in the bunkhouse. Bonnie's right about one thing, you don't need to be by yourself after dark in such a remote place."

"I don't need your help," she said, glowering at him.

"Yes, you do. Your husband wouldn't have liked having you try to run that ranch alone," he added quietly, even though he didn't mean it, and he hoped that his distaste for the late Walt Monroe didn't show. He still recalled watching Lisa heft a huge bale of hay while her husband stood not ten paces away flirting with a pretty blond woman. It was a miracle she hadn't miscarried, the way she hefted heavy things around. He wondered if she even knew the chance she was taking...

She was looking at him with different eyes now. The concern touched her despite her hostility. She sighed. "I guess you're right," she said softly. "He wouldn't have."

He hated the way that softness made him feel. He'd lost so much. Everything. He wouldn't admit, even to himself, how it felt to have those dark eyes look at him with tenderness. He swallowed down the ache in his throat.

She let her gaze fall to his arm, the one that had just been stitched, and her soft gasp was audible. "You've been hurt!"

"Two prescriptions, Mr. Parks," Bonnie said with a grin, holding up a prescription sack. She bent to pick up the package, a strand of her short blond hair falling around her pretty bespectacled face. "And Dr. Coltrain said that if you don't take this pain medication, he'll have me flogged," she added impishly.

"We can't have that, I guess," Cy murmured dryly.

"Glad you agree." She accepted his credit card as Lisa turned to go.

"You drive into town?" Cy asked the widow.

"Uh, well, no, the car's got a broken water pump," she confessed. "I rode in with old Mr. Murdock."

"He'll be at the lodge meeting until midnight," he pointed out.

"Just until nine. I thought I'd go to the library and wait."

"You need your rest," Cy said curtly. "No sense in waiting until bedtime for a ride. I'll drive you home. It's on my way."

"Go with him," Bonnie said firmly as she waited for

Cy to put his credit card back into his wallet and sign the ticket. "Don't argue," she added when Lisa opened her mouth. "I'll phone the lodge and tell Mr. Murdock you got a ride."

"Were you ever in the army?" Cy asked the young woman with a rare twinkle in his green eyes.

She grinned. "Nope. But it's their loss."

"Amen," he said.

"Mr. Parks…" Lisa began, trying to escape.

Cy took her arm, nodded to Bonnie and herded Lisa out of the pharmacy onto the street where his big red Ford Expedition was parked. On the way they ran into the second pharmacist, a dark-eyed woman with equally dark hair.

"Hi, Nancy!" Lisa said with a grin.

Nancy gave a gamine smile. "Don't tell me, the line's two miles long already."

"Three. Want to go home with me?" Lisa asked.

Nancy sighed. "Don't I wish. See you!"

Nancy went on toward the pharmacy and Lisa turned back to let Cy open the door of the Expedition for her. "Imagine you with a red vehicle," she said dryly. "I would have expected black."

"It was the only one they had in stock and I was in a hurry. Here." He helped her up into the huge vehicle.

"Gosh," she murmured as he got in beside her, "you could kill an elephant with this thing."

"It's out of season for elephants." He scowled as she fumbled with the seat belt. "That's hard to buckle on the passenger side. Here, like this…" He leaned close to her and fastened it with finesse despite his damaged left hand and arm. It required a closeness he hadn't had with a woman since his wife and son died in the fire. He noticed that Lisa's eyes were a very soft dark brown and that her complexion was delicious. She had a firm, rounded little chin and a pretty mouth. Her ears were tiny. He wondered what that mass of dark gold hair looked like at night when she took the hairpins out, and his own curiosity made him angry. With compressed lips, he fastened the seat belt and moved away to buckle his own in place.

Lisa was relieved when he leaned back. He made her nervous when he was that close. Odd, that reaction, she thought, when she'd been married for two months. She should be used to men. Of course, her late husband hadn't been that interested in her body. He didn't seem to enjoy sleeping with her, and he was always in such a rush that she really didn't feel any of the things women were supposed to feel. She recalled that he'd married her on the rebound from the woman he really wanted, and the only thing about Lisa that really appealed to him had been her father's ranch. He'd had great ideas about starting an empire, but it was only a pipe dream. A dead dream, now. She stared out at the small town as they drove through it on the way out to their respective ranches.

"Do you have anyone managing the ranch for you?" he asked when they were on the lonely highway heading out of town.

"Can't afford anyone," she said wistfully. "Walt had big plans for the place, but there was never enough money to fulfill them. He borrowed on his salary and his life insurance policy to buy the steers, but he didn't look far enough ahead to see the drought coming. I guess he didn't realize that buying winter feed for those steers would put us in the hole." She shook her head. "I did so want his plans to work out," she said wistfully. "If they had, he was going to give up undercover work and come home to be a rancher." Her eyes were sad. "He was only thirty years old."

"Manuel Lopez is a vindictive drug lord," he murmured. "He doesn't stop at his victims, either. He likes to target whole families. Well, except for small children. If he has a virtue, that's the only one." He glanced at her. "All the more reason for you to be looked after at night. The dog is a good idea. Even a puppy will bark when someone comes up to the door."

"How do you know about Lopez?" she asked.

He laughed. It was the coldest sound Lisa had ever heard. "How do I know? He had his thugs set fire to my house in Wyoming. My wife and my five-year-old son died because of him." His eyes stared straight ahead. "And if it's the last thing I ever do, I'll see him pay for it."

"I had...no idea," she faltered. She winced at the look on his face. "I'm very sorry, Mr. Parks. I knew about the fire, but..." She averted her eyes to the dark landscape outside. "They told me that Walt only said two words before he died. He said, 'Get Lopez.' They will, you know," she added harshly. "They'll get him, no matter what it takes."

He glanced at her and smiled in spite of himself. "You're not quite the retiring miss that you seem to be, are you, Mrs. Monroe?"

"I'm pregnant," she told him flatly. "It makes me ill-tempered."

He slowed to make a turn. "Did you want a child so soon after your marriage?" he asked, knowing as everyone locally did that she'd only married two months ago.

"I love children," she said, smiling self-consciously. "I guess it's not the 'in' thing right now, but I've never had dreams of corporate leadership. I like the pace of life here in Jacobsville. Everybody knows everybody. There's precious little crime usually. I can trace my family back three generations here. My parents and my grandparents are buried in the town cemetery. I loved being a housewife, taking care of Walt and cooking and all the domestic things women aren't supposed to enjoy anymore." She glanced at him with a wicked little smile. "I was even a virgin when I married. When I rebel, I go the whole way!"

He chuckled. It was the first time in years that he'd felt like laughing. "You renegade."

"It runs in my family," she laughed. "Where are you from?"

He shifted uncomfortably. "Texas."

"But you lived in Wyoming," she pointed out.

"Because I thought it was the one place Lopez wouldn't bother me. What a fool I was," he added quietly. "If I'd come here in the first place, it might never have happened."

"Our police are good, but…"

He glanced at her. "Don't you know what I am? What I was?" he amended. "Eb Scott's whole career was in the Houston papers just after he sent two of Lopez's best men to prison for attempted murder. They mentioned that several of his old comrades live in Jacobsville now."

"I read the papers," she confessed. "But they didn't mention names, you know."

"Didn't they?" He maneuvered a turn at a stop sign. "Eb must have called in a marker, then."

She turned slightly toward him. "What were you?"

He didn't even glance at her. "If the papers didn't mention it, I won't."

"Were you one of those old comrades?" she persisted.

He hesitated, but only for a moment. She wasn't a gossip. There was no good reason for not telling her. "Yes," he said bluntly. "I was a mercenary. A professional soldier for hire to the highest bidder," he added bitterly.

"But with principles, right?" she persisted. "I mean, you didn't hire out to Lopez and help him run drugs."

"Certainly not!"

"I didn't think so." She leaned back against her seat, weary. "It must take a lot of courage to do that sort of work. I suppose it takes a certain kind of man, as well. But why did you do it when you had a wife and child?"

He hated that damned question. He hated the answer, too.

"Well?"

She wasn't going to quit until he told her. His hands tightened on the steering wheel. "Because I refused to give it up, and she got pregnant deliberately to get even with me." He didn't stop to think about the odd way he'd worded that, but Lisa noticed and wondered at it. "I curtailed my work, but I helped get the goods on Lopez before I hung it up entirely and started ranching full-time. I'd just come back from overseas when the fire was set. It was obvious afterward that I'd been careless and let one of Lopez's men track me back to Wyoming. I've had to live with it ever since."

She studied his lean, stark profile with quiet, curious eyes. "Was it the adrenaline rush you couldn't live without, or was it the confinement of marriage that you couldn't live with?"

His green eyes glittered dangerously. "You ask too damned many questions!"

She shrugged. "You started it. I had no idea that you were anything more than a rancher. Your foreman, Harley Fowler, likes to tell people that he's one of those dashing professional soldiers, you know. But he isn't."

The statement surprised him. "How do you know he isn't?" he asked.

"Because I asked him if he'd ever done the Fan Dance and he didn't know what I was talking about."

He stopped the truck in the middle of the road and just stared at her. "Who told you about that? Your husband?"

"He knew about the British Special Air Services, but mostly just what I told him—including that bit about the Fan Dance, one of their rigorous training tests." She smiled self-consciously. "I guess it sounds strange, but I love reading books about them. They're really something, like the French Foreign Legion, you know. A group of men so highly trained, so specialized, that they're the scourge of terrorists the world over. They go everywhere, covertly, to rescue hostages and gather intelligence about terrorist groups." She sighed and closed her eyes, oblivious to the expression of the man watching her. "I'd be scared to death to do anything like that, but I admire people who can. It's a way of testing yourself, isn't it, so that you know how you react under the most deadly pressure. Most of us never face physical violence. Those men have." Her eyes opened. "Men like you."

He felt his cheeks go hot. She was intriguing. He

began to understand why Walt had married her. "How old are you?" he asked bluntly.

"Old enough to get pregnant," she told him pertly. "And that's all you're getting out of me."

His green eyes narrowed. She was very young, there was no doubt about that. He didn't like the idea of her being in danger. He didn't like the idea of the man Luke Craig had sent over to look out for her, either. He was going to see about that.

"How old are you, if we're getting personal?" she asked.

"Older than you are," he returned mockingly.

She grimaced. "Well, you've got scars and lines in your face, and a little gray at your temples, but I doubt you're over thirty-five."

His eyebrows arched almost to his hairline.

"I'd like you to be my baby's godfather when he's born," she continued bluntly. "I think Walt would have liked that, too. He spoke very highly of you, although he didn't say much about your background. I was curious about that. Now I understand why he was so secretive."

"I've never been a godfather," he said curtly.

"That's okay. I've never been a mother." She frowned. "Come to think of it, the baby hasn't been a baby before, either." She looked down at her flat belly and smiled tenderly, tracing it. "We can all start even."

"Did you love your husband?"

She looked up at him. "Did you love your wife?" she countered instantly.

He didn't like looking at her belly, remembering. He started down the road again, at a greater speed. "She said she loved me, when we married," he said evasively.

Poor woman, Lisa thought. And poor little boy, to die so young, and in such a horrible way. She wondered if the taciturn Mr. Parks had nightmares, and guessed that he did. His poor arm was proof that he'd tried to save his family. It must be terrible, to go on living, to be the only survivor of such a tragedy.

They pulled up in front of her dilapidated ranch house. The steps were flimsy and one of the boards was rotten. The house needed painting. The screens on the windows were torn, and the one on the screen door was half torn away. In the corral, he could hear a horse whinny. He hoped her fences were in better shape than the house.

He helped her down out of the truck and set her gently on her feet. She was rail-thin.

"Are you eating properly?" he asked abruptly as he studied her in the faint light from the porch, scowling.

"I said you could be the baby's godfather, not mine," she pointed out with an impish smile. "Thank you very much for the ride. Now go home, Mr. Parks."

"Don't I get to see this famous puppy?"

She grimaced as she walked gingerly up the steps, past the rotten one, and put her key in the lock. "He stays on the screen porch out back, and even with papers down, I expect he's made a frightful mess... That's odd," she said when the door swung open without the key being turned in the lock. "I'm sure I locked this door before I... Where are you going?"

"Stay right there," he said shortly. He opened the truck, took out the .45 automatic he always carried and cocked it on his way back onto the porch.

Her face went pale. Reading about commandos was

very different from the real thing when she saw the cold metal of the pistol in his hands and realized that he was probably quite proficient in its use. The thought chilled her. Like the sight of the gun.

He put her gently to one side. "I'm not going to shoot anybody unless I get shot at," he said reassuringly. "Stay there."

He left her on the porch and went carefully, quietly, through the house with the pistol raised at his ear, one finger on the trigger and his other hand, in spite of its injury, supporting the butt efficiently. He swept the house, room by room, closet by closet, until he got to the bedroom and heard a sound inside. It was only a sound, a faint whisper. There was a hint of light coming from under the door, which was just slightly ajar.

He kicked the door open, the pistol leveled the second he had a clear view of the bed.

The man's face was a study in shock when he saw the expression on Cy Parks's dark face and the glitter in his eyes. Bill Mason, Luke Craig's erstwhile cowboy-on-loan, was lying on the bed in his shorts with a beer bottle in one hand. When Cy burst in the door, he sat up starkly, his bloodshot eyes blinking as he swayed. He was just drunk enough not to realize how much trouble he was in.

"You're not Mrs. Monroe," he drawled loudly.

"And you're not Mr. Monroe. If you want to see daylight again, get the hell out of that bed and put your clothes on!"

"Okay. I mean yes, sir, Mr. Parks!"

The man tripped and fell, the beer bottle shattering on the floor as he sprawled nearby. "I broked it," he moaned as he dragged himself up holding onto the bed-post, "and it was my...my last one!"

"God help us! Hurry up!"

"Okay. Just let me find...my pants..." He hiccuped, tripped again and fell, moaning. "They must be here somewhere!"

Muttering darkly, Cy uncocked the pistol, put the safety on, and stuck it into the belt at his back. He went to find Lisa, who was standing impatiently on the porch.

"I saved you a shock," he told her.

"How big a shock?"

"The great unwashed would-be lover who was waiting for you, in your bed," he said, trying not to grin. It wasn't really funny.

"Oh, for heaven's sake, not again," she groaned.

"Again?"

She was made very uncomfortable by the look on his face. "Don't even think it!" she threatened angrily. "I'm not that desperate for a man, thank you very much. He gets drunk one night a week and sleeps it off in Walt's bed," she muttered, oblivious to both her phrasing and his surprised look. "I lock him in, so he can't cause me any trouble, and I let him out the next morning. He's got a drinking problem, but he won't get help."

"Does Luke Craig know that?"

"If he did, he'd fire him, and the poor man has no place to go," she began.

"He'll have a place to go tomorrow," he promised her with barely contained fury. "Why didn't you say something?"

"I didn't know you," she pointed out. "And Luke meant it as a kind gesture."

"Luke would eat him with barbecue sauce if he knew what he was doing over here!"

There was a muffled thud and then the tipsy man weaved toward the front door. "So sorry, Mrs. Monroe," Mason drawled, sweeping off his hat and almost going down with it as he bowed. "Very sorry. I'll be off, now." He hesitated at the top step with one foot in the air. "Where's my horse?" he asked blankly. "I left him out here somewhere."

"I'll send him to you. Go back to Craig's ranch."

"It's two miles!" the cowboy wailed. "I'll never make it!"

"Yes, you will. Get in the truck. And if you throw up in it, I'll shoot you!" Cy promised.

The cowboy didn't even question the threat. He tried to salute and almost fell down again. "Yes, sir, I'll get...get right in the truck, yes, sir, right now!"

He weaved to the passenger side, opened the door and pulled himself in, slamming the door behind him.

"I'd sleep on the sofa," Cy advised Lisa. "Until you can wash the sheets, at least."

"His girlfriend must be nuts. No woman in her right mind would sleep with him," she murmured darkly.

"I can see why. I'll send a man over to the bunkhouse. And he won't get drunk and wait for you in bed," he added.

She chuckled. "That would be appreciated." She hesitated. "Thanks for the ride home, Mr. Parks."

He hesitated, his narrow green eyes appraising her. She'd taken her husband's death pretty hard, and she had dark circles under those eyes. He hated leaving her alone. He had protective feelings for her that really disturbed him.

"I'll want to meet that pup when I come back again."

She managed a smile. "Okay."

"Go in and lock the door," he instructed.

She clutched her heating pad and her purse to her chest and glared at him, but he stared her down. *Oh, well,* she thought as she went inside, *some men just didn't know the meaning of diplomacy.* She'd have to make allowances for that little character flaw.

He waited until she got inside and locked the door before he climbed into his truck. He wondered why she'd said Walt's bed and not *their* bed. The question diverted him as he drove the intoxicated but quiet cowboy over to Luke Craig's house and showed him to Luke. The blond rancher cursed roundly, having closed the door so that his new wife, Belinda, wouldn't overhear.

"I'm very drunk," the cowboy said with a lopsided grin, swaying on the porch.

"He was stripped to his shorts, waiting for Lisa in her bed," Cy said, and he didn't grin. "I don't want this man sent over there again."

"He won't be. Good God, he's hidden it well, hasn't he?"

"I'm very drunk," the cowboy repeated, and the grin widened.

"Shut up," Cy told him. He turned back to Luke. "I'm sending one of my own men over to sleep in the bunkhouse. Can you handle him?"

"I'm *veerrryy* drunk," the cowboy interjected.

"Shut up!" chorused the two men.

Belinda Jessup Craig opened the front door and peered out at the tableau. "He's very drunk," she pointed out, and wondered why they looked so belligerent.

"You'd better bring him inside, Luke. We can sober him up in the kitchen. You can't leave him stumbling around like that. I'll phone the Master's Inn and see if they've got room for him." She glanced at Cy's puzzled expression. "It's a halfway house for alcoholics. They offer treatment and continued support."

"She wants to save the world," Luke muttered, but he grinned at her.

"And he wants to control it," she shot back with a wink. "Care to come in for coffee, Mr. Parks?"

"No, thanks," he replied. "I have to get home."

"I'm sorry about the trouble," Luke said.

"Your heart was in the right place. She's special," he added in spite of himself.

Luke smiled slowly. "Yes. She is."

Cy cleared his throat. "Good night."

"Good night," Luke answered.

"Good night!" the cowboy echoed before Luke propelled him firmly into the house.

CHAPTER TWO

CY TOOK HIS MEDICINE and had the first good night's sleep he'd enjoyed in days. He'd sent a capable, older cowboy over to Lisa's ranch the night before to sleep in the bunkhouse and keep an eye on things. He'd also arranged covertly for sensitive listening equipment to be placed around her house, and for a man to monitor it full-time. He might be overly cautious, but he wasn't taking chances with a pregnant woman. He knew Manuel Lopez's thirst for revenge far too well. The drug lord had a nasty habit of targeting the families of people who opposed him. And Lopez might not know Lisa was pregnant. Cy wasn't willing to risk leaving Lisa out there alone.

The next day he drove over to Lisa's house and found her struggling with a cow in the barn, trying to pull a calf by hand. He couldn't believe she was actually doing that!

He'd barely turned off the engine before he was out of the big sports utility vehicle and towering over her in the barn. She looked up with a grimace on her face when she realized what a temper he was in.

"Don't you say a word, Cy Parks," she told him at once, wiping the sweat from her forehead. "There's nobody but me to do this, and the cow can't wait until one of my part-timers comes in from the lower pasture. They're dipping cattle…"

"So you're trying to do a job that you aren't half big enough to manage. Are you out of your mind?" he burst out. "You're pregnant, for God's sake!"

She was panting, sprawled between the cow's legs. She glared up at him and blew a stray strand of hair out of her eyes. "Listen, I can't afford to lose the cow or the calf…"

"Get up!" he said harshly.

She glared at him.

For all his raging temper, he reached down and lifted her tenderly to her feet, putting her firmly to one side. He got down on one knee beside the cow and looked at the situation grimly. "Have you got a calf-pull?"

She ground her teeth together. "No. It broke and I didn't know how to fix it."

He said a few words under his breath and went out to his truck, using the radio to call for help. Fortunately one of his men was barely two minutes away. Harley, his foreman, came roaring up beside Cy's truck, braked and jumped out with a length of rope.

"Good man, Harley," Cy said as he looped the rope around the calf's feet. "If we can't get him out ourselves, we can use the winch on my truck. Ready? Pull!"

They were bathed in sweat and cursing when they managed to get the calf halfway out.

"He's still alive," Cy said, grinning. "Okay, let's go again. Pull!"

Three more firm tugs and the calf slipped out. Cy cleared his nose and mouth and the little black-baldy bawled. The cow turned, gently licking away the slick birth membranes covering her calf.

"That was a near miss," Harley observed, grinning.

"Very near." Cy glowered at Lisa. "In more ways than one."

"Excuse me?" Harley asked.

"It was my cow," Lisa pointed out. "I thought I could do it by myself."

"Pregnant, and you think you're Samson," he said with biting sarcasm.

She put her hands on her hips and glared up at him. "Go away!"

"Gladly. When I've washed my hands."

"There's a pump over here," Harley reminded him, indicating it.

"You go ahead, son," Cy muttered, glancing at his stitched arm. "I've got a raw wound. I'll have to have antibacterial soap."

Harley didn't say anything, but his face was expressive. He thought his poor old crippled boss was a real basket case, barely fit to do most ranch work.

"Antibacterial soap, indeed. The germs would probably die of natural causes if they got in you!" Lisa muttered.

"At least my germs are intelligent! I wouldn't try pulling calves if I was pregnant!"

Lisa almost doubled over at the thought of a pregnant Cy Parks, which only served to make him angrier.

"I'll get back to your place and start the men culling cattle for the next sale, boss man. I can wash up there!" Harley called, and didn't wait for an answer. The amused expression on his face was eloquent—he wanted to get out of the line of fire!

"Craven coward," she muttered, staring after the

cloud of dust he and the truck vanished in. "Are all your men like that?"

He followed her into the kitchen. "He's not afraid of me," he said irritably. "He thinks I'm pitiable. In fact, he has delusions that he's soldier of fortune material since he spent two weeks having intense combat training with a weekend merk training school," he added with pure sarcasm. "Have you got a hand towel?"

She pulled one from a drawer while he lathered his arms, wincing a little as the water and soap stung the stitches.

"You don't want to get that infected," she said, studying the wound as she stood beside him with the towel.

"Thanks for the first-aid tip," he said with failing patience. "That's why I asked for antibacterial soap!" He took the towel she offered, but his eyes were on her flat belly even as he dried away the wetness. "You take chances," he said shortly. "Dangerous chances. A lot of women miscarry in the first trimester, even without doing stupid things like heavy lifting and trying to pull calves. You need to think before you act."

She studied his quiet, haunted face. Discussing pregnancy didn't seem to make him feel inhibited at all. "You must have been good to your wife while she was pregnant," she said gently.

"I wanted the baby," he replied. His face hardened. "She didn't. She didn't want a child until she was in her thirties, if then. But I wouldn't hear of her terminating the pregnancy," he added, and there was an odd, pained look in his eyes for an instant. "So she had the child, only to lose him in a much more horrible way. But despite everything, I wanted him from the time I knew he was on the way."

She felt his pain as if it were tangible. "I won't have anyone to share this with," she said, her voice husky with remembered loss and pain. "I was over the moon when they did the blood test and said I was pregnant. Walt wouldn't even talk about having children. He died the night after I conceived, but even if he'd lived long enough to know about the baby, he would have said it was too soon." She shrugged. "I guess it was."

She'd never told that to another soul. It embarrassed her that it had slipped out, but Cy seemed unshockable.

"Some men don't adjust well to children," he said simply. It went without saying that he wasn't one of them. He didn't know what else to say. He felt sorry for her. She obviously took pleasure in her pregnancy, and it was equally obvious that she loved children. He sat down at the table with her. Maybe she needed to get it out of her system. Evidently she could tell him things that she couldn't tell anyone else.

"Go on," he coaxed. "Get everything off your chest. I'm a clam. I don't tell anything I know, and I'm not judgmental."

"I think I sensed that." She sighed. "Want some coffee? I have to drink decaf, but I could make some."

"I hate decaf, but I'll drink it."

She smiled. She got up and filled the pot and the filter and started the coffeemaker while she got down white mugs. She glanced at him with pursed lips. "Black," she guessed.

He gave her an annoyed look. "Don't get conceited because you know how I take my coffee."

"I won't."

She poured the coffee into the cups and sat back down, watching as he cupped his left hand around it. "Does it still hurt?" she asked, referring to the burns on his hand.

"Not as much as it used to," he said flatly.

"You don't have anyone to talk to, either, do you?"

He shook his head. "I'm not much for bars, and the only friend I have is Eb. Now that he's married, we don't spend a lot of time together."

"It's worse when you hold things inside," she murmured absently, staring into her coffee. "Everybody thinks I had a fairy-tale marriage with a sexy man who loved danger and could have had any woman he wanted." She smiled wryly. "At first I thought so, too. He seemed like a dream come true. Boy, did my illusions leave skid marks taking off!"

"So did mine," he said flatly.

She leaned forward, feeling daring. "Yes, but I'll bet *you* weren't a virgin who thought people did it in the dark fully clothed!"

He burst out laughing. He hadn't felt like laughing since…he couldn't remember. Her eyes bubbled with joy; her laugh was infectious. She made him hungry, thirsty, desperate for the delight she engendered.

She grinned. "There. You look much less intimidating when you smile. And before you regret telling me secrets, I'd better mention that I've never told anybody what my best friend did on our senior trip to Florida. And I won't tell you now."

"Was it scandalous?"

"It was for Jacobsville." She chuckled.

"Didn't you do anything scandalous?"

"Not me," she popped back. "I'm the soul of propriety. My dad used to say that I was the suffering conscience of the world." Her eyes darkened. "He died of a stroke while he was using the tiller out in the garden. When he didn't come in for lunch, I knew something was wrong. I went out to find him." She moved her coffee cup on the table. "He was sitting against a tree with his thermos jug of coffee still in his hands, his eyes wide-open, stone dead." She shivered. "Mom had died when I was in sixth grade, of cancer. Dad loved her so much. He loved me, too." She lifted her sad eyes. "I suppose I'd rather have had him for a short time than not to have had him at all. Walter felt sorry for me and asked me to marry him, because I was so alone. He'd just lost the woman he loved and I think he wanted to marry me just to spite her. The ranch was a bonus. I was really infatuated with him at first, and he liked me and loved this ranch. I figured we had as good a chance of making a marriage work as people who were passionately in love." She sighed again. "Isn't hindsight wonderful?"

He leaned back in his chair and looked at her for a long time. "You're a tonic," he said abruptly. "You're astringent and sometimes you sting, but I like being around you."

"Thanks. I think," she added.

"Oh, it's a compliment," he murmured. "I wouldn't offer you anything except the truth."

"That really is a compliment."

"Glad you noticed."

"What happened to the drunk cowboy?" she asked.

"Luke's wife is getting him into a halfway house,"

he mused. "A real crusader, that lady. She is a bleeding heart."

"She likes lost causes," she countered. "I've heard a lot about her, and I like what I've heard. If I can get this ranch back on its feet, I'd like to help her."

"Another latent crusader," he teased.

"A lot of people need saving, and there aren't a lot of reformers around," she pointed out.

"True enough."

"Thanks for sending that other man over to keep a lookout. He's very nice. Did you know that he likes to do needlepoint?" she asked matter-of-factly.

He nodded. "Nels does some exhibition-quality handwork. Nobody teases him about it, either. At least, not since he knocked Sid Turpen into the water trough."

She chuckled. "He looked like that sort of man. I knit," she said. "Not very well, but it gives me something to do when I'm by myself."

"You're always by yourself," he said quietly. "Why don't you come home with me one or two evenings a week and we can watch television after I've finished with the books. I could come and fetch you."

Her heart jumped. She didn't need telling that he'd never made that invitation to anyone else. He was like a wounded wolf in his lair most of the time. "Wouldn't I be in the way?" she asked.

He shook his head. "I'm alone, too. You and the baby would be good company; before and after he's born. You don't have a husband anymore. I don't have a family," he said bluntly. "I'd like to help you through the next few months. No strings," he added firmly. "And absolutely no ulterior motives. Just friendship."

She was touched. He made her feel welcome, warm and safe. She knew that a lot of people were intimidated by him, and that he was very standoffish. It was a huge compliment he was paying her. "Thanks," she said genuinely. "I'll take you up on that."

He sipped his coffee and put the cup down. "It might be good for both of us to spend less time alone with the past."

"Is that what you do, too, thinking about how it might have been, if…" She let the word trail away.

"If," he agreed, nodding. "If I'd smelled the smoke sooner, if I'd gone to bed earlier, if I'd realized that Lopez might send someone after me even from prison…and so forth."

"I kept thinking, what if I hadn't got pregnant so soon after I married," she confessed. "But I'm not sorry I did, really," she added with a tiny smile. "I like it."

He searched her dark eyes for longer than he wanted to and dragged his attention away. All at once, he glanced at his watch and grimaced. "Good Lord, I almost forgot! I've got a meeting at the bank this morning that I can't miss—refinancing a loan so that I can replace my combine." He got to his feet. "No other problems except for drunk cowboys in your bed?" he asked whimsically.

She glared at him. "Don't look at me, I didn't put him there!"

His eyes roamed over her and he smiled slowly. "His loss."

"You get out of here, you fresh varmint," she said, rising. "And there's no use trying to seduce me, either. I'm immune."

"Really?" he asked with raised eyebrows and a twinkle in his green eyes. "Shall we test that theory?" He took a step in her direction.

She flushed and backed up a step. "You stop that," she muttered.

He chuckled as he reached for his hat. "Don't retreat. I'll keep to my side of the line in the sand. Keep that door locked," he added then, and not with a smile. "I'm having you watched, just in case Lopez does try something. But if you need me, I'll be as close as the telephone."

"I know that. Thank you."

"Your car has a busted water pump," he added, surprising her that he remembered. "I'll have one of my men come get it and overhaul it for you."

She was all but gasping. "But, you don't have to…!"

"I know I don't have to," he said, eyes flashing. "You can't be stuck out here without transportation, especially now."

She didn't want to accept what she knew was charity, but the temptation to have her little red car fixed and running again was too much. She couldn't afford an extra spark plug. "Thank you," she said a little stiffly. It hurt her pride to know that he was aware of her financial situation.

He searched her face quietly. "No need for thanks. I'll take care of you. And the baby."

She stared at him while confusing sensations washed over her like a gentle electric current. She'd never felt such a surge of emotion, with anyone.

"I don't have any ulterior motives, Lisa," he said, speaking her name for the first time. It sounded soft, mysterious, even beautiful in his deep, measured tones.

"Then thanks, for seeing about my car," she said gently. "And if you get sick, I'll take care of you. All right?"

His heart ran wild. He'd never had anybody offer to look after him. His wife hadn't been compassionate. It hit him right in the gut that Lisa thought of him with such kindness. He searched for an answer and couldn't find one.

"I'm sure you never get sick," she said quickly, a little intimidated by his scowl. "But just in case."

He nodded slowly.

She smiled, reassured.

He turned and went out the door, speechless for the first time in recent memory. He couldn't have managed a single word to save his life.

Lisa went onto the porch and watched him drive away with confused emotions. She shouldn't let things intensify. She was a recent widow and he hadn't been widowed all that long ago. People would gossip, if for no other reason than that Cy Parks was the town's hermit. On the other hand, she was lonely and a little afraid. She remembered what Walt had told her about Manuel Lopez and the men who worked for him in the narcotics underworld. She knew what they did to people who sold them out. A shiver ran down her spine. They'd killed Walt and they might not stop until they wiped out his whole family—that was the reputation that Lopez had. She wasn't going to put her baby at risk, regardless of what people thought. She touched her flat belly protectively.

She smiled. "I'm going to take such wonderful care of you."

The smile remained when she thought how Cy would

care about the baby, too. He wasn't at all the sort of man he seemed on first acquaintance. But, then, who was? She went back inside to work in the kitchen, careful to make sure the doors were locked.

CY USED HIS CELL PHONE to have a local wrecker service take Lisa's small car over to his ranch, where he had one of his two mechanics waiting to fix it. Harley was good with machinery, but he had the mechanic do the work instead. For reasons he didn't understand, he didn't like having his good-looking foreman Harley around Lisa.

He went to the meeting with his banker and then on to Ebenezer Scott's place, careful to phone ahead. There were men on the gate who didn't like unexpected company and might react instinctively.

Eb met him at the front door, more relaxed than Cy had seen him in years.

"How's it going?" he asked the newly married man.

Eb grinned. "Funny how nice a ball and chain can feel," was all he said, but his eyes were twinkling with delight. "How's it going on your end?"

"Let's go inside," Cy said. "I've found out a few things."

Eb took him into the kitchen and poured coffee into mugs. "Sally's teaching. I don't usually do more than grab a sandwich for lunch…"

Cy held up a hand. "I haven't got time, thanks. Listen, they've got the beehives on site around that new warehouse on the land adjoining mine. There's a lot more activity there, panel trucks coming and going and deliveries after dark. I've spotted a number of unfamiliar faces. They don't look like beekeepers to me. Besides," he added curtly, "I saw a couple of Uzis."

"Automatic weapons at a honey plant," Eb murmured thoughtfully. "They must have armed, militant bees." He grinned at his own whimsy. "I'd hoped that Lopez might hesitate after his failed attempt on Sally's family." Sally, along with her aunt Jessica and Jessica's young son, Stevie, were targeted for vengeance by the drug lord. Luckily Lopez hadn't succeeded in his mission.

"We knew that Lopez had mentioned to one of his slimy followers that he needed a new distribution center. What better place than a little Texas town not far from the Gulf of Mexico, with no federal officers around?"

"He knows we're around," Cy pointed out.

"He only knows about me," came the reply. "Nobody locally knows about you. And he thinks I won't do anything because he's backed away from harming Sally's family. He figures the two guys who are taking the fall for him will keep the wolves from his door."

"I don't like it."

"Neither do I, but unless we can prove he's channeling drugs instead of honey through here, we can't do anything. Not anything legal," he added slowly.

"I'm not going up against Uncle Sam," Cy said firmly. "This isn't the old days. I don't fancy being an expatriated American."

Eb sighed. "We're older."

"Older and less reckless. Let Micah Steele go after him. He lives in Nassau and has connections everywhere. He wouldn't be afraid of getting kicked out of the States. He doesn't spend much time here anyway."

"His stepsister and his father live here," Eb pointed out. "He isn't going to want to put them in harm's way."

"From what I hear, his father hates him and his stepsister would walk blocks out of her way to avoid even passing him on the street," Cy said curtly. "Do you think he still cares about them?"

"Yes, I do. He came back with the express purpose of seeing his father and mending fences, but the old man refused to see him. It hurts him that his father won't even speak to him. And I've seen the way he looks at Callie, even if you haven't."

"Then why does he live in Nassau?"

Eb glanced around warily. "He's over here doing a job for me, so watch what you say," he cautioned. "I don't want him on the wrong side of me."

Cy leaned back in his chair and sipped coffee. "I suppose we all have our crosses to bear." He narrowed one eye at his oldest friend. "Do you think Lopez will make a try for Lisa?"

"It's possible," he said flatly. "Down in Mexico, a 'mule' crossed him. He killed the man's whole family except for one small child."

"That's what I thought. I sent Nels Coleman over to her ranch to stay nights in the bunkhouse. He used to work for the Treasury Department back in the late seventies."

"I know him. He's a good man."

"Yes, but not in Lopez's class. Your guys are."

Ebenezer nodded. "I have to have good people. The government and I are more than nodding acquaintances, and I run a high-tech operation here. I can't afford to let my guard down, especially now that I've got Sally to think of."

"It's been a long time since I've had to consider a woman," Cy replied, his green eyes quiet and thoughtful.

"Lisa Monroe is sweet," Ebenezer said. "She'll love that child to death."

"She's like that," Cy agreed, smiling. "I wish she wasn't so bullheaded. I went by to see her this morning and found her out in the barn, trying to pull a calf all by herself with her bare hands."

Ebenezer chuckled. "I won't turn your hair white by mentioning some of her other exploits, before she got pregnant."

"This isn't the first time she's done something outlandish?"

"Let's see." Ebenezer pursed his lips, recalling gossip. "There was the time she stood in the path of a bulldozer that was about to take down the huge live oak in the square that a peace treaty with the Comanche was signed under. Then she chained herself to a cage in the humane society when they were going to put down half a dozen dogs without licenses." He glanced at Cy. "The Tremayne brothers suddenly developed dog fever and between them, they adopted all six. Then there was the time she picketed the new chain restaurant because they refused to hire immigrants…"

"I get the idea," Cy murmured dryly.

"We were all surprised when she married Walt. He was a real man's man, but his job was like a religion to him. He didn't want anything to tie him down so that he couldn't advance in the agency. If he'd lived, that baby would have broken up the marriage for sure. Walt said often enough that he wasn't sure he ever wanted children." He shook his head. "He wasn't much of a husband to her, at that. Most of us felt that he married her on the rebound from that model who dropped him. He felt sorry for Lisa when her dad died and she was left all alone. Even after the wedding, he flirted with every pretty woman he saw. Lisa went all quiet and stopped staying home when he was around. He wasn't around much of that two months they were together, either. He volunteered for the undercover assignment the day they married. That shocked all of us, especially Lisa, and he got killed the same day he was introduced to Lopez."

"They knew who he was," Cy guessed.

"Exactly. And it was Walt's first undercover assignment, to boot. The only reason Rodrigo hasn't been discovered infiltrating Lopez's distribution network is that he's still a Mexican national and he has at least one cousin who's been with Lopez for years. The cousin would never sell him out."

"Lucky man," Cy remarked. "I hope we don't get him killed."

"So do I," Eb said with genuine concern. "Rodrigo's been in the business for a lot of years and he's the best undercover man I know. If anybody can help us put Lopez away for good, it's him. But meanwhile, we have to keep Lisa safe."

Cy went thoughtful. "She's a kind soul."

"Kind and naive," Eb replied. "People take advantage of her. That baby will wrap her right around its finger when it's born."

"I love kids," Cy said. "I miss mine."

"Lisa will love hers," came the quiet reply. "She'll need a friend, and not only because of Lopez. She can't run that ranch by herself. Walt was good with horses, and the men respected him. Lisa can't keep managing those two cowboys who work part-time for her, and she can't get a foreman because she hasn't enough capital to pay the going rate. Besides all that, she doesn't know beans about buying and selling cattle."

"Didn't her father teach her?"

"Not him," Ebenezer chuckled. "He didn't think women were smart enough to handle such things. He ran the ranch until the day he died. She was kept right out of it until then. Walt proposed to her at her father's funeral and married her shortly after."

"She loved her father, I gather."

"Of course she did, and he loved her. But he was a nineteenth-century man. He would have fit right in after the Civil War." He shook his head. "That ranch isn't solvent. Lisa's going to lose it eventually. She needs to go ahead and put it on the market and get the best price she can."

"I might see if she'll sell to me. I could rent her the house and have my own men work the ranch."

Ebenezer grinned. "Now, that's constructive thinking." He leaned forward, emptying his coffee cup. "As for those so-called beehives, I think we'd better send somebody over to have a quiet look after dark and see if there are really any bees in them."

"Good idea. Then we can start making plans if it looks like Lopez is sending drugs through here." Cy got to his feet. "Thanks for the coffee."

"Anytime. Watch your back."

Cy smiled. "I always do. See you."

WHEN CY GOT HOME, Harley was out in the front yard having an animated conversation with a foreigner in an expensive pickup truck. He turned as Cy drove up in front of the house. He cut off the engine and eyed the newcomer's vehicle with knowing eyes. Here was an opportunity not only to meet one of Lopez's executives, but to throw them off the track about him as well.

"Hey, boss, this is Rico Montoya," he said with a grin. "He's our new neighbor with the honey export business. He just dropped by to say hello."

Sure he did, Cy thought, but he didn't reply. He got out of the utility vehicle slowly and deliberately favored his left arm as he moved to the pickup truck.

"Glad to meet you, Mr. Montoya," Cy said with a carefully neutral expression. "My men noticed the warehouse going up." He tried to look worried. "I don't really like bees close to my purebred Santa Gerts," he said without preamble. "I hope you're going to make sure there aren't any problems."

The man's eyebrows rose, surprised at Cy's lack of antagonism. Surely the rancher knew who he was and whose orders he was following. Or did he? His dark eyes narrowed thoughtfully. Parks was holding his crippled left arm in his right and he had the look of someone who'd seen one tragedy too many. Lopez had been worried about interference from this rancher, but Montoya was certain there wouldn't be any. This wasn't an adversary to worry about. This was a defeated man, despite his past. He relaxed and smiled at Cy. "You're very straightforward," he said with only a trace of an accent. He was wearing a silk suit and his thick hair was not only cut, but styled. There was a slight bulge under his jacket. "You have nothing to fear from our enterprise," he assured Cy. "We will be meticulous about our operation. Your cattle will be in no danger. I give you my word."

Cy stared quietly at the other man and nodded, as if convinced. Near him, Harley was gaping at the lack of antagonism that Mr. Parks showed to most visitors. It wasn't like him to favor that burned arm, either.

"I am very pleased to make your acquaintance, Mr. Parks," Montoya said with a grin. "I hope that we will be good neighbors."

"Thank you for taking the time to stop by and introduce yourself," Cy said with a noticeable lack of animation. He got a firmer grip on his injured arm. "We don't get many visitors."

"It was my pleasure. Good day, *señor.*" Montoya smiled again, this time with faint contempt, and pulled his truck out of the driveway. Cy watched him go, arrow-straight, his mouth making a firm line in his lean, taut face.

"Mr. Parks, you are the oddest man I know," Harley said, shaking his head. "You weren't yourself at all."

Cy turned to him. "Who do you think that was?"

"Why, our new neighbor," Harley said carelessly. "Nice of him to come over and say howdy," he added with a scowl. "Your arm bothering you?"

"Not in the least," Cy said, both hands on his lean hips as he studied the younger man. "What did you notice about our new hardworking neighbor?"

The question surprised Harley. "Well, he was Latin. He had a bit of an accent. And he was real pleasant..."

"He was wearing a silk suit and a Rolex watch," he said flatly. "The truck he was driving is next year's model, custom. He was wearing boots that cost more than my new yearling bull. And you think he makes that kind of money selling honey, do you?"

Harley's eyes widened. Once in a while, his boss threw him a curve. This was a damned big curve. He frowned. How had Cy noticed so much about a man he only saw for a minute or two when Harley, a trained commando he reminded himself, hadn't?

"That was one of Lopez's executives," Cy told the younger man flatly, nodding at his wide-eyed realization. "I want you to go work cattle over near that warehouse and take a pair of binoculars with you," Cy told his foreman. "Don't be obvious, but see who comes and goes for a few days."

"Sir?"

"You told Eb you wanted to help keep an eye on Lopez's operation. Here's your chance."

"Oh, I see, Mr. Scott told you to send me out there." Harley grinned from ear to ear. "Sure. I'll be glad to do it!"

"Just make sure you aren't caught spying," Cy told him flatly. "These people are killers. They won't hesitate if they think they're being watched deliberately."

"I can handle myself," Harley said with faint mockery.

"Yes, I know, you're professionally trained," Cy drawled.

The tone made Harley feel uncertain. But he put it down to jealousy and grinned. "I know how to watch people without getting noticed," he assured his boss. "Does Mr. Scott want tag numbers as well as descriptions of the people?"

"Yes, and pay attention to the trucks that come in."

"Okay."

Cy wanted to add more to those instructions, but he didn't want Harley to know everything. "Be sure you keep your mouth shut about this," he told Harley. "Eb won't like it if he thinks you're gossiping."

"I wouldn't want him mad at me!" Harley chuckled. "I'll keep quiet."

"See that you do."

Cy walked back to the house with a quick, sharp stride that reflected his anger. He'd just met a new link in Lopez's chain, probably one of his divisional managers. It would work to his advantage that he had just convinced the drug lord's associate that he was a crippled rancher with no interest in the bees except where his cattle were concerned.

Lopez thought he had it made with his "honey business" as a blind, here in little Jacobsville. But Cy was going to put a stick in his spokes, and the sooner, the better.

CHAPTER THREE

HARLEY DROVE THE LITTLE red car with its new water pump back to Lisa Monroe early the next morning, with Cy following in his big utility vehicle.

Lisa was overjoyed at the way the engine sounded as Harley pulled up at the front porch and revved it before he turned it off.

"It hasn't ever sounded that good before!" she enthused. "Thank you, Harley!"

"You're very welcome, ma'am," he said, making her a mock bow with his hat held against his chest. "But I didn't fix it. I'm just delivering it."

She laughed and Cy glowered. She and Harley were close in age, or he missed his bet. The man, despite his bravado, was honest and hardworking and basically kind. Cy wondered how old Lisa was. Well, at least she was young enough to find Harley's company stimulating—probably much more stimulating than the company of an aging mercenary who was half-crippled and cynical....

"Won't you both come in for a cup of coffee?" she invited.

"I will," Cy told her. "Harley, go take a look around and see what needs doing. Then find Lisa's part-time help and get them on it."

"My pleasure, Mr. Parks," he said with a wicked grin and turned to follow the tersely given instructions.

Lisa gave Cy a speaking look.

"Go ahead," he invited. "Tell me that chores are getting done by people other than you. Tell me that the south pasture is being hayed before the predicted rains day after tomorrow. Tell me," he added mockingly, "that you've got your new calf crop vaccinated and tagged."

She got redder by the minute. She didn't want to tell him that she couldn't get the men to take her suggestions seriously. They were throwbacks to another age, most of them were twice her age, and the madder she got, the more indulgent they became. Once they threatened to quit, they had her over a barrel and she gave up. Hands were thin on the ground this time of year. She could barely afford to pay her employees as it was.

"Harley will get them moving," he told her.

Her lips compressed and her eyes sparked. She looked outraged.

"I know," he said helpfully. "It's a new age. Men and women are equals. You pay their wages and that means they need to do what you say."

She made a gesture of agreement, still without speaking.

"But if you want people to obey, you have to speak in firm tones and tell them who's the boss. And it helps," he added darkly, "if you hire people who aren't still living in the last ice age!"

"They were all I could find to work part-time," she muttered.

"Did you go over to the labor office and see who was available?" he asked.

The suggestion hadn't occurred to her. Probably she'd have found young, able-bodied help there. She could have kicked herself for being so blind.

"No," she confessed.

He smiled, and that wasn't a superior smile, either. "You aren't aggressive enough."

"I beg your pardon?"

"If you're going to hire that type of man, you have to have the whip hand. I'll teach you."

"If that means I'll end up being a local legend like you, I'm not sure I want to learn it," she replied with a twinkle in her dark eyes.

"Old lady Monroe," he recited, chuckling, "carries a shotgun and emasculates men in the barn."

She flushed. "Stop that."

"Isn't that a nicer image than sweet little Lisa who hasn't got the heart to fire a man just because he lies in wait in her bed dead drunk and stinking?"

"Cy!"

He grinned as she curled one hand into a fist. "Much better," he said. "Now hold that thought when you speak to your lazy hands next time. In fact, don't smile at them ever again. Be decisive when you speak, and don't ask, tell. You'll get better results."

She had to admit, she wasn't getting any results at all the way she was. On the other hand, she was still young, and feeling her way through leadership. She wasn't really a drill sergeant type, she had to admit, and the ranch was suffering because of it.

"I don't suppose you'd like a ranch?" she asked whimsically, and was startled when he replied immediately that he would.

"Oh." She stared at him, poleaxed.

"I'll give you the going market price. We'll get two appraisals and I'll match the highest one. You can rent the house from me and I'll manage the cattle. And the cowboys," he added wryly.

"It's not in very good shape," she said honestly, and pushed her glasses back up onto her nose.

"It will be. If you're willing, I'll have my attorney draw up the papers tomorrow."

"I'm very willing. I'll be happy to sign them. What about the appraisals?"

"I'll arrange for those. Nothing for you to worry about now."

"If only my father hadn't been such a throwback," she murmured, leading the way into the ramshackle house. "He thought a woman's place was in the kitchen, period. I'd much rather be working in the garden or doctoring cattle than cooking stuff."

"Can you cook?"

"Breads and meats and vegetables," she said. "Not with genius, but it's mostly edible."

She poured black coffee into a mug and handed it to him. When she sat down across the table from him, he noticed the dark, deep circles under her eyes.

"You aren't sleeping much, are you?" he asked.

She shrugged. "I'm still halfway in shock, I guess. Married and widowed and pregnant, and all in less than two months. That would be enough to unsettle most women."

"I imagine so." He sipped his coffee. She made the decaf strong and it tasted pretty good. He studied her narrowly. "You haven't had any more problems at night, have you?"

"None at all, thanks." She smiled. "And thank you for having my car fixed. I guess if people are going to own old cars, they need to be rich or know a lot about mechanics."

"They do," he agreed. "But I'll keep your little tin can on the road."

"It's not a tin can," she said. "It's a very nice little foreign car with an—" she searched for the right words "—eccentric personality."

"Runs when it feels like it," he translated.

She glared at him. "At least I don't have to have a ladder to get into it."

He smiled. "Remind me to have a step put on just for you."

She didn't reply, but that statement made her feel warm and safe. God knew why. She was certain he wasn't really going to modify his vehicle just for her. She'd only been in it once.

"Do you like opera?" he asked out of the blue.

She blinked. "Well, yes…"

"Turandot?"

"I like anything Puccini composed. Why?"

"It's playing in Houston. I thought we might go."

She pinched her jean-clad leg under the table to see if she was dreaming. It felt like it, but the pain was real. She smiled stupidly. "I'd really like that." Then her face fell. She moved restlessly and averted her eyes. "Better not, I guess."

"You don't have to wear an evening gown to the opera these days," he said, as if he'd actually read her mind. He smiled when her eyes came up abruptly to meet his. "I've seen students go in jeans. I imagine you have a Sunday dress somewhere."

"I do." She laughed nervously. "How did you know I was worried about clothes?"

"I read minds," he mused.

She sighed. "In that case, I'd love to go. Thank you."

He finished his coffee. "Friday night, then. I'll go round up Harley and see what he knows about your place." He got up, hesitating. "Listen, there are some things going on around here. I don't want to frighten you, but Lopez has men in and around town. I want you to keep your doors locked and be careful about strangers."

"I always am," she assured him.

"Do you keep a gun?"

She grinned. "No. I have Puppy Dog."

"Puppy Dog will get under a bed if there's trouble," he assured her flatly. "I've still got Nels staying in the bunkhouse at night, and he's armed. All you have to do is yell. He'll hear you. He's a very light sleeper."

"You can't be sure that Mr. Lopez means me harm."

"I'm not. But I'm a cautious man."

"All right," she said. "I'll keep both eyes out for trouble."

"I'll pick you up Friday night about five. Okay?"

She nodded. "I'll be ready." She went with him to the front door and stood behind the screened door to study him, frowning. "Cy, is it too soon for this?"

"Because you've been a widow such a short time?" He shook his head. "I know you miss Walt. I'm not offering anything heavy, just a trip to the opera. It's very unlikely that we'll see anybody who knows us in Houston."

"I guess you're right." She folded both arms around herself. "The walls are beginning to close in on me."

"I don't doubt it. A night at the opera isn't exactly a cause for gossip."

"Of course not." She smiled. "I'll see you Friday, then. And…thanks."

"I get lonely, too," he said with surprising candor. He gave her one last grin and walked out to find Harley.

HIS FOREMAN WAS TIGHT-LIPPED as he came striding out of the barn. When Harley forgot to be irritating, he was a cowboy and a half. Most of the men walked wide of him in a temper already. "The whole damned place is about to fall to pieces," he said without preamble. "The hay hasn't been cut, the corn hasn't been put in the silo, there are breaks in half the fences, the calves don't even have a brand…. What the hell kind of men did Mrs. Monroe hire?"

"Lazy ones, apparently," Cy said tightly. "Find them and put them all on notice. Lisa's selling me the place. We'll put on four new men to work this ranch and share chores with my own."

"That's a wise decision on her part," Harley said. "She doesn't seem to know much about the business end of cattle ranching."

"Her father thought women weren't smart enough to learn it," Cy mused.

"What an idiot," Harley replied. "My mother can brand cattle right along with the cowboys, and she keeps the books for Dad."

"A lot of women are big-time ranchers, too," Cy

agreed. "But Lisa doesn't really have the knack, or the love, for it. Cattle ranching is hard work even if you do."

Harley nodded. "I'll put her part-timers on notice and get the boys over here with a tractor and a combine to hay those fields and harvest the corn."

"When you get that organized," Cy said, "I want to know what you saw over at the honey warehouse last night."

"Not much," Harley had to admit. "And I got challenged on your land by a man with a rifle. Good thing there was a cow down in the pasture for me to show him," he added with a grin. "I told him we had a problem with locoweed and offered to show him where it grew. He went back on his side of the fence and didn't say another word."

"That was a stroke of luck," Cy remarked. "Because we don't have any locoweed."

"We do now," Harley murmured. "I set out a couple of plants and netted them, just in case I get challenged again. Now that I have a legitimate reason to be out there, they won't pay much attention to me. And if they go looking for locoweed," he added with a mocking smile, "why, they'll find it, won't they?"

Cy smiled at the younger man. "You're a treasure, Harley."

"Glad you noticed, boss, and how about that raise?"

"Don't push your luck," came the dry reply. "I'll talk to you later."

"Sure thing."

CY DROVE TO THE LAWYER'S OFFICE the next morning to discuss the land buy. Blake Kemp was tall, thirtyish, with a gray streak in his black, wavy hair, and pale blue eyes. He was the terror of the Jacobsville court circuit, although he looked mild-mannered and intelligent. Deceptive, Cy mused, studying him, because Kemp had a bite like a rattlesnake in court.

"I'm going to buy the Monroe place," Cy said without preamble. "Lisa can't run it alone, and she hasn't the capital to make improvements or even necessary maintenance."

"Good decision on her part," Blake told him. "And on yours. It's good land, and it adjoins your property." He pursed his chiseled lips. "Is that the only merger you're contemplating?"

Cy's eyes narrowed. "She's only been widowed two weeks," he pointed out.

Blake nodded. "I know that. But she's going to have a hard time paying rent. She doesn't even have a job anymore."

Cy studied him evenly.

"Well, I guess I could use a receptionist," he said. "Callie Kirby is my paralegal, and she can't really handle the research and the phones at the same time. Besides, Lisa worked for a colleague of mine last year. She knows her way around a law office."

"What happened to the brunette who works with Callie?" Cy asked.

"Gretchen's gone off to Morocco with a girlfriend from Houston," Blake said with a chuckle. "She spent the past few years nursing her mother through a fatal bout of cancer," he added solemnly. "And then the first man who took a shine to her insurance money broke her young heart. She needed a change of scene, and she said she doesn't want to work in a law office when she comes back. So there's a job available, if Lisa wants it."

"I'll tell her. Thanks."

He shrugged. "We all like Lisa. She's had a rough deal, one way or another."

"She has indeed. Now, about those appraisals…"

WHEN CY CAME TO PICK Lisa up for their trip to the opera, he was wearing a navy sports coat with dark slacks and a white shirt. His tie combined red and navy in a paisley print. He looked dignified and very handsome. Lisa was glad he hadn't worn a dinner jacket, because she had nothing that dressy in her small wardrobe. The best she could find was a simple gray jersey dress with long sleeves and a skirt that fell to her calves. She covered it with her one luxury, a lightweight black microfiber coat that was warm against the unseasonably cool autumn winds. Her hair was in a neat, complicated braid and she wore more makeup than usual to disguise her dark-circled eyes. She slept badly or not at all lately, and not completely because she missed Walt. She was having some discomfort that concerned her. She knew that pregnancies could fail in the early weeks, and it bothered her. She really needed to talk to her doctor when she went for the next visit. It might be nothing, but she didn't want to take any chances with her baby.

"Not bad at all," Cy mused, watching her pull on the coat over her clinging dress. She had a pretty figure.

"Thank you," she said, coloring a little. "You look nice, too."

"I talked to my attorney about the property," he said after he helped her into the utility vehicle and started the engine. "He's contacted two appraisal firms. They'll be out next week to see the ranch and give you an estimate."

That worried her. She hated seeing the family ranch go out of the family, but what choice did she have? She smiled wanly. "Walt was planning a dynasty," she recalled. "He talked about all sorts of improvements we could make, but when I mentioned having kids to inherit it, he went cold as ice."

Cy glanced at her. "Not much point in working yourself to death just to have the empire go on the market the minute you're in the ground."

"That's what I thought." She turned her small purse over in her lap. "It's just as well that you'll have the ranch," she added. "You'll know how to make it prosper."

"You'll still be living there," he pointed out. "I'll be a damned good landlord, too."

"Oh, I know that." She stretched. "I'll still have to get a job, though. I'll want to put what I get for the ranch into a savings account, so the baby can go to college."

She surprised him constantly. He'd thought she might want to brighten up the house, even buy herself a decent car. But she was thinking ahead, to the day when her child would need to continue his education.

"Nothing for you?" he asked.

"I've got everything I really need," she said. "I don't have expensive tastes—even if Walt did. Besides, I've got a little nest egg left over from some cattle Walt sold off before he…before he died."

"I know of a job, if you want it."

He distracted her, which was what she supposed he'd intended. "Really?"

"Kemp needs a receptionist," he said. "Gretchen's

gone off to Morocco and she isn't coming back to work
for him. So now Callie Kirby's up to her ears in work.
Kemp said you'd be welcome."

"What a nice man!" she exclaimed.

"Now there's a word that doesn't connect itself with
Kemp," He gave a soft laugh. "Or didn't you know that
people talk in whispers around him?"

"He doesn't seem that bad."

"He isn't, to people he likes." His eyes softened as
they searched her averted face. "He'll like you, Lisa
Monroe. You're good people."

"Thanks. So are you."

"Occasionally."

She glanced in his direction and smiled. "It's funny,
isn't it, the way we get along? I was scared to death of
you when you first moved here. You were so remote and
difficult to talk to. People said you made rattlesnakes
look companionable by comparison."

"I moved here not long after I buried my wife and
son," he replied, and memories clawed at his mind. "I
hated the whole world."

"Why did you move here?" she asked curiously.

He wasn't surprised that she felt comfortable asking
him questions. He wouldn't have tolerated it from anyone
else. But Lisa, already, was under his thick skin. "I needed
someone to talk to, I guess," he confessed. "Eb lived here,
and he and I go back a long way. He'd never married, but
he knew what it was to lose people. I could talk to him."

"You can talk to me, too," she pointed out. "I never
tell what I know."

He smiled at her. "Who would you tell it to?" he
drawled. "You don't have close friends, do you?"

She shrugged. "All my friends got married right out of high school. They've got kids of their own and, until fairly recently, I didn't even date much. I've been the odd one out most of my life. Other girls wanted to talk about boys, and I wanted to talk about organic gardening. I love growing things."

"We'll have to lay out a big garden spot for you next spring. You can grow all sorts of stuff."

"That would be nice. I've got a compost pile," she added brightly. "It's full of disgusting things that will produce terrific tomatoes next summer."

"I like cattle, but I'm not much of a gardener."

"It's a lot of work, but you get lovely things to eat, and they aren't poisoned by pesticides, either." She glanced out at the long, flat dark horizon. "I guess you aren't big on people who don't like to use chemicals."

"Haven't you heard?" he chuckled. "I go to cattlemen's association meetings with J. D. Langley and the Tremayne brothers."

"Oh, my," she said, because she'd heard about the uproar at some of those gatherings, where the Tremaynes had been in fistfights over pesticides and growth hormones. Their position against such things was legendary.

"I enjoy a good fight," he added. "I use bugs for pest control and organic fertilizer on my hay and corn and soybean crops." He glanced her way. "Guess where I get the fertilizer?"

"Recycled grass, huh?" she asked, and waited for him to get the point.

He threw back his head and roared. "That's one way of describing it."

"I have some of that, too, and I use it in my garden. I think it works even better than the chemical ones."

The subject of natural gardening and cattle raising supplied them with topics all the way to Houston, and Lisa thoroughly enjoyed herself. Here was a man who thought like she did. Walt had considered her organic approach akin to insanity.

The parking lot at the arts center was full. Cy managed to find one empty space about half a city block away.

"Now that's a full house," he remarked as he helped her down from the vehicle and repositioned her coat around her shoulders. "This thing sure is soft. Is it wool?" he asked, smoothing over it with his fingers.

"It's a microfiber," she told him. "It's very soft and warm. The nights are pretty chilly lately, especially for south Texas."

"The weather's crazy everywhere." He nudged a long, loose curl from her braided hair behind her ear, making her heart race with the almost sensual movement of his lean fingers. "I thought you might wear your hair loose."

"It's…difficult to keep in place when it's windy," she said, sounding and feeling breathless.

His fingers teased the curl and slowly dropped to her soft neck, tracing imaginary lines down it to her throat. He could feel her pulse go wild under his touch, hear the soft, broken whip of her breath at his chin. It had been far too long since he'd had anything warm and feminine this close to him. Restraints that had been kept in place with sheer will were crumbling just at the proximity. He moved a full step closer, so that her body was right up against him in the opening of her coat. His hands were both at the back of her neck now, caressing the silky skin below her nape.

"I haven't touched a woman since my wife died," he said in a faintly thick tone, his voice unusually deep in the silence. The distant sound of cars and horns and passing radios faded into the background.

She looked up, straight into his green eyes in the glow from a streetlight, and her heart raced. That look on his face was unfamiliar to her, despite her brief intimacy with her late husband. She had a feeling that Cy knew a lot more than her husband ever had about women.

Cy's thumbs edged around to tease up and down her long, strained neck. Her vulnerability made him feel taller, more masculine than ever. He wanted to protect her, care for her, watch over her. These were new feelings. Before, his relationships to women had been very physical. Lisa made him hungry in a different way.

She parted her lips to speak and he put a thumb gently over them.

"It's too soon," he said, anticipating her protest. "Of course it is. But I'm starving to death for a woman's soft mouth under my lips. Feel." He drew one of her hands to his shirt under the jacket and pressed it hard against the thunderous beat of his heart.

She was more confused than ever. This was totally unfamiliar territory. Walt had never said anything so blatantly vulnerable to her, not even when they were most intimate.

His free hand went around her waist and drew her slowly closer, pressing her to him as his body reacted powerfully to the touch of her soft warmth. He lifted an eyebrow and smiled wickedly at her frozen expression.

"Why, Mrs. Monroe, you're blushing," he chided softly.

"You wicked man...!"

His nose brushed lazily against hers in a tender nuzzling. "I've probably forgotten more about women than Walt ever knew in the first place," he said. "You don't act like a woman who's ever known satisfaction."

That was so close to the truth that it hurt. She stiffened.

He lifted his head and searched her eyes. His own narrowed. He moved her lazily against him and felt her breath catch, felt her hands cling to his lapels as if she were drowning.

"Oh...no," she choked as a surge of pure delight worked its way up her spine. She hated herself. Her husband was only buried two weeks ago...!

While she was thinking of ways to escape, and fighting her own hunger, Cy backed her very gently against the big utility vehicle and edged one of her long legs out of his way to bring them into more intimate contact.

"This is the most glorious thing a man and a woman can do together," he murmured as his mouth lowered to hers. "He cheated you. I won't. Open your mouth."

Her lips parted on a shocked little gasp, and his mouth ground into them, parting them. He wasn't hesitant or tentative. He demanded, devoured. His mouth was a weapon, feinting, thrusting, biting, and all the while her body rippled with a thousand stings of new pleasure as she clung hard to his strength. Sensations she'd never known piled one upon the other until a hoarse moan tore out of her strained throat and went up into his mouth.

Another minute and he knew he wouldn't be able to

pull back at all. He had her hips pinned with his, and his body ached for satisfaction.

With a rough curse he dragged his head up and moved away from her. She looked at him with dazed eyes in a flushed face, her mouth swollen from his kisses, her body shivering with new knowledge.

He drew himself up to his full height. His eyes glittered like green diamonds in a face like stone. He had to fight to get a normal breath of air into his lungs.

She tried to speak, but she couldn't manage even a whimper. Her body was still flying, soaring, trembling with little shivers of pleasure that made her knees weak.

He reached out and caught her small hand in one of his big ones, linking their fingers. "We'd better go inside," he said quietly.

"Yes." She let him pull her away from the truck and lead her toward the arts center. She was amazed that she could walk at all.

CHAPTER FOUR

TURANDOT WAS BEAUTIFUL. Lisa cried when the tenor sang "Nessun Dorma," one of her favorite arias. The sets were elegant, colorful, the Chinese costumes glittery and resembling fantasy more than reality. The dragon was a masterpiece of sound and fury and color. All in all, it was a magnificent production, and Puccini's glorious music brought it alive. Lisa had never seen an opera except on the public broadcasting television channel. She knew that she'd never forget this for as long as she lived, and every time she remembered it, she'd remember Cy sitting beside her in the dark.

Meanwhile, Cy was cursing himself silently for what had happened in the parking lot. It was months too soon for that. She was a pregnant, newly widowed woman and he'd let his emotions get out of control. His jaw tautened as he remembered the silky feel of her in his arms. He wanted to take care of her, and it looked as though she was going to need protection after all—from him.

Somehow he was going to have to get them back on a simple friendly footing. It wouldn't be easy. He had no idea how she felt about what had happened. She sat quietly beside him, obviously enjoying the opera. She even smiled at him from time to time. But if she was angry, it didn't show. He remembered her soft moan, her clinging arms. No, he thought, she'd gone in headfirst, too, just as he had. But he had regrets and he suspected that she did as well. He had to draw back before he put the delicate new feeling between them at risk. Lisa was off-limits in any physical way, and he was going to have to remember that.

Lisa saw his scowl and wondered if he had regrets about what had happened. Men got lonely, she knew, and he was a very masculine sort of man to whom women were no mystery. He was probably wondering how to tell her that it wasn't about her a few minutes ago, that any woman would have produced that reaction in a hungry man.

She would save him the trouble, she decided, the minute they started home. He'd already done so much for her. She couldn't expect him to take over where Walt had left off; not that Walt had ever really felt passion for her. Walt had enjoyed her, she supposed, but there hadn't been any sizzling attraction between them. It shamed her to admit that what she'd felt in the parking lot with Cy had been infinitely more pleasurable than anything she'd ever done with her late husband. She didn't dare think about how it would be if they were truly intimate...

Her hand jerked in Cy's as the final curtain fell and the applause roared. She clapped automatically, but made sure that both her hands were tight on her purse when they started to leave.

"It's a beautiful opera," she remarked as he escorted her to the exit.

"Yes, it is," he agreed pleasantly. "I've seen it in a dozen different cities, but I still enjoy it."

"I guess you've been to the Metropolitan Opera in New York City?" she mused wistfully.

"Several times," he agreed.

She imagined him there, with some beautiful woman in an expensive evening gown and wrapped in furs. It wasn't far to imagine them going into a dark room together, where the coat and the evening gown were discarded. She swallowed hard and tried not to think about that.

He could feel tension radiating from her. She was clinging so hard to that tiny purse that she was leaving the indentations of her nails in the soft leather.

When they reached the Expedition, he opened the door for her, but held her back when she started to climb inside.

"I'm sorry about what happened earlier," he said gently. "I've made you uncomfortable."

Her wide eyes met his. "I thought I'd made you uncomfortable," she blurted out.

They stood just looking at each other until his lean face went harder than ever with the effort not to give in to the hunger she kindled in him.

"You poor man," she said huskily, wincing as she saw the pain in his eyes. "I know you're lonely, Cy, that you just needed someone to hold for a few minutes. It's all right. I didn't read anything into it."

His eyes closed on a wave of pain that hit him like a bat. She reached up and pulled his face down to her lips. She kissed him tenderly, kissed his eyes, his nose, his cheek, his chin, with brief undemanding little brushes of her mouth that comforted in the most exquisite way.

He took a ragged breath and his lean hands captured her shoulders, tightening there when he lifted his face away from her warm mouth. "Don't do that," he said tersely.

"Why not?" she asked.

"I don't need comforting!" he said curtly.

She moved back a step. He looked as if she'd done something outrageous, when she'd only meant to be kind. It irritated her that he had to be antagonistic about it. "Oh, I see," she said, staring up at him. "Is this how it goes? 'Men are tough, little woman,'" she drawled, deepening her voice and her drawl, "'we can eat live snakes and chew through barbed wire. We don't want women fussin' over us!'" She grinned up at him deliberately.

He glared at her, his eyes glittering.

She raised her eyebrows. "Want me to apologize? Okay. I'm very sorry," she added.

His broad chest rose and fell heavily. "I want you to quit while you're ahead," he said in a tight voice.

She stared at him without guile. "I don't understand."

"Don't you?" His smile was full of mockery and he was seeing a succession of women from his wild days who liked to tease and run away, but not too far away. His lean hands tightened on her shoulders as his eyes slid down her body. "Your husband didn't tell you what teasing does to a man?"

"Teasing…?" Her eyes widened. "Was I?" she asked, and seemed not to know.

That fascinated expression was real. He did scowl

then. "What you were doing…it arouses me," he said bluntly.

"You're kidding!"

He wanted to be angry. He couldn't manage it. She did look so surprised…. He dropped his hands, laughing in wholesale defeat. "Get in the damned truck."

He half lifted her in and closed the door on her barely formed question.

She was strapped in when he pulled himself up under the steering wheel, closed the door and reached for his seat belt.

"You were kidding," she persisted.

He looked right into her eyes. "I wasn't." He frowned quizzically. "Don't you know anything about men?"

"I was married for two months," she pointed out.

"To a eunuch, apparently," he said bluntly as he cranked the vehicle and pulled out of the parking lot and into traffic.

"I *am* pregnant," she stated haughtily.

He spared her an amused glance. "Pregnant and practically untouched," he replied.

She sighed, turning her attention to the city lights as he wound south through Houston to the long highway that would take them home to Jacobsville. "I guess it shows, huh?" she asked.

He didn't say anything for half a block or so. "Did you want him?"

"At first," she said. Her eyes sought his. "But not like I wanted you in the parking lot," she said honestly. "Not ever like that."

A flash of ruddy color touched his cheekbones. He was shocked at her honesty.

"Sorry, again," she murmured, looking away. "I guess I haven't learned restraint, either," she added.

He let out a long breath. "You take some getting used to," he remarked.

"Why?"

His eyes met hers briefly before they went back to the highway. Rain was beginning to mist the windshield. He turned on the wipers. "I don't expect honesty from a woman," he said curtly.

She frowned. "But surely your wife was honest."

"Why do you think so?"

"It's obvious that you loved your little boy," she began.

His laugh had the coldest ring to it that she'd ever heard. "She wanted an abortion. I threatened to take away her credit cards and she gave in and had him."

"That must have been a difficult time for you," she said softly.

"It was." His jaw clenched. "She was surprised that I wanted her baby."

"Hers, and not yours?" she ventured.

"Hers by one of her lovers," he said bitterly. "She didn't really know which one."

There was an abrupt silence on the other side of the truck. He glanced at her frozen features with curiosity. "What sort of marriage do you think I had? I was a mercenary. The women you meet in that profession aren't the sort who sing in church choirs."

"How did you know I sang in the choir?" she asked, diverted.

He laughed, shaking his head. "I didn't, but it figures. You're her exact opposite."

She was still trying to understand what he was saying. "You didn't love her?"

"No, I didn't love her," he replied. "We were good together in bed and I was tired of living alone. So, I married her. I never expected it to last, but I wanted a child. God knows why, I assumed it was mine."

"Why did she marry you if it wasn't?"

"She liked having ten credit cards and driving a Jaguar," he said.

That produced another frown.

"I was rich, Lisa," he told her. "I still am."

She pulled her coat tighter around her and stared out the window, not speaking. She was shocked and more uncertain about him than ever. He was such a complex person, so multifaceted that just when she thought she was getting to know him, he became a stranger all over again.

"Now what is it?" he asked impatiently.

"I hope you don't think I agreed to come out with you…that I was eager to let you buy the ranch because…" She flushed and closed her mouth. She was so embarrassed that she wanted to go through the floor.

"If I'm rich, it's because I know pure gold when I see it," he said, casting her an amused glance. "Do you think I'll assume that you're a gold digger because you came out with me?"

"I kissed you back, too," she said worriedly.

He sighed with pure pleasure and relaxed into the seat, smiling to himself. "Yes, you did."

"But it was an accident," she persisted. "I didn't plan it…"

"That makes two of us." He pulled up at the last streetlight before they left the city behind and turned to her.

His eyes were narrow and very intent. "There are things in my past that are better left there. You'd never begin to understand the relationship I had with my wife, because you don't think in terms of material gain. When I was your age, you were the sort of woman I'd run from."

"Really? Why?" she asked.

He cocked an eyebrow and let his eyes run over her. "Because you told me once that you hadn't slept with Walt before you married him, Lisa," he drawled.

She glared at him. "I would have if I'd wanted to," she said mutinously.

"But you didn't."

She threw up her hands, almost making a basketball of her small purse. She retrieved it from the dash and plopped it back into her lap.

"You're the kind of woman that men marry," he continued, unabashed. "You like children and small animals and it would never occur to you to be cruel to anyone. If you'd gotten involved with me while I was still in my former line of work, you wouldn't have lasted a day with me."

"I don't suppose I would have," she had to agree. She looked through the windshield, wondering why it hurt so much to have him tell her that. Surely she hadn't been thinking in terms of the future just because of one passionate kiss? Of course, her whole body tensed remembering the pleasure of it, the exciting things he'd said…

"And you weren't Walt's usual date, either," he said surprisingly. "He liked experience."

She grimaced. "I found that out pretty quick. He said I was the most boring woman he'd ever gone to bed with. Except for our wedding night, and the night before he was killed, he slept in a separate bedroom."

No wonder she was the way she was, he mused as the light changed and he sent the big vehicle speeding forward. She probably felt like a total failure as a woman. The child must have been some sort of consolation, because she certainly wanted it.

"I'll bet you hate admitting that," he said.

"Yes, I do. I felt inadequate, dull, *boring*," she muttered. "He liked blondes, but not me."

"He liked that parcel service driver plenty," he recalled, his eyes narrowing. "You were pitching hay over the fence to the cows and he was flirting with her, right under your nose. I never wanted to hit a man more."

Her lips parted on a quick breath. "You saw...that?"

"I saw it," he said curtly. "That's why I stopped by later and said something about the way you were pitching hay by yourself."

She shifted in the seat. "He said they were old friends," she replied. "I guess he really meant they were former lovers. He never treated me to that sort of charm and flirting. He really wanted Dad's ranch. It was a pity I went with the deal."

"It was his loss that he took you for granted," he corrected. "You're not inadequate. You proved that earlier tonight, in the parking lot."

She cleared her throat. "An incident best forgotten."

"Why?"

"Why?" She stared at him. "Walt's only been dead two weeks, that's why!"

He stopped at a four-way stop and turned in his seat on the deserted road to look at her. "Lisa," he said quietly, "it wouldn't have mattered even if he'd still been alive, and you know it. What happened was mutual and explosive."

"It was a fluke…"

His hand reached out and his fingers traced her lower lip. She couldn't even speak. "Would you like me to prove that it isn't?" he asked quietly. "There are plenty of dirt roads between here and home, and the seats recline all the way."

"Cy Parks!"

"Best of all," he mused, "we wouldn't even have to worry about pregnancy, would we?"

Her face was scarlet; she knew it was. He was making her breathless with that torturous brush of his fingers, and she was vulnerable. She'd never really known desire until tonight, and she wished she could turn the clock back a day. Life was difficult enough without this new complication.

He drew in a long breath and lifted his hand back to the steering wheel. "God knows I want to," he said shortly, "but you'd die of shock and never speak to me again afterward."

"I…certainly…would," she faltered, pushing her hair back unnecessarily just for something to do.

He shook his head. He'd known her such a short time, really, but she seemed to hold his attention even when he wasn't with her. Every future event he thought of these days, he considered her part in. It was disturbing to know that he considered her part of his life already.

She fiddled with the top button on her coat. Her eyes were restless, moving from the dark horizon to the occasional lighted window flashing past as the utility vehicle picked up speed. What he'd said disturbed her, mostly because she knew it was true. She'd have gone anywhere with him, done anything with him. It made her guilty because she should be mourning Walt.

"Don't brood," Cy told her. "You're safe. No more torrid interludes tonight, 1 promise."

She fought a smile and lost. "You're a terrible man."

"You have no idea how terrible." He paused to look both ways before he crossed a lonely intersection. "Harley's fired your part-time hired hands, by the way."

"He's what?"

"Calm down. They were being paid for work they didn't do. That's economically disastrous."

"But who'll get in the hay and brand the calves…?" she worried.

"You didn't hear the noise? Harley got the tractors out in your hay field early this morning. The haying's done. The corn crop is next. I'm hiring on four new men. Harley will supervise them, and your place will live up to its promise." He glanced at her. "You haven't decided not to sell it have you?"

"I can't afford to keep it," she confessed. "I'm glad you don't plan to build a subdivision on it or something. It's been in my family for a hundred years. Dad loved it with all his heart. I love it, too, but I have no idea how to make it pay. I'd like to see it prosper."

"I think I can promise you that it will."

She smiled, content with just being next to him. He turned on the radio and soft country music filled the cab. After a few minutes, her eyes slid shut as all the sleepless nights caught up with her.

She was vaguely aware of being gently shaken. She

didn't want to be disturbed. She was warm and cozy and half-asleep.

"No," she murmured drowsily. "Go away."

"I have to," came a deep, amused voice at her ear. "Or we'll have a scandal we'll never live down. Come on, imp. Bedtime."

She felt herself tugged out of the seat and into a pair of warm, hard arms. She was floating, floating…

Cy didn't wake her again. He took off her shoes, tossed the cover over her, put her glasses on the bedside table and left her on the bed in her nice dress and coat. He didn't dare start removing things, considering his earlier passionate reaction to her. But he stood beside the bed, just watching her, enjoying the sight of her young face relaxed in sleep. He wondered how old she was. She never had told him.

He turned and went back out into the hall, pausing to check the lock on the back door in the kitchen before he went out the front one, locking it carefully behind him. He still wasn't convinced that Lopez wouldn't make a beeline for Lisa if he thought his men could get away with harming her. Cy was going to make sure that he didn't.

He stopped by the bunkhouse to have a word with Nels before he went home and climbed into his own bed. He stared at himself in the bedroom mirror, his eyes narrow and cynical as he studied his lean, scarred face and equally scarred body. He was only thirty-five, as Lisa had already guessed, but he looked older. His eyes held the expression of a man who'd lived with death and survived it. He was wounded inside and out by the long, lonely, terrible years of the past. Lisa soothed the part of him that still ached, but she aroused a physical need that he'd almost forgotten he had. She was a special woman, and she needed him. It was new to be needed on a personal level. He thought about the child she was carrying and wondered if it would be a boy or girl. She'd need someone to help her raise it. He wanted to do that. He had nobody, and neither did she. They could become a family—for the child's sake.

He turned off the lights and went to bed. But his dreams were restless and hot, and when he woke up the next morning, he felt as if he hadn't slept at all.

HARLEY GOT THE CALVES branded and the corn in the silo in quick order.

"You've got a knack for inspiring cowboys to work, Harley," Cy told him one afternoon a few days later.

"I get out there and work with them, and make them ashamed of being lazy," Harley told him with a grin. "Most of them can't keep up with me."

"I noticed." Cy leaned back against the corral fence and stared at the younger man evenly, without blinking. "You were out near the warehouse last night. What did you see?"

"Three big trucks," Harley said solemnly. "One had some odd stuff on the back. Looked like oil drums lashed together."

That was disturbing. Cy knew that drug dealers threw portable bridges across rivers to let trucks full of their product drive to the other side. What Harvey was describing sounded like a makeshift pontoon bridge. Cy and the mercenaries he'd worked with had used them, too.

"Did you get a look at what was in the trucks?" he asked.

Harley shook his head. "The doors were closed and locked. I was afraid to risk trying to pick a lock, with all that hardware around. Those guys had Uzis."

"I know," Cy said without thinking.

Harley's eyebrows went up, and he grinned in a fairly condescending way. "Do you now? Are you using Uzis to load cattle these days, boss?"

Cy realized what he'd said and chuckled. "I wasn't listening. Sorry."

"No problem. I noticed a couple of new faces over there," he added. "Tough-looking men, and they weren't wearing suits."

"Get back out there tonight," Cy told him. "And be very careful, Harley. I've got a bad feeling about this whole thing." He didn't add that he was worried about Lisa. He saw her every other day, and the paperwork had just been completed and signed, ready for the transfer of money and deeds. He wouldn't be surprised to learn that Lopez had an informant in town who'd tell him that. It might prompt the drug lord to hasty action, if he thought Lisa was selling the ranch in order to move away. He couldn't know that Cy planned to rent her the ranch house. He wouldn't like having to search for her.

Knowing that bothered him, and he mentioned it to Lisa when he stopped by to see her the next day. Harley had seen yet another unfamiliar face on the warehouse property, and he'd also seen flat after flat of jars being moved inside the structure. The drug dealers were getting ready to begin operations. Things would heat up very soon, or Cy missed his guess. He didn't want Lisa in the middle of it.

"Have you got family you could visit out of state?" he asked without preamble as he joined her in the living room, where she had gas logs burning in the fireplace.

She curled up on the sofa in her jeans and knit turtleneck white sweater and stared at him curiously. "I don't have family anywhere," she confessed. "Maybe a cousin or two up around Fort Worth, but I wouldn't know where to look for them."

He sighed heavily and leaned forward in the chair with his arms crossed over his knees. "All right," he said, seeming to come to a decision. "If you leave the house from now on, I want to know first. If you can't get me, you call Eb Scott."

"Why?"

He knew she was going to ask that. He didn't have a very logical reply. "I don't know what Lopez is up to," he said honestly. "He may have given up on ideas of targeting you. On the other hand, he may be lulling us into a false sense of security. I'd rather err on the side of caution."

"That suits me," she said agreeably.

"Do you have a phone by your bed?"

"Yes," she said. "It makes me feel more secure."

He stood up. "Don't forget to keep your doors locked, even in the daytime, when you're home alone."

"I'm not, much," she said without thinking. "Harley comes by every day to check on me, sometimes twice a day."

His eyes narrowed. He didn't like that, although he said, "Good for Harley."

She caught a nuance of something in his tone. "Do

you mind?" she asked deliberately. He'd been remote and she'd hardly seen him since the night of the opera. She wondered if he'd been avoiding her, and she concluded that he was. His manner now was standoffish and he seemed in a hurry to leave. She wanted to know if he was the least bit put out by Harley's attentiveness.

"It's your life," he said nonchalantly, tilting his wide-brimmed hat over one eye. "He's a steady young man with a good future."

He couldn't be thinking…or could he? She started to tell him that Harley was friendly, and that she had no romantic interest in him. But before she could, Cy was already on his way out the door.

She went after him, trying not to be undignified and run. She didn't catch up to him until he was going down the steps.

"When do we close on the sale?" she asked, having no other excuse for following him.

He turned at the door of the utility vehicle. "The first of next week, Kemp said. It will take that long to get the paperwork filed."

"Okay. You'll phone me?"

"I will. Or Kemp will."

That sounded less than friendly. She wrapped her arms around her chest and leaned against one of the posts that held up the long porch. "That's fine, then," she said with forced cheer. "Thanks."

He opened the door and hesitated. "Are you in a rush to close?"

She shrugged. "Not really. I just wanted to know when I'd need to start paying rent. I was going to go see Mr. Kemp next week about that job."

She thought he didn't want her around, and that was so far from the truth that it might as well have been in orbit. But he didn't want to rush her, frighten her. Hell, he didn't know what he wanted anymore.

"I'll see you Monday," he said, and got into the vehicle without another word. He didn't even look back as he drove away.

Lisa stared after him with her heart around her ankles. So much for her theory that he was attracted to her. She supposed that he'd had second thoughts. It might be just as well. He was mourning his son, whom he'd obviously loved even if it wasn't his own child, and she was a recent widow expecting a child of her own. She'd been spinning daydreams and it was time to stop and face reality. Cy wasn't her future even if she'd hoped he was hers. She turned and went back into the lonely house, pausing to close and lock the door behind her.

CHAPTER FIVE

THE FIRST TIME SHE HEARD the noise at the window, Lisa thought it was a squirrel. The old house seemed to attract them. They often scurried over the roof and came leaping down into the limbs of the big pecan trees that surrounded the porches. But she usually didn't hear them in the wee hours of the morning, and so loud that they woke her up. She tried to go back to sleep, but then the noise came again. This time it didn't sound like a squirrel. It sounded more like a window being forced open.

Lisa slipped out of bed in her sweatpants and white cotton top, hesitating at the door that led into the hall. The noise had come from the room next door, the one Walt had occupied for most of their married life.

She heard a faint rubbing noise, like one a man might make climbing in a window. Her heart began racing and she dashed down the hall in her bare feet, down the wooden steps and into the kitchen. Her glasses were still in the nightstand drawer by her bed, and she could barely make out familiar objects in the dim light. She was headed for the back door when she was caught and lifted and a big, gentle hand was clapped over her mouth while she struggled pitifully in an embrace of steel.

"It's all right," Cy Parks whispered at her ear. "It's

all right, we know there's someone trying to break in upstairs. Micah's rappeling from the roof down to the window of the room across the hall. He'll have him in a minute. Don't scream or you'll give him all the warning he needs to get away. Okay?"

She nodded.

He eased her back onto her feet, taking her soft weight against the black sweater he was wearing with black jeans, one lean arm holding her just under her breasts. She saw the glimmer of metal in his other black-gloved hand. Her frightened eyes drifted up to his face, and all she could see of it was his eyes. He was wearing some sort of black mask.

While she was studying him, she heard a loud thud, followed by a louder groan.

"All clear!" came a loud, deep voice from upstairs.

"Stay here." Cy let her go and went past her and up the staircase with an economy of motion that made her very glad she wasn't the enemy.

She leaned back against the counter and almost jumped out of her skin when the back door opened and Eb Scott came in pulling his mask off, grinning.

"Sorry," he said quickly. "But the man Cy had staying in the bunkhouse spotted two suspicious figures outside your window. Unless you're expecting Romeo, it's a bit late for social calls."

"I was asleep," she said, shaken. "I heard the noise and thought it was a squirrel. I was trying to get out the back door when Cy grabbed me." She whistled. "I thought my number was up."

"Good thing you slept light," Eb said solemnly. "We barely got here in time."

"Who is it, do you think?" she asked.

"One of Lopez's goons," Eb told her flatly. "And this definitely confirms our worst fears. Lopez is after you."

"But I didn't do anything!" she said, still shaken from the experience. "Why is he after me?" She brushed back the long, tangled curtain of hair from her flushed cheeks. She felt sick.

"He's going to set an example for anybody else who might consider trying to infiltrate his organization," Eb told her. "It doesn't matter what you did or didn't do. He doesn't care. Your husband betrayed him and he wants you to pay for it, too. He wants all the government agencies to know the price for selling him out—their lives and their families' lives."

The fear made a tight knot in the pit of her stomach. She sank down into one of the kitchen chairs with a protective hand over her belly. She felt twice her age.

She heard heavy footsteps on the staircase and out the front door before Cy came back into the room, tearing off his mask. He looked even more formidable than usual, and that said something about his present demeanor, Lisa thought.

"Micah's taking the guy over to the sheriff," he said. "He suddenly doesn't speak English, of course, and his friend lit a shuck while he was breaking into the house. We won't be able to prove a thing beyond the obvious."

"He'll be out on bond by tomorrow afternoon and out of the country an hour later," Ebenezer added.

Cy's expression was homicidal before he turned his glittery green eyes on Lisa. "You can't stay here a day longer," he said flatly. "Lopez doesn't make the same mistake twice. You've been put on notice. The next time, there won't be a near miss."

She ground her teeth together. "This is my ranch. I haven't sold it to you yet, and I'm staying here," she said furiously. "I'm not going to let some sleazy drug king-pin force me into hiding out like a scared kid!"

"Commendable courage," Cy remarked with a stoic expression. He reached into his belt and pulled out something dark. "Here."

He tossed her his automatic. She caught it and then dropped it with a gasp of pure horror.

"You'd better pick it up and learn to shoot straight and under fire," he said coldly. "You'd better learn to shoot to kill while you're at it. Because that," he indicated the gun, "is the only way you'll survive if you insist on staying here alone. We were almost too late tonight. Next time, we might not be so lucky."

She glared at him, but she didn't argue. "I hate guns."

"Good God, so do I," Cy told her. "But when you get in a war, you don't throw potatoes at the enemy."

"Then what do I do?" she asked Cy.

Cy told her. "Go pack a bag. You're leaving."

"Leaving for where?" she demanded, standing up with both hands on her hips. "I told you already, I've got no family, no close friends, and no place to go to!"

"Yes, you have. The Expedition's outside. I'll send Harley over in the morning to pick up your VW and bring it over, too."

Her dark eyes widened. It didn't help much, her glasses were upstairs on the bedside table and all she could see of Cy was a blur. "I can't go home with you. I've only been widowed a short time!"

"I've only been widowed three years," he reminded her. "So what?"

"I can stay with Callie Kirby!"

"Callie's apartment isn't big enough for Callie, much less Callie and you," he said. "I've got three bedrooms. You can even have a bathroom of your own."

She didn't want to give in. But the memory of someone trying to break in the house scared her. She knew that she couldn't shoot an intruder. That left her few options.

"When you make up your mind, I'll be in the truck," Cy told her.

He actually walked out the door. Eb followed him with an amused grin that he didn't let Lisa see.

Lisa glared after him, hesitant and bristling with hurt pride. But in the end, she went upstairs, changed into jeans and a shirt and packed a small bag. Ten minutes later, he opened the door of the utility vehicle so that she could climb in with her tote bag.

"If Harley so much as grins, I'll kick him in the shins," she said after she'd fumbled her seat belt together.

"So will I," Cy promised her.

She glanced at him from the warm folds of her flannel-lined denim jacket. "Would you have shot that man?"

"If there hadn't been another way to stop him, yes."

"I couldn't shoot anybody," she said.

"I know. That's why you have to stay with me until we get Lopez." He glanced at her. "It won't be so bad. I can cook."

"So can I."

"Good. Fair division of labor." He glanced at her with a faint smile. "When the baby comes, we'll take turns getting up for his meals."

She felt a warm glow wash over her. She smiled, too. "Oh, I wouldn't want to sleep if he was hungry," she mused dreamily. "I'd get up, too."

He remembered his wife complaining bitterly about lost sleep, making formula, giving bottles. She hated everything to do with the baby, and couldn't begin to understand his affection for the tiny little boy, who wasn't even...

He closed his mind to the anguish that memory fostered, and concentrated on his driving instead.

Apparently Cy's men were asleep in the bunkhouse, because the ranch house was quiet when they arrived. He helped Lisa out of the vehicle and carried her suitcase into the house.

"You'll probably like this room. It faces the rose garden," he added with a smile.

She looked around at the simple, old-fashioned room with its canopied double bed and gauzy white curtains and white furniture. "It's very pretty," she murmured.

"The house belonged to an elderly woman, who was the last living member of her family," he said. "She had to go into a nursing home. I learned the history of the house from her. It belonged to her father, who was one of the better known Texas Rangers. She raised two kids and three grandkids here. One of her grandsons was a congressman, and another worked for the U.S. Secret Service. She was very proud of them."

"Is she living in Jacobsville?"

He nodded. "I go to visit her every other week. You might like to go along occasionally. She's a walking history of Texas."

"I'd like that." She was studying him with open curiosity. He looked so different in that stark black outfit that she wondered if she would even have recognized him if she'd seen him on the street. Her husband had been in law enforcement, but even he hadn't looked as dangerous as Cy Parks in commando gear.

He lifted an eyebrow.

"Sorry," she murmured with a shy smile. "You look different, that's all."

"Think of it as a covert ops business suit," he mused. "The object is to blend in with the night."

"Oh, you did that very neatly," she agreed.

He chuckled. "Get some sleep. There won't be anybody to bother you here, and you can sleep as late as you like."

She grimaced. "What about Puppy Dog?"

"What?"

"Puppy Dog," she said. "He's all shut up on the back porch…"

"I'll fetch him at daybreak," he said. "But if he eats one of my chickens, he's dog bone stew. Got that?"

"You've got chickens?"

"Five," he said. "Rhode Island Reds. I like fresh eggs."

She smiled. "I like them, too."

"A woman after my own heart." He moved toward the door. "The windows are electronically wired, by the way," he added with the doorknob in his hand. "If anyone tries to open them from the outside, they'll think we're being bombed."

"That's reassuring."

"So it is. Sleep tight."

"You, too."

He spared her a glance. "Don't get up until you want to. I'll haul Puppy Dog over here at daybreak."

"He likes to chew up things," she said worriedly.

"You shouldn't let him eat heating pads, while we're on the subject."

"He can reach the shelf I keep them on," she said. "I didn't realize it until I saw him jump up to pull it down. By then I'd lost two and I thought I'd left them on the sofa." She shook her head. "He's already very tall. His father, Moose, is almost five feet tall when he stands on his hind legs."

"He'll be good protection for you when he's trained."

"He seems to be training me," she said on a wistful breath.

"I'll take care of that. 'Night."

She smiled. "Thanks for rescuing me."

"I had good help," he told her.

She stood staring after him even when the door closed. Her life had just gone up two notches on the complications scale. She forced herself not to think of how hungry he'd made her the night they'd gone to Houston to the opera, of how much she liked being close to him. He'd been very standoffish since, so it was obvious that he didn't like the small taste of her he'd had. She was safe with him. Safe, pregnant and a widow. She shouldn't be thinking about kissing Cy. The thought made her uncomfortable, but she slept soundly all night long.

HARLEY WALKED IN THE kitchen door with a wicker basket full of eggs and a disgusted look on his face. He stopped short when he saw Lisa, in jeans and a sweatshirt with her dark blond hair in an unruly bun, making coffee.

She gave him a challenging look back. "Where's Cy?" she asked.

"Gone to town to have his truck cleaned."

That sounded intriguing. "Does he do that a lot?"

"Only when dogs throw up in it."

"Oh, dear," she said.

"Seems your puppy doesn't like to go for rides," he murmured with a grin. He put the basket of eggs on the table. "He's out in the barn with the boss's collie."

"I didn't know Cy had a dog."

"He didn't know he had one, either, until it got run over week before last," he remarked. "He picked it up and took it to the vet. It was a stray that somebody had put out, half-starved, full of fleas, almost dead from lack of care. Amazing what some dog shampoo, flea medicine, regular meals and attention can do for a mangy old cur." He shook his head. "For a hard-nosed man, he sure has some soft spots. He'd never make a soldier, let me tell you." He held up a hand when she started to speak. "Don't tell him I said that," he added. "He pays me a good salary and he's a fine man to work for. He can't help it if he isn't exactly G.I. Joe. Considering what he's been through, I guess he's got some grit in him somewhere."

She almost bit her tongue through trying not to tell Harley what she knew about his soft-centered employer. But that was Cy's business, and she didn't want to get on his bad side when she'd only arrived.

"I rode over to your place with the boss and drove your little VW back with me. It's in the garage. None of my business, but are you staying awhile?" he asked curiously.

"I guess so," she sighed. She poured coffee into a cup. "A man broke into my house last night. Cy let me come over here."

"Broke into your house? Why?"

She grew pensive. "My husband was an undercover DEA agent," she told him. "He was infiltrating a drug lord's organization when he was exposed and executed. Apparently the drug lord likes to set examples, like wiping out whole families of people who oppose him. I'm on his list."

"Then you sure came to the right place," Harley said with a beaming grin. "As it happens, you'll be safer here than anywhere else in the county, except maybe with Ebenezer Scott." He seemed to stand two feet taller. "I was in the Army Rangers for two years and I've had commando training. Nobody can slip by me."

"I can't tell you how much better I feel, knowing that," she said, smiling pleasantly.

He almost blushed. "Good. Well, I'll get back to my chores. Glad you're okay, Miss...Mrs. Monroe," he corrected, tipping his hat on his way out.

"Thanks for bringing my car," she said.

"No problem." He shot a grin back at her as he left.

She sat down at the kitchen table beside the eggs and shook her head. He didn't have a clue what was going on. His life was apparently so dull that he couldn't live without the illusion of bravery. She wondered how he would respond to a real threat, and hoped she never had to find out. He seemed a nice sort of man, but she had a feeling that he wasn't quite as formidable as he made out.

CY CAME IN FOR LUNCH, helping himself to bread, mayonnaise and luncheon meat while Lisa poured iced tea into tall glasses.

"I can make sandwiches," she offered.

He gave her a grin. "I'm used to doing it myself. Want a couple?"

"Just one, thanks," she agreed and sat down at her place beside his at the small table. "I'm sorry about Puppy Dog messing up your truck."

His eyebrows lifted under disheveled black hair. "Who told you?"

"Harley." She gave him a gamine look. "He said that he'd be glad to protect me from potential attackers, seeing as how he's a trained commando."

Cy chuckled softly. "I was his age once. Seems like fifty years ago, now."

She put her elbows on the table and propped her chin on her hands, watching him make sandwiches. "Did you swagger, too?"

"Probably. At least, I did until I saw combat for the first time. Nobody tells you that people scream when they get shot. On television they just grunt or groan and hold the part that's been shot." He shook his head. "It's a lot more…vivid…in real life."

"Were you afraid, the first time?"

"I was afraid every time," he corrected with a level stare. "Only a fool pretends he isn't. You learn to face the fear and deal with it, just like everyone else does."

"It's difficult, isn't it?"

"Difficult to watch people die, yes," he told her. "Difficult to live with what you do, too. I remember a young boy in Africa who was fighting the rebels. He carried a

carbine in his hands and ammunition belts that probably weighed more than he did, strapped around his
chest. His name was Juba." He smiled as he worked.
"He had a passion for chocolate bars. We always had a
few in our packs, just a taste of something sweet to remind us of civilization. One day, Juba ran ahead of us
into a building the rebels had just evacuated. We hadn't
swept it for traps and he wouldn't stop when we tried
to warn him. He broke a trip wire right in the doorway
and blew himself up." His hand hesitated on the knife
as he spread mayonnaise on the bread. His eyes were
solemn and quiet. "He didn't die right away," he added
grimly. "We gave him morphine from one of our medical kits. Then I sat under a silk cotton tree with him in
my arms and talked to him until he died." His eyes fell
back to his task. "He was eleven years old."

She winced. "That's very young to be fighting a war."

"He'd already lost his parents and two sisters in the
crossfire," he recalled. "He was alone in the world, except
for us. We'd thrown in with the government forces. They
were overwhelmed by the rebels and advertised for mercenaries. My unit went in. I started with thirty men and
came back with three." He passed her a plate with a sandwich on it and started making two more for himself. "The
rebels took over the capital and formed a government of
their own. It stood for two months before outside troops
joined forces with the overthrown government, moved in
and took back possession of their country. Before they did,
ten thousand people were shot or blown up in the streets."

"I'm sure I wouldn't make a good soldier, even if
Harley thinks he would," she remarked somberly.

"I wanted to make enough money to retire while I

was still a young man," he mused. "I planned to come back home, buy a ranch, get married and settle down." He finished his own sandwiches and took a sip of his iced tea. "It almost worked. But along the way, I helped a government agency get hard evidence on that drug lord Lopez," he said, searching her eyes. "As I mentioned a while back, he had my house in Wyoming set on fire. The hitch was, my son was supposed to be rescued before the incendiary device was placed. Lopez's henchman didn't think one kid more or less would matter." He traced an invisible pattern on his coffee mug. "The only consolation I had was that Lopez had the assassin eliminated for that slipup. He doesn't kill children."

"I'm so sorry," she murmured, watching him.

"So am I. But all the regrets in the world won't bring back that little boy."

His face was harder than rock. She sketched it with her eyes. "You can help me take care of my little boy."

He glanced at her. "What makes you think it's a little boy?"

"Wishful thinking, I guess. I love baseball and soccer and working around the ranch. I know girls can do those things, too, but I'd love a son."

"You'd love whatever you get," he chided.

"Yes. I would." She grimaced.

"What's the matter."

"I don't know." She laughed nervously. "I have these mild cramps sometimes. I read a book about being pregnant, and it said some women have fleeting cramps during early pregnancy."

He scowled. "That doesn't sound good."

She picked up her sandwich. "Maybe it's just nerves. It's been a rough few weeks."

"Sure it has. But if those cramps get any worse, you go see a doctor."

"I will."

After lunch, he took her out to the huge, airy barn to see Puppy Dog, who was comfortably contained in a huge stall with a drain in the concrete floor, and fresh wheat straw making a comfortable place for him to sleep.

"Hello, Puppy Dog," she said, going into the stall to pet the frisky, enormous puppy. "Did you miss me?" She glanced past him at the clean containers of dog food and water, and the dog toys liberally scattered along the wall. "Maybe not, considering all the toys."

"Dogs need something to play with. Keeps them active and healthy. I got half a dozen for Bob, too."

"Bob?"

He motioned to her. She gave Puppy Dog a last hug and went out of the stall. He whined for a minute and then went back to pick up a ball he liked.

In the stall next door was a huge white-and-tan collie with an intelligent face and soft brown eyes. There were still traces of malnutrition in the coat, but Bob was beginning to shape up into a beautiful animal.

"He's a doll," she said, smiling at him.

"*She's* a doll."

She hesitated. Turned. Raised her eyebrows.

"*She's* a doll," he repeated.

"Bob is not a female name…"

"If a boy can be named Sue, a girl dog can be named Bob."

"You listen to too many Johnny Cash songs," she accused with a chuckle.

"He's great, isn't he?" he asked. "'A Boy Named Sue' was great, but I loved everything he ever recorded."

"I have two of his albums myself," she confessed.

He grinned. "I knew you had good taste."

She liked the way his eyes twinkled when he smiled. He was something of a curiosity around town, because he had a reputation for being a hard case and unsociable. But here, on his home ground, he was relaxed, pleasant, even amusing. She wondered how many people ever got to see this side of him. Probably not many.

"What happened to that man who broke into my house?" she asked abruptly.

"Sheriff's got him locked up," he told her. "We left the crowbar right where it dropped. The man wasn't even wearing gloves. There are enough fingerprints on it to convict him. He'll make bond, of course, and then he'll go home."

"Home?"

He turned toward her. "A man wearing an Armani suit drove up here a few days ago and introduced himself as my new neighbor. There's a honey packing warehouse on my border. But it's not honey they're distributing, if you understand what I mean."

She stilled. "Drugs?"

"Raw cocaine," he replied. "Or, rather, cocaine paste. At least, that's what we suspect they're stockpiling in that warehouse."

"Here, in Jacobsville?" she gasped.

"Right here," he said.

"Then tell the sheriff and let him send some men out to arrest the owners!"

"They won't find cocaine if they do," he said carelessly. "In fact, I'd bet my boots that they'll phone in a tip about themselves just to draw the law out there to check around. And while they're checking, all the honey in the jars will be real honey, and even a drug-sniffing dog won't find a trace of cocaine. Having searched the place once and found nothing, local law enforcement will logically hesitate before they go back out there a second time. At least, not without some concrete evidence of malfeasance. It's easy to get sued for harassment, and believe me, Lopez would howl at the idea of taking our sheriff to court over it."

"You sound very cynical," she told him.

"I know how these people operate. In my checkered past, I've dealt with drug dealers, gun runners, diamond smugglers, hit men…"

Her eyes were growing wider by the second. "You outlaw, you."

"Count on it," he told her. "I did what the job called for. Wars make strange bedfellows. Got to have guns and ammunition, you know, not to mention explosives, communications equipment, medicines. You can't walk into the nearest superstore and buy those."

"You can buy guns," she began.

"Registered guns," he emphasized. "They're required by law to do a background check before they sell a gun, and there's a waiting period. If you know where to go, you can get everything from Uzis to C-4, and no waiting."

"I had no idea," she murmured, shaking her head.

"It's almost impossible to shut these drug cartels

down. They are run on a corporate structure. In a sense, they're multinational corporations. They have a hierarchy, complete with divisional managers and regional distribution networks. When you understand the way they work, you also understand why it's such an uphill battle. You can't arrest every gang member in the country. That's what it would take to stop it. And even then," he added, "there would still be dealers. You know why? Because where there's demand, there's supply. As long as there are people willing to pay for illegal drugs, there will be people who sell them."

"That's very demoralizing," she pointed out.

"Of course it is. But you can't fight a war unless you know the enemy. Every time we shut down one of the cartels, we come one step closer to cutting off the supply. It's discouraging to see the statistics, but there are a lot of dedicated people trying to stop the drug trade. I like to think that one day, they'll succeed."

"I'd be very happy if they could put Mr. Lopez someplace where he can't shoot me," she told him.

He smiled. "At least," he said, "we've got *you* someplace where he can't. Now eat that sandwich. Waste not, want not."

She laughed softly and bit into the sandwich.

CHAPTER SIX

LISA SETTLED IN AT THE RANCH, much to the interest of Cy's cowboys, who walked around with stunned expressions every time they saw her. Most people around Jacobsville had the same attitude, because of Cy's remoteness. Of course, he had dropped the charges against Belinda Craig's rebellious young charge at her summer youth camp when the lad had been caught trespassing on his property. And he'd taken Candy Marshall, that nice young woman from the local cattlemen's association, out to the bar to look for Guy Fenton when he'd been drunk for the last time before he fell in love with Candy and married her. But other than those two incidents, he kept to himself and had little if anything to do with women. Now here was Lisa Monroe, a young widow alone and pregnant, living with him. It was delicious gossip.

As Cy had predicted, the man who was arrested for breaking into Lisa's house had skipped bond and left the country. That didn't let her out of the woods, though, he assured her. Lopez wouldn't stop until he accomplished whatever goal he'd set. Since it was common knowledge that Lisa was staying with Cy, the drug lord wouldn't have far to look to find her.

Also, as Cy had predicted, an anonymous tip led sheriff's deputies to the "honey warehouse" behind Cy's ranch. The flats of jars and the beehives Harley had watched them unload were searched and searched again, by deputies, DEA agents and drug-sniffing dogs. Predictably, they found nothing illegal and went away. It didn't take a genius to realize that it would be hard to get the law enforcement people out there again without vivid concrete evidence of illegal operation. Gossip was that the owners of the new "business" had already threatened a multimillion-dollar lawsuit against the various agencies for just setting foot on the property. Jacobsville was a small town in a small county and its sheriff's department already had such a tiny budget that they hadn't had a raise in two years. The county commissioners went pale at the thought of even a small lawsuit. Like it or not, the sheriff was constrained by politics and capital.

There was one encouraging new development. Rodrigo, the Mexican national who'd successfully infiltrated Lopez's distribution network, managed to get a brief message to Eb Scott, saying that a huge shipment of cocaine paste was scheduled to be shipped into the country soon through Mexico. He had few details as yet, but would keep his eyes and ears open and report anything pertaining to the shipment as soon as he heard it.

Lisa overheard Cy talking with Eb Scott on a shortwave radio—an odd way to communicate, she thought, when the telephone was right beside him.

When he gave his call sign and cut the unit off, she asked him about it.

"This—" he indicated the set "—has a scrambler. It's high-tech, not a conventional shortwave device."

She shook her head as she studied the array of electrical gadgets in the study where Cy did his bookwork. "I've never seen so many strange-looking things."

"Didn't Walt have equipment like this?" he asked curiously.

"If he did, he kept it someplace else." She sighed, thinking of Walt's horrible end and their very brief marriage. Absently her hand went to her belly.

"You were up walking the floor last night," he commented. "Why?"

She shifted. "I had some more cramps," she murmured. But she wasn't too concerned. When she called the doctor she was told it wasn't so unusual to have twinges now and again.

He scowled, watching her. "This isn't the first time you've had cramping. You need to call a doctor."

"I did, day before yesterday," she reminded him. "He said it's a fairly common complaint in early pregnancy, and as long as there's no bleeding there's no reason to worry. Actually I feel better than I have for weeks."

Cy managed not to say that she looked delectable, but she did. Her long, soft hair was loose around her shoulders and even with glasses on, she was pretty. He liked the little tip-tilted nose and the full, soft bow of a mouth. He liked the way she watched him, like a curious little bird, when he worked around the ranch. He especially liked the way she looked in cutoff jeans that showed the curves of her legs up to the thighs, and the way her knit blouse outlined her firm, small breasts. He remembered the feel of her in his arms, the softness of her young mouth, and his whole body clenched. She didn't know, couldn't know, what an ordeal it was for him to be in the same house with her and never touch her. But he didn't want her to feel threatened. She was at risk, and she had no place else to go.

She lifted both eyebrows when she saw that the dark scowl over his green eyes was getting more ominous by the minute. "What's wrong?" she asked.

"Don't go out in the yard like that," he said abruptly.

She looked down at herself and then back at him, puzzled. "I beg your pardon?"

"You heard me." He stood up, towering over her. That was a mistake because now he could see the upper curves of her breasts that her knit blouse left visible. "I don't want my men leering at you." Especially Harley, he thought angrily.

Her eyes kindled with humor. "You're leering at me right now," she pointed out, grinning because he obviously found her attractive. Her knees suddenly felt wobbly.

"I'm not leering. I'm noticing. But I've got some young men with bucking hormones and to them a woman in a steel drum would probably look sexy. Wear jeans and a blouse that buttons to your throat."

"Bucking hormones," she mused. "That's a new one."

"You aren't that naïve," he grumbled. "You were married. You can tell when a man wants you."

Not really, she wanted to tell him. Walt had only slept with her twice, and apparently had to force himself both times. He wasn't really attracted to her physically, and the feeling had been mutual. It wasn't that way with Cy. She looked at him and her knees went weak.

"I'm not wearing a steel drum around the place to do housework," she informed him. "Hormones or no hormones. Heavens, I'm pregnant! Who's going to make a pass at a pregnant woman?"

"Any man under eighty who sees you dressed like that," Cy said flatly. "Up to and including me."

Her heart jumped into her throat as her eyes lifted to his and were captured. She felt the breath rush past her parted lips as the look intensified, making her feel odd in the strangest places, even more strongly than the night at the opera. She remembered the taste of his mouth on hers, and no matter how disloyal it might have been to her late husband, she wanted it again.

"Would you really?" she asked.

He looked uncomfortable. "We were talking about how you dressed. When you go outside around the men, don't wear shorts and low-cut blouses."

"Are you telling me that grown men can't control themselves and I have to go around in a coat all summer to keep from disturbing them?" she wanted to know. "That's not fair."

"Oh, hell, of course it's not fair! But men are going to look when there's something to see. All the legislation in the world won't kill a basic human instinct, and that one is hundreds of thousands of years old!"

Her eyes dropped to his hard mouth and she remembered, not for the first time, how delicious it felt when he kissed her. Then she felt guilty for even the thought. She was forgetting Walt, something that Cy hadn't. He hadn't touched her again since she moved in. He was respecting her husband's death. She was sorry about Walt, but when she got close to Cy, her emotions were all over the place.

"Harley seems to spend a lot of time in the house lately," he remarked unexpectedly.

"He gathers the eggs for me," she replied, fighting down the excitement she felt as his green gaze slid over her once again. "Ever since you found that chicken snake in the henhouse, I've been nervous about putting my hand in the nests."

"We moved the chicken snake into the barn," he reminded her.

"Well, it isn't in handcuffs or anything, now is it?" she demanded. "It can go wherever it wants to, and I've noticed that snakes seem to feel violent attractions to anyone who's scared of them."

"In that case, I don't suppose even the house is safe."

She immediately started looking around her feet and he burst out laughing.

"Never mind," he said on a sigh. "I guess Harley's better than a snake, at that."

"I know he isn't what he pretends to be," she replied with a smile. "But he's nice. Besides," she added with a calculating look that he missed, "isn't he helping to keep an eye on those people who set up the honey warehouse next door to you?"

He didn't like that, not one bit. Eb had agreed to let Harley spy on the drug dealers if he kept his mouth shut. Quite obviously he'd been bragging about his exploits to Lisa.

"Did he tell you that?" he asked quietly.

She didn't quite trust the look in his eyes. She didn't want to get Harley in trouble. On the other hand, she didn't like telling lies.

"He mentioned that he was watching them to make sure the bees didn't threaten your purebred cattle," she said, which was the truth. Or, at least, what Harley had told her.

"I see." He relaxed visibly and she knew she'd said the right thing. She wondered why he was so concerned about bees, when plenty of people around Jacobsville kept them. Maybe he had a hidden fear of flying insects.

Cy's green eyes narrowed. Harley was young, in his late twenties, and despite his bravado, in peak physical condition. Cy was thirty-five and scarred, inside and out. Perhaps Lisa couldn't help liking the younger man. And he had been kind to her.

"If you'd rather I asked someone else to fetch the eggs, I can," she began, trying to find a way to erase that dark scowl on his lean face.

"Of course not," he said at once. "Why should I mind?"

He left her wondering about that, and she went back to what she'd been doing.

TWO DAYS LATER, CY CAME into the kitchen and found Harley holding Lisa's hand in the living room.

Both of them turned and jerked at his sudden appearance. Harley's high cheekbones colored as Cy's green eyes glittered at him like a poisonous snake uncoiling.

"Hi, boss!" he said with forced enthusiasm. "I was, uh, just showing Lisa...Miss...Mrs. Monroe how to break a hold."

"Yes, he was," Lisa said quickly. She had on those same tight jeans and a yellow sweater with a vee neck that was much too low when she bent over. Cy's unsmiling scrutiny made her feel as if she'd just committed adultery. She'd put on the outfit deliberately, not for

Harley, but for Cy. He hadn't been near her until now. Harley had.

"I'd better get back to the garage now, I guess," Harley said, still flushed. He was wearing a white T-shirt and jeans with a red rag sticking out of his back pocket. "I'm overhauling the cattle truck, boss."

"Good. Hadn't you better go do it?" Cy asked with a bite in his voice that he seldom used these days. He looked dangerous, something Harley noted with surprise.

"Sure thing!" Harley went through the kitchen and out the back door without another word.

"He really was showing me how to get out of a hold," she told Cy with her hands on her hips.

Cy moved toward her, too jealous to think properly. "Was he now? And you've learned the lesson? Show me. Let's see you get out of this hold!"

He had her around the waist and flush against every line of his lean, powerful body before she could speak. She opened her mouth to protest and his lips claimed hers, hungry and rough and demanding.

She wanted to fight. She really did. But the closeness of him, the warmth, the strength of him drained her of every semblance of protest. With a tiny little cry, she slid her arms under his and pushed as close as she could get, answering that hard kiss with all the pent-up longing of the weeks since he'd touched her. She felt a shudder go through him even as her own body rippled with passion.

He said something against her mouth that she didn't hear, didn't understand. Her mouth pushed up against his, answering the devouring fierceness of his hard lips. It wasn't a practiced sensuous kiss at all. It was flash-fire need, hunger, desire, out of control. It gave her an odd feeling of pride that she could throw him off balance. And as much as it shamed her to admit it even in the privacy of her mind, his jealousy of Harley made her even hungrier for him.

His body began to swell and old instincts jerked him out of her embrace. He stepped back, fighting the desire that tautened every muscle he had. The unexpected explosion left him shocked and uncertain.

They were both breathing unsteadily, staring at each other more like combatants than lovers.

"I don't like Harley touching you," he said bluntly, bristling with possessive instincts he hadn't known he had.

"I noticed." She sounded breathless.

His green eyes slid down her body and back up again with desire and possession equally mixed. "You're pregnant."

She nodded. Somewhere deep in her mind she wished it was Cy's baby. That was disloyal to Walt and she should be ashamed. Her hand went protectively to her waistline.

He muttered something under his breath and stepped back. "I shouldn't have touched you," he bit off. "God knows, I'm trying not to! I might manage it if you'd stop tempting me with tight jeans and shirts cut to the navel in front!"

So that was why he'd kept his distance. She was pregnant and he felt that he should be trying to take care of her, not make love to her. But he wanted her. She knew it in every cell of her body. It made her glow with new delight; with hope.

He got his breath back and glared at her. "Harley's fixing the truck. Make sure he stays out of here. If you don't tell him, I will, and I won't be diplomatic."

She wasn't offended by the possessive note in his deep voice. She liked it. "All right, Cy."

His eyes narrowed. Her compliance, unexpected, knocked the fire off his temper. "Stay inside and keep the doors locked."

"Okay."

"Don't assume that you're safe just because Harley's in the garage," he added tautly. "He isn't half as savvy as he thinks he is, and he's never dealt with men like Lopez."

"Okay," she repeated with a smile.

He drew in a heavy breath. "There's a loaded pistol in my middle desk drawer. Just in case."

"I'll remember."

Her mouth was swollen from the pressure of his, and it gave him a feeling of pride to see her disheveled and flustered because of him. He didn't smile, but his eyes did.

"Are you leaving?" she asked breathlessly.

"Yes." He dragged his eyes away from her to check his watch. "I've got to drive up to Kingsville to see a man about some new bulls."

She knew where he was going the minute he mentioned the town, and her soft sigh was all too audible. "I went on a tour of that ranch once, with Dad," she said. "It made our little operation look like a milkmaid enterprise. They had some beautiful breeding stock."

"I like Santa Gertrudis cattle," he said. "No better place to buy them than where the foundation herd originated." His eyes narrowed again as he studied her. "While I'm gone, don't go out of the house for any reason. Harley will have the house in sight all the time, and I've got surveillance equipment linked to Eb Scott's place. If anything happens that Harley can't handle, Eb can be here in five minutes. You aren't afraid by yourself?"

"By myself?" she exclaimed. "Cy, have you noticed those fifteen cowboys who work for you…?"

"Only six of them work here full-time. And none of them are around the ranch house for most of the day, except early in the morning and late in the afternoon," he told her. "Harley's working on one of the cattle trucks, which is the only reason that he'll be nearby. If you need him, push the intercom button and he'll come right up." He indicated the button next to the wall phone in the dining room. He hated having to tell her that. He hated the idea of Harley anywhere near her. "And keep all the doors locked."

"You're worried," she gathered.

"I've heard a few things. Yes, I'm worried. Humor me."

She shrugged and smiled up at him. "Okay, boss."

His eyebrow lifted and he smiled back. "Oh, that sounds sweet," he drawled. "Pity I know it's just lip service. You smile and nod your head when I tell you, for your own good, not to do something. And then you go right out and do it the minute my back's turned."

"It always worked with Dad," she mused. "It's a waste of time to argue with some men," she added.

He reached for his hat on the wall rack. "And some women," he countered. "Watch yourself."

"You do that, too," she returned smartly. "You're not on Lopez's good list, either."

He propped his hat on his head as the back door opened to admit Harley. He glanced at Lisa from under the wide brim. "Yes, but Lopez doesn't like to take unnecessary chances, and he's already had one bad brush with the law," he began as Harley's footsteps became audible behind him. "He won't come here unless he gets pretty desperate..."

"Because he knows I'm here, Mrs. Monroe," Harley interrupted with an irrepressible grin at his boss and their houseguest. "Nobody's going to lay a finger on you while I'm on the job."

"Of course," Lisa said and didn't dare look at Cy.

"I just came in to get a soft drink. It's thirsty work. You, uh, don't mind, boss?" he asked Cy warily.

"I don't mind," Cy lied. "But don't get careless," he told his young foreman, and with more than usual caution. "Lopez won't."

Harley dismissed Lopez and his entire organization with a flick of his hand. "All the same, he won't come around here."

Cy wanted to argue the point, but the younger man was in a concrete mind-set and he wouldn't listen to reason. He'd just have to hope that Harley wouldn't do something stupid.

"I'll be back late. Remember to keep the doors locked," he cautioned Lisa.

"You bet."

He left rather reluctantly. Harley got himself a cold drink out of the refrigerator and paused at the back door. Lisa went to the kitchen counter and got out a bowl and a knife and some potatoes and began peeling them for potato salad. "I wanted to make sure I hadn't got you in trouble," Harley said sheepishly. "Mr. Parks was pretty hot when he came in."

"It's all right," she assured him with a smile. "He's protective of me because of the baby," she added.

Harley grimaced. "I should have realized that. He isn't a man who has much to do with women, you see." He shrugged. It had seemed like violent jealousy to Harley, but now Mr. Parks's ill temper seemed justified. He wouldn't want anybody making passes at her when she was pregnant. Of course, he added silently as he looked at her, she did seem somewhat flustered and her mouth was swollen. He wondered…

"Don't you want that soft drink in a glass with some ice?" she asked. His scrutiny was making her nervous.

"No, thanks, this is fine. Well, if you need me, just call, Mrs. Monroe. I'll be trying to find the oil leak in that engine."

He looked as if he'd found several, she mused, judging from all the black stains on his once-white sweatshirt. It never ceased to amaze her that Harley always found something white to put on when he was going to do a dirty job.

"I know where the intercom button is," she assured him. "But I don't think I'll need to use it."

"You never know. I'll lock the door as I go out. See you later."

"Sure."

He locked the door and moved slowly toward the garage. Lisa watched him walk back to the garage with a slight frown between her eyes. Cy was unusually worried about Lopez, and it made her uneasy. Surely the man wasn't going to risk having any more men picked up by the sheriff. After all, he'd lost two in the midnight raid on Lisa's house that had prompted Cy to bring her here to stay with him.

On the other hand, she had to admit, if the man based

his reputation on keeping his word, he couldn't afford not to make good on a threat. But she was fairly certain that Lopez was long gone. Otherwise why would Cy have gone off in the first place?

Reassured, she went to the kitchen, put Lopez forcefully out of her thoughts and peeled the rest of the potatoes.

Harley finished most of his repairs on the truck and came back into the house for another drink, liberally stained with grease and a noticeable cut on the back of one lean hand. It was bleeding. There was even a little grease in his crew-cut sandy hair.

"Here," Lisa said at once, leading him to the kitchen sink. "Wash that with antibacterial soap while I find a bandage."

"It's nothing much, Mrs. Monroe," he protested, but very weakly.

She smiled to herself as she fetched adhesive bandages from the kitchen cabinet and began peeling one apart to cover the deep scratch after it was clean.

"I wish you'd been with us in Africa," he observed wryly, his blue eyes twinkling. "Several of us got banged up out in the bush."

"In the bush? With the lions?" she exclaimed.

He held out his dried hand for her to put on the bandage. "Didn't see any lions," he remarked. "But there were plenty of guerrillas. Not the furry kind, either." He sighed and smiled dreamily. "That's the life, Mrs. Monroe, fighting for principles and a king's ransom in loot. When I get another two or three training courses under my belt, that's what I'm going to do; I'm going back to Africa to make my fortune."

"Or get yourself shot," she observed.

"Not a chance. I'm too handy with close quarter weapons." He looked as if he could strut sitting down as he said it. "My instructor said he'd never seen anybody who was such a natural in martial arts. And I can throw a knife, too."

"It wouldn't do you much good if the other guy had a gun, would it?" she asked innocently.

"It isn't so hard to disarm a man, if you know how," he said confidently. "They taught us a lot of tricks. I guarantee there isn't a man alive who could threaten me with a gun. I know my business."

Lisa almost winced at the certainty in his tone. He was young, probably not much older than she was, and she couldn't help thinking that a little knowledge could be a dangerous thing.

"Thanks for patching me up," he told her with a grin. "I found the leak. Now all I have to do is put all the parts back on the truck without having any left over."

She laughed as she put away the bandages. "I'd have bagsful left over," she mused. "I can cook and work horses and cattle, but I don't know a thing about engines."

"My dad's a mechanic," he told her. "He has his own garage. I grew up learning how to fix things. It comes in handy on a ranch this size, even though we have a full-time mechanic on the payroll." He shook his head. "It must cost a fortune to run a place like this. I guess Mr. Parks inherited his."

She went back to her potatoes, her head down as she asked, "You don't think he might have worked for it?"

"Not many professions that pay the kind of money he has, from what I've heard," he said. "Besides, he's not exactly a risk-taker. He doesn't do much of the heavy work around here and he really favors that left arm from time to time. I guess it still hurts him sometimes."

"I guess." She didn't add that he might change his mind about Cy if he ever saw him dressed in black and carrying an automatic weapon.

"Thanks for the first aid," he told her as he retrieved another soft drink from the refrigerator and closed it. "Better get back to work."

He went out and the door locked behind him. Lisa forced herself not to think about that hungry kiss she and Cy shared in the living room or if Cy was going to draw back into his shell again. He was a complex and attractive man, but she seemed to be off-limits. Pity. They had so much in common....

CHAPTER SEVEN

IT WAS LATE AFTERNOON when Lisa heard a truck pull up out by the barn. She was sure it was Cy. Without thinking, she got up from the kitchen table where she'd been rearranging a messy kitchen drawer and went right out the back door.

It wasn't Cy. It was three men, all foreign-looking. Harley saw them and came out of the garage, wiping his hands on a red work cloth.

"Can I help you boys?" he asked with faint menace.

"We are looking for Mr. Parks," the flashily dressed one said with an ear-to-ear grin.

"He's gone to Kingsville to look at bulls," Harley said obligingly. "I don't know when he'll be back."

"How convenient," the man drawled, and pulled an automatic weapon from under his jacket.

Harley froze in place and his jaw dropped.

Lisa realized the danger immediately. She closed and locked the back door and ran to Cy's study, locking herself inside. She grabbed the mike of the shortwave set, already positioned to the Scott ranch, and gave out a Mayday call.

"Stay in the house," Eb's calm but very hushed voice came over the air instantly. "Cy's on his way."

He left before she could ask what he meant. She didn't know whether to lock herself in and wait, or go to a window and try to see what had happened to poor Harley. She felt guilty that she hadn't been able to do anything for him, but she was one person against three men, one of whom was dangerously armed.

In the end, she grabbed the loaded pistol Cy had told her he kept in his center desk drawer and went cautiously down the hall. She peered out the curtain that covered the upper, glassed portion of the kitchen door. Harley was in the grip of a man at least his physical equal, a pistol at his throat. One of the other men was looming with that automatic weapon and she just glimpsed the third wandering into the garage, out of sight.

She ground her teeth together and held the huge .45 automatic pistol tighter, wondering what she should do. She'd never fired a pistol in her life, but if she had to use it, she thought she could. Shivering with nerves, her heart pounding, her mouth dry, she heard the sound of a truck approaching very fast. Cy's big red Expedition roared up in the yard. He was out of it seconds after the engine died.

But it wasn't the Cy she was used to seeing. He walked slowly toward the two visitors in plain sight, his tall figure bent slightly forward, and he was cradling his burned left arm in his right hand.

"You are Cy Parks," the man with the automatic weapon called in a cold tone.

"Yes," Cy replied quietly. He glanced at Harley, who was red-faced and nervous, held securely in the grip of the second man.

"We want the woman," the flashily dressed visitor continued. "You will bring her out to us. Now."

"She's a widow. She's pregnant," Cy began.

"This is nothing to us," the man replied. "We were told to bring the woman back. It will cost us our lives not to comply with the instructions we were given."

Cy sighed audibly. "I'll go get her," he said with resignation.

"Mr. Parks!" Harley burst out, horrified. "Man, you can't…you can't let them have Mrs. Monroe!"

"They'll shoot us if we don't, son," Cy told the other man in a subdued tone that matched his bent stance. As he spoke, he let go of his burned arm and let it dangle at his side. The right hand moved, just a fraction, but his limping posture had the full attention of the armed men. They didn't notice the movement under his long sleeve. "You might let poor old Harley go," he added. "He just works for me."

"Let a trained mercenary loose on the three of us?" The man laughed. "We heard him talking to the woman in the kitchen about his exploits in Africa."

Which meant, Cy deduced, that they had the house bugged. He'd have to do something about that, and quickly. He glanced at Harley and prayed that the younger man wouldn't panic and do something stupid.

"It was a lie. Honest!" Harley swallowed hard. "I'm not a merk. I'm just a simple, working cowboy…!"

"Why, of course he is. And do I look like any sort of threat to armed men?" Cy asked softly. "I mean, look at me. I'm just a poor cripple."

Harley grimaced. It hurt him to see poor old Mr. Parks grovel like that. If only he could get that pistol away from his throat. He might be able to do something to save Mrs. Monroe and his boss! His fears were still present but subsiding a little as he realized the danger his boss and Lisa were in. He had to conquer the fear. He knew what to do. Even if he'd had little training, he remembered the moves. And he'd been an army ranger when he was in the service, only a short time before he came to work for Cy Parks. He wasn't a coward. He could do what he needed to do, to protect Cy and Lisa. He could do it. His head lifted and new purpose narrowed his eyes as he watched the armed men.

The man with the automatic weapon shrugged. "I see that you are injured. But this man told the woman that he had commando training and would not hesitate to use it," he told Cy. "Am I to believe now that he is harmless?"

"No," Cy drawled. "It's more than enough if you believe I am," he said enigmatically and glanced at Harley. "You just stay put, Harley," he added in a tone that made Harley frown. "I'll just go get Mrs. Monroe…" His head turned abruptly to the left of the gunman and he pointed. "Good God, look at that!!"

The man with the automatic weapon reacted predictably and was diverted for a few precious seconds. It was enough. Cy's hand moved so fast that his knife was in the man's shoulder before he could turn his head back, causing him to drop the automatic weapon as he groaned in shock and pain. Even as that knife hit the target, Cy whirled and sent a second knife slicing through the air. It hit the man holding the pistol at Harley's neck, pinning his forearm, pistol, sleeve and all, to the wood of the barn wall behind him. The man cried out and Harley ducked and got out of the way immediately.

Green eyes blazing, Cy rushed forward, aimed an explosive high kick at the first man's stomach, bringing him down instantly. He fell, trying to extricate the knife from his shoulder at the same time, with little success.

"There's…another man…in there!" Harley called urgently through his shock.

"There was." A deep chuckle accompanied the words. Eb Scott came out of the barn with a miserable-looking man in denims held at gunpoint. "He made a fatal error. Never turn your back to a dark corner. Nice timing, Cy."

Cy didn't answer. He jerked up the automatic weapon and spared a glance for the groaning man on the ground and the other one, pinned to the wall of the barn.

"I didn't want to do it like this," Cy said calmly, walking to the man his second knife had pinned to the barn wall. "But if you're going to set a trap, it's best done on your home ground and in your own time. Oh, shut up for God's sake," he growled at his victim as he jerked the knife out and wiped it on the man's shirt-sleeve. "You're barely nicked! When you get a Bowie knife sticking out of your arm, you can complain."

Harley was still staring at his boss with wide eyes. He hadn't said a single word. He felt his head to make sure it was where he'd left it.

"You all right, Harley?" Cy asked curtly.

"Shh…sure," he stammered.

"I'll just check on Lisa." Cy strode off toward the house.

Harley stared after his boss as if he'd never seen him before. "Did you see that?" Harley asked Eb Scott. "Did you see it? He had the second knife in the air even before the first one hit its target!"

"You said he was no threat!" the assailant with the formerly pinned forearm growled at the man in the suit. Both were holding their wounds.

"I thought he was crippled!" the flashily dressed man growled. The knife was still in his shoulder, and he didn't dare pull it out for fear it might hemorrhage at withdrawal.

"So did I," Harley murmured, but only Eb heard him.

"Cy's not quite what he seems," was all Eb had to say about it.

ON THE PORCH, LISA HAD watched with surprise and disbelief as Cy easily took care of the two armed men, while Harley stood shellshocked nearby. If she'd ever worried about him, her mind rested easier after she saw the ease with which he subdued the armed assailants. She watched him with covetous, protective eyes, almost limp with relief. She'd been so worried that he might die right in front of her eyes. She opened the door as Cy mounted the steps and rushed out to throw herself against his chest, oblivious to his shocked delight. She was still holding the gun in one hand.

He took it from her, keeping the other arm around her, and put the safety back on. "Were you going to come out shooting and rescue me?" he asked with a grin.

"If I got the chance, I was," she said huskily, clinging harder. "I certainly wasn't going to cower in the house and let them kill you."

His eyes were warm with affection as he lifted his dark head to search her flushed face. "Nice to know I can count on backup when I need it," he told her, tracing a soft pattern down her flushed cheek.

She smiled at him and only looked away when she heard sirens and saw two sheriff's cars pull up in the driveway with their lights flashing. "Speaking of backup," she gestured. "Did you plan this?"

He shrugged. "Eb planned it and convinced me to go along," he said quietly. "All those surveillance gadgets paid for themselves this afternoon. Eb was already in the barn when I left here. He waited to act after the guns were drawn because he didn't want to get Harley killed." He shook his head as he saw Harley standing morose and miserable against the barn with his arms folded while the deputies handcuffed the three men. Barely two minutes later, an ambulance joined the patrol cars. "What I didn't know was that Lopez had the house bugged," he added curtly. "When we get these guys in custody, I'm going to sweep the house and get rid of them."

"They can hear what we do in the house?" she asked worriedly.

He glanced down at her and knew she meant what they were doing in the living room before he left. He smiled slowly. "Not all of it," he murmured wickedly. "Probably they only had listening devices in the kitchen, since we spend so much time in there."

"Oh." She sighed with relief.

"I'd better go and have a word with the deputies," Cy told her. "You okay?"

She grinned. "Never better. Are you?"

"Can't hurt a weed," he replied, winked and walked back down the steps.

Eb and Cy explained what had happened to the deputies. Cy agreed to swear out a warrant so that the three men could be held. He was furious that Lopez had dared to send men onto his own place after Lisa. He wasn't ever going to get the chance to do that again. He swore it.

As the two wounded prisoners were being loaded up in the ambulance and the other one confined in the patrol car for the trip to jail, Cy joined Harley at the barn door.

"I'm all hot air," Harley said with cold self-contempt. He couldn't meet the older man's eyes. "All that damned bragging about what I could do, and how I could take care of everybody. And look at me! I was taken by surprise and overpowered by a man half my size. I'm a fraud, Mr. Parks. You ought to fire me on the spot."

Cy only smiled. Harley was showing the first signs of wisdom. And even if he'd been overpowered, he'd conquered whatever fears he had. Cy knew that the younger man's pride was in shreds at being surprised and captured. He'd been in similar situations himself. No need to rub it in, just because he'd overreacted at Harley holding Lisa's hand.

"If I fire you, who's going to gather Lisa's eggs every morning?" Cy asked.

Harley couldn't believe he'd actually heard that droll question. He forced his shamed eyes up, and found his boss's eyes twinkling.

"You don't want to fire me?" he asked.

"Not today," Cy replied. "Get back in there and finish getting that cattle truck fixed. We'll need it tomorrow to haul calves."

"It's finished," Harley said with a faint smile. "I was just putting it back together when those guys drove up and caught me off guard."

Harley still felt a little disoriented. Mr. Parks, on the other hand, didn't have a hair out of place and seemed supremely calm. Despite the cool weather, Harley felt perspiration on his forehead. He wiped his sweaty brow on his arm and let out a heavy breath. He even managed a grin. "I guess you learned how to throw a knife when you were in the military. You, uh, were in the military?"

"Somewhat."

"Well, it was amazing, what you did with those knives," Harley continued. "That's some aim you've got, Mr. Parks."

"I get in a little practice now and then."

Harley moved away from the barn. "You sure had those guys foxed about how helpless you were," he said, chuckling. "They bought every word."

"To their cost," Cy said easily, without breaking stride. "You never underestimate an adversary, if you want to live."

"You've, uh, been in a few fights then?"

Cy's green eyes were enigmatic as he glanced back at the younger man. "Stop fishing, Harley. Get that truck running."

He turned again and started toward the house. Harley watched him go with raging curiosity. On an impulse he didn't even understand, Harley picked up the pistol his captor had dropped where it lay forgotten in the straw. He tossed it toward Cy Parks's back.

As if he sensed danger, Cy whirled immediately and caught the weapon in midair. He had it cocked and leveled at Harley's nose in the space between one heartbeat and the next. Harley stopped breathing as he looked down the barrel for seconds that seemed like hours.

Cy cursed harshly and lowered the gun. "If you ever do that again, so help me, I'll shoot you in the foot, Harley!" he growled, furious. He snapped on the safety and walked toward the sheriff's deputies to leave the weapon with them.

Harley let out the breath he'd been holding. He'd served two years in the army himself, in the rangers. He didn't know a single man who could have done what Cy Parks just had. That was a sort of training that men only got in some elite fighting force, and it wasn't regular military. He forced himself to walk back to the garage without casting another glance at his enigmatic boss. He felt as if his legs had turned to rubber.

LISA WAS UNEASY ALL NIGHT. She kept hearing noises. She dreamed that Cy was in front of the man with the machine gun, but that he hadn't managed to throw those knives in time. She woke up crying, in a cold sweat.

The door opened, the light came on and Cy stood over her, dressed in pajama bottoms with his broad, hairy, scarred bare chest. His dark hair was tousled, his eyes narrow with concern.

"You screamed," he said.

She sat up in her sweatpants and pullover white cotton T-shirt and hugged her knees. She couldn't quite see him because her glasses were in the drawer of the bedside table. She could imagine how she looked with her eyes red and wet with tears and her long hair tangled all around her.

"Sorry if I woke you," she said miserably. "It's been a rough day."

"For me, too," he replied. "I'm sorry you ever got mixed up in this business."

"So am I, but there's not much we can do about that now." She pushed back her long, sweaty hair. "Now Lopez seems to be after you, too."

"No. He's after you. This was a test run, to see if he could get to you on my ranch."

"He didn't."

"No, he didn't."

"You think he'll try again."

"They say Lopez will follow a man to hell to get even with him," he said quietly. "I believe it."

"What am I going to do? I can't keep on staying here…"

"Why not?"

"Well…"

He came around the side of the bed. "Move over," he said, sitting down beside her on the bedspread. "Now listen. I've got a big house and plenty of room. As long as you're here, right here, I can protect you, and I will. You've got a baby coming and you need someone. There's no reason you can't stay."

She looked worried. She picked at the cover. "Cy, people are already talking about us…"

"They'll stop when we get married."

She didn't seem to breathe for a space of seconds. She looked up at him with a curious mixture of shyness, excitement and pleasure. "Married."

"Married."

She picked at a fingernail while she turned the proposal over in her mind. She was barely widowed. Whatever would people think of her?

"We don't advertise what's going on in this town, but the people who count know that you're staying here because you're in danger," he said quietly. "As for all the rest, if we marry, no one will have any reason for talk. I'm not proposing for any hidden agenda," he added. "We'll have a marriage of convenience. Period."

That was vaguely disappointing, and she hoped she could keep him from seeing how it affected her.

"Okay," she said after a minute. "But you can kick me out when this Lopez thing is over," she added and managed a smile.

"Fair enough," he agreed, his face carefully schooled not to let any hint of emotion show through. "But only if you want to leave by then. I wouldn't make that offer to any other woman. I've had a bad time with marriage. If Lopez hadn't decided to target you, I wouldn't have proposed in the first place."

"I know that," she said.

"Not that you aren't attractive," he said unexpectedly. "I think you know that under different circumstances, you'd be first on the endangered list. I haven't made a secret of the way you affect me. But you're pregnant and a very recent widow. Under the circumstances, it would hardly be appropriate to take advantage of the situation."

He was talking in riddles and she was very puzzled by the look in his eyes when he spoke to her. Odd, how reluctant he sounded to have her leave. But surely he was marrying her for the reasons he'd mentioned. He'd been through his own time of pain. She knew that there must be times when he ached for the child who had died in such a terrible manner. But for whatever reason, he was offering Lisa a marriage of companionship, protection for her baby. She couldn't have turned it down to save her life. Living with him would be heaven, even if he kept her at arm's length.

"Are you sure it's the right thing to do?" she asked worriedly.

"Yes, I am," he said firmly. "And the sooner, the better."

She toyed with a fold of her sweatpants. "I might be in the way."

His chest rose and fell heavily. His eyes narrowed. He looked at her with such hunger that it was blatant when she met his eyes.

Involuntarily she let her knees down. The T-shirt was thin and his eyes went instantly to the thrust of her breasts against it. Her mauve nipples were very noticeable, making soft peaks under the fabric.

His breathing changed. Her own eyes went to that broad chest and she wondered how it would feel against her.

"Don't push your luck," he said in a husky tone. "It's been three years. More than that. I didn't want her after my son was born, and the feeling was mutual."

Her eyes lifted to his. "You want me."

He nodded, very slowly. His eyes went back to the T-shirt and her own roamed over his bare chest like seeking, exploring fingers. In the silence of the bedroom, the sound of their breathing was harsh and loud. She could hear her own heartbeat in her ears, see his at the base of his strong throat.

She shivered and his teeth clenched.

"That baby is just starting to develop," he said, almost choking on his own voice in a throat as dry as desert sand. "And you've had cramping. I won't risk it."

"I wasn't offering, really," she managed unsteadily.

She bit her lower lip and frowned as she searched his lean, hard face. "I don't understand. I never…felt like this. I'm scared."

"Felt like what?" he asked, not at all embarrassed. "Tell me, Lisa."

She flushed. "I can't!" she bit off.

He took her by both arms and pulled her gently across him, so that her head lay in the crook of his powerful arm. His free hand went to her throat and caressed its way under her long, loosened dark blond hair. She relaxed against him helplessly, her breath coming in tiny little jerks as she looked up into his quiet, gentle eyes.

"Then I'll tell you," he said softly. "You want to pull the fabric out of the way and show yourself to me," he whispered. His thumb moved slowly over her parted lips. "You feel hot and swollen all over, and you aren't quite in control. That's what frightens you."

She shivered again. "It wasn't like this with Walt."

His big warm hand slid from her neck down to her collarbone and as he held her wide eyes, it moved blatantly over the hard peak of one small breast and pressed there.

She whimpered, closing her eyes with a faint shudder. Her hand pressed hard into his hair-roughened chest and she leaned her hot face against the cool, hard muscle of his upper arm.

His cheek lay gently against hers. He caressed her almost absently, with a slow, restrained tenderness that made her whole body tremble with passion.

Her nails bit into his chest as the hunger grew with every soft brush of his fingers.

She felt his mouth on her closed eyelids as his hand found the hem of the T-shirt and moved under it. She arched helplessly to the sensuous delight of that expert touch.

He smiled against her mouth as he kissed her very tenderly. All the while his hand explored the softness of her silky skin, arousing a need that made her moan helplessly.

She moved closer, her eyes opening, wide, dazed, soft as a doe's.

He slid the fabric under her chin and looked at the firmness of her young breasts while he traced them. Odd, he thought, that her breasts showed no evidence of a pregnancy that should be approaching its fifth week. He'd seen his wife's body, and he remembered the changes pregnancy made in it. He wondered if women differed in the physical signs.

"I'm very small," she whispered unsteadily.

"Do you think size matters?" he murmured with a wicked, soft smile.

"If it didn't, men wouldn't buy those picture magazines…"

He bent and brushed his mouth against hers. "The men who buy those magazines don't have real women to practice on."

"Is that why?" she asked, laughing breathlessly through her shyness.

"You're just right," he breathed, letting his fingers sketch her body. "And if you weren't five weeks pregnant, I'd do more than talk about it."

"Would you?"

He lifted his head and looked down at the soft thrust of her creamy pink breasts. His eyes narrowed as he imagined the feel of them under his mouth. He felt his body tense with desire. It made him ache.

"You want to put your mouth on me, don't you?" she asked daringly. "I...would let you."

"I know," he said in a choked tone. His eyes met hers. "And what do you think would happen then?"

Her face colored helplessly as images flashed through her whirling mind.

His eyes narrowed. "I haven't wanted a woman for a long time. I want you very badly. Don't make it hard for me to walk away."

She forced herself to breathe slowly, to deny the ache inside her. She was suddenly ashamed of the way she'd behaved, and she grimaced as she tugged her T-shirt down and lifted herself out of his loosening arms.

"I'm sorry," she said without looking at him.

"No need to apologize." He got to his feet. His arousal was noticeable but he didn't turn away. He looked down at her with lingering traces of desire, and she looked at him the same way.

"First, we get married," he said in a subdued tone that didn't match his stormy eyes. "Then we talk to your obstetrician. If it's safe, I'll make love to you. Assuming that you want me to."

"I want you to," she said honestly, avoiding his probing gaze.

"That makes two of us."

She slipped back under the covers and only then lifted her eyes back up to meet his. "I'm glad those men didn't hurt you," she said.

"Harley took it hard," he replied.

"Of course he did. He's not so bad," she added with a smile.

He didn't like hearing her say that. She was young

and she had all the normal urges. He wanted to marry her right away, before Harley got to her. Maybe she'd have felt the same desire for anyone who offered her tenderness. She'd barely been married and she hadn't wanted her husband. She was ripe for an affair. If it happened, it was going to be with him. He wasn't letting Harley near her.

"You look angry," she commented.

He forced a smile. "Frustrated," he said, deliberately letting his gaze slide over her.

"Oh."

"Your breasts aren't swollen," he remarked bluntly, "and your nipples aren't enlarged or dark. Has the doctor explained the normal changes pregnancy will make in them?"

"Well, yes," she said, fighting embarrassment. "I imagine I'm not far enough along for it to show much."

"That makes sense." He moved back to the door. "If you need me, sing out."

"Would you like musical comedy or grand opera?" she mused. "Because I can start right now and save you the trip back to your own bed."

He chuckled softly. "Not yet," he told her deliberately. "First the ring, then the doctor. First things first."

She sighed. "Okay. You're the boss."

"Yes, I am," he mused. "But that won't last much longer, I imagine," he murmured, and left her sitting there with puzzlement all over her face.

CHAPTER EIGHT

A WEEK LATER, with Eb and Sally Scott for witnesses, Cyrus Jonathan Parks married Lisa Jane Taylor Monroe in a quiet civil service in front of a justice of the peace. She wore a simple beige dress and carried a small bouquet of orange autumn maple leaves and yellow chrysanthemums that seemed just right for an autumn wedding.

They'd discussed rings and chose simple gold wedding bands with no ornamentation, just right for a marriage of convenience.

Except that it was more than that. Lisa began to tremble every time she got within five feet of her handsome, taciturn new husband. He knew that she wanted him. He wanted her, too. But despite the flare of desire between them, all he'd really offered her was a refuge, not love eternal. He'd said quite bluntly that he wouldn't have married her at all unless she'd been in danger, and he didn't plan to stay married to her after Lopez was arrested or subdued. She had to remember that.

There was time for a small reception at the Jacobsville Methodist Church fellowship hall, where friends still suffering from belated shock at the sudden wedding of Jacobsville's most reclusive rancher had laden a table with delicious tidbits while cakes for both bride and groom graced a side table. Cy and Lisa were required to cut the bride's cake together and share the first piece. As she looked up into his eyes, the photographer Cy had hired took a photograph so revealing that when Lisa would see it a week later, she would be too embarrassed to show it to anyone. She'd looked like a woman absolutely besotted with the man beside her.

They went back to his ranch together after the reception, and she went inside quickly, to spare him the humiliation of not being able to carry her over the threshhold with his damaged arm. Incredibly, the well-meant action ignited an argument that had explosive consequences.

The front door slammed audibly as Lisa went down the hall. He caught up with her in the bedroom she'd been occupying.

Green eyes blazing, he closed the door behind him. And locked it.

"Why didn't you paint a sign and have it hung on the front door?" he asked in a menacing tone. "We both know I have limited use of this," he extended his left arm. "But I could have carried you over the threshold. You aren't exactly a challenging weight!"

She just stared at him, stunned by the furious anger in his lean face. "I was only trying to spare your pride," she said tightly. "I never meant to insult you."

He threw off his jacket and tossed it onto a chair. His strong fingers went to his tie. That followed the jacket. He unbuttoned his shirt, all the while walking deliberately toward Lisa.

She'd never had cause to be afraid of him. She wasn't

now, although her knees felt weak as water under her. He was devastatingly attractive to her, and if her heartbeat was shaking her, it wasn't out of fear. She wondered if he knew.

His hands caught her by the waist and brought her against him firmly. His glittery eyes searched her wide, surprised ones. His fingers contracted. He wasn't behaving rationally, and it wasn't much of a surprise. He'd gone without a woman for over three years and here was Lisa, his wife, who made him hungry as he'd never been hungry before. He thought briefly of the child she was carrying, and hesitated.

"Did you speak to the doctor about the baby…?"

"Since I haven't had any more cramps, he said it's all right," she said huskily, drowning in the strong arms enfolding her.

She was hardly aware of meeting him halfway when his head bent. He kissed her slowly, softly, and then with a hunger that made fires in her blood. She reached up on tiptoe to press hard against his strong body, clung as the kiss deepened and became slow and hungry, devouring her soft mouth.

Her submissive moan made him wild. He lifted her quite easily with his right arm, catching her neatly under her knees with the left one, and carried her to the bed with his mouth still demanding and rough on her eager lips.

It was broad daylight. The sun filtered in through the blinds, but she didn't feel inhibited by the light. Walt had always wanted the darkness, but Cy didn't seem to care at all. He caressed her out of her neat beige dress and the things under it, his mouth ardent and expert in a way she'd never experienced with her husband. Walt had always been in a hurry. Cy wasn't. Long before his shirt came off, she was twisting under him in a veritable orgy of pleasure, her nails biting into his shoulders, her gasps audible as each pleasure was eclipsed by a new one. It was like the night he'd proposed, but without his stoic restraint. He didn't seem to mind her knowing that he was desperate to have her, although he was patient and tender and restrained.

She wouldn't have believed that a man who'd gone without a woman for so long could be so patient. He acted as if he had all the time in the world. He laughed softly at her obvious desire, but he didn't satisfy it. His mouth worked its way lazily down her soft body to her breasts while she trembled in the wake of new and mysterious pleasures. She seemed to hang in midair as his mouth hovered over the hard peak of her breast. Then, tenderly, his mouth worked its way completely over it and began to suckle her, and she cried out in surprised ecstasy.

Her headlong response delighted him. She'd mentioned once that her husband hadn't been patient, and now he was willing to believe it. Despite her marriage and her pregnancy, she acted like a woman who'd never been intimate with anyone. Her ardent clinging, her soft cries of pleasure, her trembling made him feel more like a man than ever before. His own wife had hated this part of marriage, hated her child, hated him. In the old days, before his marriage, there had never been a shortage of women. But since he'd been widowed, there had been no one. Not until now. And this soft, eager woman beneath him was his wife. He groaned harshly against her breast as a wave of hot pleasure swept over him. His control was suddenly gone.

He wrestled the rest of his clothes off and jerked back the bedspread, moving Lisa onto the cool, crisp sheets. His body covered hers, feeling the heat and eagerness of it. He heard her faint gasp and felt the ripple of her soft body as she moved to accommodate him.

"Cy...!" she whispered, her nails gripping his upper arms.

His mouth closed her lips as he eased down. "Don't be afraid. I'll be careful with you," he whispered, reading the helpless fear in that soft exclamation. "Very, very careful. I won't hurt the baby."

That wasn't at all what she was thinking, to her shame, but she was too shy to tell him that she wasn't sure her slender body could adjust to his. He wasn't made like Walt, she could tell...

She gasped again as he moved lazily and a violent spasm of pleasure shook her entire body. Her nails bit into him and when he lifted his head to look at her, she knew her eyes must be like saucers. She was aware of her legs relaxing, her slender hips arching, her body trying to incite him to repeat that lazy movement of his body, to give her that shock of ecstasy again.

His soft, possessive eyes met hers. "Is this what you want me to do?" he whispered lazily, and he smiled as he moved and she tensed again, trembling.

She couldn't get the words out, but he didn't seem to need them. He shifted their positions and the next time he moved, she closed her eyes on a shuddering moan of exquisite pleasure. Never like this. She hadn't dreamed that a woman could feel such...!

He heard her voice, barely audible, pleading with him, sobbing at his throat. He was near the end of his endurance, but from the sound of her, he needn't be patient any longer. He caught her mouth firmly under his and moved deliberately, roughly, quickly, feeling her body take up the rhythm and echo it. The silken brush of her skin took the last of his control. He could feel her going up the spiral with him, he could hear the pleasure in her choked sobs, feel it in her clinging hands and arching body, in the grip of her long, elegant legs as they curled around his and tightened in spasms.

It was more than he'd hoped for. She fell with him into the white-hot heat of ecstasy, throbbed with him as reality became nothing more than a glimpse of light somewhere in the distance. He felt his body stiffen even as hers convulsed under the pressure of him. It was like being buried in warm, soft velvet...

"No!" she cried out as the pleasure fell away from her just as she'd grasped it. "No, no...!"

"What is it?" he asked huskily at her ear, his body shivering a little in the aftermath as he lay heavily above her. "Did I hurt you?"

"It didn't last," she sobbed, clinging. "I couldn't... make it last...!"

He understood at once. His mouth moved softly over her damp eyes, across her wet cheek and down to her parted lips where her breath came in husky little jerks. "Pleasure like that would be lethal in long doses," he whispered into her lips. He bit at her lower lip gently and then rubbed his mouth over it in soft little caresses.

She moved experimentally and felt the intimate pressure of him. Her eyes lifted to his, a little shy, and very soft.

His thumb brushed her lower lip while he searched her eyes in a silence so profound that she could hear their accelerated heartbeats.

"It was like making love to a virgin," he said in a deep, slow tone.

"It was like being one," she whispered honestly. Her fingers smoothed over the hard muscles in his upper arms. The one that had been damaged was only noticeable from the elbow to the hand, she observed. The rest of him, despite a few scars and depressions, was absolutely perfect.

He brushed back the loose strands of blond hair and, impulsively, took all the hairpins out to let it fall around her shoulders.

"That's better," he murmured, smiling.

They were still intimately joined, and her eyes searched over his lean, dark face with wonder.

His hips moved very sensuously and her whole body clenched visibly.

He reached to put the hairpins on the side table. He looked down into her eyes and moved again, with deliberate sensuality, watching her lift toward him helplessly.

He bent and put his mouth tenderly over hers, shifting onto his side with both lean hands on her hips as one long, powerful leg slid between both of hers. He felt her shiver as the pleasure began all over again. His last sane thought as she pressed into his body was that he hoped he had the stamina to survive what they were going to do to each other this time...

MUCH LATER, AFTER A SHOWER and a change of clothes, they had a small wedding supper of bacon and eggs and toast and coffee at the small kitchen table. Cy couldn't force himself to take his eyes off Lisa, and the attraction seemed to be mutual just at first. She couldn't stop touching him, even just to pass him the sugar or refill his cup. It was more than physical desire. It was a sort of intimacy he'd only seen in old movies. He'd had brief affairs, liaisons, even a wife. But with none of the other women had he felt this deep emotional bond.

His green gaze dropped to her belly and a surge of jealousy caught him unaware. She was carrying another man's child. When he'd first taken her in, protected her, it had been more out of pity and affection than anything else. But slowly desire and the need to possess had replaced his initial attraction, and jealousy had become a constant companion since he'd seen Harley holding her hand. But after what they'd shared in bed, he was unexpectedly jealous of her late husband and the baby as well. He didn't understand his own riotous feelings. He was upset at the level of intimacy they'd attained and disturbed by the sense of possessiveness he felt for her. This hadn't been the plan at all. He'd married her to protect her and the baby from Lopez, not with any long-term relationship in mind. He'd proposed a marriage of convenience, which was interesting when he considered how quickly he'd maneuvered her into bed with the flimsiest of excuses. Abstinence alone wouldn't have caused hunger that sweeping.

He didn't understand his sudden lack of restraint, and because he didn't, he was broody. At least he'd had the presence of mind to ask about the risk to the baby first. But that wasn't much comfort at the moment. He'd crossed the line, his own line, and he couldn't put her at risk again. He'd have to keep his uncontrollable urges to himself. As that thought persisted, he forced himself not to stare at Lisa. If he was going to practice restraint, he'd better get a head start, and right now.

She noticed the faint scowl on his heavy brow and looked at him quizzically as she sipped her second cup of coffee. "Is something wrong?" she asked.

He made a dismissing gesture with a movement of his shoulder. He smoothed his thumb absently over the fork he was holding. He seemed deep in thought and he was even more silent than normal.

She was getting more insecure by the minute. In bed, she'd felt as if she belonged to him completely, as if no two people on earth could have been any closer, any more intimate. Now, she was as far away from him as if they were still just neighbors. She wondered if she'd done something wrong. Maybe she'd been too...eager. She flushed, remembering her passionate, wanton behavior. He might be one of those men who didn't like aggressive women in bed. She swallowed the lump in her throat and averted her eyes from his taciturn expression. He hadn't complained, but he was very remote since they'd left the bedroom. She'd have to remember that he didn't like her undisciplined ardor, and not be so uninhibited again. Maybe if she could curtail her headlong response, it would ease the sudden tension between them.

She forced a smile to her face. "Would you like some more coffee?" she asked pleasantly.

He pushed his cup toward her to let her refill it, and finished the last of his eggs. He was furious at himself for the jealousy that had attacked him so unexpectedly.

He'd married her to protect her from Lopez and help her take care of the child, and that was just what he was going to do. He'd be better off if he could keep in mind that passionate interludes in the bedroom weren't part of their deal, and stop trying to create new problems for himself and Lisa in the first days of their marriage. He'd broken faith with her by seducing her. Besides, he reminded himself, they still weren't out of the woods where Lopez was concerned. The man wouldn't stop just because Cy had married Lisa. In fact, he was willing to bet that the marriage would tempt Lopez to even further improvisation.

Meanwhile, he still had the problem of Lopez's warehouse behind his property. Since the blatant attack on Harley and Lisa, Cy had pulled Harley off the night surveillance, certain that Lopez's people would have night scopes now that would catch anyone spying on them. That excuse about locoweed worked once, but it wouldn't work again. Still, there was surveillance equipment that was undetectable by infrared glasses, and Cy initiated it. He hadn't shared it with Harley. The younger man hadn't quite recovered from the shock of seeing his supposedly crippled boss take down two professional assassins. He'd stopped asking questions, but he watched Cy from a safe distance and did nothing to upset him. He wouldn't even talk to Lisa unless Cy was around lately. It was almost comical.

She got up to put the dishes in the sink and he stacked his cup and saucer on his plate to simplify the chore for her. She smiled as she finished clearing the table and began to fill the sink with soapy warm water.

"I need to buy you a dishwasher," he said abruptly.

"There wasn't much need for it when I lived alone, but we'll have dinner guests from time to time…"

"I don't mind washing dishes in the sink, Cy," she faltered, her wide dark eyes in their big lenses searching his.

He leaned against the counter, watching her deliberately, his face scowling and remote. "I wasn't as gentle as I should have been. Do you feel okay? Any queasiness or discomfort?" he asked bluntly.

"I feel great!" She smiled. "No cramping and I haven't had a hint of morning sickness since I've been pregnant."

Cy frowned. It had been a long time since his late wife had been pregnant, but he remembered everything he'd read on the subject. It was hard to overlook the lack of visible changes in Lisa's soft body, especially her breasts. He felt suddenly uneasy. Pregnancy tests weren't foolproof. Maybe she wasn't pregnant after all. But if she wasn't pregnant with her late husband's child, she could quite easily be pregnant with his right now. Especially, he thought ruefully, after his exhaustive lovemaking. He hadn't held anything back and he hadn't tried to protect her—useless when she was already pregnant, which he'd thought at the time. He'd proposed a temporary marriage to protect her. Making her pregnant with his own child wasn't part of the plan. He didn't want a binding relationship…did he?

She noticed his curious stare. "Why are you looking at me like that?" she asked uneasily.

"I like your hair loose around your shoulders," he said evasively.

"Do you?" She pushed the heavy fall of it back over her shoulders with a tiny smile. "It's a nuisance to wash and dry."

"I had Harley bathe Puppy Dog, by the way," he mentioned, searching for a neutral subject.

"Did you? That was nice."

"Bob needed a bath, too," he said. He didn't add that putting Harley to work bathing dogs had made him feel pretty good. He was still brooding about the way Harley had tested his reflexes with the pistol. He hadn't wanted any of his men to know about his old life. That was wishful thinking, he supposed.

She hesitated, washing the same plate until it threatened to rub the pattern off.

"Speaking of Puppy Dog," he said, "didn't he stay in the house with you before you moved over here?"

"Yes," she agreed, "but he's big and clumsy, like his father, and you've got lots of breakable stuff. Anyway, he seems to like being out in the barn with Bob. It's almost as warm in there, with the doors closed, as it is in the house. And it's amazingly sanitary. For a barn."

"I like healthy stock. Sanitation is important." He glanced around the kitchen. "I thought I was a fairly decent housekeeper, but you've brightened the place up considerably."

"I like housework," she said absently. "I do know a few things about the cattle business, but I enjoy cooking and cleaning and even ironing shirts." She fingered his. "I always thought I'd take to family life like a duck to water. I just never had the chance to prove it."

He scowled, thinking of the difference she'd made here. He'd gotten used to finding her in the kitchen or the living room when he came home every evening. He liked the little touches, the frilly curtains in the kitchen, the silk flowers on the table, the visible signs of her presence in his life. He thought about having her move back into her old house, and it was distasteful. He refused to pursue that line of thought.

His eyes went to her waistline and quickly away. She noticed and bit her lower lip while she finished washing utensils and put them in the other side of the sink to rinse.

"Does it bother you that I'm pregnant?" she blurted out.

He hesitated. He didn't know how to answer her. "The baby must be a comfort to you," he said slowly, "with your husband gone."

She didn't even feel as if she'd been married, she thought to herself. She'd slept with her husband exactly twice and the rest of the time he'd either been away from home or pretending that she wasn't there. He'd married her on the rebound.

He'd proposed to Lisa, having already confessed about the woman he'd loved leaving him. Lisa had no hope of marrying anyone else and she'd been very lonely since her father's death. A marriage of convenience wouldn't be so bad, she'd told herself. But Walt couldn't love her, and she couldn't love him. Now here she was in a second marriage of convenience with a man who didn't want her permanently any more than Walt had.

"I've always wanted children," she said noncommittally.

He was remembering the little boy who hadn't been his, and how painful it had been to lose him in such a violent manner. That led him to thoughts of Lopez and revenge.

Lisa saw the expression on his face and frowned. He hadn't wanted to harm her child, but it was obvious that he regretted their intimacy. She wished she could, but it had been the only time in her life she'd felt as if she belonged to someone.

"I'm sorry, by the way," she said quietly. "About not letting you carry me over the threshold," she added, avoiding his sudden intent gaze. "I really was trying to spare your pride."

He stared at her for a few seconds before he spoke. "There was some nerve damage and loss of muscle tissue to my arm after the fire," he said. "But I can do almost anything I could before. I don't advertise it," he added slowly. "It gives me a psychological advantage if people think I'm less capable than I am—especially since Eb's line of work became public knowledge."

"You don't want people to know what you did," she said with understanding. "Well, you may fool everyone else, but Harley goes out of his way not to upset you these days," she murmured.

"He's lucky I didn't shoot him," he muttered. His eyes narrowed. "Did you see it?"

She nodded.

"And you still didn't think I could carry you into the house."

She cleared her throat. "I was terribly shy of you, if you want the truth," she told him. "Walt was an ordinary man who never made me nervous. But my knees started shaking the minute I saw you. I didn't know what you'd expect of me. I was a little afraid of you."

"Why?"

Her shoulders rose and fell. "I haven't been completely honest with you about a few things. Not important things," she was quick to emphasize. "But I'd only been intimate with Walt twice and it was uncomfortable and quick and embarrassing. I…knew you were experienced, and that you'd expect more from a woman than Walt had. I thought I wouldn't be enough for you. If you meant us to have a real marriage, I mean, and not just one on paper."

So that was why. She hadn't been challenging him at all. She'd been afraid of the very thing her behavior precipitated.

"I'm sorry. I didn't understand," he added irritably.

"Not your fault. I sort of got carried away, too." She blushed.

A lot of things were becoming clear to him, predominantly her total lack of experience with intimacy. If she'd only slept with her husband twice and hadn't liked it, the past few hours must have shocked her speechless. Funny, most women weren't naïve these days. His gaze darkened as he stared at her. She seemed mature sometimes. And then she'd throw him a curve, from out of nowhere. He couldn't fathom her.

"Are we going to sleep together at night?" she asked before her courage failed.

"No," he said flatly. "This afternoon should never have happened. I'm not going to put your baby at risk a second time."

She worked not to let her disappointment show. Now she was certain that she hadn't pleased him. She seemed to be an ongoing disappointment to men in bed, and she didn't know how to change it. "Okay," she said with forced carelessness.

He was glad she was taking it so calmly. She might not have loved her husband, but she genuinely wanted the baby and there was still a chance that she was pregnant, despite the lack of symptoms. He recalled now that some women did have cramping in the early stages, and it usually went away, just as hers had. And a lot of women never had morning sickness.

If she really was pregnant with Walt's child, he wasn't going to be the cause of her losing her baby. Nor was he going to touch her for the duration of their marriage of convenience. Once the threat of Lopez was removed, he was going to let her go back home and go to work for Kemp. They could have the marriage quietly annulled and it would be the best thing for both of them. He wasn't going to let himself love anyone ever again. He couldn't go through the hell of losing anyone else.

Lisa felt embarrassed, but she didn't let it show. It shouldn't have surprised her that she'd disappointed him in bed, considering the sophisticated women he'd probably attracted before his marriage. She was just a country woman with no experience, and thank God he didn't know her real age or he'd be doing more than clamming up when they talked. "I'll have supper when you come in," she said.

"I'll be late."

She nodded. "Okay."

He went to the door, hesitated, looked back and a flash of possessiveness showed in his green eyes as he stared at her. Her face colored and he forced himself to look away. She wasn't the first woman he'd taken to bed, and she wouldn't be the last. He had to stop seeing her as some sort of permanent fixture in his life. There was simply no future in it. He grabbed his hat off the rack, slanted it over one eye and walked out without another word.

Lisa went back to her dishes on shaky legs. She wondered if he had any idea what that smoldering look of his did to a woman.

CHAPTER NINE

TWO MORE WEEKS PASSED with the occupants of the Parkses' house being polite to each other and not much more. Cy had swept the house for "bugs" the same day Lopez's men made their assault, making sure that he didn't miss any of Lopez's little listening devices. He had no idea how long the drug lord's men had been eavesdropping, but there hadn't been that many opportunities for them to get into the house. He didn't imagine it had been long.

He checked his surveillance tapes periodically as well, noting that the warehouse on the land behind his property had been joined by what looked like a small processing plant, supposedly for honey from the row upon row of beehives on the property. He saw nothing to indicate a drug presence, but Lopez had added several more men to the site, and there were several big eighteen-wheel trucks on the premises now. It looked very much as if Lopez planned to start shipping his product fairly soon.

Meanwhile, Cy had gone to see Eb Scott to check on Rodrigo's progress, and the status of the cocaine shipment he'd already reported.

"Narcs got it down in the Gulf," Eb murmured coolly. "The Coast Guard homed in on the boats that were carrying it and strafed them with gunfire. Needless to say, they gave themselves and their shipment up. The DEA made several arrests and confiscated enough cocaine paste to addict a small country."

"Damn," Cy murmured angrily. "So here we sit."

"Don't knock the confiscation," Eb mused. "I'd love to see them make that kind of haul on a daily basis."

"So would I, but I want to catch Lopez with his fingers in the cookie jar," the other man said. And soon, he could have added, because his hunger for his wife was growing less controllable by the day. He looked at her and ached. Anger made new lines in his lean face. "Meanwhile, he sits on the edge of my property like a volcano about to erupt and I can't do a damned thing about it. I suppose you know that the sheriff's department and the DEA were all over it because of an 'anonymous' tip."

"I know," Eb replied. "One of Lopez's men phoned in the tip, apparently, and then the man in charge of the honey operation threatened to sue everybody for harassment if they came out again and did any more searches." He shook his head. "You have to admire the plan, at least. It was a stroke of genius. Nobody's going to rush out there again to look around unless there's concrete evidence of drugs."

"And that," Cy agreed, "will be hard to come by now."

"Exactly." He leaned forward in his chair and studied Cy intently. "You look older."

Cy scowled. "That's what marriage does to a bachelor."

"It had the opposite effect on me," his friend replied. "I've had a streak of good luck since I married Sally."

"I noticed. Is Micah Steele still in town?" he asked abruptly.

"He's in and out. He had an assignment and he's due back next week. Had an apparently disastrous argument with his stepsister Callie Kirby over his father before he left."

"Callie isn't much for arguments," Cy pointed out. "If there was an argument, he started it."

"Could be."

"I wish we could nab Lopez and get Rodrigo out of there before he gets himself shot," Cy said, changing the subject. "He's good people. I don't want him killed on our account."

"Same here. He's been in the business at least as long as Dutch and J.D. and Laremos," he replied. "And they taught him everything he knows."

"They were the best."

"We weren't bad, either," Eb said on an amused laugh. "But I suppose we either settle down or die. Personally I consider marriage an adventure."

"Some do," he said without enthusiasm and changed the subject.

"Did you hear that Sally's aunt Jessica married Dallas and moved back to Houston with their son Stevie?" Eb asked unexpectedly. "Nobody was exactly surprised about it."

"At least she'll be looked after," Cy remarked.

"That's true." Eb frowned as he stared at his friend. "It's none of my business, but is it true that Lisa's pregnant?"

He was going to say yes, but Eb was watching him with the insight of years of friendship and he let his guard drop. "That's a good question," Cy replied, leaning forward. "I thought that she was, just after Walt was killed," he added. "But she had some symptoms I don't like and she doesn't show the normal signs of pregnancy." He grimaced. "We don't talk about it."

"She's young," Eb agreed. "I don't imagine she knows very much about pregnancy, since she was an only child more or less raised by her dad. He wasn't the sort to discuss intimate issues with her."

"She's young, you said," Cy returned quickly. "How young?"

"You mean to tell me that you're married to her and you don't know how old she is?"

"She hid the marriage license," he muttered. "Put her thumb over the birthdate while I was signing it and confiscated it as soon as the JP signed it. Every time I've asked, she's changed the subject."

"I see."

"Well?" Cy prompted.

Eb grimaced. "She ought to tell you."

"Eb!"

The other man shifted restlessly. "She's twenty-one. Barely."

Cy's face went white. He leaned back in his chair as if he'd been shot. He took off his hat and wiped his sweaty brow on his sleeve. "Dear God!"

"That's legal age," Eb pointed out. "And you don't need me to tell you that she's amazingly mature for that age. Some women grow up quicker than others. She never really had a childhood. From what I've heard, from the age of six, she was riding horses in competitions and working around the ranch. For all that her dad wouldn't teach her management, there isn't much she doesn't know about the daily routine of ranch hands."

"Fourteen years my junior," Cy groaned. "I could never get her to tell me."

"Now you see why," his friend remarked. "You'd never have married her if you'd known."

"Of course I wouldn't have married her if I'd known, Lopez or no Lopez! I don't rob cradles!"

Eb chuckled. "She's no kid. Around Jacobsville we pay more attention to family than we do to age differences. Lisa comes from good people. So do you."

Cy had his face in his hands. "Walt wasn't even thirty," he remarked. "And damned Harley is barely twenty-eight. He's still in and out of the house all the time flirting with her when he doesn't think I see him. I caught him a couple of weeks ago showing her how to break handholds, right in my own living room."

"You know how to handle that," Eb said easily.

Green, glittery eyes came up to meet his. "I can't handle it. She's too damned young for me and I don't want to stay married to her!"

Eb's eyebrows went up at the vehemence of the statement. "What do you plan to do, then, kick her out and let Lopez…"

"Oh, for God's sake, you know I wouldn't do that! I just don't want her getting comfortable in my house," he added irritably. "I think she's still in shock at Walt's death and latching onto the first pair of comforting arms she can find."

"So that's it. And you don't want to take any chances until you know for sure."

Cy glared at him. "Don't psychoanalyze me!"

"Wasn't trying to," Eb said with a grin. "But she and Walt didn't marry for love eternal. He'd just lost Becky Wayne and his heart was broken. Everybody knew he married Lisa on the rebound. And she'd never been in love with anybody. She assumed it came naturally when you put on an engagement ring. That isn't the case."

"You ought to know," Cy said. "You got engaged to Maggie Barton, and I know for a fact you didn't love her."

"I was lonely," he said simply. "But until Sally stormed back into my life, I didn't know what love was. I do now."

Obviously. It was written all over him. Cy turned his eyes away.

Eb's expression became covertly amused. "If you don't want Lisa for keeps, you might let Harley get on the inside track. He's got potential..."

"Damn Harley!" Cy burst out, his eyes were blazing. "If he goes near her again, I'll feed him to my chickens!"

So much for Cy's true feelings, even if he wouldn't admit them. Eb chuckled. "I haven't forgotten what happened at your place when Lopez's men made a try tor Lisa," Eb murmured. "Talk is that Harley's given up throwing pistols at you and he walks a mile around you lately."

"Some men have to learn the hard way that they aren't invulnerable. Harley got overconfident. It almost cost him his life. You know that the two assailants made bond and left the country?"

"I know. What was it, a million in bond, each?"

"Yep. Pocket change to Lopez, but the judge set bond as high as she could. I don't blame her."

"She's a good judge at that," Eb agreed.

Cy stood up, feeling shaky. "I've got to get back home. If you hear from Rodrigo, let me know. I'm still trying to keep an eye on the honey plant. Nothing's shown up so far."

"Wouldn't it be a hoot if Lopez had decided to turn respectable and it's a real honey processing plant?" Eb mused.

"Sure, and pigs will fly."

"Not on my place, they won't," Eb said. He got up, too, and walked the other man to the front door. "But bullets may, before this mess is over," he added in a somber tone. "I don't like all this sudden quiet from Lopez's warehouse. They're up to something."

"That's exactly what I'm afraid of," Cy agreed, and he didn't smile.

AS ANOTHER WEEK CRAWLED BY, Lisa could see that Cy was brooding about something. He continued to be standoffish and remote after their tempestuous afternoon in bed together, and he'd been somber and unapproachable altogether since he'd gone to see Eb Scott. But his eyes always seemed to be on her. She caught him watching her when she worked in the kitchen, when she washed clothes. He'd bought her a dishwasher, as he'd promised, and every sort of kitchen utensil and cookware any gourmet would have cherished. He surprised her with the romance novels she liked to read, and even scarce out-of-print editions of authors she enjoyed. He was forever buying toys for Puppy Dog and Bob, and coaxing Lisa into stores where he had accounts. She was spoiled constantly. But he never touched her.

One evening when they'd just finished watching the news, she cut off the television and followed him daringly into the office where he kept his computer and printer and fax-modem. He looked up from behind the massive oak desk with an expression of surprise.

"Can I come in?" she asked from the doorway.

He shrugged. "Help yourself."

That didn't sound welcoming, especially from a man to his new wife, but she smiled and walked up to the desk.

"Something bothering you?" he asked quietly.

"Yes."

"What?"

She stuck her hands into the pockets of her pretty embroidered purple apron. "I feel like an unwanted houseguest lately," she said flatly. "I want to know what I'm doing wrong."

He scowled and put down the pencil he was holding over a spreadsheet of figures. "You haven't done anything wrong, Lisa," he said.

"I must have. You can't seem to force yourself to come within five feet of me." Her voice sounded raw and she didn't quite meet his eyes.

He leaned back in the chair. A harsh sound came out of his throat and his lips made a thin line as he studied her. "You didn't tell me you were just twenty-one."

She looked suddenly uncomfortable. "Does it matter?"

"Good God in heaven!" he exclaimed, explosively pushing himself up and out of his desk chair. "Of course it matters! You're still a kid and I'm thirty-five years old!"

She let out an expressive breath.

"You don't look your age," he muttered, walking away from her to stand in front of the dark window. The horizon was a faint silhouette in the distance, flat and cold-looking.

"That's what Walt used to say," she recalled. She leaned her hip against his desk and stared at his long back. "But I'm not as immature as you're making me out to be."

His shoulder moved jerkily. "If you were ten years older…"

"But I'm not. So what do you want to do about it?" she demanded, blowing a wisp of loose hair out of her mouth. "Do you want me to move back over to Dad's ranch and go to work for Mr. Kemp and pay rent? I'm willing."

He felt his heart stop. His expression was vulnerable for those few seconds, and he actually winced.

"Don't look so tormented. It won't cause any gossip if I go back home, wedding ring or no wedding ring. We can get an annulment."

"The gossips would have a field day over that!"

"I can't believe you care what people might say," she bit off. "I certainly don't."

"It isn't that." He rammed his hands into the pockets of his jeans and stared at her worriedly. "You've never been out of Jacobsville. You don't know beans about men." He drew in a slow breath. "You should have gone to college or at least seen a little more of the country and the world before you married."

"There was never enough money for travel," she said shortly. "My dad was a small rancher, not an aristocrat. If I went to college it would be to study veterinary medicine or animal husbandry, and I don't really see how I could do that with a baby on the way!"

He hesitated. Should he tell her what he suspected about the baby? It might be the best time to do it. But he couldn't think clearly. All he could think about was her age. He should have realized how young she was. He felt as if he'd taken unfair advantage of her, even if it had been the only way to protect her from Lopez. She had been married already, he reminded himself. It wasn't as if he'd snatched her from a cradle.

Her hand went to her waistline. "I'd much rather have the baby than a degree, if you want the truth," she said.

His face hardened. He couldn't tell her. Not yet. For all he knew, she might truly have loved her late husband. What would it do to her if she wasn't pregnant? He turned back toward the desk. "I don't want you to move out. Lopez may be laying low, but I guarantee he hasn't gone away. I won't risk your life."

She stood glaring at him. "Fair enough. When he's finally caught, I'm out of here," she said flatly. "I am not living with a man who can't bring himself to touch me because I'm pregnant with another man's child!" she added, making a stab in the dark. It seemed to have paid off when he went rigid all over.

She turned and started out the door, sick at finally knowing the truth he hadn't wanted to tell her. It wasn't her age that bothered him, not really—it was Walt's baby!

"Damn it, that's not why!"

She whirled. "Then what is?"

He glared at her. She had a temper that easily matched his, despite her youth, and with her dark eyes flashing and her face flushed, she gave him a very inconvenient ache.

"It's strange that you don't have any pregnancy symptoms," he said flatly.

She didn't answer him for several tense seconds. "All right," she said finally. "I'll make an appointment first thing tomorrow."

"See that you do," he returned curtly.

She searched his drawn face, seeking answers to questions she didn't want to ask. "We were so close, the day we married," she said hesitantly. "You were…different. I thought you cared about me."

He managed a smile that mixed equal parts of self-contempt and mockery. "Didn't anyone ever tell you that men get sentimental after sex?"

She seemed to close up like a flower. She turned away from him without another word and left the room, quietly pulling the door closed behind her.

He ran an angry hand through his dark hair and cursed himself silently for that cruel remark. He'd never been so confused. He didn't know if she was carrying Walt's child or not. He didn't know how he really felt about her. He was sick at heart to realize how very young she was. On top of that, he was frustrated because Lopez wouldn't come out in the open and make a move. One thing he was sure about, though, was that Lisa had to be protected. He was going to take care of her the best he could. Then, when it was over, and she was safe, she could have a chance to decide whether or not she wanted to spend her life with a maimed ex-mercenary.

He wasn't going to continue to take advantage of her, even if it was killing him to stay out of her bed. If she wasn't pregnant, he wasn't going to take the slightest chance of making her that way. She was going to be completely free to decide her future. Even if it was with damned Harley.

LISA WENT TO THE DOCTOR and had the pregnancy test, and came back to the ranch looking more disturbed and worried than ever.

Cy was waiting for her in the living room. He stood up, his face strangely watchful. "Well?" he asked abruptly.

She moved restlessly, dropping her purse into a chair. She was wearing the same beige dress she'd worn the day they married, with a lightweight brown coat, and her hair was in a bun. She looked pale and quiet and not very happy.

"The test was positive," she said, avoiding his eyes. "He said pregnancy symptoms sometimes don't show up right away. He said there was nothing at all to worry about."

Cy didn't say anything. Apparently he'd been wrong right down the line. She was pregnant, and her child was Walt's. It was uncharitable of him to be disappointed about that, but he was.

She'd noted the expression that crossed his face and it wounded her. She knew that men were said to grow possessive once they'd been intimate with a woman, and it wasn't totally unexpected that he resented Walt's place in her life. It wouldn't be easy for a man to accept and raise a child that wasn't his.

"Are you sure you don't want me to leave?" she asked in a subdued tone.

"Of course not," he said automatically.

She lifted her eyes to his. "I won't get in your way."

"You aren't in my way."

She moved jerkily away. "Okay. Thanks."

She seemed to hesitate at the door, but only for a second. She went out, leaving Cy to watch her exit with a tangle of emotions.

He stopped by his office to check his messages before he retrieved his shepherd's jacket and slanted his hat across his green eyes. He went out by way of the kitchen so that he could tell Lisa where he was going.

Harley had just come in with the eggs, and he was leaning against the counter smiling at Lisa, who was smiling back. They were both so young...

"Sorry I didn't get them in first thing this morning," Harley was telling her, "but I had some work to do on the fence line."

"That's okay. I had an appointment in town," Lisa replied.

"I'll be late tonight," Cy said from the doorway. They both jumped, surprised by his sudden appearance. Harley cleared his throat, nodded at Lisa and went rushing down the steps toward the barn.

Cy didn't understand why until Lisa actually backed up against the sink.

"Now, what, for God's sake?" he demanded shortly.

"You ought to see your face in a mirror," she retorted.

His green eyes narrowed. "Harley spends too much time in here," he said flatly. "I don't like it."

Her eyebrows arched. "How would you know? You're never here!"

His lips made a thin line. He was bristling with unfamiliar emotions, the foremost of which was pure jealousy.

She glared up at him from her safe vantage point at the sink. "I didn't cheat on Walt and I won't cheat on you," she said coldly. "Just in case you wondered."

He glared back at her. His eyes, under the wide brim of the hat, glistened like green fire.

"I never should have agreed to come here," she said after a minute, her breath sighing out as she leaned back against the counter. "I've never been so miserable in my whole life."

That was worse than a slap in the face. His whole body tightened. "That makes two of us," he lied. "Don't worry. It won't be much longer before we'll have everything resolved. Once the sale of the ranch goes through, you'll have enough money to do what you please."

He turned and walked out. He didn't look back.

LISA FELT LIKE BREAKING THINGS. She was crazy about the stupid man, and he wouldn't give an inch. He didn't want her talking to Harley, he was resentful of her baby because it was Walt's, he alternately ignored and spoiled her. Now he'd offered to let her leave. She didn't want to. She'd grown used to living with him, even if it was like being alone most of the time. But he had said that she could go when things were resolved. Did that mean they were close to dealing with Lopez? She hoped so. The memory of the assault on her bedroom and then the attempted assault here still worried her. She felt safe with Cy, even with Harley. If she went home, she'd be watched, but she wouldn't feel safe.

Cy, driving toward town in his truck, was fuming. So she wanted to go home. Well, he'd see what he could do to hurry things up for her. First he went to Kemp's office and told him to push the paperwork through as fast as possible. Then he started toward Eb's place. There had to be some way to force Lopez to stick his neck in a noose.

But on the way, he decided to swing by the old Johnson house. It would be deserted now, of course, and there was only one other house on the stretch of outlying road. He didn't really know why it occurred to him to go that way. Maybe, he considered, his old instincts still worked at some level.

He pulled off the paved road and turned down the small county road that led to the Johnson place. He remembered Eb talking about the members of Lopez's cartel who had rented a house nearby and had accosted Sally Johnson before she'd married Eb. It was a crazy notion, and he needed his head read. All the same, he told himself, it never hurt to play a hunch.

He noticed the lack of traffic on the road, which was nothing unusual. This far out, there weren't a lot of people who opted for the badly kept county road instead of the newer highway that led to Victoria. The late autumn landscape was bleak and uninviting. All the leaves were off the trees now, and the last bunches of hay were cut and stacked in barns for winter forage. The weather had a nip in it. Nights were cold. He remembered winter nights when he and Eb were overseas, trudging through ice and snow. Life was much simpler here, if not overly comfortable.

He was watching the scenery, not paying a lot of attention to anything, when he noticed two huge tractor-trailer rigs parked near an old Victorian house. He didn't slow down or show any obvious interest in the once-deserted dwelling. But it was painfully clear why Lopez's "honey operation" was sitting still. He had a distribution center up and running already, only it wasn't behind Cy's property. The beehives were only a blind. Here was the real drug operation, complete with huge renovated barn and dangerous-looking employees sitting around the big rigs, which were backed up to the barn. Cy knew without looking that there would be locks on those barn doors and men with automatic weapons patrolling around it. He knew, too, that it wasn't hay that was being loaded into the trucks.

They'd been foxed. And now it was almost too late to close down the operation. He'd have bet money that this was Lopez's follow-up shipment to the one that had been confiscated down in the Gulf of Mexico. The odd-looking oil drums were scattered around, and had obviously been used to bridge rivers between Texas and the Gulf so that the men hauling the cocaine had been able to cross at places where the border patrol wouldn't be waiting for them.

He drove straight past the place without looking again. As he passed the deserted Johnson homestead, with its For Sale sign standing awry and uninviting, he knew that what they'd all dreaded was already taking place. Lopez was back in business, right here in Jacobsville. And if Cy and his friends were going to stop them, there wasn't much time to plan an assault.

At the end of the road, he turned back into the highway and burned rubber getting to Eb's place.

CHAPTER TEN

EB WAS SURPRISED BY THE NEWS.

"Right under our damned noses," he exploded. "No wonder we couldn't find any evidence of drug smuggling at the honey warehouse. That was a blind, and we fell for it, just like raw recruits!"

"The question is, what do we do now?" Cy asked coldly. "And since Rodrigo didn't warn us about this, have they found him out and disposed of him?"

"I hope not," Eb said sincerely. "But I can't help thinking that he would have warned us if he'd been able to." He ran his hand through his hair. "Hell of a time to make this sort of discovery, when Lopez is ready to ship his new supply out to his distribution network."

"It gets worse. From what I saw, I'd say he's ready to go tonight."

"We'll have to go in now," Eb said at once. "Or we'll miss the chance. And we'll have to have help," he added. "I counted at least twelve men. Even with our experience, we won't be able to take that many men armed with machine guns."

"I know. But we can't do it without authorization, either," Cy returned. "We live here. I don't know about you, but I don't want to end up as an ex-patriated American."

"Neither do I." Eb's eyes narrowed. "There's another consideration, too. If Rodrigo's with them, still undercover, the feds won't know and they'll shoot him. We have to go in with them. I have a few contacts. I can call in favors."

"So can I," Cy agreed. "Let's compare notes. With a little luck, we may be able to bring down Lopez's local network and save Rodrigo all at once."

IT WAS RUSHED AND HECTIC to get the necessary people notified and in place, but they managed it, just. The sheriff pulled two deputies off patrol and called in two more special deputies. The DEA only had three men who could get to Jacobsville in time to assist with the surprise attack, but they were dispatched immediately. Two of the best officers from the local police department, Palmer and Barrett, volunteered to go along with the sheriff's force to help. They might still be outnumbered, but hopefully it would be possible to take the drug dealers by surprise and close down their operation. Nobody wanted a drug cartel operating out of Jacobsville.

Cy was putting on his night gear when Lisa came into his room and gasped.

"Where are you going?" she exclaimed.

He turned, black face mask in hand, to study her. She was wearing sweats, yellow ones that made her blond hair look more blond. It was loose, around her shoulders, and she had that peculiar radiance that pregnancy bestowed on a woman's face.

"Lopez's goons are ready to haul their shipment out tonight. We're going to stop them," he said honestly.

Her worried eyes never left her taciturn husband,

from his tall, powerful figure in black to his lean, scarred face and glittery green eyes. He was devastating to her, physically as well as mentally. He took her breath away. She hated knowing what he meant to do.

She went right up to him, her dark eyes looking even darker through the lenses of her glasses. "No," she said shortly. "No, you don't! There are plenty of people in law enforcement who do this for a living. I'm not letting you go after those drug dealers!"

He took her by both shoulders, pulled her against him, and bent and kissed the breath and the protest right out of her. His arms enfolded her, cradled her, while his hard mouth devoured her soft, parted lips. It was a long time before he lifted his dark head.

"If Lopez is allowed to set up an operation here, none of us will ever be safe again, especially you," he said quietly. "If we don't stop it now, we never will."

"You could be killed," she said miserably.

The worry on her face made him feel funny. He couldn't remember anyone caring if he lived or died, especially not his erstwhile wife who'd only wanted creature comforts. His welfare was of supreme unimportance to her. But Lisa was cut from another sort of cloth. She was brave and honest and loyal. He searched her face and realized with a start that he could give up anything, even his own life, easier than he could give up Lisa. She was too young for him, of course…

He kissed her again, long and hard, ignoring all the reasons why he should do his best to send her out the door and out of his life. For her own good, of course, he rationalized. Sadly, none of those reasons made any difference when he was within five feet of her. Her arms curled around him and she gave him back the kiss with every bit of strength in her body. It was like walking on hot coals. She couldn't get close enough.

She was breathless when he lifted his head, but the resolve was still there, in those narrow green eyes. "It amazes me," she whispered huskily, "what lengths you're willing to go to…in order to stay out of my bed."

He laughed despite the gravity of the situation. "Is that what you think?"

"Walt was my husband," she said quietly. "I was fond of him. I'm not sorry that I'll have his child, so that a part of him will live on. But you and I could have children of our own as well. It isn't biology that makes a man a father; it's love. And you aren't ever going to convince me that you wouldn't love a baby, even if it wasn't yours genetically."

He sighed gently and smoothed back her disheveled hair. "I keep mixing you up with the past, when you're nothing like my late wife. I don't resent Walt's baby." He shrugged. "It's not the age difference, either, really. But you're young and I'm older than my years make me. Maybe you need someone closer to your own age."

"Someone like Harley?" she asked deliberately.

His face hardened and his eyes flashed dangerously. *"No!"*

Hope, almost deserted, began to twinkle in her eyes. "That's what I thought you said." She pulled his head down and kissed him tenderly. "I know you can take care of yourself. I've seen you do it. But don't take chances. I want to be married a very long time."

"You do?" he murmured.

"Yes. I'm not going back to Dad's ranch. If you won't

let me live in the house, I'll live in the barn with Puppy Dog and Bob and tell everybody in Jacobsville that you won't let me live with you...."

He was kissing her again. It was sweet and heady, and he didn't have time for it at all. He just couldn't seem to stop. He was starting to ache and that would never do.

"And I'm moving into your bedroom while you're gone," she added, her voice thready with passion. "So there."

"Maybe I can think up an objection before I come back," he murmured against her lips.

"You try to do that." She grinned.

He loosened her arms and put her gently away from him, his strong hands tight on her shoulders. "While I'm gone, stay in the house with the doors locked. I've got Nels on the front porch and Henry watching the back door. They're both armed. Stay away from the windows and don't answer the phone. You know where the spare pistol is," he added, and she nodded. "It's loaded."

She bit her lower lip, realizing from his demeanor how dangerous it would be for both of them. "Okay. I'll use it if I have to. But don't you let yourself get shot," she told him firmly.

"I know, come back with my shield or on it."

She smiled and nodded. "That's right. Because you're not a 'summer soldier' like Thomas Paine wrote about. You're a winter soldier, fighting through blizzards. But you have to come back to me in one piece."

"I'll do my best to oblige," he mused, smiling back. Her eyes were soft and dark. He almost got lost in them. His gloved hand came up to touch her flushed cheek.

"What did I ever do in my life to deserve someone like you?" he asked in a breathlessly tender voice. He moved away from her before that softness captured him. "I'll be home when I can."

She put up a brave front. "Okay," she said, and without further protests.

He paused at the doorway for one long, last look at her. She was a hell of a woman. And he wasn't giving her up, whether or not it would have been for her own good. He read the same resolve in her own face. She didn't cry or complain or try to stop him. She stood there very bravely and kept smiling, even though her eyes were too bright to be normal. She was still standing there when he went out into the hall and disappeared.

HARLEY WAS SITTING ON the front porch with Nels, waiting for him with a lit cigarette and a scowl. He got to his feet when Cy came out the door dressed in black and wearing a face mask. Harley had on jeans and boots and a camo jacket left over from his army ranger days.

"You aren't leaving here without me," Harley said belligerently.

"Who says I'm leaving?"

"Don't insult me." Harley opened his jacket to disclose a .45 automatic. "I may not be a full-fledged merk, but I was a crack shot in the Rangers," he added. "And no matter how many men are going, I might still be useful."

That was much better than bragging that he had combat training, Cy supposed. He hesitated, but only for a minute.

"All right. Let's go. Nels, guard her with your life," he added to his man on the porch, who nodded solemnly.

Harley headed for the Expedition, but Cy shook his head. He indicated a black Bronco of questionable vintage, parked under a tree. There were two men already in it. Harley was shocked that he hadn't seen it at all until now.

He wasn't surprised to find Eb Scott in the front seat with an unfamiliar man much bigger than Eb or Cy, and both of the newcomers dressed similarly to Cy.

"Here," Eb said, handing a small container of black face paint to Harley. "You'll shine like a new moon without a mask."

Harley at least knew how to use camouflage paint. He wanted to ask half a dozen questions, the foremost of which was why his boss was going along on what was obviously a search and destroy mission. Then he remembered the way Cy had used that knife on the two intruders and the way he'd caught the pistol Harley had thrown at his retreating back. It had long since dawned on him that his boss hadn't always been a rancher.

"Stubbs and Kennedy are going to rendezvous with us at the old Johnson place," Eb said tautly. "We've got the sheriff's department out in force, too. You and Micah and I will set up a perimeter with the deputies and let the feds go in first."

"Who are Stubbs and Kennedy?" Harley asked.

"DEA," came the cold reply. "Walt Monroe was one of theirs. They get first crack at these mules."

Mules, Harley recalled, were the drug lords' transportation people. He handed the face paint back to Eb. "You said the old Johnson place," Harley began. "But the warehouse is right behind Mr. Parks's place."

"That was a damned blind," Cy said shortly. "To

draw attention away from the real distribution point. I could kick myself for not realizing it sooner."

"No wonder we never saw any drugs changing hands," Harley realized.

"Listen," Eb said as he eased the Bronco off the main highway and down the back road that led first to the Johnson place and then to the rental house near it, "I want a promise from you, just on the off chance that Lopez is around. No storm trooper stuff."

"Mr. Scott, I wouldn't dream…!" Harley began.

"Not you," Eb said impatiently. "Him!"

He was staring in the rearview mirror straight at Cy, whose eyes were glittering.

"He set fire to my house," Cy said in a menacing tone, "killed my wife and my five-year-old son. If he's there, he's mine, and no power on earth will save him. Not even you."

"If you kill him, the DEA will string you up on the nearest courthouse lawn!"

"They're welcome," Cy returned grimly.

"And what about Lisa, when you're gone?" Micah Stecle interjected. "This isn't Africa. You're not on your own. You have to think about Lisa and her baby."

"Africa was a long time ago," Cy said irritably, noting Harley's intent stare.

"None of us have forgotten it," Micah persisted. "You walked right into a nest of snipers with machine guns firing. Your clothes were shot to pieces and you took ten hits in the body, and you kept right on going. You saved us from certain death. We won't forget how much we owe you. That's why we're not letting you near Lopez. If I have to knock you down and sit on you, I'll do it."

"They were lousy shots," Cy muttered.

"They were crack shots," Eb countered. "But you psyched them out by walking right into the gunfire. It won't work with Lopez's men. We have to let the DEA take point. We aren't even supposed to be in on this. I had to call in markers from all over Texas to get even this far. And to boot, I had to confess to Kennedy why we're here—to protect Rodrigo from everybody in case he's among these guys. Don't forget that we haven't heard a word from Rodrigo. He may also be with them and unable to get a message to us."

"They may have killed him already, too," Cy added.

"We won't know until we get there. Harley—" Eb glanced over the seat "—you stick close to Cy."

Harley was weighing the dangers of that position when Micah Steele began to chuckle. "That's all he'll be able to do, or don't you remember that it took Laremos and Brettman and Dutch all together to bring him down just after Juba was killed, and he went right after a company of crack government troops?"

Harley's gasp was audible. "Laremos and...!"

"Who do you think taught us all we know?" Eb mused. "Now put a sock in it, Harley. This is where things get dicey."

He pulled up at the old Johnson place and cut off the engine. He handed out high-tech night scopes and listening devices to Micah and Cy. Cy gave Harley a level stare.

"This isn't a weekend at a merk training school," he told the younger man in a firm tone. "If there's a fire-fight, you stay out of it. Eb and Micah and I are a team. We know to the last ditch how far we can trust each other and we work as a unit. You're the odd man out. That being the case, you could get somebody killed. You're backup, period. You don't shoot until and unless one of us tells you to."

Harley swallowed. He was getting the idea, and an odd sickness welled up in his stomach. He could hardly talk, because his mouth was so dry. "How will we know the bad guys from the good guys?"

"The DEA boys will have that imprinted on the back of their jackets in big letters. Palmer and Barrett from the police department and the deputies from the sheriff's department will all be in uniform. The bad guys will be trying to protect their product. This is important," he added intently. "If you should be captured, make damned sure that you're on the ground when we come in. Because if that happens, if we have to storm the house, the first thing we'll do is to take out everybody standing. Have you got that?"

"I've got it," Harley said. "But I'm not going to get myself captured."

The others synchronized watches, and piled out of the Bronco. With Eb in the lead, they made their way so stealthily that Harley felt like an elephant bringing up the rear. He realized at once that his so-called training session was nothing but a waste of money. And that his inexperience could prove deadly to his comrades.

Eb deployed Micah and Cy at the edge of the woods behind the barn. One of the feds motioned to them, and to the five sheriff's deputies. As he waved, four other men in DEA jackets split and went around both sides. Everybody hesitated.

Harley crouched with his heart beating him half to

death. He'd been in the United States for his entire tour of duty with the Rangers, except for a brief stint in Bosnia, where he hadn't managed to get out of headquarters. He'd seen people who'd been in combat and he'd heard about it. But he had no practical experience, and now he felt like a high school freshman getting ready to give a book report in front of the whole class—on a book he hadn't read. His knees felt like rubber under him.

Time seemed to lengthen as the seconds ticked by. Then, quite suddenly, one of the government agents raised his arm high and brought it down.

"Move out!" Eb called to his team.

It was pandemonium. Lopez's men were in civilian clothing, not the black gear that Cy and the others were wearing. The sheriff's deputies and the police officers were in uniform, and the DEA boys had visible identification on their jackets. Everybody seemed to be firing at once.

Harley hesitated at the sharp firecracker pop of guns going off, the sound so ominous and deadly in real life, so unlike the enhanced gunfire used in movies and television. He got a grip on his nerve, clutched his pistol in both hands and moved out a few seconds in the general direction where Cy and Eb had just vanished. He started to run, but he wasn't quick enough to get to cover. He ran right into the path of a submachine gun, and it wasn't held by one of his team. He stopped, his breath catching in his throat as he looked certain death in the face for the first time in his young life.

The small, dark man in jeans and checked shirt facing him ordered him in perfect English to drop his pistol. The leveled automatic weapon he was holding looked very professional. Harley's pride took a hard blow. He'd walked right into that by being careless and he steeled himself for what was coming. He knew that the man wouldn't hesitate to fire on him. With a muffled curse, he dropped his automatic to the ground.

"One less to worry about," the foreign man said with a vicious smile. *"Adios, señor…!"*

Harley heard the loud report as a shot was fired and he tensed, eyes closed, waiting for the pain to start. But the weapon spilled out of the other man's hands an instant before he crumpled and fell forward.

"Get the hell out of there, Harley!" Cy raged.

Harley's eyes opened to find his opponent lying very still on the ground, and Cy standing behind him. Cy picked up Harley's .45 and threw it to him.

"Get around in front of the barn. Hurry!" Cy told him.

Harley felt shaky, but he caught the pistol and walked rapidly past the downed man. He glanced at him and had to fight the rise of bile in his throat. He'd never seen anyone like that…!

His heart was racing crazily, his mouth felt as if it had been filled with cotton. As he cleared the side of the building, he saw firefights. Some of the drug dealer's men were undercover, firing from behind the big transfer trucks. Others were in the barn. They were cornered, desperate, fighting for their lives if not their freedom.

The DEA guys moved in, motioning to their backup, their own weapons singing as they brought down man after man. Most of the wounds were nonlethal, but the noise from the men as they fell made Harley sick. Groans, screams…it wasn't like that in the movies. He watched the police officers, Palmer and Barrett, walk right into the gunfire and drop their opposition neatly and without killing them. He envied them their cool demeanor and courage. He reminded himself never to tick them off once this was all over!

His whole body seemed to vibrate as he followed his boss. What had he been thinking when he enrolled in that mercenary training school? It was all just a lot of baloney, which had made him overconfident and could have gotten him killed tonight. The comparison between himself and these professionals was embarrassing.

Cy went into the barn alone, but now Harley didn't hesitate. He took a sharp breath, ground his teeth together and went right in behind him, ready to back him up if he was needed. He fought the fear he felt and conquered it, shaky legs, shaky hands and all. He'd made a fool of himself once. He wasn't about to do it twice. He wasn't going to let Cy and the others down just because he had butterflies in his stomach. His lean jaw tautened with new resolve.

There was a man in an expensive suit with an automatic weapon firing from behind several bales of odd-looking hay in the barn. Harley noted that he was the man who'd come to Cy's ranch in the pickup truck to "introduce himself."

Cy's instincts were still honed to perfection. He pushed Harley to one side and stepped right into the foreign man's line of fire and raised his own weapon, taking careful aim. Not even the head of the other man was visible now as he crouched behind the bales.

"Drop the gun or I'll drop you, right through your damned product," Cy warned.

The foreign man hesitated, but Cy didn't. He fired.

The bullet went right through the hay and into the man, who cried out, clutching his shoulder as his weapon fell.

"Same arm I got with the knife, wasn't it?" Cy asked coldly as he approached the man and dragged him to his feet. He pushed him back against one of the wooden posts that supported the hayloft and held his pistol right to the base of the man's neck. "Where's Lopez?"

The drug dealer swallowed. He saw his own death in Cy's masked face, in those terrible glittering green eyes.

Harley felt that familiar cold sickness in the pit of his stomach as the muzzle of Cy's .45 automatic pressed harder into the adversary's neck just for a few seconds. It wasn't a training exercise. The gun was real. So was the threat. He looked at his boss, at the man he thought he knew, and realized at once that Cy wasn't bluffing.

"Where's Lopez?" Cy repeated, and he pulled back the trigger deliberately.

"Please," the foreigner gasped, shivering. "Please! He is in Cancún!"

Cy stared at him for just an instant longer before he jerked the man around and sent him spinning away from the protection of the bales.

"Hey, Kennedy!" he called.

One of the DEA men came forward.

"Here's the site boss," Cy told him, pushing the injured man ahead. "I think you'll find him more than willing to talk. And if he isn't, just call me back," he added, watching the drug lord's man go even paler.

"I'll do that. Thanks," Kennedy said. "The sheriff's deputies and those police officers have most of them cuffed and ready to transport. We're going into the house. At least three of them managed to hole up in there. And there's a fourth man still missing. Watch your back."

"You do the same," Cy said. He glanced at Harley. "Let's check out the perimeter of the barn."

"Sure thing, boss," Harley drawled, but he was pale and somber and all traces of his former cockiness were gone. He held his pistol professionally and followed his boss out the door without a trace of hesitation. For the first time, Cy was really proud of him.

They trailed around back, watching as shadows merged with other shadows. There was a sudden crack of twigs and Harley spun around with his .45 leveled as another man carrying an automatic weapon stepped suddenly from behind one of the big trucks. His lean face was unmasked, and he was definitely foreign.

Harley fired, but Cy's hand shot out and knocked the barrel straight up.

"Good reflexes, Harley," Cy said, smiling, "but this guy's on our side. Hi, Rodrigo," he called to the un-masked newcomer. "Long time no see."

"*Muchas grácias* for the timely intervention," Rodrigo replied on a husky chuckle. He moved forward, his white teeth showing even in the darkness. "It would be a pity to have come this far and be shot by a comrade."

"No danger of that," Cy said with a smile as he clapped the other man on the shoulder. "We were afraid they'd killed you. How are you?"

"Disappointed," came the reply. "I had hoped to ap-prehend Lopez, but he remained in Cancún and refused to participate. Someone is feeding him information about the movement of the government agents. He knew you were coming tonight."

"Damn!" Cy burst out.

Eb Scott and Micah Steele, the taller man who'd accompanied them, came forward. "Rodrigo!" he greeted, shaking the other man's hand. "We thought you'd been killed when we didn't hear from you."

"Lopez was suspicious of me," he said simply. "I couldn't afford to do anything that might tip my hand." He waved his hand toward the barn. "As it is, he was warned in time to divert the cocaine shipment and substitute this for it," he added, indicating the neat bales. "This has a significant street value, of course, but it is hardly the haul we hoped for."

Harley was inspecting the "hay." He frowned as he sniffed a twig of it. "Hey! This is marijuana!"

"Bales of it," Cy agreed. "I noticed when we came in that the barn had a padlock on it."

"Now that's what I call keeping a low profile," Harley murmured dryly. "Locking a barn full of hay."

"It would have been coca paste, if Lopez hadn't been warned," Rodrigo told Cy. "What he'd set up behind your ranch was a small processing plant that would have turned coca paste into crack cocaine. If I'd had just another week…!"

Cy smiled. "We'd rather have you alive, Rodrigo. We aren't through yet."

"No, we aren't," Micah Steele said coldly. "I have a contact in Cancún who knows Lopez. He can get someone in the house."

"An inspired idea," Rodrigo said. "Just don't share it with your friends over there," he added bitterly. "They don't have much of a track record with infiltration. Someone else infiltrated Lopez's home once before and died for it."

"Excuse me?" Micah asked.

"They lost an agent who worked for Lopez as a housekeeper," Rodrigo said. "He pushed her off his yacht." His face tightened. "Then he took a fancy to my sister, who was singing in a night club. He assaulted her, and she committed suicide at his house by throwing herself…onto the rocks below."

Eb's eyes narrowed. He was remembering some of the crazy things Rodrigo had done before he took this assignment, behavior that had marked him as a madman. Now they made sense. "I'm sorry," Eb said simply.

"So was I." Rodrigo glanced at the government agents rounding up the stragglers. "I'd better get out of here before that guy with Kennedy recognizes me."

"Who, Cobb?" Eb asked, frowning.

Rodrigo nodded. "It was his office I ransacked," he murmured. "They say he'll follow you to hell if you cross him. I'm inclined to believe it."

Rodrigo murmured, "Well, whether or not Cobb recognizes me, I don't want to risk being apprehended while Lopez is still loose. I can't do any good in prison."

"You were never here," Eb replied, tongue-in-cheek.

"Absolutely," Cy agreed. "I haven't seen you in years."

Micah Steele lifted one huge hand to his eyes. "Forgot my glasses," he murmured. "I couldn't recognize my own brother without them."

"You don't wear glasses, and you don't have a brother," Cy reminded him.

Micah shrugged. "No wonder I couldn't recognize him." He grinned.

Harley listened to the byplay, wondering how these men could seem so calm and unconcerned after what they'd all been through. He was sick to his stomach and shaking inside. He was putting on a good enough front to fool everyone else apparently, though. That was some small compensation.

"Get going," Eb motioned to Rodrigo. "Kennedy's heading this way."

Rodrigo nodded. "I'll be around if you need me again."

"We'll remember," Cy said. "But it won't be infiltrating Lopez's gang next time."

"No, it damned sure won't," Micah Steele said with ice in his deep voice. "Next time, we'll go at him head-on, and he won't walk away."

"I will count the days." Rodrigo melted back into the darkness before Kennedy came around the barn and paused beside the small group.

"The four of you had better do a quick vanishing act," Kennedy told them. "Cobb's over there asking a lot of questions about you guys, and he won't overlook a breach of departmental procedure. Since he outranks me, that wouldn't be good. As far as I'm concerned, officially, you were special agents undercover and I don't know who you are for your own protection. You infiltrated Lopez's gang and took a powder the minute the firefight was over. Since I never knew your names, I couldn't confirm your involvement." He gave them a big grin. "Unofficially, thanks for your help. At least we've managed to shut down one of Lopez's little enterprises." His eyes narrowed. "The man you dropped in the barn," Kennedy added, talking to Cy, "was the one who popped a cap on Walt Monroe. We've been hoping to happen onto him. Cobb says he'll go down for murder one, and I guarantee he'll make it stick. Monroe was one of his new recruits. He doesn't like many people. He liked Walt."

"I'll pass that along to his widow," Cy said. "She'll be glad."

He nodded. "Walt was a good man." He looked around. "I only wish we'd had something really nasty to pin on these guys. Distribution of cocaine would have suited me better than distribution of marijuana."

"Yes," Cy agreed, "but even if this was small pickings, it will hurt Lopez to have a hefty portion of his transportation force out of action, not to mention the lab he set up next to his beehives on my back property line. He's lost a big investment here tonight, in manpower, material and unrecoverable goods. He'll really be out for blood now. None of us will be safe until we get Lopez himself."

"Dream on," Kennedy said quietly. "He's more slippery than a greased python."

"Even pythons can be captured." Micah Steele's eyes glittered through his mask. "I've got a few friends in Nassau. We'll see what we can do about Lopez."

"I didn't hear you say that," Kennedy replied.

"Just as well," Micah chuckled. "Since I was never here."

"There's a lot of that going around," Kennedy murmured. "Get going before Cobb gets a good look at you. I'll take it from here."

Eb nodded and the others joined him for a quick jaunt back to the Johnson place where they'd left the truck.

Harley hadn't said a single word. Eb and Cy and Micah talked about Lopez and discussed options for getting to him. Harley sat and looked out the window.

It wasn't until Eb dropped the two men off at Cy Parks's ranch, several hundred yards from the house, that Cy was able to get a good look at his foreman.

Harley had the expression now, the one any combat veteran would recognize immediately. The experience tonight had taken the edge off his youth, his impulsive nature, his bravado. He'd matured in one night, and he'd never be the same again.

"Now," Cy told him quietly, "look in a mirror. You'll see what was missing when you were talking about your 'exploits' on the mercenary training expedition. This is the real thing, Harley. Men don't fall and then get back up again. The blood is real. The screams are real. What you saw tonight is the face of war, and no amount of money or fame is worth what you have to pay for it in emotional capital."

Harley's head turned. He looked at his boss with new eyes. "You were one of them," he said. "That's what you did before you came here and started ranching."

"That's right," Cy said evenly. "I've killed men. I've watched men die. I've watched children die, fighting in wars not of their making. I did it for fame and glory and money. But nothing I have now is worth the price I paid for it." He hesitated. "Nothing," he added, "except that woman in my house right now. She's worth dying for."

Harley managed a wan smile. "I could have gotten you all killed tonight, because I didn't know what I was doing."

"But you didn't get us killed," Cy returned. "And when the chips were down, you conquered your fear and kept going. That's the real definition of courage." He put a big, heavy hand on the other man's shoulder. "You have a way with ranch management, Harley. Believe me, it's a better path than hiring yourself out to whatever army needs foreign help. At the very least, you accumulate fewer bullet wounds."

Harley nodded. "So I saw. Good night, boss."

"Harley."

The younger man turned.

"I've never been prouder of you than I was tonight," Cy said quietly.

Harley tried to speak, couldn't, and settled for a jerky smile and a nod before he walked away.

Cy walked on toward the house, smiling faintly as he contemplated the movement of the curtains in the living-room window.

Before he even reached the porch, Lisa was out the front door and flying toward him. He caught her easily as she propelled herself from the second step. He folded her close, whirled her around and kissed her with his whole heart.

She held on to him for dear life, tears raining down her face as she thanked God that he'd come back to her in one piece.

"Can I keep you?" she whispered at his lips as he picked her up and carried her inside.

His heart jumped wildly. "Keep me?" he murmured, kicking the door shut with his foot. "Try to get rid of me…!"

She smiled under the fierce hunger of his mouth, savoring its coolness, its beloved contours, as he carried her into the bedroom and kicked that door shut as well. She could feel the adrenaline surging through his powerful body even before she felt the aftereffects of passion in his hungry, devouring kisses. She had a feeling that it was going to be the most explosively sensual night of their married lives. And she was right.

CHAPTER ELEVEN

TWO FEVERISHLY EXCITING hours later, Lisa lay trembling against the powerful body beside hers in the tangled covers of Cy's big bed. She stretched and moaned helplessly as the movement triggered delicious little aftershocks of pleasure.

"If you weren't already pregnant," he murmured huskily, "you would be, after that."

She lifted herself up and propped her forearms on his damp, hair-roughened, deeply scarred chest. She brushed her mouth against one of the scars lovingly. "I went back to the doctor again yesterday," she confessed.

"Why?" He was concerned now, his green eyes narrowing on her face.

She traced his hard mouth with her fingertips. "To have a sonogram to date the pregnancy and to have some blood work done." She looked straight into his eyes. "The baby is yours, Cy."

He shivered. She could feel the ripple of muscle go right down him. "What?" he asked.

"I'm only a few weeks along. That means the baby is yours—not Walt's." She slid down beside him and pillowed her cheek on his chest, letting one slender, pretty leg slide over his muscular, hairy one. "He told me he did some checking and the results from my first pregnancy test after Walt died were switched with someone else's. It was a mix-up at the lab. That explains why I haven't had any pregnancy symptoms until now."

He stroked her long hair absently. "I can't believe it."

"Me, either. But it makes sense. I didn't know, but before we married, Walt…had a vasectomy. I checked with his doctor to get information on Walt's RH factor."

Every tendon in his body pulled tight. He rolled over and looked down into her flushed face incredulously.

"He said he didn't want children," she confessed. "The doctor said that he wanted to make sure he didn't have any. The doctor wanted him to tell me. He never did."

He was speechless with wonder. His baby. She was carrying his baby. He thought of his late wife and the child she'd borne that belonged to another man. He'd married Lisa believing that she was pregnant with her dead husband's child. But here he was with a miracle. He was going to be a biological father, for the first time in his life. He felt moisture sting his eyes as his big, lean hand smoothed over her flat stomach gently.

The expression on his face made her feel warm inside, safe, cocooned. "No need to ask if you're pleased," she said in a tender, amused tone.

He laughed self-consciously. "Pleased? I'm ecstatic. I don't suppose my feet will touch the ground for weeks."

She smiled and pressed close. "Mine won't, either, and not only because of the baby."

"Why else, then?" he teased.

She sighed, drawing her fingers across his mouth. "Because you love me."

He didn't hesitate or deny it. He only smiled. "Sure of that, are you?"

"Yes."

"How?"

She linked her arms around his neck and pressed her mouth gently to his damp throat. "It shows, in so many ways. All the time."

His fingers tangled contentedly in her long hair. "Like what you feel about me shows," he murmured, holding her closer.

"Does it?"

"We nurture each other," he said softly. "I never realized married people could be close like this, tender like this, loving like this. I've been standing outside warm houses all my life, looking in, and now I'm right inside by the fireplace." His arms contracted. His face nuzzled gently against hers. "I love you with all that I am, all I ever will be. More than my life."

She moaned and pressed closer, shivering. "I love you more than my life, too," she breathed at his lips. "I'm going to give you a son, Cy."

"And a daughter," he whispered back, delighted. "And a few others, assorted."

She smiled against his mouth. "You'll be a wonderful daddy."

He kissed her with aching tenderness, almost overwhelmed with emotion. Out of such tragedy and anguish had come this woman, this angel, in his arms. He was still amazed that she could love him, want him, need him as she did, with his past, with his scarred body and scarred emotions. He'd never dared hope for so much in his life. He closed his eyes and thanked God for the biggest miracle he'd ever had.

"I'll take care of you as long as I live, Lisa."

"And I'll take care of you as long as I do," she murmured happily. "I hope we live a hundred years together."

He laughed softly and agreed, drowning in the warm delight of her body curled so close into his. It was unbearably sweet to love, to really love, and be loved in return.

Her leg moved sensuously against the inside of his and she felt his breath go jerky. She was more sure of herself now, eager for new lessons, new techniques, new adventures with this man, this winter soldier, she loved.

"Cy?" she whispered as her hand smoothed over his chest and then steadily down.

It was hard to talk. "What?" he managed in a husky tone.

"I want you to teach me."

"Teach you…what?" he bit off as her hand moved again.

"How to please you."

He would have answered her, if he'd been able. But his soft groan and the shivering of his powerful body as he eased over hers were more than enough to convince her that she was pleasing him already. She stretched like a contented cat under the warm, sinuous press of his lean hips and then moaned as the fever burned so high that she thought she might become ashes in his arms. Life had never been so sweet. And this was only the tip of the iceberg, the very beginning of their marriage. She pressed her mouth into his and held on tight, following him into the fire.

WITH LOPEZ'S JACOBSVILLE connection closed down, and all his local assets seized by the feds, it seemed a good guess that the drug lord would set up operations elsewhere. But he still had people, unknown people, acting as his eyes and ears. He also had someone inside the federal agency, Rodrigo had said, to tip him off about drug busts. Cy worried about who it was. Cy worried more about another possible attempt on Lisa, after the successful sneak attack on Lopez's shipment of marijuana.

Cy had gone to Eb's ranch at his friend's request to discuss future plans, and they were talking over cups of black coffee in the living room when Micah Steele came into the room. He was taller, bigger than both the other men. He had thick, straight, medium blond hair cut conventionally short. He was wearing a beige Armani suit that seemed perfect for his tall frame. It made his dark eyes look even darker. He wore a watch like Eb's on his left wrist and no other jewelry. Thirty-six years old, the former CIA agent spoke several languages fluently and had a temper that was explosive and quiet. Dutch van Meer used to say that Micah could get more results with a steady look than he could with a weapon.

"Why are you still in town?" Cy asked curiously.

"That's what I asked you over to tell you." Eb grimaced. "We've still got problems."

"When have we had anything else lately?" Cy said with resignation.

"The word is that Lopez's bosses in Colombia think he's slipping. First, he got arrested. Then he lost a shipment to the Coast Guard. We cost him a tidy sum in men and equipment here, not to mention marijuana. Yesterday, another group of his men were driving plastic bags of cocaine paste in several transfer trailer trucks bearing the logo of a grocery store chain. The DEA was tipped off, probably by Rodrigo, and the feds got all the trucks plus their cargo. The haul would have been worth millions, if not billions, in crack cocaine sales if it had been processed and put out on the streets. It's the largest confiscation by the DEA in years. Lopez's bosses are furious. They're ready to dump Lopez, and he's cut some sort of deal to keep his connection. The word is, he's making plans to eliminate the obstacles to his local smuggling traffic."

"That's no real surprise," Eb pointed out.

Micah's dark eyes narrowed. "No. But I didn't expect this quite so soon. He can't get to either of you without some difficulty, now that his operation here has been shut down. Any group of strangers in town would stick out like sore thumbs, and the local authorities are on alert. But one of my contacts said that Callie and my father might become targets, and that the last he heard, Lopez was going to call in a mechanic. One man, alone, might succeed where a larger group failed."

It went without saying that a "mechanic" meant a professional killer. "Why your family and not ours?" Cy asked.

Micah leaned against the mantel above the fireplace in Eb's study. He smiled mockingly, looking more elegant than a male model with his striking good looks. "You only helped shut down a small operation of Lopez's. But I tipped the DEA guys about the multimillion dollar cocaine shipment that was confiscated."

Cy whistled. "Did Rodrigo pass that tidbit along?"

"Not Rodrigo," came the reply. "It was a last act of defiance by his cousin, who," he added grimly, "is now dead. They pulled him out of a vat of industrial chemicals. They were only able to identify him by dental records."

"Any idea where Rodrigo is?" Eb wanted to know.

"Hiding out in Aruba, I gather from my sources. But he may not be safe, even so. Lopez has a long reach. He's got people everywhere."

"Plus an informant with the feds who's spilling the beans to Lopez about our government's attempts to bring him down," Cy added.

"That's how Lopez knew I blew the whistle on him. You'd better believe that Kennedy and Cobb are doing their best to find out who it is," Micah replied. "But I expect it's someone in a high position who's beyond suspicion. It won't be easy to ferret him out."

"He's risking a lot on Lopez's account, whoever he is," Eb mused.

"Lopez is paying him a million a tip," Micah interjected.

"Well, that would make it worth the risk for most people, I'm afraid," Eb said.

Micah dropped down into an easy chair and lit a cigar. Eb turned on the smokeless ashtray and handed it to him. Micah chuckled, taking it in one big hand.

"That will kill you," Eb said with a grin.

"In my line of work, bullets will probably get me long before smoking does. Besides, I don't expect to be here long." He checked the big watch on his wrist. "Callie gets off work in five minutes. I'm going to waylay her before she goes to pick up Dad at the senior citizen center."

His face changed when he mentioned his former

stepsister. His dark eyes narrowed and his jaw went taut. He smoked absently, his mind obviously far away.

"If worse comes to worst, you could take her and your father down to Nassau with you and keep her out of Lopez's reach," Eb suggested.

Micah gave him a hellish glare. "Neither of them will talk to me right now, much less agree to go to Nassau. Haven't you heard?" he drawled. "I'm anybody's friend but theirs."

"You always start the fights," Eb pointed out. "You can't blame Callie for defending herself."

Micah took another draw from the cigar and thumped ashes in the ashtray. "I blame her for everything," he said icily. "If it hadn't been for her and her damned mother, my father would want to see me occasionally."

"Surely he doesn't still blame you for his divorce?" Cy remarked.

"He blames me for everything." He put out the cigar impatiently and turned the smokeless ashtray off. "I blame her mother."

"Whatever happened to her?" Eb asked.

"I have no idea," Micah said abruptly. "She dumped Callie and left town even before the divorce was final. She hired a lawyer to bring the papers to her in England so that she wouldn't have to see any of us again. Some mother."

"Callie never talks about her," Eb said thoughtfully. "It's not surprising. Her mother treated her like the hired help. Callie wasn't pretty enough or sophisticated enough to please her mama."

"There's nothing wrong with Callie," Micah replied absently. "She's naïve, of course, but looks aren't that important. She's a good woman, in the true sense of the word. I should know," he added with a harsh laugh. "I've left a trail of the other kind behind me over the years."

"I won't argue with that," Eb had to agree. "They used to follow you around like flies after honey. Really beautiful women."

"Window dressing," Micah said carelessly. "Underneath they all had one thing in common—greed. Being rich and single has its drawbacks as well as its perks."

There was a brief silence while all of them recalled other times, other places.

"How's Lisa, by the way?" Micah asked. "Is the baby all right?"

"The test results got mixed when she had the first test, just after Walt was killed," Cy replied. He began to smile. "But she's pregnant now."

Eb scowled. "With Walt's baby. I know."

Cy shook his head. "Not Walt's baby. Mine." His eyes were brimming with pride, joy, delight. "Walt had a vasectomy before they married. He didn't want kids at all."

The other two men chuckled softly. "I thought you said she was too young for you," Eb said mischievously.

"I changed my mind. She's old for her age and I'm young for mine." He couldn't seem to stop smiling. "It's like a second chance. I never thought I'd get one."

"I'm glad for you," Eb said. "Glad for myself, too. We've made good marriages."

"I wish you could stop talking about it," Micah said disgustedly, glancing from one of them to the other. "I'll break out in hives any minute."

"Mr. Confirmed Bachelor," Eb said, jerking a thumb at the blond man.

"Napoleon before Waterloo," Cy agreed.

Micah got up out of his chair. "I'm going to see Callie. I brought Bojo over here with me, but he flew to Atlanta to see his brother. I guess it's just as well. If I had him tail her, he'd probably attract a little attention."

"Dressed in a long white silk robe and babushes on his feet? Who'd notice that in Jacobsville, Texas?" Eb asked dryly.

"He's Berber. The beard and mustache are traditional, like the accoutrements. He wouldn't blend, that's for sure," Micah said. He sighed. "I've had a hard time replacing Dallas since he got shot up and then left to marry Sally's aunt Jessica. Good men are really hard to find these days."

"They were just as hard to find back when we started out, too," Eb said. "Well, there's always Harley. He's hooked on adventure."

"No, he isn't," Cy said firmly. "He's the best foreman in two counties and I'm not recommending him for a target."

"He did pretty good that night," Eb said. "When the chips are down, he can keep his head."

"I want him to keep his head," Cy said. "That's the whole point of keeping him at home."

"How about Rodrigo?" Eb suggested.

Micah nodded slowly. "He could come to Nassau. He'd be safer there, with Bojo and me. I'll see if I can find him on my way home."

"Take care of yourself," Cy said.

Micah shook hands with him. "You do the same."

He left the two of them still talking about Rodrigo and climbed into the racy black Porsche he drove. It was like him, power and grace conventionally packaged and deceptively straitlaced. Micah was a law unto himself.

Micah drove to the side street near Kemp's law office, where Callie's little yellow VW beetle was sitting. He liked the updated style of the body, and the color suited her. She was bright and sunny. Or she had been, until her mother ruined all their lives.

It was five o'clock on the dot, and he waited and watched the rearview. Sure enough, less than a minute later, Callie Kirby came out of the law office and went down the sidewalk toward her car, lost in thought as she dug in her purse for her car keys. It amazed him that everything didn't fall out on the pavement at her feet. He remembered Callie being all thumbs, a gangly teenager suffering from embarrassment, lack of social graces and a bubbly personality despite her drawbacks.

But this Callie had changed. She had pale blue eyes and an ordinary sort of face, but it had a gamine charm all its own. She wore her dark hair short. She was only medium height, a little thing compared to him. But for her size, she packed a wallop when she lost her temper. He was sorry they couldn't be friends. He didn't have many, and she would have had the distinction of being the only woman among them. His affairs had tarnished him in Callie's quiet eyes. She had no use for playboys. Especially Micah Steele. Like his father, she blamed him for the divorce and the anguish that came after it. She thought that he'd been having an affair with her mother. That was ironic, when her mother was the one woman on earth he'd ever considered totally repulsive.

Well, you couldn't go home again, they said. They were right. That door was closed forever. His father was old and weak and illness had taken much of the spirit out of him. He hated the separation between them. He loved his father. He was glad that Callie did, too, and that she took such good care of the old man. He thought about Lopez and the possibility of a hit man with those two gentle people as the targets, and his blood ran cold. He didn't want them to die for his actions. Lopez would know that, and it would please him. His teeth clenched as unwanted pictures of some nebulous tragedy began to take shape in his mind.

Callie came toward her car, noticed the low slung Porsche and stopped dead in her tracks, staring at it.

Micah climbed out of the car with his usual elegance of movement and went to join her beside her car.

"We need to talk."

She clutched her purse against her small breasts and looked up at him with faint hautcur. Her heart was racing. He could see her blouse move jerkily above her breasts. He remembered vividly the feel of her in his arms that once...

"*We* never talk," she informed him. "You say what you want to, and then you walk away."

She had a point. He pulled the half-smoked cigar from its holder and lit it.

"That's illegal in the mall," she said with unholy glee. "Light up there, and they'll arrest you."

"You'd love that, wouldn't you?"

She wasn't going to be drawn into another verbal firefight with him. She straightened. "I'm tired and I still have to pick up Dad at the senior center. He stays with me now."

"I know." He hated the thought of Callie being his father's nurse and protector. It was one of many things he resented. "Have you heard from your mother?" he added mockingly.

She didn't flinch. But her eyelids did, just barely perceptibly. "I haven't heard from my mother since the divorce," she said calmly. "Have you?" she added with pure venom.

His dark eyes glittered at her.

She decided to cut her losses. "What do you want?" she asked bluntly.

Now that he had her attention, he didn't know how to put it. She had no idea what he did for a living. Even his father didn't know. He'd kept his profession secret from both of them. He'd inherited a large trust from his mother, which would never have been enough to furnish him with Porsches and Armani suits. They didn't seem to realize that, so he left them to draw their own conclusions. Now, with Lopez looming over him, his profession might get them both killed. He had to find a way to protect them. But how?

"I don't suppose you and Dad would like to come down to Nassau for a vacation?" he asked speculatively.

Her chin lifted proudly. "I'd rather holiday in hell," she said with a cold smile.

He let out a husky, hollow laugh. "That's what I thought."

"Your father is all right," she said, anticipating what she thought was wrong. "It was just a mild stroke."

"When did that happen?" he asked abruptly, with concern.

"No one called you?" She shifted her purse. "Sorry.

We've all watched him carefully since that heart attack. It was two weeks ago, he lost the feeling on the left side of his face and couldn't move it. As I said, it was mild. It was a light stroke. But they were actually able to clean out the artery that was clogged and put a shunt in it. He's on blood thinners, and he has a good prognosis. You don't have to worry about him. I'm taking good care of him."

"On your salary," he said flatly, angered.

She stiffened. "I make a decent living and he's an economical guest. We struggle along together just fine. We don't need financial help," she added firmly. "In case you wondered," she added, reminding him that he'd accused her of being money-hungry just like her mother. It was one of many things he'd said to her that still hurt.

The words went right through him, but he hid his reaction. He wished he could forget the accusations he'd made, the hurtful things he'd said to her. But there was no going back. "Did you know your own father?" he asked, curious.

Her face grew taut. "I don't know who my father was. My mother's first husband was positive that it wasn't him. That's why he didn't press for custody when she divorced him."

She said it with savaged pride, and he was sorry he'd forced the admission from her. "So my father's standing in for him?" he probed gently.

"Jack Steele was kinder to me than anyone else ever was," she said tightly. "It's no great burden to look after him. And you still haven't said why you're here."

He fingered the burning cigar and tried to find the words. "I've made an enemy," he said finally. "A very bad man to cross. I think he might target you and my father to get back at me."

Callie frowned. "Excuse me?"

His dark eyes met hers. "He's a drug lord. He heads one of the Colombian cartels. I just cost him several million dollars by tipping the DEA about a massive shipment of cocaine he sent over here."

Her blood ran cold. She worked in legal circles. She knew about drugs, not only their dangers, but also the penalties for using or selling them. She also knew about the Colombian cartels, because they were on the news most every night. They were graphic about how drug dealers got even with people who cost them money. She couldn't even shoot a gun, and Jack Steele, Micah's father, was practically an invalid despite his remarkable recovery. The two of them together would never be able to protect themselves from such an adversary, and she couldn't afford to hire a bodyguard.

She stared at Micah blankly. "Would he be that ruthless?" she had to ask.

"Yes."

Her chest rose and fell heavily. "Okay. What do we do?"

Straightforward. No accusations, no rage, no exaggerated fear. She simply asked, trusting that he'd know. And he did.

"I'm going to send someone over here to watch you and Dad," he replied. "Someone trustworthy."

"And what are you going to do?" she wanted to know.

"That's my business."

He looked, and sounded, harder than nails. She felt exposed, vulnerable. She was eighteen again, hearing him accuse her of setting him up with his father. He'd already been angry at her for what had happened when they'd been alone that last Christmas they'd all lived together. He'd given in to temptation and it had taken all his willpower to get away from her at all. He'd lectured her about being so free with her kisses, so wanton and forward. He'd left her in tears. It had only dawned on him much later that she'd had something alcoholic to drink. He'd walked out into the hall, where her mother had seen him in a state of unmistakable arousal and had made a blatant play for him, thinking *she'd* aroused him in her low-cut dress.

In the seconds it took his dimmed brain to react, his father had come out of the study and found him in the hall with Callie's mother, in a compromising position. Micah and his father had almost come to blows. Callie and her mother were summarily booted out the door and Micah had accused Callie of sending her father out there to catch him with his stepmother, out of revenge because he wouldn't kiss her. It had broken Callie's heart. Now, she withdrew from Micah Steele as if he were molten lava. She had no wish to repeat the lesson he'd taught her.

"Very well," she said demurely. "I'll look after Dad while you do…whatever you're going to do. I've got my grandfather's shotgun and some shells. I'll protect him at night."

He looked at her in a different way. "Can you shoot it?"

"If I have to," she replied. Her face was very pale, but she wasn't flinching. "Was there anything else?"

His dark eyes slid down her slender, graceful body and he remembered Callie in bathing suits, in flimsy gowns, in her one fancy dress at her birthday party—

her eighteenth birthday party. She'd been wearing deep green velvet, cut low and sensuous, and he'd refused her invitation to attend the celebration. Like so many other things he'd said and done, he'd hurt her that day. She still looked impossibly young. She was barely twenty-two, and he was thirty-six, over a decade her senior.

He wanted to prolong the meeting. That was unlike him. He shrugged one shoulder indifferently instead. "Nothing important. Just watch your step. I'll make sure nobody gets close enough to hurt either of you."

She gave him one slow, eloquent look before she turned to her small car and unlocked it. She got in and drove off, without another word. And she didn't look back.

CHAPTER TWELVE

CY AND LISA WERE HAVING a late supper at the kitchen table. They watched each other hungrily with every bite as they discussed the changes the baby would mean in their lives. They were delightful changes, and they spoke in low murmurs, smiling at each other between bites. The loud squeal of tires out front caught them unaware and made them tense. Surely it wasn't another attack by Lopez or his men...!

Cy was out of the chair and heading for the front door seconds later, his hand going automatically to the phone table drawer where the loaded .45 automatic was kept. He made a mental note to himself to keep his gun locked up once the baby arrived. He motioned Lisa back and moved cautiously out onto the porch. Seconds later, he lowered the weapon. It was Micah Steele, but he was hardly recognizable.

His thick blond hair was disheveled, and he needed a shave. He looked as if he hadn't slept.

Cy didn't waste time asking questions. He caught the taller man by the arm and pulled him inside. "Coffee first. Then you can tell whatever you need to."

"I'll bring it to the study," Lisa offered.

Cy smiled at her and bent to kiss her cheek. "I'll

bring it to the study," he corrected tenderly. "Growing mamas need their rest. Go watch TV."

"Okay." She kissed him back, sparing a curious and sympathetic glance for Micah, who nodded politely before he preceded Cy into the kitchen.

When Lisa was out of earshot, Cy poured coffee into two mugs and put them on the table.

"Would you rather talk in the study?" Cy asked him.

"This is fine." Micah cupped the mug in both hands and leaned over it in a slumped posture that said all too much about his mental condition.

Cy straddled a chair across from him. "Okay. What's wrong."

"Lopez has Callie," he said in a husky, tortured voice.

Cy sat stock-still. "When? And how?" he exploded.

"Yesterday, not five minutes after I spoke to her outside her office building," he said dully. "We had a brief conversation. I warned her that someone I knew might possibly target her or my father. She listened, but she didn't pay much attention. I told her I was going to have someone watch them for their own safety. But I'd barely gotten back to my motel when Eb phoned and said he'd had an urgent message from Rodrigo that Callie was going to be snatched. I phoned the adult day care where she leaves Dad every day and they said she hadn't picked him up." He looked absolutely devastated. "You can set your watch by Callie. She's always early, if she isn't right on time. I went looking for her, and I found her car about a block from the senior center on a side street. The driver's door was standing wide-open and her purse was still in it."

Cy cursed roundly. "Did you call the police?"

Micah shook his head. He ran a big hand through his hair restlessly. "I didn't know what to do." He looked at Cy in anguish. "Do you know what that snake will do to her? She's untouched, Cy. Absolutely untouched!"

He had a pretty good idea what Lopez would do, and it made him sick to consider it. Judging by Micah's behavior, his stepsister meant a lot more to him than he'd ever admitted; possibly, more than he'd realized himself.

"The first thing we do is call Chet Blake."

"A lot of good a local police chief is going to do us," Micah said miserably. "By now, Lopez has her out of the state, if not out of the country."

"Chet is a distant relation of our state attorney general, Simon Hart," Cy interrupted, "and he has a cousin who's a Texas Ranger. Lopez's men left some sort of trail, even if it's just a paper one. Chet has connections. He'll find out where Lopez has taken her. If she's in Mexico, we can contact the Mexican authorities and Interpol…"

Micah's steely glare interrupted him. "All I need to know is where she is," he said tautly. "Then I'll pack up Bojo and Rodrigo, and we'll play cowboys and drug dealers."

Cy wanted to try to reason with him, but the man was too far gone. He'd seen Micah in this mood before, and he knew there was nothing he could say or do to stop him. He spared a thought for Callie, who was probably terrified, not to mention Micah's father. The old man had already had a major heart attack and a stroke, and the news might easily be too much for him. Micah would have to make up a story and tell it to whoever was nursing him. He said as much.

"I've already taken care of that," Micah said heavily. "One of the freelance homebound nurses who sometimes visits him at the center went home with him. I've arranged for her to stay there until I come back—or until Callie does. I told her to say that Callie had an emergency out of town, a cousin in a car wreck. He doesn't know that she has no cousins. He'll believe it, and he won't have to be upset."

"Good thinking," Cy said. "What can I do?"

Micah finished his coffee. "You can keep an eye on Dad for me while I'm out of the country. You and Eb," he added. "If you don't mind."

"Certainly I don't mind," Cy told him. "We'll have somebody watch him constantly. I promise."

"Thanks," Micah said simply. He stood up. "I'll let you know when I've got her safe."

"If there's anything else you need, all you have to do is ask," Cy told him.

Micah smiled wanly. "Remember that old saying, that we don't appreciate what we've got until we lose it?"

"She'll be all right."

"I hope so. See you."

"Good luck."

Micah nodded and went out as quietly as he'd come in. Cy poured himself another cup of coffee, took out a glass and filled it with milk for Lisa before he closed up the kitchen and went to join her in the living room.

Her eyes lit up when he sat down on the sofa beside her, put the drinks down and slid his arm behind her to watch her knit.

"What was wrong with him?"

"Lopez got Callie," he said.

She grimaced and groaned. "Oh, poor Callie! Can he rescue her, do you think?"

"As soon as we find out where she is. I've got to make some phone calls in the study. Go on to bed when your program goes off. I'll be there in a little while."

She put her hand on his cheek and caressed it softly. "I love going to bed with you," she said softly.

He smiled at her, bending to kiss her lips tenderly. "I love doing everything with you," he said.

"Will it be enough for you, me and the baby?" she asked solemnly. "Will it make up for what you've lost?"

He drew her close and hugged her. "I'll always miss Alex," he replied, naming his five-year-old son who died in the Wyoming fire. "And I'll always blame myself for not being able to save him. But I love you, and I want our baby very much." He lifted his head and looked down into her dark eyes hungrily. "You'll be enough, Lisa."

She smiled again, and kissed him hungrily before he got up from the sofa. "I love you."

"I love you, too." He ruffled her long hair and grinned at her. "You've changed my whole life. I look forward to waking up every morning. I have such a pretty view in my bed."

She chuckled. "I have a very nice one of my own." She sobered. "Will Lopez hurt Callie?"

"I wish I knew. We'll do what we can to help Micah find her."

"Even when Lopez is not here, he's still here," she said. "One of these days, he's going to be called to account for all the evil things he's done."

"And he'll pay the price," Cy assured her.

He went to make his phone calls. He paused in the doorway to take one long look at his wife. Despite his sympathy for Micah Steele, he was grateful that he hadn't lost Lisa to Lopez's violence. His life was new again, fresh, full of promise and joy. After the storm, the rainbow. He smiled. The winter soldier had found a warm, loving home at last.

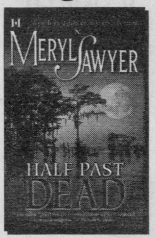

If you enjoyed what you just read,
then we've got an offer you can't resist!

Take 2 bestselling
love stories FREE!
Plus get a FREE surprise gift!

From #1 *New York Times* bestselling author

NORA ROBERTS

come the first two stories in the classic
MacGregor family saga that has touched
readers' hearts the world over.

THE MACGREGORS:

SERENA CAINE

Serena MacGregor met Justin Blade during a Caribbean
cruise and the arrogant man wouldn't take no for an
answer in *Playing the Odds*.

The attraction was immediate between Caine MacGregor
and Diana Blade despite a strict professional relationship,
or were they merely *Tempting Fate?*

Available in trade paperback in January.